THE
TAKEN

D1634773

Also by Casey Kelleher:

Rotten to the Core
Rise and Fall
Heartless
Bad Blood

THE
TAKEN

CASEY KELLEHER

Bookouture

Published by Bookouture

An imprint of StoryFire Ltd.
23 Sussex Road, Ickenham, UB10 8PN
United Kingdom

www.bookouture.com

ISBN: 978-1-78681-077-9
eBook ISBN: 978-1-78681-076-2

For My Sons

Ben, Danny & Kyle

x x x

AUTHOR'S NOTE

When I started writing *The Taken* the European migrant or refugee crisis was of epic proportions and, unfortunately, it remains so.

'The Jungle' encampment mentioned in the book is a real place. In Calais, France, it was named by the migrants and refugees themselves in ironic reference to how they believed they were being forced to live. After extensive research, the chapters that are set in 'the Jungle' in *The Taken* have been written using inspiration from real-life accounts from migrants, refugees, and journalists who have lived there.

PROLOGUE

Albania: One year earlier

'Tariq?'

Whimpering, Lena Cona looked down at the ground to where her brother lay.

The two men were shouting now, their voices angry, intimidating.

She tried to comprehend what they were saying, but their jumbled words were muted, merging into background noise as her ears began to ring loudly, a high-pitched screech filling her head.

She was in shock.

Unable to think straight, Lena tried to move, but she couldn't.

Her legs were shaking, but her feet felt weighed down, as if her shoes were filled with lead.

She was afraid. Paralysed to the spot, all she could do was stare; her eyes fixated on the thick stream of blood that oozed out from the gash at the back of Tariq's head.

He'd been hit.

The taller of the men had whacked him around the head with the butt of his gun.

They had a gun!

Panic ripped through her at the sudden realisation.

Lena tried to shout out; opening her mouth, a strained squeak barely louder than a whisper was the only noise that crept out.

'Get in the car.'

The man pointed his gun at her now. Aiming it straight at her. His words were devoid of emotion, reflecting the same vacant hollowness that she could see in his eyes.

Stepping closer, he shoved the barrel against Lena's chest.

'Now!' This time he bellowed, his face twisting in anger as he pushed the gun harder against her skin.

Lena could see his finger hovering threateningly over the trigger. This wasn't an empty threat. She knew he was dangerous, but still she couldn't move.

A few minutes ago she and her brother had been laughing and joking together.

Tariq had been walking her home from school.

That was her parents' order: that her brother would walk her to and from school every day.

Lena had thought her parents were overreacting. Of course there were risks, but they didn't apply to her, surely. Now she'd realised she'd been stupid, naïve. She remembered, with increasing terror, Néné's harrowing tales of girls from Shkodër being snatched. Abducted and taken to the city's main port, Vlorë, before being shipped off on speedboats across the Adriatic Sea, never to be seen again.

Her parents had pleaded with her to stay at home, to accept the traditional life of a normal Albanian girl just as many of her peers had done, but Lena was anything but normal.

Strong-willed. Defiant. Unlike most of the other girls in her class who had left school at the age of twelve or thirteen due to the pressures that their families had bestowed on them, Lena had refused to follow suit, insisting on completing her education. Why should she be penalised just for being born female? Why should she submit to a life doing what was expected of her? Instead, adamant to remain, schooled in a classroom of eleven boys, Lena had strived to be top of her class.

Not only had Lena excelled in mathematics, but she was also fluent in English. Her teacher had been impressed. He had told Lena that she had mastered the language so well that, eventually, she'd be able to teach it herself.

Lena had loved that idea. Travelling the world, working as a teacher or a translator. Practising daily, she'd even started to educate her parents and her brother. Just the basic words of salutation, or naming the food they ate.

She wanted to learn as much as she possibly could, so that, one day, she could have more than just what her parents had chosen for her. She didn't want to be stuck here in Albania as just somebody's wife, or somebody's mother.

It may have been enough for Néné, but it would never be enough for her. Lena wanted so much more: to be treated as an equal; to experience the same opportunities and freedom that her brother had.

Unwilling to back down, she'd argued so intently that her parents had finally given in; insisting, in the end, that if Lena must continue with her schooling until she was nineteen then she could, on the condition that Tariq chaperone her.

Only now it seemed that fate had played out a cruel hand. Staring down at him she could see that Tariq was hurt, maybe dead.

And it's all my fault, a voice screamed in Lena's head.

'Help me! Please, somebody?' Shouting hysterically, Lena finally found her voice as she prayed that someone would come to her aid.

'Help me, please… '

Lena caught the gaze of a woman across the road, her eyes pleading with her to help her, but all that stared back at her was the woman's fear. With an apologetic look, the woman put her head down and kept walking, pretending that she hadn't seen.

Crying now, desperate, Lena scoured the street, looking for anyone that might help her, but the dusty road was almost deserted. School had finished; people were already indoors, evading the mid-afternoon scorching heat.

A single car passed by. Slowing down, the people inside stared out from behind the glass windows, but they didn't stop to help her. They didn't dare.

'Pick her up,' the taller man shouted now, directing the shorter man.

He did as he was told: grabbing her roughly from behind, clamping his hand over her mouth to mute her cries.

Lena saw their car. It was a battered-looking bright blue Mercedes, covered in flaky patches of orange rust. The back door was wide open; the engine running.

They are going to take me?

Gripped with fear, Lena dug her heels into the dry mud, trying her hardest to resist as one of the two men tried to grab at her feet, but it was no use. The men were much stronger than her.

Overpowering her, they lifted her off the ground, hauling her over to their car.

A hand came from behind her, clamping tightly across her mouth, making her gag for breath. Silencing her. Lena struggled to break free but her attempts only caused the men to hold on to her tighter.

'Stay still, you stupid bitch!'

The man's voice was commanding. He was losing patience. The sternness of his tone indicated that he'd had enough of her not complying. 'Do as you are told, or you will be punished.'

Punished?

Lena twisted her head back to where her brother lay sprawled out on the ground, motionless.

Hadn't they punished her enough already?

She had no idea who they were or what they wanted. All she knew was that she couldn't let them take her.

Her brother needed her. Despite feeling helpless, Lena couldn't just leave him like this.

Kicking and clawing at the men like a wildcat as they tried to force her onto the back seat, her body convulsing, Lena fought to break free from her abductors.

If she got inside this car, maybe she'd suffer the same fate as all the girls before her.

She had to fight.

Kicking out her heel, her foot connected with the shorter man's face. She startled him, just enough for him to lose his footing and his grip. Stumbling, he dropped her legs. But her small victory was short-lived.

A massive thud exploded at the back of her skull. The almighty blow from the man behind her immobilised her in an instant.

'I warned you.'

Lena flopped forward like a rag doll.

She felt the man grab at her roughly, breaking her fall just before she hit the ground.

She felt herself being lifted up, thrown into the back of the car. She was dizzy, her head pounding.

A sharp burn of her scalp as the man seized a fistful of her long auburn hair. Wrapping it around his fist, he twisted her around to face him.

He was just inches away from her now; his face almost touching hers. He was so close that she could smell his stale rancid breath, see the glistening beads of sweat forming on his forehead. His face was puce from the heat and the struggle to get her into the car.

Still woozy from the blow she'd received to the back of her head, she tried to focus. Her vision blurred; she was surprised at how young her abductor looked. She had expected someone older. This man looked only a few years older than Tariq. No more than twenty, she guessed.

'So, you think you're a wild one huh?'

The man's steely grey eyes flickered then, and Lena thought that she saw the tiniest hint of amusement behind them as he yanked at her hair even harder, ripping a clump from her scalp as he did so. The pain so acute, it forced Lena alert once more.

'Well, it won't take me long to tame you.'

Lena kept eye contact. Refused to let him see her pain; she stared back at him with nothing but pure contempt.

'Stupid little girl.'

He punched her again, this time his fist locking hard with her cheek, her neck snapping back, her head smacking against the window behind her.

Slumped in the car now, Lena had nothing left. She was exhausted; her body weak and broken.

'Tie her up,' the man commanded, as the shorter of the men slid in beside her.

The man did as he was told. He bound her legs together tightly with coarse brown rope before wrapping thick black strips of tape firmly around her wrists. He was obviously taking no more chances with her.

The car began to move.

Petrified, Lena sat slumped in silence as she stared out of the window. Her gaze fixed on Tariq's body, motionless, on the ground.

Move! Please, let me know that you're okay?

Only Tariq didn't. He remained completely still, lifeless, as the car continued off into the distance.

Lena watched until her brother was completely out of sight. All hope from her now gone.

She could feel the stream of blood pouring from her nose; the metallic taste mixed with the saltiness of her tears, filling her mouth.

Silent tears ran down her face as she wondered what fate was ahead of her.

She thought of Néné's words once more.

About those girls. About what happened to them after they were taken.

How they were trafficked around Europe like cattle.

Her mother hadn't been able to bring herself to tell her young daughter why the girls had been taken, but Lena knew. Rumours in Shkodër were rife. People in the village had spoken of how the girls that were taken were used for sex. Forced to earn money for men in ways so disgusting it was almost unimaginable to Lena.

Except maybe now she didn't have to imagine it.

Maybe she was destined to experience the horror of it all herself, first hand.

Lena sobbed as she thought how she should have listened to her parents.

They only wanted the best for her, to keep her safe, but she'd been so foolish, so pig-headed. She'd put Tariq in danger.

These men were savages, animals.

Capable of anything.

Resting her head on the window as the car made its way out of Shkodër, out towards the rural mountains of the countryside, Lena closed her eyes and said a silent prayer.

She had no idea what fate lay ahead of her, but one thing she knew for certain, her nightmare was only just beginning.

CHAPTER ONE

Saskia Frost's eyes snapped open.

With a sharp intake of breath she sat up in her bed.

Something had woken her.

A noise. Startling her from sleep.

She hadn't meant to fall asleep; she'd just closed her eyes for a few minutes. Exhausted from the week's harrowing events, her body must have finally given in. Yet even in sleep she hadn't been able to escape the torment of her father's death.

He haunted her dreams. He'd been back here at home with her. Sitting at the table having dinner. Laughing at something she had said, one of her stories. His eyes twinkling; his face lit up.

But as she had awoken to complete darkness in the cold, empty room, the realisation had hit her with full force once again.

He was gone.

Death was so cruel, so taunting.

Sitting up, her eyes fixed on the alarm clock next to her bed. She shook her head, dazed. It was past three a.m.

She must have dozed off. That was the longest she'd slept all week.

Saskia was annoyed with herself. She'd been determined to see the day through, to give her father the send-off that he deserved, but when she saw the measly scatter of acquaintances that attended his funeral, she had known it was never going to be that.

The day had been heartbreaking; the dismal turnout like the final twist of the knife.

Her father deserved so much more than a small cluster of people standing over his graveside – than the handful of mere strangers huddled afterwards in his kitchen. The stilted awkward conversations; their words full of clichés.

'He'll be at peace now.'

'In time, you'll be okay.'

She knew she'd never be okay, not now her father was gone.

Their empty meaningless words made her want to scream.

What did they know? What did any of these people know?

They didn't know her. They didn't know her father, how close they both were. It had been just the two of them. Always.

Saskia had held her tongue – determined to see the day through – to hold herself together, but the pretence had been too much.

Sneaking up into the sanctuary of her bedroom she had just wanted to escape. To have a few minutes alone with her thoughts.

That's when it had caught her. Her grief.

She'd crumbled.

Falling down onto her bed she'd sobbed uncontrollably. The weight of her grief so immense that all she had wanted to do was curl up and die too.

She'd been in denial. She knew that now.

Up until the day of her father's funeral she'd just been going through the motions, desperate to carry on as normal – trying to convince herself that somehow her father's death wasn't real. That there had been some kind of mistake.

You can't deny death when you're standing over a graveside, though. The memory of her father's coffin being lowered into the ground would haunt her forever.

Wincing now, she squeezed her eyes shut, trying to shut out the bittersweet words spoken by the vicar that kept playing over and over inside her head.

'Angeline and Daniel Frost – Reunited.'

Afterwards, other people had tried to console her with those same words.

At least her parents were together again now. As if it was some kind of comfort.

Saskia felt the tears threatening once more.

She had no one now. No family. No uncles or aunts. No cousins.

She was completely and utterly on her own now – and that thought alone scared her stiff.

She heard the noise again. Downstairs. Wiping away her tears, she wondered if someone was still down there. Maybe someone had stayed behind from the wake?

Rigid, totally still, she strained to listen.

There it was again. Louder this time.

A loud clang.

Someone was in the house? Frozen with fear, she couldn't move, couldn't breathe, her heart racing in time with her mind.

Shaking, she stepped out of bed, wrapping her dressing gown around herself, and tiptoed over to the doorway. Unsure of what to do, she pressed her ear up against the thick oak door.

There was nothing. Just silence.

Waiting just a little longer, she wondered if perhaps her mind had been playing tricks. If maybe she'd been hearing things.

This big old house could do that. The high vaulted ceilings and marble floors magnified every noise into an echo.

About to go back to bed, Saskia heard a creak from a door downstairs. She was certain now; sure she'd heard it.

Her mind went into overdrive.

What if it wasn't a guest from the wake? What if someone had broken in?

Filled with fear, she stared over at the phone next to her bed, cursing silently to herself as she remembered it had been cut off. The bill unpaid. The line disconnected.

Shit!

She couldn't even ring someone for help; she'd have to go downstairs and investigate. She tried to calm her nerves, convince herself she was probably just freaking herself out over nothing. It might be nothing. Just a window she'd forgotten to close banging in the wind. The cool draught pushing at a door.

She needed to check though, make sure that everything was secure. She'd never get anymore sleep tonight otherwise.

Slowly, gently, she pulled down the door handle and carefully crept out onto the landing.

Moving slowly along the thick pile carpet, Saskia's eyes searched through the shadows as she scanned the long corridor of bedrooms. Checking that each door remained closed as they had been earlier.

She looked down then, her eyes following the sweeping curve of the marble staircase.

Nothing.

No movement.

'Hello?'

Her voice quaking as she called out, betraying her.

She shouted again, this time determined to sound in control.

'Hello? Is anyone there?'

Her question, echoing off the walls, met with only silence.

Nothing.

Silently she berated herself. She needed to get a grip. She couldn't just hide away upstairs like a frightened little girl every time she heard a noise. This house was hers now. She needed to pull herself together.

She was halfway down the stairs now. She could do this.

Ensure that the house was empty, safe. She'd get herself a drink of water while she was at it. Her mouth was dry, her throat parched.

As her feet hit the cool marble tiles of the entrance hall, a loud shrill rang out to the left of her.

A loud crash, this time in the kitchen.

She could see the sliver of light shining through from under the kitchen door.

Shadows shifted as someone moved around; then she heard footsteps.

She wasn't alone.

Someone was in the house.

Fuelled with adrenaline, her heart pounded inside her chest.

Saskia scoured the entrance hall for something she could use as a weapon, to protect herself. A small ornate letter opener was lying on top of a pile of unopened mail.

Grabbing it, she held the silver blade out in front of her.

'Whoever you are, the police are on their way,' Saskia called out; impressed that her bravado masked the fact that inside she was a trembling wreck.

She waited for some movement, for whoever was on the other side of the door to panic and leave at the sound of her words. Instead she heard the scrape of a kitchen stool. A clang of a cup as it was placed on the granite worktop.

Alone in the darkness of the hallway, she pushed her back up against the wall, confused.

She waited. It was a stand-off.

She'd have to go in there. What other option did she have?

Saskia felt physically sick now as she stepped forward, anxiously pushing at the kitchen door.

Standing in the doorway now, the silver letter opener gripped tightly in front of her body, Saskia looked at the man sitting at the breakfast bar, perplexed.

She recognised him from earlier.

He'd been here, at her father's funeral. At the wake. Saskia had assumed he was an ex-work colleague.

Now, in the dark of night, with him sitting in her kitchen, grinning at her with an unfaltering look in his eyes, Saskia wasn't so sure.

'Who are you?'

'My name's Vincent. Vincent Harper.'

Picking up his cup of coffee, the man took a sip, holding Saskia's gaze. Unperturbed by her sudden presence.

'Why are you still here?' She wondered if perhaps the man was drunk.

'I could ask you the same thing?' Vincent smiled, then taking another mouthful of coffee he held the cup up, grimacing. 'By the way, this stuff tastes like shit! I take it your old man couldn't afford any of the decent stuff though eh? Seeing as he owed fucking thousands to half of London.'

'Excuse me?'

Saskia shook her head, even more confused. She had no idea who this man was, or what he wanted. What she did know was that she wanted him to get the hell out of her house. Now.

'I don't know who you think you are,' Saskia said, irritated. 'But I'd like you to leave.'

The man laughed then, throwing back his head. He was mocking her, and Saskia had no idea why, which only fuelled her temper further.

'I said I want you to leave. Get out of my house!'

Waving the knife out in front of her, her empty threat only succeeded in making the man laugh even harder. Finally, he stopped, his eyes twinkling with amusement as he shook his head in wonderment.

'You don't have a fucking clue do you? You've got no idea?'

'Don't have a clue about what?' Unable to hide her irritation, Saskia shouted. 'You are trespassing. You need to leave. I've phoned the police; they'll be here any minute… '

Saskia stared with defiance. Letting her words hang in the air between them, hoping that the threat of the police would be enough to deter the man; that he'd finally leave.

He didn't.

Instead, he sat back on the stool. Staring at Saskia, his expression cold.

His eyes unwavering from hers.

'Is that so?' He smirked.

Saskia nodded.

He knew she was lying. She hadn't called anyone.

He'd already checked the house phones. They were dead. He'd been pleased because it had meant that he hadn't needed to cut them, and she'd left her mobile phone down here. He knew because he'd already looked through it.

Reading through all her pathetic messages between her and daddy dearest. The photos of her with her posh-looking school friends. Pretentious little girls wearing too much make-up.

She was calling his bluff.

Only, Vincent Harper was too fucking smart to fall for it.

'Well, you'll be shit out of luck if the Old Bill do turn up, darling, 'cos I think you'll find that technically it's you who's trespassing.'

Taking a sip of his coffee, Vincent screwed his face up once more at its bitterness before placing his cup down on the counter.

The girl looked confused. He was really starting to enjoy this.

'Let me spell it out for you sweetheart! Your "daddy dearest" was up to his neck in debt! He owed a shitload of money to people all over the place. One of those people being my brother, Joshua Harper. You might have heard of him? No? Well, Joshua was nice enough to help your dad out. Only, the small matter of your father snuffing it means that the agreement they made is now null and void, isn't it, seeing as your dad won't be making any deposits into Joshua's account anytime soon. So, it looks like we're going to have to call in the debt. Just as it says in our contract here.'

Pulling out the envelope from the inside pocket of his leather jacket, Vincent waved it in front of Saskia.

'This house is ours.'

Vincent smiled then, the insincere gesture not reaching his eyes.

'But I don't understand.'

Saskia's voice shook now as the feeling of dread consumed her. Racking her memory, she was trying to remember her father mentioning the Harpers. She couldn't. Joshua and Vincent Harper? She'd never heard of them and she was convinced her father hadn't either. She would have known.

'I think there's been some kind of a mistake… ' She faltered. 'I don't understand who you are?'

Standing up, Vincent threw the paperwork down onto the kitchen worktop.

'You can just call me the messenger, darling. I'm here to let you know, politely on this occasion, that you have seven days to vacate this property.'

Vincent pushed his way past Saskia, both of them facing each other inside the doorway.

Leaning in, filled with arrogance, he raised his brow.

'And trust me sweetheart, I only do "polite" once.'

CHAPTER TWO

Her hands were still shaking uncontrollably even though Vincent had left hours ago. Still, Saskia Frost couldn't let that deter her. She needed to keep looking.

Slipping the knife between the gap in the wood, she levered the blade's edge on the wooden lip of the drawer. The lock of her father's desk was still not budging.

She'd been trying for almost ten minutes now.

Determined not to let it beat her, she leant against the silver handle, driving the metal into the gap again, using every bit of strength she had.

The contract that Vincent had taken great pleasure in delivering to her was sprawled out in front of her on the desktop.

The words were there in black and white. The deeds to the house signed over into Joshua Harper's name.

Her stomach knotted. It couldn't be true.

The paperwork was forged. A trick. They were lying. They had to be.

Pushing harder now, forcefully, the metal handle of the knife dug into her skin, indenting her palm, but she didn't care.

She had to get inside this desk. It was the only part of the house that she hadn't yet ransacked. Everywhere else had been ripped apart; every room, every cupboard, every box.

She was desperate to find something that would prove that it wasn't true.

This was the last place to check, but without a key, getting inside her father's desk was easier said than done.

Straining with all her might, Saskia gave the knife one last almighty push.

It wasn't working.

She couldn't open it.

Tears of frustration were streaming down her cheeks now.

Looking around her father's office at the pictures of her mother, Saskia felt overwhelmed with sadness.

The house was a shrine to her mother. Every room the same. Her father had been obsessed. Every wall, every mantle, adorned with pictures of her late mother.

Saskia had grown up under her mother's watchful gaze. Unable to escape those beautiful green eyes that stared back at her from every corner. Haunting her.

Saskia often wondered why her father had never blamed her. Resented her.

Because she'd been the one who had killed his beautiful Angeline.

Her mother had died during childbirth. She'd taken her last shallow breath just as Saskia had entered the world and taken her very first. It had been all Saskia's fault. If she hadn't been born, her mother would never have died.

Her father had never seen it that way, though. Instead of treating Saskia with any kind of resentment, the tragedy bestowed on them all had only made her father love her more. To him, Saskia was a precious miracle. His wife's last passing gift to the world.

He cherished this house. The memories inside these walls.

'You are not taking my house,' Saskia shouted, rage suddenly filling her as she gave one last almighty stab.

Her eyes opened wide at the sound of the click of metal as the lock popped open. Tossing the knife down on the floor, Saskia pulled at the drawer and dragged out the mass of paperwork that was packed down inside. A thick, heavy pile of papers.

Searching through them, Saskia felt a sense of dread wash over her once more.

The words coming out of the pages at her… final demands, bailiffs' letters, court summonses.

It was true. Her father really had been up to his eyes in debt.

Flicking through the letters, she noticed the dates. Some went back months ago, some dated almost a year ago.

How could her father have kept this from her for all that time? How could she not have known?

Her head was spinning.

Her heart told her that her father wouldn't lie to her; he wouldn't hide anything from his only child. They had always told each other everything. They were close.

But there were other papers too.

Betting slips. Bank statements.

Her father had been gambling.

Big money, too. Every day, hundreds of pounds deposited to places like Betfair and BettingWorld.

It didn't make sense to Saskia. As far as she knew, her father never gambled.

Fingering a pile of papers that had been neatly bound in an elastic band, separate from all the others, Saskia immediately recognised the fancy royal crest emblazoned on each letterhead.

The Royal Ballet School. Every single invoice had been paid in full.

Confused, she searched through the rest of the pile of bills. The house had been remortgaged. A loan. Credit cards. Yet her school fees had been paid in full. They were the only payments that her father had managed to keep up with.

She felt a sinking feeling in the pit of her stomach then as she finally understood.

This was why her father wouldn't have wanted her to know.

He knew if Saskia had even an inkling of the trouble he was in she would have given up her schooling. That was why he never told her.

He'd been so proud of her when she had first been accepted into The Royal Ballet School: 'My baby, a professional dancer. Just like your mother had been.'

He used to beam when he talked about the career that lay ahead of his daughter.

Placing down the invoices, Saskia continued to rummage through the rest of the paperwork. She needed to find the final piece of the puzzle, then she could prove that these men were lying. As much as her father was in debt there was no way that he'd ever give up their home.

Lifting up the final brown envelope, she looked inside.

Bingo!

The deeds of the house. Her father's copy.

She scanned the paperwork, her legs weakening beneath her as she saw Joshua Harper's signature. Dated just a few days before her father's heart attack.

My God, it was true. Her father really had signed the house over to those people.

Slumping down into the chair, she held on to her father's desk to steady herself as her uncontrollable sobs shook her body.

She'd lost everything. Her father, the house, it was all gone. Taking a deep breath, she wheezed, the walls suddenly closing in on her, suffocating her.

Getting up out of the chair, Saskia pushed the pile of paperwork across the desk, every piece of paper crumpling to the floor.

She needed to get out of here; her head was spinning. She needed some fresh air.

Her dad had always told her that he'd live out his days here in this house. The house no longer being in his name had been the catalyst that had brought on his heart attack.

That's what had killed him in the end, Saskia was sure of it.

Right up to the end, he'd tried to protect her from it all.

Closing the office door behind her, Saskia was hit by the bittersweet irony of her father's kept word.

He *had* lived out his days here. But he hadn't just willingly walked away.

Instead, he'd been carried out in a body bag.

Her father had paid the highest price of them all.

CHAPTER THREE

Pressing down the handle of the studio door, Saskia stalled. She didn't want to go in. She didn't know what to say. Instead, she stood staring in through the glass, watching, as the girls lined up against the barre, perfecting their pointe work.

They looked like a row of robots. Each girl pulling her body up straight; taking turns at twisting their bodies around into a beautifully executed arabesque. Each girl moving gracefully, perfectly composed, as she extended her legs backwards, torso bent forwards, arms outstretched.

Miss Godfrey's shrill voice spoke over the music.

'Come now girls, lean forward more! What have I told you all? Lean too far forward and break your noses, or lean too far back and break your backs? Lean forward, at least your noses can be fixed.'

Obedient. Disciplined. The girls all did as they were told, pushing themselves to their most flexible point. Each was desperate to outdo the other. To be the best.

'Keep your hands light, girls. I wish to see no white knuckles. It's all about the balance.' Irritated that the girls were slacking today, Mrs Godfrey berated them. 'This is just the rehearsal, girls. You need to do better than this… '

Saskia stared at the girls' faces.

Determined, they stood in a line in their uniform black leotards and leather ballet shoes. The same plain buns in their hair.

Their faces were etched with concentration as they listened intently to every instruction.

Staring in through the glass Saskia felt like an intruder, as if she'd just seen a glimpse of a world in which she no longer belonged.

A world she'd never belonged to in the first place.

Ballet had never been her dream.

It had been her father's.

He had so desperately wanted Saskia to be a world-class ballet dancer – just as her mother had once been, years ago, before Saskia was born.

Her thoughts were interrupted as a familiar voice called out from behind her.

'Well, well, well. Saskia Frost. I wasn't expecting to see you back here again!'

Turning, Saskia took a deep breath. It was Lauren Durand.

The French girl had been at the school for just over six months, and she had taken an instant dislike to Saskia on her very first day.

Daughter of an oil tycoon, Lauren liked to think that she had an air of importance about her, and the other girls, sensing the girl's high social status, had flocked around her like sheep.

'We heard that you weren't coming back,' Lauren said, raising her eyes questioningly. 'Because of your… circumstances.' The French lilt to the girl's voice only added to her patronising tone.

'My circumstances? You mean because of my father passing away?'

Saskia's back was up now. Bristling at the girl's lack of tact and sympathy, she was trying her best not to rise to Lauren's spitefulness, knowing it was exactly what the girl wanted from her.

'Yes, that, and your other circumstances. Like not being able to pay your school fees. Is it true that you're going to have your house taken away from you? Only Jessica Walters said you had debt collectors at your door. Loan sharks? She said that a man had actually broken in? No wonder you went around to Jessica's house, crying your eyes out. It must have been so horrible for you... ' Lauren was on a roll now, but spoke in a faux-sweet voice, eyes wide.

Trying her hardest to hold herself together, Saskia didn't let the girl know how much her words hurt.

She'd confided in Jessica and was bitterly stung that her so-called friend had spread her private business around the school. She felt stupid now for thinking she could have trusted the girl.

Desperate to save face, Saskia didn't give Lauren the reaction she was so clearly waiting for, instead, she just shrugged.

'I've only came back here to collect some things from my locker. I was going to pop in and say goodbye—'

'Such a shame that you're leaving. You probably would have been an okay ballet dancer – with a lot more practice, of course. The girls are a bit busy right now. We have auditions for the role of Juliet at the London Coliseum. Can you even imagine?'

Lauren had already pushed past Saskia, opening the door of the studio. Now, she turned back and sneered.

'I'll tell the girls that you popped by though, shall I? Though I'm sure they've already forgotten all about you... '

Lauren sashayed back into the room with an air of confidence: a gaggle of girls gathering around her as she shared with them her latest snippet of gossip.

Saskia watched as Lauren, Jessica and the rest of the girls all turned to face her as they whispered amongst themselves.

She'd stupidly expected looks of sympathy, a friendly wave; instead, they all just stood staring at her before bursting into laughter at something Lauren said.

Stepping away from the doorway, Saskia felt her face burning, humiliated. She never told her father about how the girls here had looked down their noses at her. She'd just got on with it, desperate to make her father proud.

He'd always thought that the school was elegant. Becoming.

A place where dreams were made.

Only, they had been her father's dreams, not hers.

Making her way down the corridor to collect her belongings from her locker, Saskia was glad that she was leaving. This place had never been any of those things for her.

It was fake, just like the girls that attended it.

It was all just an illusion, mirroring everything else in her life lately.

Saskia Frost couldn't wait to get out of the place. For good.

CHAPTER FOUR

Drita was here.

Lena hadn't heard the woman let herself in, but she could hear her now. Her low mumbled drone filling Ramiz's head.

Drita had a way of doing that. Of goading Ramiz, causing him to work himself up into an almighty rage. His mother was his puppet master; all she had to do was pull the right strings… and Drita always knew which ones they were. It didn't take much for Ramiz's temper to get the better of him.

As Ramiz's loud angry shouts filled the house once more, Lena closed her eyes in despair, praying that he wouldn't wake Roza again. The poor child had been terrified earlier. Picking up on the tension building in the house, Roza had screamed inconsolably for what felt like hours until Lena finally managed to settle her.

If Drita had been summoned to the house tonight, then that only spelled trouble for Lena.

Knowing Ramiz, her punishment was probably far from over.

The safest place for Roza right now was tucked away in her crib.

Hearing footsteps in the hallway, Lena busied herself in the kitchen, stirring the *chomlek* that bubbled away on the stove.

Ramiz and Drita's thick Albanian accents floated through the thin cottage walls as they continued their loud, animated conversation.

Catching her reflection in the broken mirrored tile on the wall, Lena winced. Her fingers reached up to her swollen right eye, flinching, as she pressed the dark purple bruise that circled it.

The wrath of Ramiz.

The man lived like a caged animal, constantly pacing the house, resentful and irritated by everything.

Lena tried her hardest to keep out of his way: keeping herself busy with the chores, cooking, cleaning, but trapped here like a prisoner, confined inside these four decaying walls, staying out of the man's way was proving an impossible task.

Besides, today's attack had actually been all her fault for once.

Lena knew that she was never to venture out of the house; she wasn't even allowed to go as far as the main gate. She'd learned her lesson the hard way.

She should never have gone down to the village, knowing that she would never get away with it, but it had been like a moment of madness, born out of pure desperation.

After a whole year of being kept here against her will it had been her first real attempt at trying to escape, and she had failed miserably.

Ramiz had been asleep, passed out on the sofa, drunk on the *Rakia* that he spent most of his days drinking.

He'd been drinking more and more lately.

Lena had been watching him, biding her time.

He'd drunk himself into his usual stupor and, knowing that he'd be out cold for hours, Lena had seized her opportunity.

Only, when she got down to the village, she had felt overwhelmed with fear, scared of who she could actually trust.

If she spoke to the wrong person, the Gomez's would know. They would find out. Drita always found out everything.

Then they would kill her, or worse, they would kill Roza.

Ramiz had threatened it often enough.

Filled with panic, Lena had wandered around the market in the end. Begging for scraps from the stall holder so that, at least, she wouldn't have to go home empty-handed. If Ramiz had already woken she'd have some kind of an alibi. Ramiz might believe that.

By the time she'd reached the farmhouse, Ramiz had long awoken from his afternoon nap. Prowling the house like a lion ready to pounce on his prey, he'd attacked her as soon as she walked through the door.

His punishment had been brutal as always. He'd been consumed by it; she had seen it in his eyes. He got a sick kick out of the sadistic violence he inflicted on her.

'You will obey me. You *will* show me respect!' he had screamed as the blows had rained down on her body. 'You do not leave unless I give you permission.'

Despite her bruises, Lena had carried on as normal, feeding and changing Roza, even though it had taken ages to settle the hysterical child.

Lena had stayed in the kitchen after that, desperate to stay out of Ramiz's way.

She'd kept herself busy: chopping vegetables and small cuts of the fatty lamb she had managed to haggle for nothing from the street market.

Chomlek. It was Båbå's favourite dish.

Closing her eyes, Lena was suddenly overcome with emotion as the familiar aromatic scent of garlic and onion-infused lamb filled the room; the smell instantly transporting her to memories of back home.

She thought of Néné standing in their family kitchen, cooking the stew for them all.

Båbå would be sitting at the table laughing at one of Tariq's jokes.

A heaviness pulled at her chest. Oh, how she missed them all.

It had been a whole year since she had been taken.

She thought of her family always. Wondering what her parents would think of their little granddaughter, what Tariq would think of his only niece.

Tariq.

The image of him lying on the ground, injured, unmoving, haunted her.

She had to believe that he was okay. That he'd survived that fateful day.

Right now she would give everything she had to be back there with them, back home with her family. Tariq, Néné and Bábá. Surrounded by love, laughter.

Anywhere but here, stuck in this neglected farmhouse with Ramiz. Locked away like his slave.

It wasn't a life; it was merely existing.

'Lena.'

Jumping at the sound of her husband's shrill voice, his tall, burly frame looming in the doorway, Lena tried to compose herself. He'd caught her off guard.

'Get a bag for Roza's things. Drita's taking her.' Speaking through gritted teeth, Ramiz glared at her, his eyes still flashing with anger.

'Your mother is taking her? Where?'

Holding onto the kitchen worktop, the quiver in Lena's voice betrayed the bravado she displayed as she answered her husband back.

'Do not question me. Just do as you are told!'

Lena could hear the nursery door opening along the hallway as Drita went in to the baby's bedroom.

She listened as the woman padded back down the hallway towards the kitchen.

'Please. No.'

Unable to stop her hands from shaking as Drita entered, Lena stared at Roza snuggled in the crook of the woman's arm.

'You can't do this,' Lena begged.

'That is where you are wrong, Lena. Ramiz is your husband. He owns you. He can do as he pleases.'

The stony expression on Drita's face was final. Glaring at Lena, the permanent scowl etched on her face highlighted the mass of deep-set wrinkles: the remnants of every sneer, every harsh word the woman had ever spoken.

'You caused this, Lena, and now you must be punished.' The older woman didn't raise her voice. She didn't have to. When Drita Gomez spoke you shut up and listened.

The woman was tiny, five foot nothing, her bony frame making her look almost skeletal, but her frail looks were deceiving; if Lena had learned nothing else this past hellish year it was that Drita was a force to be reckoned with.

Like mother, like son – Drita had brought her son up to be just like her: a monster.

'It's all a mistake, Drita. I promise, I meant no harm.' Lena's voice was a whisper now. She knew that once Ramiz and Drita had made up their minds there would be no persuading them otherwise, but she didn't know what else to do. They couldn't take Roza. 'Please, I beg you… '

'Silence!' Drita ordered, her face twisted with revulsion as she spoke, emphasising her ugliness. 'What you did could have jeopardised everything. So tell me why? Why would you put Ramiz's life at risk, you stupid girl?'

'I only went there to get us some food,' Lena lied.

'Your selfishness could have cost Ramiz his life. What if you'd been seen?'

Roza had started to cry again now. Irritated, Drita stared down at the small baby as if she was nothing more than an inconvenience.

'My milk is running dry. I'm hungry; I can't feed Roza.' Lena blushed as she continued to explain herself. Mortified that she had to admit to her husband and her mother-in-law that she wasn't able to feed her own baby, she felt her tears threatening. 'I was desperate. I'm sorry. It will never happen again.'

'What sort of a woman can't even feed her own child?' Drita smirked as she rocked Roza back and forth in a vain attempt to quieten her. 'This child has no hope with you as its mother. Roza will be better off with me. Get me a bag, Ramiz.'

Watching as Ramiz grabbed a straw bag from behind the kitchen door and gathered up Roza's belongings, Lena caught the twisted sneer that crossed his lips, the flash of malice in his eyes.

He was enjoying this.

She knew it was his new way of punishing her; using Roza as his pawn.

'Please don't do this, Drita? I'm telling you the truth. I went down to the village for food. Look, I'm making *Chomlek* with the meat I got. You can't punish me for that… '

The Gomezes had taken everything from her. Stripped her bare – her family, her freedom, her life – but she refused to let them take her child.

'Please! I do everything that is expected of me and still it's not good enough… ' Lena said bitterly.

'Everything that is expected of you – except to bear me a son.' Ramiz spoke quietly now, his eyes still flashing with anger.

Lena shook her head.

This was madness.

'A son?' Lena screeched.

Ramiz didn't want the child that he had. He'd barely acknowl-edged Roza's presence in the four weeks since she'd been born. It was as if he couldn't bare the sight of her, couldn't stand her.

Sons were of value here in Albania. What use were daughters?

'What good would a son be to you, Ramiz? A son to continue the Gomez name? Another victim to add to the list?'

The fear of her mother-in-law and husband was suddenly lessened by the fear that, if she didn't speak up, they would take her child from her.

Drita was leaving. She was taking Roza. For how long?

Lena was sobbing now, and her body shook. She had to try and fight. 'All the men in your family are doomed, Ramiz, just like you are. Just like we all are! This is no life; it's nothing more than a slow death sentence for us all. I hope the Bodis come for you, and soon. Then maybe we can all be put out of our misery!'

'Shut up.'

Ramiz crossed the room in two strides, slamming his head into hers; the force of his head-butt sending her flying across the room, collapsing in a heap on the floor.

Placing her shaking hand up to her forehead, Lena could feel the sticky patch of fresh blood. The pain in her skull was intense, as if it had been cracked open.

Drita loomed over her.

For a second Lena thought that the woman was going to help her up. Check that she was okay. But the woman took this chance to berate the girl too.

'You think we choose to live this life?' Twisting her lips into a sneer, Drita spat her words with venom. 'The ancient *Kanun* law incites that spilt blood must be met with spilt blood! This blood feud is our fate. We must accept it.'

'Accept it? Why must I accept it? I didn't choose this life! You kidnapped me. Forced me to marry this animal, to bear his child.'

They were taking Roza regardless of what she did or said, so what else was there to lose? She was finally speaking the truth.

'This is your fate, not mine. It's you that needs to accept it, Drita. Give Ramiz up to the Bodis, hand him over. Why prolong all of our suffering any longer? If we should accept our fate, why are you hiding him up here in the mountains like a coward?' Raising her voice, Lena knew that her words would only make her punishment a hundred times worse, but she no longer cared.

'Do not tell me about cowards,' Drita hissed. 'I have lived through five decades and in that time I have seen my uncles, my brothers, my nephew all slain by the Bodis. I'm not ready to let them take my only son too. Not yet.'

Drita shook her head sadly.

The girl in front of her knew nothing about struggle, about the sacrifices that this family had made. How dare she jeopardise everything that they had done to protect Ramiz's location?

'It's my wish that he hides away. Mine! What's a little more time?' Drita's voice quivered as she fought to hide the emotion behind her words. 'I have watched too many men from this family slaughtered at the mercy of the Bodis. Murdered savagely over a dispute that happened so far back in our family's history that even my own Néné had trouble remembering how it all started. You are a Gomez now; you owe it to Ramiz to honour his wishes. Without honour for your own husband, Lena, you may as well be dead.' Furious at Lena's disrespectful outburst, Drita struggled to control the tremor in the back of her throat. 'Your husband had forbidden you to go down to the village, yet you disobeyed him. You put his life at risk.'

'Mother to mother, Drita, I beg you, please don't take my baby from me… I made a mistake. It will not happen again.'

Drita was quiet. Taking a second to compose herself, she shook her head.

'Sorry isn't good enough.'

Waving her hand in the air, she dismissed Lena's plea.

Turning on her heel, with Roza clutched tightly to her chest, the child's bag in the other, she addressed her son.

'I'll keep the child with me until you have got your house back in order. However long it takes.'

Lena felt physically sick as she watched the exchange between mother and son. She was leaving now. Taking her baby.

Roza was crying.

'No!' Lena ran then, shrieking.

Leaping off the floor, she grabbed Drita roughly on the shoulder and swung the woman around, almost causing her to fall as she desperately tried to snatch her baby back from the woman's grasp. She wouldn't let them do this to her. They couldn't.

'Enough!' Ramiz bellowed as he pulled his distraught wife back from his mother, restraining her by her wrists and slamming her up against the wall behind her.

'You have your work cut out with that one,' Drita sneered, and with one last look, she was gone.

'No, please, Ramiz, please. Don't let her take our baby. I'm sorry for what I did.' Begging now, she saw the glimmer of amusement in her husband's eyes as he gripped her arms tighter.

The front door had barely shut behind Drita and Ramiz was already on her.

Beating her once more.

All Lena could do now was pray for peace. For her punishment to be over.

Curled in a heap on the floor, trying to protect herself from Ramiz's vicious punches, Lena Gomez passed out.

CHAPTER FIVE

Wrapping her cardigan tightly around her as she walked down Battersea Road, Saskia scanned the road for a taxi.

The traffic was at gridlock, as usual: a typical Friday evening in London. Picking up her pace, she decided she'd be quicker walking, despite the bitterly cold wind.

Passing the endless queue of irritated drivers making their painstaking commute home, Saskia thought it was ironic really, the fact that this time of the evening was referred to as rush-hour, when it was anything but. In fact, at the moment, every vehicle for about a mile was at a standstill.

Slipping in between the halted traffic, Saskia crossed the road, reaching the ornate Albert Bridge.

She always found the view of the Thames breathtakingly beautiful. Especially at night when the usual dirt and grime of the city suddenly became invisible – hidden under the blanket of a million twinkly stars set in the darkened skies.

Stopping for a few minutes so that she could take it all in, Saskia cast her gaze out across the water, hypnotised by the luminous coloured lights that danced on its surface. Across the bank, clusters of people hurried about: the bars and restaurants crowded, buzzing.

Even from here she could feel the charged atmosphere. London was electric.

Saskia was soaking it all up, mesmerised; even the sound of the traffic behind her fading into almost nothing now. Just a gentle constant drone. Background noise.

This was the London that she loved the most: night, when everything seemed to come alive.

For a few minutes there was nothing else. Just her, standing on the bridge. Her hands holding onto the icy cold metal railings; the chill of the evening wind sweeping over her.

A few seconds of peacefulness overwhelmed her and it took all she had to stop herself from crying.

Turning her head back towards Battersea she looked in the direction of her house, where it stood nestled away under the steely shadow of the power station's iconic silhouette. Saskia felt the familiar heaviness in her gut at the thought of losing it.

She remembered her father once telling her that he hadn't been keen on moving there at first. How Saskia's mother had talked him into it. She'd fallen in love with the house. Detached, and set on the edge of Battersea Park, she'd described it as a diamond in the rough.

Her father had been approached by investors several times in the past few years, offering him large amounts of money to sell up. Battersea was a sought-after location to live in now, and everyone was cashing in. There were tower blocks and flats popping up everywhere. Even Battersea Power Station itself had been sold to developers.

Saskia smiled to herself wistfully.

A diamond in the rough. That's how she used to think about her dad.

Even with all his debt, all his money worries, her father had refused to sell their home. That's how much it had meant to him.

Closing her eyes, as if trying to block out the reality that she was facing, Saskia felt the familiar surge of anger rip through her.

In the space of just a few weeks she'd lost everything that mattered to her; nothing would ever be the same again.

That's why she didn't have anything else left to lose.

Glancing at her watch, it was almost half past five. She needed to get a move on.

Taking a deep breath, she continued walking, making her way to the end of Albert Bridge, towards Chelsea Embankment.

Taking the business card out of her pocket, she eyed the black swirly writing. Though she didn't need to keep reading it. She'd stared at the card for so long that the details were etched on her brain: *Harper's Palace, Kings Road, Chelsea.*

She was almost there.

Turning onto the infamous King's Road, Saskia weaved her way through the hordes of late-night shoppers and restaurant goers, grateful for the noisy distraction as she made her way towards what its website had deemed as 'London's most prestigious gentleman's club'.

She could see it just up ahead now. The purple neon uplighters illuminating the brickwork of the building; the neat row of topiary trees lining the front entrance.

Harper's Palace.

The place looked plush. Nestled between the flurry of shops and restaurants, the club took prime location in the centre of the King's Road.

Reaching the red carpeted steps that led up to the main entrance of the club, Saskia stood at the bottom. It was early. The club wasn't open yet. Saskia was glad; she wasn't sure that she'd have the nerve to go in there if it had been packed with people.

She stalled for time; scanning the road once more. The bravado she had felt earlier had gone now and her nerves were starting to get the better of her.

Am I doing the right thing?

Vincent Harper was dangerous.

Unhinged.

She'd seen it in his eyes and she had no doubt that he meant every word he said about 'not being so polite' the next time he came back. And he would be back. Of that she had no doubt.

So what other choice did she have?

She was on borrowed time. A week, he had said. Then she was out.

Taking a deep breath, she silently cursed herself. She had to do this. She had no other choice. She needed to face these people once and for all. To show them that she wasn't scared. That she wouldn't be bullied out of her home.

Gulping down one last lungful of dense London air, Saskia made her way up the steps, her eyes focusing on the burly bouncer who was guarding the main door.

She smiled.

'Can I help you, darling?'

Towering above her, the man looked Saskia up and down suspiciously. A questioning look in his eyes. Saskia realised that she probably didn't look like the usual sort that frequented Harper's Palace.

'Are you lost?'

Staring the bouncer straight in the eyes, Saskia shook her head, speaking with more confidence than she felt.

'I'm here to see Joshua Harper actually. My name is Saskia Frost. He's expecting me.'

Unable to hide his amusement, Joshua Harper smiled as he leant back in his chair listening to the continuous nervous chatter of the girl opposite him.

So this was Daniel Frost's daughter. What a turn-up for the books! The girl was simply stunning: model material. Her skin was clear, even devoid of make-up. Her hair scraped up into a messy bun on top of her head.

She was a looker all right; only she seemed completely unaware of her natural beauty.

Somehow her presence lit up the room, yet it was effortless. It was no wonder that Daniel had kept her as far away from Joshua and his business dealings as he possibly could. Especially knowing what kind of establishment Joshua ran here.

'So that's it, Mr Harper. That's my proposal.'

Joshua Harper zoned back in now that the girl's incessant talking had finally stopped. Raising his brow, he checked that he had heard her correctly.

'So let me get this straight. You want me to sign the house back over to you?'

Saskia nodded.

'The house that your father signed over to me in order to clear his substantial debt?'

Joshua eyed the girl curiously. She may be stunning, but she was deluded it seemed.

That was a real shame, Joshua thought, but then, wasn't it always the way? The prettier the girl, the more of a fucking head-case they generally were.

He could see now why Saskia had been so nervous. The girl was completely out of her depth.

'You do realise that I'm running a business here, Miss Frost, not some kind of charity, don't you?'

Saskia nodded again, shifting uncomfortably in her seat as she caught the mocking tone in Joshua Harper's voice. He made her request sound suddenly ridiculous. Maybe she hadn't explained herself properly?

'I'm not asking you to just hand the house back over to me, Mr Harper. I'm asking that you reinstate my father's debt. Give me the chance to pay it off, and in return I get to keep my home.'

Joshua pursed his lips.

This had to be some kind of a joke? If Daniel Frost hadn't been able to keep on top of his finances, then how the hell did this young woman think that she could?

'I'm serious, Mr Harper.' Saskia spoke now with assertion, determined that the man realised she was deadly serious about her proposal.

Joshua frowned.

Saskia Frost either had some serious front on her, or the girl was just completely naïve. Joshua just couldn't put his finger on which it was. He could normally read people like books, but not this time. Baffled, he wondered if he was perhaps losing his touch.

'So, exactly how do you expect to pay me back £700,000, Miss Frost?' Joshua asked, intrigued.

Leaning back in his chair, he watched the girl flinch as she learned exactly how much money was involved.

'Seven hundred thousand pounds?' Saskia repeated, her voice barely a whisper.

It was an obscene amount of money, but the house was worth four times that, at least. Her father must have been desperate to agree to handing the house over.

Shit!

How would she find that kind of money?

Joshua was bored now.

Saskia Frost clearly had no idea what she was dealing with here. The girl didn't even know how much money her father owed. She was out of her depth; she knew it too. She had fear written all over her face. It was laughable. Coming here, making grand gestures that she would never be able to meet.

Saskia Frost was clearly as delusional as her father had been.

'Look, I'm sure you can appreciate, Miss Frost, that I am a very busy man. I'm very sorry about your circumstances, but I'm afraid there's nothing that I can do. The deeds are all signed. It's all above board. I'm really sorry… Truly.' Joshua's voice was clipped, irritated that he'd even entertained this meeting.

If anyone else had waltzed in here requesting something so ridiculous, they'd have been out on their ear before their arse had even touched the seat, but for a reason that he couldn't fathom, Joshua was still sitting here – still tolerating this absurd conversation.

'Please?' Saskia was begging now, obviously desperate. Holding Joshua Harper's gaze, unflinching under his obvious scrutiny, she no longer cared what he thought of her. If she walked out of here she'd lose everything. She had to at least try. 'I give you my word that I will pay you back every single penny that my father owed you. I will work seven days a week. I'll do whatever it takes, but I promise you, I will get you your money.'

'And how do you propose to make that kind of money, Miss Frost? What line of work are you in?'

Joshua Harper shook his head in dismay. The girl was starting to irk him now.

'I'll take the first job that I'm offered.' Clearing her throat, Saskia shuffled nervously in her chair.

Joshua Harper was staring at her so intently it was almost like he was looking straight through her.

'So you haven't even got a job?' Joshua could feel himself losing his temper. This girl was wasting his time. It would take her years to pay him back that kind of money.

This conversation was getting them both nowhere.

'I'll get one easily. I have auditions already lined up… '

'Auditions? So, you're an actress?'

Saskia shook her head.

'A dancer.'

'You're a dancer?' Joshua laughed then. 'Well, this really is just getting better and better... '

Stung by his laughter at her expense, Saskia rose to her feet, her temper finally getting the better of her.

'Mr Harper, my father has just passed away, and I'm about to lose the house that I grew up in.' Saskia fought back her tears, adamant that she wouldn't show this man any sign of weakness. How dare he sit and laugh in her face. She shouldn't have come here. 'Last night I woke up to find one of your thugs had broken into my house to threaten me. This isn't a joke. This is my life—'

'Calm down, Miss Frost.' Raising his hand to silence the girl – Joshua didn't have the patience for melodramatics. 'Please, sit.'

Realising that she had been shouting, that her hands were trembling, Saskia felt foolish. Joshua had barely raised his voice, but there something commanding about his tone that made her do as she was told.

'Let's get something straight, shall we? First of all, that thug that you are referring to is my brother, Vincent. He did not break into your house. He has a key. The reason why he has a key is because I gave it to him. I own that house. Secondly, I think you'll find that at no point were you threatened. Vincent was simply informing you that you have seven days to vacate the property. Was he not?' Joshua's tone was neutral now.

'Well, yes, but—' Saskia nodded.

'No buts! It's a real shame. I was quite fond of your old man as it goes.' Joshua meant it too. Unlike some of the down-and-outs that Joshua had loaned money to over the years, Daniel Frost was a decent man. He'd just let everything get out of control, and when it all had become too much he'd buried his head in the sand. Still, that was what this business was all about. One man's loss was Joshua Harper's gain.

He'd built an empire out of other people's misfortunes.

Joshua had an eye for knowing when to strike a deal and something in his gut was telling him to cut this girl a chance. *Fuck knows why though*, he thought, as he continued to scrutinise her. Whatever it was made Saskia Frost waltz in here and ask him outright for her house back – be it boldness or naïvety – Joshua really wasn't sure, but the girl had certainly made quite an impression. She was ballsy, he'd give her that.

'How old are you, Miss Frost?'

'I'm eighteen.' Saskia spoke quietly now. He was patronising her. Saskia knew what he was thinking: that she was just some stupid, naïve little girl.

She was beginning to feel like one too.

'Eighteen. Hmm!' Joshua nodded. Deep in thought. He knew better than anyone that there was nothing more attractive in this world than youth. Especially in his line of work. Fuck it! In for a penny, in for a pound. 'And you're willing to take the first job that you're offered?' Testing her now, trying to gauge how serious she was, Joshua raised his brow questioningly.

'You have my word.' Saskia nodded, full of determination.

Silent for a few moments, Joshua clasped his hands together across the desk before finally speaking. 'Okay.'

'Okay?' Confused at Joshua Harper's sudden change of heart, Saskia shook her head. 'What? You mean you're going to help me?'

'I'm going to give you one chance, Miss Frost. If you fuck it up, then that's it. Done. There will be no negotiations.'

'Thank you so much, Mr Harper. Thank you so much… ' Sitting forward in her chair, Saskia was so grateful for this opportunity that she felt like crying.

She had her house back. All she had to do now was find the money.

'Whoa. Whoa.' Holding up his hands, afraid that in her excitement the girl was going to run around the desk and hug him, Joshua looked at her sternly. 'You haven't heard my terms yet. There are conditions, of course!' His tone was serious now, forewarning.

Saskia nodded in agreement as she watched Joshua pick up his phone and tap in a number. It was answered immediately.

'Misty, can you come in here please?'

Replacing the handset, Joshua sat back in his chair. Tapping his fingers noisily on the desk as they waited; his eyes remained fixed on her.

Pretending not to feel awkward as they sat together in silence, Saskia concentrated on the music – the thud of the bass making the floor vibrate.

Finally, she spoke, her nerves kicking in again. 'I know that I won't get the deeds back until I've paid you off, but it would be helpful if you could put our agreement in writing.' Seeing the blank look on Joshua Harper's face, she continued, 'though I expect you know what you are doing. Being that this is your job I mean. Sorry, I'm babbling. I'm just so grateful for this opportunity. You have no idea what that house means to me.'

There was a knock at the door then.

Saskia was silenced as the door swung open.

'Saskia, this is Misty,' Joshua told her.

Saskia stared, unable to tear her eyes away from the stunning woman that had entered the room, followed by an overpowering cloud of sweet, heady perfume that filled the air around them all.

'Hi,' Saskia mouthed, smoothing her hands down the front of her black knee-length dress. Suddenly self-conscious of how frumpy she looked in comparison, Saskia eyed the girl's sharp, pointy-toed stilettos and the black lace fitted dress that barely covered her bottom.

'Misty is the House Mother here at Harper's Palace. She looks after all of the girls.'

Misty smiled at Saskia.

The gesture curt, unfriendly.

Undeterred, Saskia smiled back as she tried to gauge how old the girl was. A few years older than her she guessed. Her face was heavily painted with a thick mask of make-up and her clothes were provocative. Scanty.

Misty certainly didn't look like any kind of 'mother' that Saskia had ever seen before.

'Misty, I want you to give Saskia a tour of the place. Introduce her to some of the other girls. Make her feel welcome.'

'No problems, boss. Is this the new cloakroom girl?' Misty asked inquisitively, looking Saskia up and down with vague curiosity.

'No, actually. Saskia is a dancer. I want you to put her on a trial. Show her the ropes, so to speak. See how she gets on.'

'Hold on,' Misty said, her face flashing with anger. 'I thought recruiting the girls was my domain? We aren't taking anyone on right now? We've got a full house.'

Misty glared at Saskia like she was something she had stepped in; the disapproval clear on her face.

'Oh no, no, no,' Saskia interrupted. 'I'm not a dancer. Well, I am, only I do ballet. I'm not here for a job…' Looking back over towards Joshua Harper, Saskia frowned. Her face reddening. She wasn't sure what was going on here, but it appeared that someone had their wires crossed. That someone being Mr Harper. 'I think there's been some kind of a misunderstanding.'

'There is no misunderstanding, Miss Frost. These are my terms.' Joshua leant back in his chair, amused now. 'You said that you would take the first job that you were offered. Well, here it is. Working here, for me. It's good money too. You'll earn triple what you could earn anywhere else in London, trust me.'

'But this is a lap-dancing club.' Saskia shook her head. Screwing her face up at the thought of working here at Harper's Palace. 'I didn't mean somewhere like this, I meant a proper job—'

'A "proper job"?' Misty piped up, offended at the young girl's dismissive attitude. Misty had seen girls like her a thousand times before: stuck up bitches that had somehow managed to convince themselves that their shit didn't smell. 'Sweetheart, you have no idea!'

Turning to her boss, Misty shook her head, eyeing him like he'd lost the plot. 'Are you kidding me? This girl wouldn't last five minutes here. She's gonna go down like a dose of the clap, and that's just with the other girls, never even mind the punters.'

Joshua pursed his lips. He knew Misty well enough to know that she wasn't going to be happy about him overriding her authority, but as far as he was concerned it was tough shit.

'Well, seeing as it's my name above the door, I think ultimately it's for me to decide who gets employed here, don't you?' Joshua curtly reminded Misty.

Misty pouted. She was House Mother; that meant she was in charge of recruiting the girls. Still, she wasn't stupid. She knew when to keep her mouth shut. Once Joshua got an idea in his head there would be no persuading him otherwise. Besides, he was right, it was his club. If he wanted to employ any old plain Jane from the streets, that was his call.

When it all went tits-up it wouldn't be down to her.

Feeling the tension in the room, Saskia interjected. 'I'm sorry, I didn't mean to offend you, it's just that, when I said I needed work, this wasn't the sort of place I had in mind. I'm sure it's really… lovely. It's just that I've never danced in front of, well, men before. Not in that way…'

Saskia could feel her face burning.

She sounded pathetic.

She should be biting Joshua Harper's hand off for the chance he was giving her, but she felt so far out of her depth, suddenly, she was barely treading water.

'You're not going back on your word already, Saskia?'

Joshua had wondered how far he could go along with it; how far he could push the girl to see if she really meant what he said about doing anything to pay the debt off. Well, here was her chance. He was handing it to her on a plate.

Would she take it though, that was the question... ?

'Well, you can't say I didn't try and offer a solution to the predicament you found yourself in,' Joshua said, no longer bothering to suppress his smugness. 'If you change your mind, my offer's on the table for you. You work for me for one month. On a trial basis. Then and only then will I be happy to sit down once more and discuss your little proposal. They're my terms; take them or leave them.'

His tone was condescending as he challenged her. He obviously didn't think that she would do it. He knew that she would turn a job down here at the club. That's why he had offered it to her in the first place.

Who was she kidding, Saskia thought to herself. Even she didn't think that she would do it. What other choice did she have though? If she didn't step up to the plate now, she'd lose everything.

She had to at least try didn't she?

'Okay.' The word rolled from Saskia's tongue so softly that Joshua barely heard it.

'Okay?' he repeated.

Saskia nodded. Scarcely believing that she was actually agreeing to this madness herself.

'I'll do it, but I get to stay in my house during the trial.' Her voice betrayed her. Her words shaky, nervous.

'Done.' Joshua nodded in agreement.

He was impressed.

The girl really did have balls; he'd give her that.

Joshua had nothing to lose. Misty was right. Saskia wouldn't last five minutes in a place like this. She'd be chewed up and spat out before she even got her kit off.

He needn't worry about the house. It wouldn't be going anywhere. In the meantime, Joshua decided, he was going to have a bit of fun. He wanted to see how far Saskia would go to get her precious house back.

'Misty will show you around so you can get a feel for the place. Watch and learn, because tomorrow you're out on the main floor.'

Saskia's face paled.

Joshua had a feeling that he was going to really enjoy this.

'Well, there's no time like the present, is there?' Opening his arms out, Joshua smiled. 'Saskia Frost, Welcome to Harper's Palace!'

CHAPTER SIX

Flinging herself forward in the bed, Lena sat up, disorientated, trying to gather her bearings. Something had woken her. Perhaps it was the screeching noise of the metal farm gate? It needed oiling. Another of the many jobs around the farmhouse that never got done because Ramiz couldn't venture out any further than the front porch.

Straining to hear who had opened the gate, Lena listened carefully.

Drita?

The woman wouldn't come up here this late at night though. Not unless something bad had happened.

No one would.

Set in the vast green plain, surrounded by nothing but trees and shrubs, the farmhouse was so far up a dirt track it was rare for anyone to come this far up the mountain. Especially at this time of night.

Her heart thudding inside her chest, she could hear a vehicle pulling up outside her bedroom window. It sounded like a truck, but she couldn't see any lights. Why couldn't she see its headlights?

The realisation suddenly hit her then. Horror engulfing her body, she felt the tiny hairs at the nape of her neck stand on end, a surge of adrenaline rushing through her veins.

They had come.

The Bodis were here.

'Ramiz, wake up. Wake up… ' Screaming, Lena reached over to wake her husband, but his side of the bed was already empty.

Scrambling from the bed, Lena knew that there wasn't much time. Fleeing the room, she needed to get to her daughter; she needed to protect Roza.

Drita had finally brought her back after a week of torturous separation. She was asleep in the nursery.

Running down the hallway, in her haste, she slipped. Losing her footing on a cracked floor tile; her body slammed forward against the wall.

Somehow, she managed to regain her balance as she pulled herself upright.

Engulfed with panic, she continued to run down the corridor that stretched the length of the house; Roza's bedroom door in her sight now.

But then she was down again. Her body smacking with force against the tiles this time. Two strong arms gripped her body tightly, pinning her down on the floor.

'Let me go.'

Screeching, Lena struggled to break free, desperate to wriggle out of the hold she was in. She had almost made it to her daughter; just another few steps and she would have reached her.

'Don't move.' It was Ramiz. His voice deep, whispering, thick with fear.

He pulled her to him then. She could feel his heart pounding inside his chest.

He was scared.

Of course he was. This was his time.

The Bodis had come for him.

'Please Ramiz, I need to get to Roza. Please, let me go to her… ' Whimpering as she stared through the darkness, Lena focused on the front door before looking back towards the baby's bedroom.

She still had time. The Bodis weren't here for her. They wanted Ramiz. She could still make it if she ran. Just a few strides and she'd be there. She didn't want the child to be left on her own.

'Quiet!' Ramiz ordered sharply.

Silenced by a noise outside, Lena did as she was told.

She could hear the heavy crunching on the gravel around the perimeter of the house.

Anxiously, they waited. Lena could feel Ramiz's heart pounding in his chest; his breath heavy, laboured.

Then the footsteps stopped.

There was a moment of silence – and then the bullets came.

Screeching in terror as the house suddenly filled with the deafening sound of gunfire, Lena fought mercifully to loosen her husband's grip, which only made Ramiz hold onto her tighter, refusing to let her go.

A shower of bullets rained down around them, puncturing holes in the thin wooden walls, covering them both in dust and debris. Lena's only thought was to get to her daughter.

She could barely breathe. Ramiz was squeezing her up against him so hard that her chest felt like it was being crushed. The coward. He was using her as a human shield.

Above them, a bullet tore through the thin glass windowpane. Instinctively, Lena turned her head, pressing her face to the floor. But Ramiz hadn't been so quick.

Jagged shards of glass plummeted violently down on top of him; the large chunk breaking over Ramiz's head imploding on impact.

Caught off guard, Ramiz shrieked in pain as a pointed sliver of glass was embedded in his cheek. Distracted by the intense agony, he loosened his grip.

It was all Lena needed; struggling free, she jumped to her feet. Dodging the spray of bullets around her, she ran towards the frantic cries from Roza's bedroom.

Pushing the door open, Lena ran to Roza's crib.

'Shh, Roza, it's okay. Néné is here.' Whispering as she scooped her daughter up into her arms, Lena quickly crouched down in the corner, seeking refuge behind the wooden dresser.

The gunfire was still going on, destroying the house. Closing her eyes, Lena whispered her silent prayers over and over.

She felt guilty, then, for all the times she'd prayed for the Bodis to come and kill her husband. Now they were here, but the Bodi family were so desperate for their vengeance that they had no concerns about sparing her or the baby in the crossfire.

Drita had warned her about this.

She'd said how women and children were no longer being spared in the bloodshed. The ancient *Kanun* was being disrespected. The feuds were no longer about honour any more; they were just an excuse for brutal violence. Only, Lena hadn't believed her.

She'd thought her mother-in-law had just been trying to scare her.

That would have been typical of Drita: to deliberately make Lena fear the Bodis so that she would never be tempted to alert them of where Ramiz was hiding.

Now though, huddled on the floor as bullets tore through her home, Lena knew that Drita had been telling the truth.

The Bodi family were after blood – Ramiz's blood – and they would take it any way they could get it.

As the loud gunshots continued, Lena knew that she needed to try and stay calm; Roza was picking up on her fear, crying, shaking. Lena kissed the child tenderly on her forehead. Closing her eyes, she took slow steady breaths.

As quickly as it had started, the shooting stopped. There was silence then.

But still Lena didn't move.

She could hear the muffled grinding of the gravel outside: the footsteps retreating.

Then the truck's engine started back up, the truck driving away. Then silence once more.

She stayed where she was, cowering behind the unit.

Was it over?

Jumping, she heard a bang.

Followed by another heavy thud.

They were *inside* the house.

Desperate to keep Roza quiet so that they wouldn't be found, Lena covered Roza's face with the blanket. Smothering the child's cries.

Lena was petrified now. If the Bodis found her they would kill her. She was convinced of it.

The noise was getting louder. Coming towards Roza's bedroom.

Squeezing her eyes shut, Lena held onto Roza as the bedroom door burst open.

She saw Ramiz standing in the doorway, blood dripping from the deep gash in his cheek.

'Get dressed,' he ordered.

Realising that she was in only her underwear, Lena was incensed, full of frustration that her husband was still alive. The enormity of what had just happened suddenly hit her, and all he could do was tell her to cover herself up.

'That's all you have to say? Get dressed? Are you not even going to ask how your daughter is?' The force of the hatred in her tone surprised even her. 'She could have been killed, Ramiz.'

'And whose fault is that?' Ramiz sneered.

'What?' Incredulous at his denial, Lena wanted to scream. 'They came for you?'

'And you think that it is just a coincidence do you? That the Bodis have found me a week after you went down to the village. You stupid little girl. You led them straight to us.'

Ramiz sounded angry, but there was something else in his voice too.

A new-found determination.

'We are no longer safe here. Get your things together; we are leaving.'

'Leaving? To go where?' Lena asked.

'We're going to make our way across the borders. To England.' Ramiz glared at Roza now, as the child whimpered. 'I want her silenced on the journey though.' Pulling out a small plastic bag from his jeans, Ramiz chucked it down on the floor next to Lena. She knew it contained opium.

'She won't need it. I will keep her quiet,' Lena begged, pushing the bag away from her.

The drug was common here in Albania, some mothers using it daily to sedate their children while they worked, weaving carpets. Lena remembered seeing babies back home in her village near the city of Shkodër. Heavily medicated, their eyes vacant, their bodies limp. Enough so that their parents could do a day's work without burden. Enough to quieten the child's cries of sickness – of hunger.

She didn't want to use opium on her child. Not ever.

'Do as you are told, or I will leave her here with Drita. I will not allow her to jeopardise our journey.'

Lena couldn't bear the thought of leaving Albania, but she knew she had no choice. Ramiz was in charge. She had to do as she was told.

'She's only crying because she is scared,' Lena pleaded with her husband. 'She will be fine. I will make sure of it—'

'Very well. I will call for Drita—'

'No. Please… ' Lena shouted, desperation in her voice. There was no way that she was leaving Roza behind with Drita. She'd never see Roza again. Not if they were fleeing to England. 'I'll do it.'

Lena picked up the packet.

Ramiz smiled.

'Shut that little bitch up. We leave in twenty minutes.'

CHAPTER SEVEN

Cowering in the bushes at the back of Greenwood Cemetery, Colin Jeffries stared out from the thick green foliage as tiny droplets of rain fell from the leaves above him. Wiping the splashes of water from his beard, he stepped back just enough to ensure that he remained firmly out of sight.

At least the rain had eased off a bit now. It had been pouring down earlier this morning when he had dug the grave out, lashing down around him; his boots caked in slushy thick mud; his overalls soaked, clinging to his skinny frame. Grave digging might sound like a morbid line of work to some people but to him it was an honour. It was the very last act that was carried out for the deceased. Their final resting place was down to him, and it was imperative that every detail of the task be executed to perfection.

Today's grave had taken three hours to prepare. The heavy downfall slowed him down, but he had persevered; clawing up the pieces of turf with the excavator before carefully placing the sods of grassy earth into a neat pile.

Perfect precision.

If it wasn't done properly it looked messy. You could tell.

Even when the turf was covered with the green matting it still had to be just so.

That's where the other workers all went wrong.

Shoddy preparation.

Unlike him, they hurried the groundwork. Not valuing how crucial every step of the process really was.

People turned their nose up at his job, he knew that, but he loved it and, despite the heavy downpour, he had been determined to do his absolute best as always.

His perfectionism made up for his biggest downfall: his refusal to backfill the graves.

He knew it was strange, a gravedigger who wouldn't fill the graves back in, but he just couldn't bring himself to do it.

Burying the deceased under a thick mound of soil was too final, too disturbing.

It fucked with his head. Gave him anxiety. Panic attacks.

He'd been so busy concentrating on digging the grave, shoring up the side walls so that they wouldn't collapse during the downpour, he hadn't given much thought to the grave's occupant until he reached for the sack of sawdust.

He'd thought of the little girl then.

The local council insisted that children's graves were lined with sawdust: psychological reasons, they said. As if, somehow, in some small way for the family, seeing their child's grave lowered down onto a bed of sawdust instead of the cold, hard ground would ease their suffering.

Maybe it did? Colin doubted it though.

Dead was dead, no matter how you dressed it up.

Violet. That was the girl's name. Violet Jackson.

Colin had read her green ticket when it had been faxed through to the cemetery's office earlier that morning.

It was tragic. Ten years old – victim of a car accident.

Children's burials didn't happen here very often, but when they did, the mood in the cemetery was always charged, and today was no exception. The atmosphere was dark and heavy, mirroring the threatening sky above him.

Shuddering, Colin sighed as he watched the black clouds dancing around overhead.

Rain at a funeral was supposed to be a sign of good luck; that's what people often said. A downpour signified the Heavens opening.

More empty, meaningless words to ease the consciences of the people who have been left behind.

Funerals were for the living, not for the dead.

Hearing a noise, Colin looked over towards the gate. The ceremony was beginning. Intrigued, he eyed the procession of mourners.

The pall-bearers, shouldering the slim white casket, were leading the way. A couple walked directly behind the coffin, crestfallen, defeated, following Violet to her final resting place. The dead child's parents, Colin assumed.

The man's stocky frame appeared slumped; his shoulders sagging as if he'd had all his strength zapped out of him.

Colin's eyes flickered to the face of the mother standing next to him. Her demeanour was weak too. She looked as though, without her husband beside her to physically hold her up, her legs would have just crumpled beneath her.

Watching as the other mourners gathered around the graveside, huddling into each other for comfort, Colin eyed every single one.

He wanted to see the pain on their faces. The loss. To feel that it was real.

The prayers were read out. The final committal beginning.

The service was short. Bittersweet, as the rain poured down around them.

It was all over so quickly.

The coffin was lowered into the ground, and the mother finally gave in to her grief as she collapsed onto the wet, sodden ground, her raw cries echoing out around the cemetery. Her husband rapidly scooping her back up onto her feet – cocooning her in his arms.

It was an award-winning display. They didn't fool Colin, though. In fact, they sickened him.

Violet was the victim here. Not them. She was the one being put in the ground. She was the one who was dead.

'Earth to earth, dust to dust, ashes to ashes,' mumbling now.

Colin rubbed his head frantically. He could feel the pressure building behind his eyes as if his brain was swelling inside his skull.

When he looked up again, people were leaving.

His breath shortened as he watched.

The parents were trailing behind the crowd; the last ones to drag themselves away.

How very noble of them, but they'd still gone, hadn't they? They'd still left Violet down there all on her own.

Unable to contain his anger any longer, the familiar surge of rage ripped through Colin like a fierce boiling heat.

This wasn't right at all.

Violet. Such a precious name. Violets were Colin's favourite flowers too. The tiny heart-shaped leaves looked so delicate, fragile even. In contrast, their colour was so vibrant it was almost fierce.

Violets bloomed in spring. They'd never survive a cold October. Not buried in the dark ground.

A ball of panic gripped his stomach tightly as he heard the sound of the JCB starting up. His colleague had already started the backfill.

But it was too soon: the mourners hadn't even reached the gate yet.

Colin hadn't wanted to be here for this bit. He didn't want to see it.

He couldn't.

His legs went weak as he stood – rooted to the spot – watching the digger fill in the grave. Staring, trance-like, as the soil poured down on top of the coffin.

She would be trapped inside now. The weight of the mud trapping her inside the casket for all eternity. He knew she'd be scared down there all on her own.

Closing his eyes, Colin imagined Violet frantically scraping her fingernails against the casket walls in a desperate bid to get out; her screams muffled by the thick mound of earth above her.

Wheezing now. Lungs constricted like they were being crushed by his ribcage.

Doubling over he placed his hands on his knees to steady himself.

Breathe, Colin. It's just a panic attack. Breathe.

Only, his body wouldn't allow him to. He was losing control. He needed to get back out of his head, away from the twisted blackness of his mind.

That's what his counsellor had taught him. All those sessions he'd had as a child.

He needed to stay grounded. Stay in the moment.

Wriggling his toes, he pushed his boots into the ground. Stamping his feet manically. Just like she showed him.

He was here. Safe, standing on the grass, breathing in the cold October air.

Somewhere, just outside the gates, he could hear the London traffic whizzing past. The rustling of leaves as they blew on the ground around his feet.

He was out of his head and back inside his body. Here in the moment again.

Concentrating on his breath for a few minutes, he steadied himself against the tree. He couldn't look up again. He couldn't bear it.

Instead he checked his watch. It was almost five p.m.

He was late.

Mother would be waiting.

He'd been so distracted by Violet that he'd forgotten the time.

He'd have to hurry.

Bundling up the heavy black sacks that were bursting with weeds and dead flowers from the graves he'd just tended to, Colin tied a knot in the top of the bag before throwing it onto the maintenance trolley.

His skin felt damp, prickly. He'd have to shower before returning. Mother hated it when he was late, but she hated it even more when he came home covered in mud.

'Filthy bastard,' she called him last time. 'What have you been doing? Rolling around with the dead?'

Hurrying now down the pathway without daring to look back, Colin dragged his cart behind him.

Mother would be waiting and he couldn't have that.

CHAPTER EIGHT

'Okay, girl, show me what you've got.'

Dressed down in her velour tracksuit, the last thing Misty wanted to do today was come to her club on her day off and teach this new girl how things worked around here, but she didn't have much choice in the matter.

She might be the House Mother, but Joshua Harper called the shots around here, and if he was insisting that Saskia go out on the main floor tonight, then that's exactly what Misty had to make sure happened. But one glance at the nervous look on Saskia's face confirmed exactly what Misty had already suspected: this girl was going to need all the help she could get.

'Show you what I've got?' Saskia repeated now, her voice shaking with nerves.

'Yeah, dance, honey. Up there.' Misty pointed to the podium. 'I wanna see your moves. See what we've got to work with.'

Reluctantly, Saskia stepped up onto the platform.

Taking her time to stretch and limber herself up for her routine, she was clearly nervous, trying to buy herself some more time.

'Look, it's just you and me here, Saskia. I know you're feeling a bit shy, but trust me. This is the easy part. Later, this place is going to be wall-to-wall punters, so the best thing you could do right now is just get on with it. The more time we have to practise the better, yeah?'

Seeing Saskia nodding her head, Misty took her cue and hit the music.

Swaying from side to side, awkwardly, Saskia could see her reflection in the wall of glass at the back of the stage. She looked ridiculous. The beat of the music was too fast; she couldn't keep up. Lifting one leg she swung herself around in a circle, but losing her footing she fell over.

Shaking her head, Misty switched the music off.

'I'm gonna take a wild guess that you've never danced anywhere else except for this fancy ballet school you keep banging on about, am I right?'

Embarrassed, Saskia shrugged.

'I've done some theatre work – a couple of shows.'

'But have you ever worked a pole?'

'A pole?' Saskia shook her head.

'Yeah, you see that big silver shiny thing hanging out of the ceiling next to you? That's a pole, and I want you to dance around it, Saskia. It's part of the main set. You need to include it in your routine.'

Looking up at the pole, Saskia wasn't sure that she could do this now.

The idea of getting out on the stage and dancing in front of a room full of men, in only her underwear, was making her feel sick with nerves. She could barely get to grips with it, even though it was just Misty here.

'Don't look so worried. Just think of it like your ballet barre, only this one's vertical. Here.' Misty climbed onto the stage. 'Watch and learn.'

Pressing her body against the cool metal bar Misty slid her body down the length of it, before jumping up high, both hands gripping the bar tightly, and twisting her body back around until she reached the floor. Slow, controlled, sexy.

'That move is called the Fireman. Go on, try it.'

Standing back, Misty watched as Saskia took her turn.

Looking up nervously at the pole she wrapped her fingers tightly around the metal bar, a look of determination spreading across her face then as she twisted herself around it; perfectly mastering the move Misty had just shown her, first time.

Misty was impressed.

'Beginner's luck? Okay how about this one… '

Misty used more speed this time. Leaping onto the bar, her legs splayed out in the air, her toes pointing outwards; effortlessly twisting and turning until she eventually came to a gradual stop.

'It's called the Corkscrew. You wanna give it a go?'

Saskia nodded, willing to give it a shot. She mimicked the move once more. Doing the best that she could.

'You got it, girl!' Misty clapped her hands, surprised that Saskia was picking up the moves so easily. The girl wasn't bad for a newbie. 'You're good. You've got good posture; you're strong too. Your fancy ballet training has clearly put you in good stead.'

She clambered back down from the podium.

'Okay we're going to do it all again. Only, this time from the top, and you're gonna strip off this time,' she shouted up to Saskia.

'Strip off? What, now?' Saskia was horrified, her eyes darting over to where the cleaner was mopping the floor. Behind her, one of the other girls, Marnie, was stocking up the fridges at the back of the main bar. 'But I thought we were only practising?'

'We are.' Misty grinned. 'But you need to know how it feels to work your body around that pole in your underwear 'cos that's all you're going to be wearing tonight. Trust me, it's good practice. It feels totally different; you have more leverage against the bar if your skin's exposed.' Misty's grin widened. 'It's only taking your clothes off, Saskia. You wanna work this club, then you're gonna have to hang up your ballet shoes and tutu and don a pair of stripper heels and a lacy thong. If you can't cut it, the door's that way… '

Not wanting to seem like a prude Saskia did as she was told. Pulling her jumper over her head, she threw it down on the floor, then, gingerly, she stepped out of her tracksuit bottoms. Self-consciously, she stood there in her plain white cotton bra and matching knickers.

'Okay, now we got ourselves a party.' Misty laughed. 'Girl, you have got an amazing figure but what is with the granny underwear?'

Seeing Saskia now blushing profusely, Misty hit the music once more.

'Okay, let's just go over the moves I've already shown you, and I want you to add your own spin to the set too.'

Saskia, determined to prove to Misty and to herself that she could do this, put everything she had into her set.

Lifting herself up, she held her weight halfway up the bar. Taking it slow, Saskia worked her way down the pole, incorporating the spins and twirls that Misty had shown her.

She was really enthralled in it now; lost in the music. Adding speed to her moves.

Spinning around almost expertly until the track finished.

'Well I'll be!' Misty whistled, impressed, as she propped herself up at the bar. 'That was spot on, girl. You dance like that tonight and you're going to be laughing all the way to the bank, girlie! You fancy a drink?'

Breathless, and beaming from Misty's compliment, Saskia nodded.

'Marnie, can you get us a couple of coffees please?'

Pulling her clothes back on so that she didn't feel so exposed, Saskia walked over and joined her.

'You seriously think that I'll do all right?' Saskia asked curiously, wondering now if perhaps she could really do this.

'Oh, I'm not gonna lie to you. When you get out on that stage tonight you're going to need nerves of steel. The punters are going to take one look at you and they are going to want to devour you whole, girl!'

Saskia's face paled. Misty didn't want to scare the girl off completely, but she felt she needed to forewarn her. Working the club was hard going and Saskia needed to be ready for it. The last thing Misty wanted was for Saskia to walk out here tonight, full of confidence, only to see a crowd full of jeering faces and to lose her bottle. The girl needed to know exactly what she would be walking into.

'Harper's is members only, exclusive, so we generally get a good crowd in. Regulars mainly. There are cameras everywhere and we have security on all the doors. The stage and booths are all covered. Unless you personally give the punters the say so, and that's solely at your discretion, then it's a strict "look but do not touch" policy.'

Saskia nodded, trying to take it all in.

'You work the pole, do your routine, and the whole time you're up there you are reeling them in. That's key. You get eye contact with a couple of punters and you make them believe that you are dancing just for them. Make them feel like they are the only man in the room. They'll be queuing up to get you dancing in the private booths for them after that and that's where you'll make your money. We don't call them "ATM's" for nothing, girl! You push the right buttons and, trust me, these fellas will chuck out the notes faster than you can catch them.' Misty smiled as Marnie brought two coffees over. Taking her cup, she stirred in a cube of sugar before taking a sip. 'Private dances are four minutes long and fifty pounds a pop. No longer than that. With your cracking little figure you're going to be killing it.'

Misty had to hand it to Joshua; despite the fact that Saskia had never danced before, he'd been right on the money. With a bit more practice this girl could be a real asset to Harper's Palace.

'So what's your story? How come Mr Harper hired you? No offence, but you're not really the usual type for this place,' Misty asked, curiously.

So far, Joshua Harper hadn't divulged much information on Saskia Frost at all. Astute as always, he was playing his cards close to his chest.

This girl had come from nowhere and suddenly she was going to be out on the main stage. Something didn't sit right with Misty.

'My dad passed away of a heart attack. Worst thing was, after he'd died, I found out that he was in a lot of debt. I don't know if he'd gambled most of it away, or he'd been gambling to try and build some funds, but he'd lost it all. The money. The house.' Saskia didn't even know where to begin. 'It turned out that Joshua Harper had bailed my dad out. Only, the house had been used as collateral, so when my dad died I lost that too.'

Misty nodded. It was all starting to make sense.

'Joshua told me that your dad passed away. I'm really sorry to hear that.'

Saskia shrugged, but she was grateful of the girl's condolences. Misty was the first person to have offered her any that actually sounded like she meant it, but now wasn't the time to start talking about her father. No matter how genuine Misty seemed. If Saskia got into it all right now – how much she missed him, how heartbroken she felt – she'd only end up crying again, and lately Saskia had done enough crying to last a lifetime.

She needed to toughen up.

If she wanted to keep her house she needed to stay focused.

'I know it sounds crazy but I just can't lose my house as well as everything else. I've got to at least try to get it back. That's why I came here, to ask Joshua to reinstate my father's debt so that I could try and salvage something back from this mess… ' Saskia was reaching out to Misty now. She could see the girl was still sizing her up, trying to work out what Saskia was about. 'I know that you think I can't do this, but I'm going to put everything I have into it. I'm not going to let you or Mr Harper down. I'm so grateful to Mr Harper for giving me this chance. I don't know what I would have done without him—'

Misty laughed then, almost spitting out her coffee.

Shaking her head, Misty could see that this poor bitch had no idea what she was dealing with. Just because Joshua Harper had offered to help Saskia didn't mean that he had good intentions. Misty would bet money on the fact that the man had some kind of hidden agenda. Besides, from where Misty was sitting Saskia wouldn't have even been in this mess if it wasn't for Joshua.

'Girl, let me give you a word of advice, and this is strictly between me and you, okay?' Misty lowered her voice then; waiting for Marnie to move down the other end of the bar before she continued. 'Joshua Harper is a smart man. Whatever deal you've cut with him you can bet your life that he's getting something out of it too. He doesn't throw in favours for anyone. The man is as ruthless as they come.'

'Well, I don't know. I mean he didn't have to give me a chance here, did he?' Saskia shrugged, wondering if perhaps Misty was just annoyed that Joshua Harper had undermined her by giving her the job in the first place.

'Well, I guess only time will tell, huh!' Misty shrugged too. Sure as hell, if anyone else had come crawling in here asking Joshua Harper for favours, her boss would have had no trouble slinging them out on their ear.

Misty knew her boss well enough to know that something wasn't quite right.

Still, who was she to start stirring the pot? Her job was sorting out the girls. Everything else that went on here was none of her business.

'You done?' Misty asked, draining the last dregs of her coffee before standing back up.

Saskia nodded.

'Good, 'cos the coffee break's over and we've got a shitload of work to do.'

CHAPTER NINE

'My friends, welcome to the Jungle.' Opening his arms widely, exaggerating his welcome to Lena and Ramiz, Korab Malik led the way through Calais's overcrowded camp. 'Follow me.'

Covering her nose with her free hand, Lena pulled Roza tightly into her chest as she followed her husband. The bitter stench of the encampment had caught her off guard, taking her breath away. Ramiz had promised her a sanctuary. Somewhere she and Roza could rest before they crossed the border to England. This place was anything but – heaving with the heady combination of rotting food, faeces, and who knew what else –– it was like nothing she'd smelt before.

'How long will we have to be here?' Ramiz asked.

Recognising the curtness in her husband's tone, Lena could tell that Ramiz wasn't impressed either.

They'd left Albania three days ago: stowing away in vehicles, hiding in the back of lorries; passing through Bosnia and Austria with surprising ease. But now they were in France, and this last part of the journey looked like it was going to prove the hardest.

'Do not worry, my friends, you will only be here for two days. Maximum.'

Two days? Lena felt nervous, catching the harsh glares that were thrown their way as they walked. The residents of the camp were emaciated, wrapped in blankets, sleeping bags and old bits of curtain as they stared out from the gloom of their hovels, eyeing the newcomers with pure disdain.

'They look angry… ' Lena whispered.

'Ignore them!' Korab waved his arms dismissively as he noted Lena's fear. 'They see you as another mouth to feed that's all. Food here is limited. We have charities who come in and give us parcels, but it's not always enough. These people would fight tooth and nail over a minuscule piece of bread; they don't want to share the little that they have. The longer they have lived here the greedier they have become.'

'They live here?'

Following Korab deeper into the cesspit that was the Jungle, Ramiz's voice was full of doubt as he looked around at the makeshift tents that were little more than slums. Korab seemed genuine, convincing them that he could get him safely over the borders undetected but, if he really did have ways of doing it, why were so many people still here?

'This is disgusting. In Albania, we treat dogs better than this and back home the dogs are vermin.'

'Well, here at the borders it is us that are the vermin. That's why they call this place "the Jungle", my friend. To the authorities we are nothing more than animals. Pests. Even dogs rank much further up the food chain than us, trust me.'

Hearing a distressed scream coming from a nearby tent, Lena turned her head, shocked to see a pregnant woman, clutching her bulging stomach, fighting with a much older man.

Shrieking obscenities at him, the woman yelled, hitting out at the man. Pounding on his chest with her fists before the older man smacked her hard around the face and grabbed her by her hair, dragging her back inside the tent.

'Should we try to help her?' Lena asked, her eyes wide with fear.

Korab shook his head.

'Don't get involved in other people's business, Lena. You will only make it worse.'

'But she is pregnant?'

Korab shrugged.

'Look around. Most of the women here are pregnant. It helps their journey?'

'Helps? How? It must be awful to be somewhere like here, carrying a child?' Lena was confused.

'On the contrary! The journey across the borders is not an easy one for a woman on her own. So they seek out a man to help them. Having a man at your side keeps the others away; it's the lesser of two evils. These women are desperate. To them a child isn't seen as a blessing. It's seen as a golden ticket. If they are lucky enough to get to England in time for the birth, they will get even more help. Citizenship perhaps? A house, money.' Korab screwed his mouth up, distastefully. 'These women are not victims, they are desperate, and desperate people have nothing to lose. So, while you're here, keep your belongings and, more importantly, your child, close to you!'

'My child?' Lena felt sick at the thought of Roza being taken. Hugging her tightly to her chest she looked around the camp, suddenly suspicious of everyone they passed.

Korab nodded his head sadly.

'Trust no one.'

'Except for you?' Lena asked warily.

'Of course! Except for me!' Korab looked back at Lena and smiled, revealing a mouthful of rotten yellow teeth.

'How can people live like this?' Ramiz shook his head. He'd heard his friend was doing well, earning good money, but now he was here Ramiz didn't know what to believe. 'There must be another way? No?'

'For some, there is no choice. They have no money to get across and the officials don't know what to do with them. They shove us all in here and leave us to fend for ourselves like scavengers. Feeding us with empty promises of help, but the help never comes.'

Weaving between the shoddy dens, Korab stopped. Turning to face his friend, he said seriously, 'if we complain, or try to make our own way across, they beat us and spray us with pepper spray; sometimes they even take our food away by stopping the charity vans from coming on site. That one often works. They like to starve us; they know keeping us hungry keeps our morale down. The people here just want asylum, but the French, they make it impossible for them. There is nowhere to go so they end up stuck here.'

Turning back to lead the way once more, Korab groaned as he looked down at his worn-looking sandals. He'd stepped in the slushy contents of an overturned slop bucket.

'As the Americans say, shit happens huh!' Korab laughed, making light of his misfortune before wiping his feet on a patch of grass. 'Watch your step, my friends, here "shit really does happen", and people like to dump it everywhere. Let that be your first lesson.'

Continuing through the squalor the group soon reached Korab's tent.

'Home sweet home.'

Lifting the blue tarpaulin, Korab indicated to his new guests to go inside.

'Please, take a seat,' he said, pointing at the grubby mattress in the middle of the floor that had been placed on top of the plastic sheeting. 'I'll see if I have any food. You both must be hungry.'

Lena sat down, grateful for some rest. Placing Roza down next to her, she looked around them, taking in her new surroundings. The shelter was larger than all the others that they had passed, cluttered with mismatched furniture: a narrow camp bed set up in the far corner, and the floor space littered with boxes of knick-knacks that Korab had somehow accumulated.

'I'm a hoarder,' Korab said, catching Lena's eye. 'It sounds crazy, I know. The camp gets so lonely, and I miss my family so much, I guess I've got a bit obsessed with surrounding myself with this junk so that the place doesn't feel so bare.' There was a look of sorrow spreading across Korab's face as he spoke.

Changing the subject, he turned his attention to the child.

'So, tell me, how old is your little one?'

'Six weeks,' Lena said proudly.

'She is very well behaved for a new-born. She hasn't made a sound.' Korab smiled warmly.

'She is quiet, isn't she?' Lena looked down at Roza, who was still sleeping, her long lashes twitching every so often.

Dreaming peacefully. Lena ran her fingers through her daughter's tiny auburn curls.

She'd been lucky, as Roza had slept for most of the journey. That had worked in Lena's favour. Ramiz didn't suspect that Lena hadn't given her the drugs.

Taking the child from her Ramiz held Roza up. Checking her over, then tugging at her blanket, he recoiled to see that the nappy was saturated, covered in a watery brown leakage.

'How could you not notice the smell? Lena, the child stinks worse than this place,' Ramiz spat, wrinkling his face in disgust as the vile smell hit him.

'I'm sorry, I don't know why I didn't notice…' Lena stuttered, mortified that Roza had been in a soiled nappy for such a long time.

'Get her cleaned up.'

Taking off his boots, Ramiz made himself comfortable on the edge of the mattress.

'I'm sorry, I didn't realise…' Lena felt her cheeks burn as she apologised to Korab then too. 'Do you have a small bowl of water?'

'Please. No need for apologies.' Korab raised his hand dismissively before passing Lena a cup of cold water.

Turning back to her child, Lena began cleaning Roza up; riddled with guilt as she noted Roza's bottom was red raw. She had no idea how long Roza had been soiled. Wrapping Roza back up in her blanket, Lena took the baby over to where Ramiz was sitting.

'It's not much, but please, you need to eat.' He handed each of them a slice of bread coated with a thick tomato sauce. Korab held out his arms. 'May I?' he asked, offering to take Roza while Lena ate.

'Thank you.' She smiled, passing Roza over.

'What's her name?'

'Her name is Roza.'

'She is beautiful, just like her mother.'

Catching the glare from her husband, Lena blushed before she lowered her head and ate her food in silence.

The bread was stale, but she was so hungry that she had devoured it within seconds.

Roza started crying again. Awake now. She was probably hungry.

'I need to feed her,' Lena said, looking to her husband for permission.

Ramiz nodded, his eyes not wavering from his bread.

'Please, you can have some privacy over in the corner there. The camp bed. If you want to rest too, you are most welcome.'

'Is that okay, Ramiz?' Lena asked. Exhausted, the thought of lying down suddenly sounded extremely inviting.

'Go! Sort the child out and then get some sleep,' Ramiz dismissed her.

Nestling down on the camp bed, Lena pulled the blanket up around her. Then, laying Roza down at her side, she tried to feed her. Her breasts were tender but she worried that her milk had dried up. It hadn't helped that Drita had taken Roza away from her for a week. Worried that there wouldn't be anything to give her child, Lena felt the rush of relief as Roza suckled on her nipple. Feeding.

Then, closing her eyes, for the first time in days Lena slept peacefully.

'So, how is everyone back home?' Korab asked as he sat down opposite his friend.

'Same as always, I guess,' Ramiz said, disdainfully.

'Drita? She is well?'

'She is good, my friend. That woman only gets stronger with age.'

Ramiz felt a stab of guilt as he thought of his mother now.

The money that he had with him his mother had stashed away in a metal box under the floorboards of his kitchen. She'd told him that if he ever needed to leave in a hurry the money was for him. The condition being that, if he fled, he would say goodbye to her before he went. In his haste to flee the Bodis he hadn't been able to keep his promise.

Drita was his weakness. They were so alike that Ramiz knew what his mother was thinking. Sometimes it felt like they were the same person. Cold, hard. Saying goodbye would have stopped him from leaving; she was the only person that he truly cared about other than himself, and his mother wouldn't have wanted that.

'What about the city? I bet it has changed so much in the time that I have been away.'

Ramiz shrugged, not wanting to admit to Korab that he had no idea because he'd been holed away in a farmhouse on the outskirts of the city.

Knowing not to question Ramiz further, Korab just nodded. But the reality was that he was just testing Ramiz, seeing how straight he would be with him. Korab already knew more than he was letting on.

Back home in their village on the outskirts of the city the vicious blood feud between the Gomez family and the Bodis family was legendary. As the last surviving male in his family, Ramiz was living on borrowed time. That was why he was running. Ramiz was desperate to escape and desperate men only meant one thing to Korab: money.

The whole world was up in arms, not just the blood feuds, but wars, terrorism; nowhere was safe anymore and business was booming for Korab because of it.

'What about you?' Ramiz changed the subject. 'I thought you were headed to England too? To make your fortune. That's what they all think back home.' Ramiz cocked his head, curiously, as he questioned his old friend. 'Drita told me that you were doing well for yourself. That you were working in a hotel here in Calais.'

Glancing around at the squalor his friend was living in, Korab clearly wasn't doing as well as he had made out.

'The camp can be a dangerous place sometimes, so I told my family that I work in a hotel.' Korab grinned then. 'But trust me, my friend, I'm doing better than it appears. I will have enough money soon to send for them all.'

Not convinced that Korab was telling him the truth, Ramiz was starting to wonder what else Korab had lied about.

'You said you can get across to England? Can you?'

'Of course, my friend.' Korab nodded. 'You said you had money? If so, you are lucky, Ramiz. Money here buys you options.'

'What options?' Ramiz asked suspiciously.

'For a fee, I can get you on a boat. Far from here, away from the main port. It's a reliable route.' Korab raised his arms out wide.

'How much is the fee?'

'It's three thousand euros. Each.' Seeing the doubt flash in Ramiz's eyes, Korab added, 'but I'm a generous man, Ramiz, and you are an old friend, so for that I will let your daughter travel for free.'

Ramiz went quiet. Deep in thought.

Korab took that to mean that the man needed further persuasion.

'Of course, you can try and make it across yourself. I won't lie to you, it's possible, but it is a huge risk. Getting into a vehicle alone is no easy feat. Only last week the authorities scraped what was left of one man from the roadside. He'd jumped from the bridge in hope of landing on the roof of a moving truck. He missed.' Korab shook his head sadly. 'Others have been killed in transit too, slipping from where they have hidden in the undercarriages of lorries, crushed beneath their colossal tyres, and even if you did manage to stow away in someone's car, or lorry, the hardest part would be getting past the border officials.'

Korab could see that Ramiz looked daunted by what he was being told, but he was only speaking truthfully. It was only fair that Ramiz knew exactly what he was up against. He might be Ramiz's best option of getting out of here, but he needed his friend to work that out for himself.

'Then you have to get past sniffer dogs, heartbeat and carbon dioxide detectors, random vehicle searches. I'd say your chances of getting through are slim to nothing, even more so with the baby. It's not impossible though. Others have made it—'

'And your way?'

'There is a collection point about six hours away from here in St Malo. It's the best chance you will have of getting across the Channel. So much security is used here, at the main ports, it opens up the smaller ones for us. There'll be a boat waiting. The crossing is not too bad. Nine or ten hours depending on the weather. When you reach England, we will have men waiting for you. They will take you to a safe place. It's a good system. The best offer you will get around here. We do several journeys a week now. It really is foolproof, my friend.'

Knowing full well that Ramiz had money to spend – Drita Gomez would have made sure of that – Korab dangled his offer in the air like a piece of forbidden fruit. He knew that Ramiz would pay, whatever the cost.

'It's up to you though.' Korab shrugged. He'd been doing this job for long enough now he knew he didn't need a sales pitch. The deal spoke for itself.

What was the alternative, to live here in the Jungle? Sooner or later, if people had the money, they always paid.

'When does the next boat set sail?'

Korab grinned. 'The next one is tomorrow night, but that boat is already full to capacity. I can get you on the next one in a few days' time.'

Ramiz was quiet. Pulling out a bag of money from his pocket, he held up his savings.

'I don't have euros. I only have lek – seventy-thousand. It's all I have.'

Pausing as he narrowly eyed the bag of money, Korab roughly totted up what the exchange rate would be. It wasn't enough.

'I'm afraid I can't do it, my friend. You're almost a thousand euros short—'

'I have nothing more to give you, this is everything I own… '

Korab could hear the desperation in Ramiz's voice. He was telling the truth. Still, this wasn't Korab's call to make.

'My boss wouldn't be happy with that price… ' Korab spoke honestly.

Taking two more passengers – three if you counted the child – without enough money was a huge risk and one that Korab was not sure that he was willing to take.

Lowering his head into his hands, Ramiz rubbed the back of his neck, frustrated.

He couldn't stay here. Not even for a few days. This place was disgusting, filthy.

He'd come so far. He needed to get on that boat; he needed to get to England, and he'd do whatever it took to get there.

'What about her?' Ramiz stared over to where Lena lay sleeping peacefully on the camp bed.

'Lena? What about her?' Korab shook his head, confused.

'How long has it been since you were last with a woman?'

Unable to hide the flicker of amusement in his eyes, Ramiz watched the cogs in Korab's head turning now as the man realised what he was suggesting. Ramiz wasn't stupid; he'd seen the way that Korab had looked at his young wife earlier. The lust in the man's eyes. The longing.

'Too long huh?' Ramiz smiled now. 'Seventy-thousand lek, and you get to do as you wish with her tonight. Lena will be my gift to you?'

Korab reddened.

He wondered if perhaps this was a test, some sick game Ramiz was playing, but his instinct told him that Ramiz was deadly serious. The man must be crazy to offer his wife like this, crazy or desperate. Probably both.

'You like her, don't you? I saw the way you were looking at her earlier. She's very pretty, isn't she?'

Ramiz looked at Korab, his face serious. He needed to guarantee himself a place on that boat. If Korab agreed to this then it would also be a lesson learned for Lena. For all those times she had called him a coward. For mocking him.

Lena needed reminding who was boss. This was the perfect solution.

'Yes, Lena is beautiful.' Korab sounded wary as he tried to read Ramiz's reaction. Still not convinced of his motives.

Ramiz was right though. He hadn't been able to take his eyes off Lena since she'd got here.

It had been a long time since Korab had lain with any woman, let alone one as beautiful as Lena Gomez. It shamed him to admit it but even Lena feeding her child had aroused him.

'Say the word, and she is yours.'

He wanted her. Of course he wanted her.

'Yes.' Korab nodded finally, seeing that his friend meant it.

'There is one condition though…' Ramiz glared now. His face stern. 'You must get us on tomorrow's boat. That is non-negotiable. We cannot go any later than tomorrow. Seventy-thousand lek and the girl and you have yourself a deal?'

Korab calculated mentally. The boat would be setting sail tomorrow night regardless. What were three more people? Two really: the child was too little to count. Money was money, maybe his boss wouldn't even notice. Korab could sneak them on.

'If you are sure, my friend, then you have yourself a deal.'

Nervously Korab offered out his hand, half expecting Ramiz to roar with laughter. To mock him, or even worse, to pounce on him in disgust and beat him, but the man did neither. Instead he extended his hand too.

Shaking, the two men finalised the arrangement.

Getting to his feet, Ramiz looked over to where his sleeping wife lay.

The deal was done.

He would take Roza now and leave Korab to his prize.

He could only imagine the horror and disgust on Lena's face when she awoke to realise that she'd been used as a bargaining tool.

It was just a shame he wouldn't be sticking around to see her downfall first hand.

It was about time the bitch realised that in order to get to England they would all have to make sacrifices, and that included his precious Lena.

CHAPTER TEN

'Jesus! I don't think I can do this. Look at them all. They're like vultures.'

Standing at the side of the stage next to Misty, Saskia stared out across the dimly lit club into a sea of hungry faces.

This was her moment.

The DJ was playing her in but, rigid with nerves, Saskia couldn't move.

She froze, her feet suddenly glued to the spot.

'Girl, you can do this.' Misty squeezed her shoulder reassuringly. 'Once you're out there, I promise you, you will be fine.'

'I don't think I can do it, Misty.' Saskia shook her head, unconvinced.

The place was packed. Crowds of men stood around the stage, waiting hungrily for flesh, for beauty – for her. Just the thought of dancing out there made her feel nauseous. 'You might have to take my slot for me?'

'Hell no, girl! Have you seen the state of me? I'll be damned if you think you are going to send me out there in your place in this outfit.' Still in her tracksuit, she and Saskia had been at the club all day practising Saskia's set. There was no way that the girl was backing out now. Not after all the work Misty had put in. 'I'd be lucky if I could turn a kettle on right now in this get-up, let alone a crowd of men. Though saying that, girl, you could make a bin-bag look sexy… ' Misty smirked, trying to lighten the mood. It wasn't working.

Saskia looked like she was about to have a panic attack, and Misty needed to do something – quick.

'Seriously, babe. You just need to own the stage. You're a dancer right? So get out there and dance! That's what we do. Don't let them see that you are nervous.'

'Why did I think that I could do this?' Saskia faltered. Her voice strained. Panic spreading through her. She was losing her bottle. 'I feel like a lamb being led to the slaughter—'

'Oh no, trust me, the ones getting slaughtered are those bunch of Neanderthals when their wives find out what they have been spending all their hard-earned money on. We play them, honey. That's all we do. We feed them an illusion, and a very expensive one at that. Trust me, from what I saw earlier you can't go wrong out there… All you have to do is dance.'

Hearing the chants around the stage getting louder as the DJ played Saskia's intro for the second time, Misty knew that she'd have pandemonium on her hands soon. Saskia needed to get her butt out there. No matter what: tonight, the show had to go on.

'Remember what I told you. It's just acting! That's all you're doing. A bit of role-play; putting on a show. You know the routine off by heart, Saskia, we practised it enough times today. Even if you messed it up, do you really think any of these punters would notice? You look hot as fuck, Saskia. The routine will be the last thing any of these men will be thinking about.'

Saskia smiled weakly as she looked down at her outfit, or lack of it. That was half her problem. Strutting out onto the stage in front of this crowd in skimpy black underwear and a pair of sky-scraping high heels was her worst nightmare come true.

Even after persuading Misty to allow her to wear a black lace bra for the set she still felt vulnerable, exposed. Completely out of her comfort zone.

'Do I have to do the stage set? Can't I just do a few private dances instead?' Saskia asked meekly.

Misty shook her head.

'The stage is what sets you up for the night. You need to get out there and dance.'

Seeing Saskia slowly coming round, she knew the girl just needed that last final bit of encouragement. Nodding to Joshua Harper on the VIP balcony above them, Misty played her ace card.

'You see him up there watching you?' Misty glanced up to the VIP section to where Joshua was waiting, and Saskia followed her gaze.

'I know and I don't want to let him down…' Saskia felt guilty.

Misty laughed. This girl really was as naïve as they came.

'Oh you ain't letting him down. You're playing right into his hands.'

Saskia looked confused then.

'You really can't see it, can you?' Misty was genuinely sorry for Saskia. 'I told you earlier that he doesn't throw favours, didn't I?'

Saskia nodded, remembering the conversation.

'You didn't hear this from me, but I overheard heard him telling one of the guys here earlier that he was going to enjoy seeing how far he could get you to go tonight. They're all placing bets on you walking… This is just another one of Joshua Harper's games. He's fucking with you.'

Shaking her head with disapproval, Misty felt awful at being the one to break the news to the poor girl, but she couldn't just stand back and let Saskia be made a fool. Not when she knew how much the girl had riding on all of this.

'He doesn't think that you're going to go through with it, Saskia. That's why he agreed to your little deal in the first place. He's waiting for you to bottle it, and you're playing right into his hands.'

Misty's words felt like a jab to her stomach. Saskia felt winded. Standing in the skimpy underwear she was suddenly humiliated that he was treating her like some kind of a joke.

It couldn't be true?

Glancing up to where Joshua Harper was standing she caught his eye. The condescending expression on his face told her everything she needed to know.

Misty was telling the truth. Joshua Harper didn't think that she was going to go through with this.

He was calling her bluff and no doubt enjoying every second of her discomfort.

Seeing the hurt on Saskia's face, Misty was straight with the girl.

'Look, the way I see it, Saskia, you've only got two options here. You either get your arse out there and wipe that smug look off Mr Harper's face. Prove to him that you meant what you said. That you want your house back, or, you see that door over there? Use it. Save yourself anymore humiliation; but you'll lose your house.'

Holding her breath now, Misty waited, unsure which way the girl in front of her was going to fold.

She didn't have to wait long.

Shrugging Misty's hand from her shoulder, Saskia's face was etched now with anger.

The girl looked thoroughly pissed off.

'Well, looks like I better get my arse out there then, doesn't it.'

Fuelled with anger, the sick feeling in her stomach replaced with fire, Saskia strutted out onto the dance floor without a second's thought.

The chanting got louder. The sound of the music thumping in her ears was almost loud enough to drown out the thump of her heartbeat, but not quite.

Standing in the middle of the stage Saskia closed her eyes as she recited Misty's words in her head.

Focus. It is just acting. Role-play.

She could do this.

The bass kicked in as the DJ started her set once more.

Unsure if it was the feeling of the floor vibrating from the music, or her legs shaking in fear, Saskia began to move – slowly, at first.

Controlled.

Reciting every step that Misty had shown her she twisted her body expertly around the pole. She could hear the crowd now too, chanting, whistling, as she finally let go.

She was really doing this.

Her body moved rhythmically in time with the beat. She was there again, lost in the dance, and the audience was captivated; every eye in the club was on her.

Glancing up at her new boss as she slid around the metal pole, Saskia smiled to herself as she saw his eyes transfixed on her.

Joshua Harper wanted a show, it seemed, and that was exactly what Saskia Frost intended to give him.

CHAPTER ELEVEN

Lying face down on the carpet clutching the empty bottle of vodka, Mary Jeffries lifted her pounding head and tried to focus on her surroundings. It took her a few seconds to remember where she was as her eyes quickly adjusted to the darkened room.

She was home. Of course she was. Where else would she be?

She should have known from the sour acidic stench that wafted through the flat; the vile smell burning at the back of her throat.

No matter how many times she'd told Colin to sort the drains the smell never bloody left the place. It was nasty, like living inside a sewer. There was no point calling the council though; those imbeciles didn't know their arses from their elbows. She'd have to get Colin out there again later.

She could still hear the banging noise too. Those bloody kids had been there all day. Deliberately trying to drive her mad.

Mary forced herself up into a sitting position. She had no idea how long had she been out? Twenty minutes maybe? Half an hour? Maybe it was a lot longer than that; it was already dark.

The nights were drawing in earlier and earlier now; the grey October sky quickly turning black, wrapping itself around the flat like a thick, dense blanket.

Licking her dry, cracked lips, she dragged herself up onto her feet as she made her way out to the kitchen, guided only by the small crack of light that poured in through the gap in the curtains from the moonlight.

There was no point in turning the light on. Her head was already banging as it was; besides, she preferred the darkness. It matched her mood, as well as the gloom helping to mask her gaunt, ageing complexion and the squalor of the flat.

Glancing at the clock above the cooker, Mary felt disorientated. It was almost five p.m. She must have really overdone it on the vodka this time. It was happening all too often lately. She'd been out cold for hours. Colin would be home soon.

BANG! BANG! BANG!

Wincing at how loud the little bastards were being now as they continued banging around, along with the godawful music they had blaring out, Mary sighed. The fact that they only ever congregated at her front door when Colin was at work made her laugh. What they thought he'd do if he was here, she didn't know. The man was about as useful as an inflatable dartboard. Middle-aged, and still living at home with his mummy, Colin was as soft as arseholes. His appearance was deceptive though. Six foot two, yet he wasn't capable of punching his way out of a wet paper bag.

The kids were out there in force today, fuelled with stories they'd heard from the mouths of their parents, she guessed. The kids on the estate were all desperate to catch a glimpse of the Greenwood Estate's notorious 'Mad Mary'.

The little bastards had been goading her all week, dying for her to give them the satisfaction of going out there and facing them.

She couldn't, even if she wanted to. Just the thought of stepping outside onto the balcony made her heart race.

Agoraphobia the doctors called it. Another one to add to the ever-growing list of ailments.

Confined to the flat, living like a recluse, she had no choice but to put up and shut up, even though the kids were relentless. Every day they got worse, more daring: pelting eggs at the windows, covering her front door in their vile graffiti. To them it was just a game, with no reprisal, no real punishment. Not around here. The estate was destitute. Run down. Just like the rest of London, no doubt. No one gave a shit about some old nut job like her. The police didn't, that was for sure. Why would they? She'd given that lot of useless bastards forty years of grief and earache.

She was Mad Mary, the very same woman who for years had roamed the estate's communal gardens half-naked, paralytic, and fighting with anyone and everyone who crossed her path.

Now it was her playing the victim card.

The irony wasn't lost on her.

Karma really did come around and bite you on the arse.

Fuck the lot of them!

She was hot now, flustered. Her long fleece nightdress stuck to her skin with sweat. Lifting it over her head, her emaciated body now completely naked, Mary rummaged through the overflowing washing machine, prising out a long black skirt. It was damp and smelt musty, but it would do for now. She'd put a top on later, when she'd cooled down a bit. Pushing her feet back into her slippers, her head started spinning.

The voices were back.

Inside her head. Whispering their cruel taunts.

She needed another drink; anything to drown the noise out.

Opening the kitchen cupboards she tried her best to ignore the sound inside her skull as she wrenched the contents out onto the worktops, slinging containers and boxes onto the sides. Empty cereal packets, mouldy bread, tins of beans.

Grabbing her ears Mary moaned inwardly, praying for the constant chants that penetrated her brain to stop, but they wouldn't – just continued like a never-ending punishment inside her head.

Why wouldn't it just stop? Why wouldn't the voices just leave her alone?

Banging her fist against her forehead, she leant over the sink, gripping the taps to steady herself.

Another drink would shut the noise up. It always did. For a little while, at least.

Where the fuck was Colin? He was normally home by five. He was late.

Grabbing a glass from the side Mary rinsed it out under the tap. Her mouth was dry, and the bitter taste of her stale breath was making her nauseous.

Ignoring the pile of dirty dishes that filled the sink, covered in hardened smears of food, she greedily gulped the water before wiping her mouth with the back of her hand. Her thirst was quenched but the noise was still there, constantly droning inside her ears.

The kids outside her flat were muted but the vicious voices inside her head screamed on.

SHUT UP! SHUT THE FUCK UP!

Her temper got the better of her and she brought the glass down hard on the counter. She gripped the broken shards tightly in her hand, welcoming the agony as sharp jagged edges sliced through her fingers.

The pain was a sweet release but all too quickly it subsided.

The voices in her head were blaring now.

It was like they knew she was near breaking point, like they were purposely fucking with her head. Crucifying her.

The kids were still outside too; she could hear them tapping on the window, mocking her.

'Mad Mary, Mad Mary.'

Then she smelt the burning. Scanning the kitchen she thought maybe she was imagining it. It couldn't be the oven. It was off; she rarely cooked, and there weren't any candles lit; no appliances that had been left on.

Staggering back into the lounge she checked the little electrical fire near her armchair. The plug wasn't even in the wall.

Then she saw it, out by the front door. A pile of papers, purposely set alight, had landed on her doormat.

The kids had gone too far this time.

Reaching the mat Mary had no time to think. No time to get any water. The fire would spread by the time she got back.

Treading the flames as they licked her cheap woollen slippers she stamped with all her might, the intense heat penetrating through the soles; the force of her foot causing a squelch as the paper bag burst open. Hot, runny dog shit exploded up her legs and the walls behind her.

There was a roar of laughter coming from outside now. They'd set this up. Posting dog shit through her letterbox purposely, to mock and humiliate her.

What if she'd still been out cold? They could have killed her. Their stupid prank could have cost her her life.

Fuelled with rage, Mary grabbed at her walking stick before flinging the front door open.

The six teenage boys that stared back at her were still laughing, but their expressions turned quickly to ones of horror as they took in the sight of the half-naked elderly woman caked in dog shit, her slippers fused to her feet, screaming like a banshee.

They wanted to see Mad Mary in all her glory? Well now they could.

'What the fuck are you all looking at? Go on, fuck off, before I wrap this stick around your bleeding heads.'

Wildly flinging her walking stick in the boys' direction with the force of a woman much younger than her sixty-five years, Mary was seething. How dare these kids think that they could torment her like this? Little bastards. She wasn't afraid of them.

They scarpered. Leaving her standing alone on her front step as they all made a run for it down the communal stairwell.

It was then she spotted Colin.

Bloody typical. Trust him to turn up after all the drama.

Mary glared at her son as he walked towards her. His body hunched. A look of confusion spread across his gormless face at the state of his mother.

Mary felt the familiar rage swell inside her.

'Finally!' Waving her arms about dramatically, Mary stormed back inside the flat, pointing to the shit that was splashed all up the walls. 'This is all your fault. I could have been fucking killed.'

'But I… I… wasn't even here? Wha… what's happened?' Colin stuttered, averting his eyes from his mother's naked sagging chest, his face flushed with embarrassment.

'Wha… Wha… What's happened.' Mimicking Colin's nervous stutter. 'Well, if you'd pulled your finger out of your arse and walked home a little bit faster, you'd know what happened, 'cos I would have bloody well sent you to deal with those bloody imbeciles instead of having to go out there myself.' Mary sneered now. 'Not that the kids would have listened to a thing you had to say. Look at the state of you. You're a fucking embarrassment, Colin. They would have fucking laughed you back inside this fucking hovel. Now, where is my bottle?' Mary asked. Pursing her lips together she held out her hand expectantly, not bothering to cover her exposed chest.

'I'm sorry.' Stuttering now, Colin reached into his rucksack. 'I left my wallet at work. I had to go back. Here…' He passed his mother the bottle of wine he'd pulled from the bag.

'What the fuck is this?' Mary screwed up her face. 'Where's my vodka?'

'It's all I could get.' Colin stared down at the floor. Shuffling his feet as he spoke. 'I don't get paid until tomorrow.'

It was better than nothing she supposed, snatching the bottle out of Colin's hand.

The wine was warm. The numbskull hadn't even picked a bottle out of the fridge. He couldn't even get that right.

'Get all this shit cleared up.' Shaking her head, Mary walked into the lounge, leaving Colin on his own, loitering awkwardly in the hallway.

The wine might be warm but it was still alcohol, and it wouldn't go to waste. Especially after the day that Mary Jeffries had just had.

CHAPTER TWELVE

'You're late!'

Narrowing his eyes as he watched Korab and the last of the passengers pile out of the back of the truck, just as it pulled up on the grass verge, Vincent Harper was in no mood for games. Glancing at his watch, his hands twitched impatiently as he stood waiting by the water's edge.

'Fuck's sake,' he muttered as he paced the sand. It was almost two a.m. and they needed to get a bloody move on if they were going to shift this lot of illegals before they aroused any suspicions.

Korab knew the score; timekeeping in this job was paramount. They might have the local plod buried deeply in their pockets, but unfortunately the same couldn't be said for the French coastguard.

Still, at least if it did all go tits-up it wouldn't be him that would be in the firing line, Vincent figured. That was the genius of the operation. That was where people like Korab came in. The brokers and the skippers. They were the mugs stupid enough to do the bulk of Vincent's hard graft for him. They were the ones taking all the risks when it came to transporting all these migrant tramps from one place to another. Blindsided by greed and the thought of a big fat pay cheque that awaited them when the boat reached British soil. The thick cunts didn't think about the repercussions if they were caught making the illegal crossing, and if they did, they were too desperate to care.

Half of them didn't comprehend how big the risks were; they were too thick to realise that the recent huge influx of migrants trying to cross the waters illegally had started to become public knowledge. The law were stepping up their game. Clamping down hard on any boat that drifted into unauthorised territory.

The boats were being seized; hefty prison sentences were being dished out. Even if the divvy cunts did know the risks they still signed up for it; to them it was easy money. Greed was a great motivator in this game.

The migrants that they shipped out of here were not much better either. Most of them could barely string a sentence of English together, yet they all spoke fluently in the universal language of cold hard cash didn't they?

It was laughable. For a price, Vincent found, you could pretty much get anyone to do your dirty work.

That was the beauty of the set-up. The reason that they were creaming it in. There were no set-up costs, no initial outlay. The goods came to them, in their hordes, and with the world and his proverbial wife wanting to seek asylum in England there wasn't going to be any kind of shortage of revenue anytime soon.

All Vincent had to do was oversee it all. Pack the fuckers onto the boats and ship them out. Three trips to England a week they were knocking out now; each one totting up just over half a million euros a go.

Fucking child's play, or at least it would be if this lot hurried the fuck up.

'Get a fucking shift on!' Vincent shouted. Grinning as he watched Korab and the rest of the group speed up, hurrying towards him now.

He loved the power that he had over people. Standing almost a foot taller than the average man and with an extremely volatile temper, Vincent Harper rarely had to ask for anything twice.

The sooner tonight was over, the sooner he'd be on English soil himself. Back in London. He couldn't wait.

It was true what they said: there really was no place like home and, as much as he loved staying at his brother's beach-front villa here in St Malo, there was only so much overrated French cuisine he could stomach. After several days of delicate cuts of fish smothered in poncy sauces, portions barely big enough to feed a hamster let alone a massive bloke like him, all he could think about was a big succulent steak and chips back home in London. Right now, standing on the beach at stupid-o-clock in the morning, freezing his bleeding nuts off as he waited for that numbskull Korab to get his arse in gear, it was that thought alone that was stopping him from getting the major hump.

That, and the large wedge of cash he'd be getting from tonight's operation.

'Five, six, seven. And a baby? What the fuck? Korab? Are you taking the piss or what!' Cursing as he carried out the final headcount of the group now standing in front of him, Vincent shook his head. 'I said I only had room for five more, and even that's a push. Who was last? They'll have to go on the next one.'

The forty-foot fishing boat was already crammed. There were over a hundred people on board; they'd be lucky if the poxy boat didn't sink before it got to the other side as it was.

'This couple were last but they are desperate, Vincent. It's their baby. She is sick. I can't send them back to camp.'

Korab lied as he pointed over to where Ramiz and Lena stood awkwardly.

Lena took her cue just as she had been instructed. Remembering what Korab had told her: that this man Vincent was in charge. If he didn't allow them to get on the boat, they'd have to go back to the Jungle. She needed to beg. To plead.

'Please Sir, my baby, she needs help. I must get to England. Please, I beg you… ' Lena meant every word. She was more desperate to get away from here, away from Korab.

Her thoughts jolted back to the previous night, when she had been abruptly woken from her sleep to find Korab's sharp bony body pinning her down to the shoddy camp bed. His repugnant stench – his filthy body – disgusting her. How she'd awoken disorientated and scared, screaming out for Roza, for Ramiz. But Korab had silenced her with his hand over her mouth, before whispering in her ear that Ramiz had given her as a gift to him. Korab even had the nerve to thank her afterwards. Just knowing that Ramiz had allowed another man to do that to her, had instigated it, made her feel violently sick. It was as if Ramiz had violated her too.

There was no way she was going back to the camp. She'd rather die.

Pleading with this man was all she had.

'Save the fucking begging routine, love, it don't fucking wash with me!'

Silencing her pleas, Vincent sneered as he eyed her and her husband. The girl looked scared, timid. The man next to her had a permanent scowl etched on his face, clutching the baby awkwardly in his arms. Vincent wasn't convinced of their story. The baby was fast asleep. It didn't look very sick to him.

'I thought we could squeeze them on, Vincent, that we could make room? I didn't think it would be too much of a problem.'

'That's just the point though, isn't it, Korab? You didn't fucking think! The boat's already over-capacity, you moron. In future stick to the numbers, okay?' Vincent squared up to Korab. 'Where's the cunting money? I take it you at least got that bit right.'

Holding out his hand, Vincent snatched the money bag from Korab's grasp and began counting the notes. 'What the fuck is this? Monopoly fucking money?' he said, holding up the green notes that were tucked down strategically in the middle of the pile of cash.

'It's lek: Albanian currency. It's for the last couple with the baby.'

'Do I look like a fucking Bureau de Change?'

Vincent shook his head. Sometimes the bloke really did take the royal piss. It was only down to the fact that Korab had done a good stint in his time working for him – that he'd pulled in a record number of passengers – that Vincent fought to keep his cool.

'How much is here?'

'Seventy thousand lek. It works out at about five thousand euros. I didn't charge for the baby—'

'You what? Five thousand euros? Are you fucking mugging me off? That's a grand short? Where's the fucking rest of it?'

'It's everything they had Vincent… '

Vincent eyed the man now. It was taking every ounce of willpower for him not to beat the living shit out of the bloke.

Korab had started out just like these migrants. Living in the squalor that was the Jungle, desperate to try his luck getting over the border. He was happy to stay behind now though, wasn't he, now he had regular money coming in. Christ, these fucking scrotes would sell their own grandmothers if the price was right.

'If I find out that you have been skimming cash off the top of my money… ' Vincent glared at Korab. He didn't need to finish his sentence. Korab knew what would happen if he was ever that stupid.

'Honest, Vincent, I haven't taken so much as a euro from you. I just felt sorry for them.' Korab pointed to where Lena and Ramiz were standing. 'Ramiz is an old friend from Albania. We go back years. The baby, she is running a fever. They are desperate.'

Vincent stared at the young couple. The woman was no more than a girl really. Sixteen at the most. Even dressed in the rags that she had on, with no make-up and her knotted hair tied up, her natural beauty could not be denied. Not his type though. Unlike some of the other men that worked for him, Vincent wouldn't touch an immigrant girl with someone else's cock, let alone his own. They were scum of the earth as far as he was concerned. Passed around in those squalid campsites like meat for the men to use at their will. Most of them willingly offering themselves up too, if it meant that they might get help to cross the border.

Vincent gobbed a mouthful of phlegm down onto the sand to emphasise his distaste.

He caught the look that Korab gave Lena then.

'You must think I'm fucking stupid. Since when did you give a fuck about some whiney bastard baby? You got your leg-over didn't you?'

Glaring at Ramiz, Vincent sneered. 'What did you do? Use your girl as part of the bargaining plea?'

Ramiz glared back defiantly, but Lena averted her gaze, quickly staring down at the sand, her cheeks turning a violent red.

Vincent laughed. He had his answer. Clutching Korab by the scruff of his neck, Vincent lifted the scrawny man clear off his feet; twisting his T-shirt so tightly around his throat that he could hardly breathe.

'She's probably riddled with all fucking sorts. Let me give you a word of advice: next time you make a deal with the illegals use your brain and not your dick. Otherwise I'll fucking chop it off, you get me!'

Unable to speak, Korab nodded.

'I hope she was worth it, 'cos you ain't getting shit from me tonight. By the sounds of it you've already had your payment, you greedy cunt.' Vincent sneered as he abruptly let go of the man, letting him fall awkwardly to the sand. 'In fact, you ain't done earning your keep just yet. The skipper can't do this drop and I need someone to steer the boat, oversee the passengers on the journey. Seeing as you're so eager to get your hands dirty, you can do it.'

'I can't. I've never sailed at sea before. You'd be better letting one of the illegals to do it.'

Korab couldn't leave the camp, couldn't leave his money. If he left the camp for more than a few hours, the others would think that he wasn't coming back. They'd ransack his tent like vultures. They'd find it.

Korab had spent months saving up that money. Every penny of his wages was stashed away, buried in the soil of his tent.

It was all he had. It was his lifeline.

'Exactly my point, Korab. You are a fucking illegal. You just seem to need reminding of the fact.'

Shaking his head, Vincent wasn't a man to take no for an answer. Losing his patience he came in close now, until his forehead was almost touching Korab's. Gritting his teeth he kept his voice low so that the passengers wouldn't hear him.

'It ain't hard. A fucking monkey could do it, and let's face it, you ain't far off! The GPS will be set up. All you got to do is man the poxy thing. You know the drill. Go as far as the fuel takes you. Then ditch them. Use the motor boat to come back. Do you think that you can at least do that?'

Korab nodded, knowing he didn't have any choice.

When Vincent Harper wanted something done it got done. There was no room for discussion.

The conversation was over.

He just prayed that his money would still be there when he got back.

'What are you lot waiting for then huh? Get this lot searched and out to the fucking boat.' Turning to his men, Vincent bellowed. 'We ain't got time to take them out on the dinghies now so make them fucking walk it.'

Stashing the money back inside the money bag, Vincent lit another cigarette as he watched his men pat down the illegals for any concealed weapons. It was his job to ensure that the job went smoothly and seeing as they were dealing with some real desperate fuckers, his men had been warned not to take any chances.

Taking a deep pull of his cigarette he watched his men escort the last of the passengers out into the water. Vincent was starting to feel a bit calmer now.

Seven more of those fuckers plus a baby would be a squeeze, but it was just about doable. Besides, he had his money and that greedy cunt Korab's cut too.

Vincent smirked. His men seemed to like Korab, but the bloke was seriously starting to get on his tits. He was getting too cocky; making decisions that weren't his to make. A trip out to sea would be just the lesson that muggy cunt needed. Maybe when he came back he'd realise his place once more. Back in the Jungle with the rest of the poncing cunts.

Glad that the drop was almost done, Vincent grinned to himself before stubbing out his cigarette in the sand. The boat could fucking sink to the bottom of the ocean now for all he cared. He just wanted to get this lot out of here so he could happily fuck off back to the villa and get in a few hours of well-earned shut-eye.

Tomorrow he was London bound and, unlike this lot of scabby fuckers, he'd be flying first class.

Following Ramiz as he trawled through the icy waters, Lena's body shook uncontrollably as she tried to keep up. The water was up to her chest now; the cutting costal winds lashing down around them all as they walked.

Pulling her bag up on her shoulders to keep it dry, she couldn't remember ever being so cold.

Squinting as a thick mist of salty seawater sprayed in her face, stinging her eyes, she could barely see the fishing boat ahead of them.

They would be in complete darkness if it wasn't for the flickering white specks of light that shone out from St Malo. The famous walled city was lit up now, its lights twinkling behind them: shining like a thousand tiny stars dancing against a dramatic black backdrop.

Focusing on Ramiz's silhouette in front of her as he waded through the water, Lena was desperate to keep Roza in her vision. Ramiz was holding her high above his head, keeping her dry. That was something.

Lena wondered if perhaps their journey was making Ramiz realise his bond with Roza. Twice now, Ramiz had offered to hold the child. It was a start, she supposed.

Terrified of the pending journey, Lena concentrated on pushing her body through the water as she walked. Every step felt like a battle against the bitter cold sting of the sea; her movement slow and heavy as her drenched clothes, as well as the rucksack on her shoulders, weighed her down.

By the time they reached the boat's ladder Lena was ready to collapse with exhaustion.

Korab climbed aboard first, then Ramiz. Holding onto the last rung of the makeshift ladder to steady herself, Lena remained at the bottom, watching, as her husband pulled himself up the vessel's side. Clutching Roza tightly in one arm, his free hand gripped each rung as he climbed. He was almost on deck, his shadowy form looming at least ten feet above her.

The boat rocked dramatically.

'Here,' Korab shouted, leaning down over the side to reach the child. 'Pass her up to me.'

Ramiz did as Korab instructed: passing Roza to him before continuing to climb; dragging himself on board as he reached the top.

Lena went next. Terrified. As her feet slipped on the wet metal bars she clutched each rung tightly with her hands. Breathing slowly. When Ramiz leant down and offered his hand she took it, despite herself – allowing him to hoist her up onto the deck – her need to get to her child was greater than her hatred for him.

Wrapping her arms around herself as she shivered with the cold, Lena looked around in horror at the cramped conditions on the boat. Row upon row of bodies took up all the space on deck. Men, women and children all huddled together like cattle; so confined that it looked like they barely had room to breathe, let alone move about.

'There is space at the back, over there. Go, get comfortable. It's going to be a long night.'

Handing Lena her baby, Korab felt her flinch as his hand brushed against hers. Guilt consumed him as he felt the hatred radiating from her in waves. Deep down he knew what he did was wrong, but he'd been unable to control himself. Craving Lena's body, her beauty. Justifying himself that Ramiz had given him permission.

Lena hadn't though.

Snatching the three brown muslin sacks from Korab's grip, she turned and followed her husband. Cradling Roza in her arms as she walked the length of the boat; weaving carefully through the throng of people until they reached the back.

Sitting down on the cold, wet deck, Lena watched others around her huddling into each other in a bid to keep warm.

She stared at Ramiz opposite her, selfishly grabbing at his own sack and wrapping it around his shoulders, before stretching his legs out so that Lena would have no choice but to squeeze into the tiny amount of space that was left in the corner.

Biting her lip angrily, Lena would rather die of pneumonia than turn to her husband for body heat.

Her only focus was to keep Roza warm.

Shivering, she wrapped one of the other sacks tightly around Roza; huddling the small girl to her chest before placing the other sack over her own shoulders. She leant back then, her head resting against the panel behind, her legs curled underneath her.

She needn't have bothered.

No sooner had she got settled than the wind picked up; an almighty thunderous wave slapped heavily against the side of the boat, sending a thick shower of icy water cascading down over everyone aboard.

Shivering at the icy blast descending down the back of her neck, Lena bent over, trying to shield the child. Lena was soaked through now, but mercifully she'd managed to save Roza from being hit by the wave that slopped over the side of the boat.

Trembling – not just from the cold and the wet but with terror too – Lena's eyes scanned the faces nearby.

She could feel the fear all around her now, thick in the air. Even with her vision impaired by the darkness, unable to see the other passengers' faces, Lena could hear their whimpers. Everyone on board was terrified. They all knew the risks of the journey that they were undertaking.

Hearing the small boat's engine fire up as they began to set sail, Lena huddled Roza in tightly to her, rocking her gently in her arms, kissing the child's forehead, desperate to settle her.

Still she screamed.

'Shut her up, Lena,' Ramiz growled.

'She doesn't seem herself, Ramiz. All she's done since we left home is cry and sleep.'

'Isn't that what babies do?' Ramiz sneered now. His voice unconcerned.

'She just seems off.' Lena was worried. Roza seemed docile. Flitting between sleeping for hours and then screaming constantly. 'I think something's wrong with her. I can't explain it.'

'Good. Then don't. I want to get some sleep. Keep her quiet.'

Lena wondered if perhaps she was just hungry. She knew that she didn't have much milk to give her daughter, but maybe a little would be enough to satisfy her. Putting Roza to her breast, Lena winced, pain ripping through her as Roza latched on to her nipple. No matter how much it hurt her, she had to try.

As the boat chugged across the waters, picking up speed as if mimicking the wind, the constant rocking motion jolted Lena's stomach. Now she knew what the man back on the beach meant when she had overheard him telling someone that the crossing would be 'choppy'.

Closing her eyes, Lena listened to the loud creaking noises, fear gripping her. The boat sounded barely seaworthy as it battled against the waves. Lena prayed that they wouldn't end up with the same fate as thousands of nameless, faceless hopeful travellers that had been lost to the sea before them.

They'd all heard the stories about the ones that never made it. Lost to the sea; their absence totally unnoticed by the rest of the world.

It was out of Lena's hands though – it was all down to fate.

Roza had quietened now, her eyes closed, her chest rising and falling gently as she fell asleep. Lena hugged the child tighter to her, rubbing her back gently.

She felt something solid.

Unwrapping the thick blanket that enveloped Roza, along with the brown muslin sack, Lena pulled at Roza's nappy. Twisting the fabric to the side she found Ramiz's pistol.

Lena stared over to where Ramiz lay opposite her, now fast asleep. Of course. That's why he had been so intent on carrying Roza aboard. Not to keep her dry... he'd used her to conceal his weapon from the men who had searched them.

Holding the gun in her hand, Lena looked at it with curiosity. All she had to do was hold it up, pull back one finger, and this would all be over.

Looking over to Ramiz now it was as if she was seeing him for the very first time.

Slouched on the deck, his head flopping about in time with the boat's jerky movements, he kept his arms folded across his chest. Even in his slumber he was guarded.

She wondered if she could do it.

It would only take a second.

One click. One single bullet to his thick, ugly skull and the man would be gone from her and Roza's lives for ever.

Shielded by darkness, Lena checked that no one could see her as she lifted her arm up just a few inches, concealing the gun as she held it tightly to her chest.

She held her arm out straight then, trying to control the shaking as her finger caressed the cold metal trigger beneath her fingertip.

Just one shot. That's all it would take.

But she couldn't do it. She couldn't shoot him here. Not in front of all these people. They might throw her overboard. Take her child from her.

Lena couldn't risk it. Not when they were so close to getting to England.

Exasperated, she tucked the gun down behind her for safe-keeping, slumping back down into the cramped space as she embraced her baby.

Glaring at her husband, she felt nothing but pure contempt. She eyed the thick jagged scar that slithered down the left side of his face where the glass had struck him. The constant reminder of the Bodis' attack.

They'd made their mark on him, yes, but one little scar wasn't good enough. Nowhere near.

An eye for an eye, that's what the *Kunan* stated. Spilt blood to be met with spilt blood. Yet once again, Ramiz had taken a coward's way out.

Escaping his fate.

For now, anyway.

One day he'd get his dues. After everything he had done to her, Lena would make sure of it.

As the waves subsided and the harsh jolts of the sea were soon replaced with a rhythmic rocking motion, she let her mind wander back to thoughts of home to pass the time. She did that often. Wondering what Néné, Båbå and Tariq would be doing right now. If they were still looking for her, or if maybe they had given up?

Her parents and Tariq would have adored Roza. She often imagined a big homecoming meal, where Båbå and Néné would greet her with open arms, hugging her as they cried with relief at her return. How her parents would adore little Roza, showering her with affection. And Tariq, he would be an amazing uncle, bringing Roza playfulness, fun, excitement.

Something deep down in the pit of her stomach told her that scene would never happen. She doubted she'd ever see any of them again. Still, she could dream.

Clutching the rucksack with Roza's belongings inside tightly to her she thought about the contents. Ramiz wasn't the only one who could hide things. She'd ripped at the bag's lining, concealing her secrets as best as she could.

Ramiz would never venture into the bag though. Nappies, baby clothes, blankets.

Nursing Roza was Lena's job. For the first time in her life she finally had some security.

All she had to do was bide her time.

Hugging the bag tightly to her, Lena closed her eyes as the journey across the Channel became smoother, the boat rocking gently from side to side.

She wouldn't fall asleep, she couldn't. She needed to stay awake for Roza.

For now, though, she'd just close her eyes and rest.

CHAPTER THIRTEEN

Slipping inside the gates to the cemetery, Colin shivered, wrapping his coat tightly around him.

At least it wasn't raining now. That was something.

Getting his torch out, he switched it on, pointing the beam of light towards the headstones as he walked the length of the cemetery, checking each grave meticulously as he passed.

His colleagues thought he was stupid, he knew, using him to do the night-time patrols just because he was the one that lived the closest, on the Greenwood Estate; the same road as the cemetery.

After the spate of vandalism that had been happening here lately, gangs of kids breaking in late at night, robbing trinkets and toys from the children's graves, they'd all agreed that they'd take the patrols in turns. But Colin had ended up doing the bulk of the checks. Not that it bothered him really.

The place was so quiet at night. Peaceful. It was just him here. No one here for him to take orders from. That was just the way he liked it.

He didn't like people. They were cruel, spiteful. Even his colleagues. Two-faced the lot of them.

Quick to make jibes about him not wanting to backfill graves after a burial; he knew they called him names behind his back.

Weirdo. Oddball.

Not that any of their words could hurt him.

He was immune to it. He'd heard it all before, and worse, from his own mother. He didn't care what any of them thought of him. He was here to work. Not to make friends.

Besides, they were the ones who were stupid. They'd given him a free pass to be here in the dead of night and do as he pleased. Away from his mother, away from the flat.

For him, tending to the graves in the dead of night was anything but a hardship.

Colin made his way over to the grave that he'd been thinking about all day long.

Violet's.

He stood there now, looking down at the perfectly displayed purple wreaths decorating the graveside. Reading the cards; his eyes drinking in the words of sorrow.

They'd all left her though, hadn't they?

Cold, alone in the ground.

Not him though; Colin had kept his word. Spreading his coat out on the ground, he sat down.

'I told you I wouldn't leave you all alone.' Whispering, he rubbed his hand across the mound of soil.

Getting himself comfortable, Colin lay down on the grass next to the grave. Switching his torch off. He knew he didn't have long.

Mother was still awake, and she'd be wondering where he was.

Another excuse for a row.

But Colin just wanted Violet to know that he was here for her now, for a little while anyway. That she wasn't on her own. He would mind her.

Lying in silence with Violet on the ground of the cemetery, there was nowhere else Colin Jeffries would rather be.

CHAPTER FOURTEEN

'Girl, are you sure you haven't danced in a club before?'

Bursting through the doors, Misty's voice echoed around the empty dressing room. Smiling, she eyed the younger girl suspiciously.

'I don't know what they have been teaching you in ballet school, but I'm gonna guess that it wasn't what I just watched you do out there! They were some serious moves!'

Misty was genuinely impressed.

Saskia had just taken everyone out there by surprise, herself included.

The girl had just worked the main floor unlike any newbie Misty had ever seen before. It pained Misty to say it, but she had to give it to the girl.

Saskia Frost could really dance.

Earlier this morning, Misty had been ready to bet her month's wages the girl would bolt.

She'd seen it a thousand times before. Girls full of bravado suddenly freezing up at the thought of going out on that stage in front of all the punters. You either had it in you to work in a place like this, or you didn't.

'You were on fire out there. Did you see the look on Joshua's face?'

Misty was laughing now.

'I just did what you showed me.'

Cleansing her face with some make-up wipes, Saskia wiped off the mask of make-up she'd been hiding behind all evening and shrugged modestly back at Misty's reflection in the mirror.

She was playing it cool, but inside the adrenaline was still surging through her body.

She couldn't believe she'd actually done it. She'd gone out there in front of all those men and danced.

'Girl, you did way more than I showed you.' Misty beamed.

The girl was beautiful. Naturally stunning, not like some of the girls that worked here that needed a complete makeover to look half decent before they went on stage. She had just taken the roof off out there. Yet, instead of buzzing about it, she was quiet, subdued.

'Tonight was a major success, you should be proud.'

Saskia shrugged.

Proud wasn't a word she'd use right now. In all honesty, she was just glad that her first night was over.

If she thought dancing up on the stage was bad, nothing had prepared her for the intimacy of dancing for men privately inside the booths. Saskia had never felt so vulnerable.

The club, the punters. Misty. Joshua. It had all been so overwhelming, and now she just wanted to get out of here, to go home and get some much needed sleep. The last few weeks were beginning to take their toll. She felt exhausted, as if she'd had all her energy zapped from her.

Jumping down from the stool, Saskia tied her hair up into a loose bun before pulling her jacket around her.

'You not staying for a drink?' Misty asked. The rest of the girls were still out on the main floor getting one last dance in before the club closed its doors for the night. 'The others will be done soon. That's the best part. We all have a well-earned nightcap at the end of a shift, while I dish out the wages.'

'I won't, thanks. My head's banging. It's been a long couple of days. Thanks for the offer and all that, but I think I just need my bed.' Bending down, Saskia shoved her clothes into her bag.

'You sure you don't want to stick around for a bit? It would be good for you to meet the other girls properly. This job can be a bastard if you single yourself out, Saskia. Trust me, friends in this place are a godsend.'

'Next time, maybe.' Saskia shrugged.

She'd seen the other girls earlier when they'd all been in here getting ready to go out on the main floor. She hadn't warmed to any of them and they certainly hadn't warmed to her. She wasn't interested in building friendships. All she wanted to do was keep her head down and earn some money.

'They're good girls once you get to know them,' Misty said, curtly now, wondering if Saskia was still feeling out of her depth. 'They may look a bit rough around the edges, but most of them here have hearts of gold.'

Saskia nodded as if agreeing, but she wasn't convinced. She'd seen the way the others girls had given her the once-over when she'd walked in the door tonight. They were thinking exactly what she had been thinking: she didn't fit in here. She wasn't from their world.

Seeing that Saskia was intent on leaving, regardless of what she said, Misty counted out a pile of £20 notes, before placing the money down on the dresser in front of Saskia.

'Well, before you do a Houdini on us all, this is for you. There's six hundred pounds there.' Misty smiled, watching the shock on Saskia's face.

'Whoa! That can't be right?' Saskia stared at the money, gobsmacked.

Shaking her head she looked at Misty disbelievingly.

'I haven't cut you short if that's what you're implying? It's all there… ' Misty's tone was sharp, offended that Saskia thought she was trying to rip her off after Misty had spent the day doing nothing but try and help the girl. 'I've taken a hundred out for your floor fee; the rest is yours to do as you please.'

'Oh God, no, I didn't mean that you cut me short. What I meant was, I've only been here a few hours… ?' Realising that her words had been taken the wrong way, Saskia quickly backtracked. 'Six hundred pounds seems like too much… '

Misty laughed now, relieved.

'Too much? When it comes to money, girl, let me tell you, there ain't no such thing as too much. Though I'm not going to lie. It's been a while since a newbie came in here and earned that kind of money on their first night. You'll be up there with the top earners before long if you keep pulling them moves like you did tonight. Oh, and by the way, Mr Harper asked if you can work tomorrow night too?'

'Tomorrow?' she asked, shoving the money into the inside pocket of her bag. 'I thought the club was closed tomorrow night?' Remembering the animated conversation that had taken place earlier that evening between the other girls as they were all getting changed earlier, Saskia was sure that they'd been saying something about a private party. 'I overheard some of the girls earlier, they sounded pretty pissed off about it. They were saying how unfair it was that he always picked the same girls. Why would he pick me? I've only been here a day.'

'Why do you think?' Misty said raising her eyes. 'He's obviously upping the stakes!'

'What will I have to do?' Saskia asked, dubiously.

'The same as tonight. Look hot and keep wriggling that little arse of yours.' Then, serious again, she added, 'The parties are a little bit more involved than the club nights. It's mainly private dancing. One on one.'

'What do you mean more involved?'

'Let's just say the parties are a little bit more hands-on.' Misty raised her eyes, suggestively. 'The usual house rules don't apply, but the money is good. Triple what you earned tonight and tips. You get to keep it all too, and because it's a private party there's no floor fee either.'

Saskia didn't need to think twice.

'No thanks, I'm not interested.'

Tonight had been bad enough. Parading around in sexy lingerie – having men leer at her and make suggestive comments as she danced – she wouldn't be able to handle being groped and manhandled on top of everything else.

'Look, no one's going to force you to do anything that you don't want to do. Just because some of the other girls like to make a bit on the side doesn't mean that you have to. You can just do the same as you did tonight. Just dance.'

Saskia wasn't sure. She'd barely got her head around the dancing bit yet; there was no way that she'd be comfortable doing anything more than that. No matter how much the money was.

'I dunno. Maybe it would be better to give my place to one of the other girls… ?'

Misty shook her head.

'Mr Harper has asked for you specifically!'

Misty was watching Saskia carefully. Her demeanour changed once more as soon as Misty mentioned Joshua's name. It was clear to them both that Joshua Harper wasn't going to make Saskia's transition into the club easy for her. Misty almost felt sorry for the girl.

'Look, don't worry about it okay? I'll just tell him that it's not for you.' Misty turned on her heel.

'No, wait.' Saskia bristled.

She'd danced her arse off tonight purely to show the man that she meant what she had said. She wanted her house back and she would do whatever it took to get it. Yet, still that hadn't been enough. She knew full well that this was another of Joshua Harper's tests. He was still pushing her. Seeing how far he could make her go. Well she wasn't going to let him get the better of her.

'Tell him that I'll do it,' Saskia said, her mind made up. 'But I'm only dancing. Nothing more than that.'

'You sure? It's going to be pretty full-on. Don't say I didn't warn you.'

Saskia nodded. Resolute now.

'Okay, girl, well get here just before nine tomorrow and I'll talk you through how it all works, okay?'

'I'll see you then.' Saskia nodded. Grabbing her bag, she made for the doors before she changed her mind.

Watching her leave, Misty smiled to herself. She had to hand it to the girl; she didn't think Saskia had it in her.

Saskia had reminded Misty of herself, back when she had started out. When she'd been younger, more naïve. The days that Misty had happily lapped up every word that Joshua Harper had fed her. Of course, she knew differently now.

Maybe she'd been wrong about Saskia too? As sweet and innocent as Saskia appeared there was more to this girl than met the eye. She'd already proved that much. Tonight, Saskia had been thrown into the lion's den, and instead of being eaten alive she'd come out fighting, determined not to let anyone get the better of her.

Misty admired that.

She had a feeling that maybe she'd underestimated the girl and would put her money on the fact that she wasn't the only one to make that mistake.

Joshua Harper was playing games with Saskia that was for sure, but Saskia Frost was giving back as good as she got.

CHAPTER FIFTEEN

Waking with a start, Lena's eyes were blinded by the harsh daylight. Taking a minute to focus, she looked over to where Ramiz was standing at the side of the boat.

Then she noticed the smell. Pungent, acidic, causing bile to shoot up and burn in the back of her throat.

Disorientated, she stared down at Roza. Her tiny daughter was still tucked in the crook of her arm, eyes staring up at her vacantly. A tiny whimper escaped her mouth.

'Roza?' Lena cried. Flinching – noticing the diarrhoea leaking out from the child's nappy – a trail of the watery excrement was smeared all over the bottom of the boat next to where she lay.

It was even worse than when she had been back at the camp.

'Ramiz! Roza, she is sick.'

Trying to clean Roza up with the muslin bag, Lena was gripped with fear. If anything happened out here at sea there would be nothing she could do. No way of helping the child.

'Ramiz?'

He was standing now, over by the side of the boat. Distracted.

Korab was balanced on the side of the boat, one leg hanging over the side, as if he was about to disembark.

'Ramiz. What are you doing?'

Confused, she noticed the gun that her husband was holding. He must have found it – taken it back without waking her.

He was pointing it directly at Korab's head.

'I said, get back on the boat!' Ramiz shouted.

People were gathering behind him, shouting in agreement. Their faces angry, twisted. Their voices were full of panic as they realised that their skipper was about to abandon the boat, and them, at sea.

'This is as far as I go,' speaking with more bravado than he looked capable of, Korab paled as he gripped the top of the ladder. His eyes focused on Ramiz. On the gun. 'You must wait here until the others come for you. They will collect you in smaller boats and take you to shore. You just need to be patient.'

Ramiz screwed up his face.

'You never mentioned other boats before? You said we'd be taken to England. That this boat would take us there.' Ramiz glared now.

Korab shook his head.

'Point your gun at me all you want, I cannot go any further, Ramiz. We're out of fuel. You must wait for the men to come… '

Ramiz stared down to the water below. Moored at the side of the fishing trawler was a motorised red dinghy. Korab was abandoning them.

Looking out into the distance, across the deep murky sea that stretched out for miles around them, Ramiz couldn't see any other boats. Not smaller boats like the ones that Korab had promised. There was no sign of anyone coming to collect them.

'And what if your men don't come?' Ramiz narrowed his eyes. 'What if this was your plan all along?'

'No Ramiz, they are coming. You must wait… ' Korab protested, but Ramiz could see the fear in Korab's eyes.

He'd been found out.

'No one is coming for us, are they?' Ramiz asked now. His anger building once more as he realised that he'd been used.

Korab and the men he'd worked for had taken their money and they were dumping them at sea. Leaving them to fend for themselves, to suffer whatever consequences came their way. They were just pawns. Bought and sold like merchandise; shipped across the sea purely to line other men's pockets.

'You promised us England. You said that your men would help us, that they would meet us. That they could find us homes, jobs? We paid you your fee. What are you going to do? Just leave us here? Abandon us?'

Korab laughed; his voice shaking nervously as he tried to talk himself out of his predicament. Everyone was looking at him now. A crowd of angry faces; harsh, accusing.

'You really think that for a few thousand euros you would get all that thrown in? What? Some kind of luxury package deal for illegals? I promised you England and you shall have it, my friend.' Opening his arms exaggeratedly, Korab pointed into the horizon.

Lena followed his gaze, her eyes settling on the chalky white cliffs and lush green foliage of Britain way off in the distance. It was a vision to behold. A vision that they had all up until now only dreamed of. They were almost there; it was close but still so far from their reach.

'How?' Ramiz growled. 'How will we get there if we have no fuel? The men you spoke of are not coming. So tell me what will become of us?'

Ramiz was enraged. Korab knew that he was best to come clean.

'The authorities will come for you.' He spoke quietly now. Embarrassed that he'd been caught out. This was the part of the plan he'd been hiding from his friend.

Of course, there were no men coming. Vincent's men had ensured that the fuel would run out before the boat had made its journey. The boat – and all its occupants – was to be abandoned a few miles out from the coastline.

The authorities would spot them in time. Then they'd be their problem. It was genius really. Only Korab hadn't realised he'd be on Ramiz's boat. He thought that, by the time Ramiz had found out his friend had duped him, he'd still be in France, counting his money.

The look on Ramiz's face told Korab all he needed to know. He was in big trouble.

'I promise you, Ramiz. It is not like France. In England they are obligated to help you; you will be well looked after. They have a better system there.' His words drifted off.

'Get back on the boat,' Ramiz spat, disgust clear in his voice as Korab's legs dangled over the side of the boat, looking ready to climb down.

'Ramiz, you must do as I ask you and wait. It is the only way,' Korab pleaded.

The atmosphere on deck was becoming increasingly charged.

Other people behind them were starting to question what was going on too.

One man, overhearing the conversation, began muttering loudly.

'He's abandoning ship. He's leaving us.'

The rumour spread quickly throughout the crowded deck; panic erupting then amongst the rest of the passengers.

Surrounding Korab, they closed in around him. All shouting above each other to be heard. Asking what was going to happen. Who was going to come for them?

Ramiz lost his patience.

Holding his gun high above his head he pointed it up towards the sky and fired.

There was silence, followed quickly by widespread panic as people started shouting and crying.

'You need to stay calm and wait for the authorities. They will come. The authorities will come,' Korab shouted now.

The situation was getting out of control.

'We're all going to die,' the elderly man that had overheard the conversation shouted to the crowd. 'He's going leave us here and we are all going to die. He's going to save himself.'

He rooted inside the bag he was holding, releasing what looked like a long red candle, striking the end. A distress flare. Extending his arm in the air, the vibrant orange flame hissed loudly, burning rapidly.

'Move out of my way!'

Waving the flame towards Korab and Ramiz, the man made his intentions clear. He was heading for the side of the boat now – brandishing the dazzling plume of fire towards Korab like a weapon as he tried to make his own bid for freedom while he still had a chance.

He wanted the motor boat.

'Move now!'

Jabbing the flare in Ramiz's direction, the man lurched forward. Ramiz moved out of his way.

Biding his time, he watched as the man clambered up onto the side of the boat. There was a second's hesitation as he looked down to where the smaller boat bobbed in the water.

That was all Ramiz needed.

A gunshot exploded, suddenly silencing the chaos.

The elderly man fell lifelessly onto the deck, a pool of thick dark blood pouring from the exposed bullet hole in the side of his head.

Lena let out a harrowing scream.

The man lay there lifeless, eyes still open, his expression pained.

'If anyone else moves I will shoot you too,' Ramiz bellowed, his hand still gripping the gun. A crazed look in his eyes.

He turned back to Korab.

'Especially you!' Ramiz aimed the gun directly at Korab's head, before shouting to his wife. 'Lena! Get over here now.'

Scrambling onto her knees, Lena quickly got up. Clutching Roza tightly, she did as she was told.

No one else moved; no one else spoke.

The only noise that punctured the deathly silence on board was the rush of the waves breaking against the side of the boat. That, and the incessant squawking seagulls overhead, alarmed by the gunshot.

'Climb down to the boat,' Ramiz instructed his wife. Turning he waved his gun in the direction of the people behind him, making sure that no one would be foolish enough to try and stop him.

Lena leant over the side. Looking down to the motorised rubber boat bouncing about in the water, a foot or so away from the bottom of the ladder, she felt sick with fear.

She was terrified of falling into the sea. Into the pitch-black pool of nothingness.

'You need to move quickly, Lena,' Ramiz commanded.

Behind them on deck a small fire had started from the discarded flare, still held in the dead man's hand. The flames had set light to his shirt. Lena could smell burning flesh.

The blaze had already reached some bags on the deck nearby. It was spreading rapidly now.

Lena eyed the other passengers, guilt flooding her as they all stood there watching her. All too scared to move, too scared to speak.

'What about Roza?'

'Give me your bag.'

Realising that Ramiz wanted to put Roza inside her bag, that he would probably tip out its contents – that her secret would be found – Lena acted fast.

Squatting down on the deck, she removed the blankets from the bag. Wrapping them around her daughter, she placed Roza inside.

There was just enough room. Turning, she allowed Ramiz to place the straps across each of her shoulders. The bag firmly on her back now.

'Move.'

Lena did as she was told.

Swinging her legs over the side, to the ladder, she turned, keeping her focus on Ramiz. Her legs were trembling. Her heart pounding inside her chest. She took one rung of the ladder at a time. The bag was heavy, pulling at her shoulders, tilting her off balance. Inside, she could hear Roza whimpering. The noise heart-wrenching.

Above she could hear Ramiz talking to Korab; pointing the gun away from her now, back to him.

'You too, move.'

Korab looked shocked.

He had thought that Ramiz was going to leave him here on the boat. To teach him a lesson.

'One wrong move and I'll kill you.' Ramiz could see the shock in Korab's eyes. The man thought he was being spared. That Ramiz was taking pity on him.

He'd forgotten that he'd mentioned having a cousin in London.

Luckily for Korab he still had his uses.

For now.

Looking down at Lena, Ramiz was starting to lose his patience.

The fire was spreading. Heavy plumes of smoke filled the sky. Some of the men on board had stepped forward, desperately trying to stamp out the inferno, but it was useless. The fire was already out of control.

'Hurry up, Lena!'

Clambering down the final few rungs, Lena could hear the noise above her.

People were screaming. Terrified.

Standing at the end of the ladder, she froze – rigid with fear as she looked down into the pool of darkest water. She'd have to jump to reach the boat but she couldn't do it.

She was too scared.

'Lena! Move!'

Looking up, Korab was scampering down the ladder towards her. If she didn't move, he'd knock her out of his way.

Leaping into the boat, she landed with a thump. Collapsing in a heap then, she realised she was crying.

She barely had time to unzip the bag and check on Roza when Korab pounced into the boat too. The force of him almost catapulted her and Roza out from the boat and into the black gloomy sea.

Screaming, Lena gripped the boat's edge with all her might. Her body on top of the bag. Her arms shielding Roza.

Ramiz was scrambling down the ladder towards them too.

Fast on his feet, others were following suit.

A stampede of people now clambered down behind Ramiz in a desperate bid to get on the motor boat.

'Hurry,' Ramiz shouted to Korab. 'Start the engine.'

Lena watched, horrified, as Korab scampered down the final two rungs.

'Move, Lena.'

Scurrying to the side of the dingy, Lena did as she was told, recognising the urgency in her husband's voice as he too made a jump for the boat.

Above her, chaos erupted.

Starting the motor, Korab untied the rope.

'Please. Take him. Please.'

A woman screamed above them, dangling her child directly over them.

The boy couldn't have been more than two years old. Kicking his legs frantically as his mother held him over the water, he looked terrified. Screaming in fear.

'Please, take him. Don't let him die. Don't let my baby die,' the woman shrieked.

'There is room, Ramiz?' Lena pleaded.

Korab looked at him too. Filled with unease.

They couldn't just heartlessly leave everyone.

'The boat can hold ten people. Maybe more if we take some of the children?' Korab asked now.

Ramiz shook his head.

'If we take one, they'll all want to come. We'll be ambushed. We need to leave now.'

'But they won't make it,' Korab said.

'Someone will come. Someone will see the smoke. We need to leave, now.'

'The child Ramiz… can't we at least take him?'

Hearing the mother still screaming, Lena looked up towards the boat. The smoke behind her was building dramatically. Their fate now sealed.

Her words were barely out of her mouth when a body plummeted into the water next to the smaller boat.

A man leapt out of the water, grabbing at Korab's arm. Desperately dragging at his shirt, he tried to hoist himself into the motor boat, almost pulling Korab overboard.

Ramiz fired, the shot ringing out loudly across the vast ocean.

The man slipped, the water next to him turning a deep red as the man's body floated lifelessly to the surface.

This time Lena didn't scream. She couldn't. Ramiz was right. They needed to get out of here now or they would be in danger themselves.

Pushing at the motor boat's throttle, Korab accelerated the boat, soaring in the direction of the cretaceous cliffs of England at great speed.

Lena looked back, unable to tear her eyes away from the harrowing scenes as they sped away, her eyes remaining focused on the distraught mother and child.

The howling noise that came from the woman's mouth was no longer human. She sounded like a wounded animal.

The boat was getting smaller now, as the distance between them increased.

Lena could still just about make out the flames licking the side of the doomed fishing boat; she could still just about hear the terrified screams and shouts of the people they were leaving behind.

She watched the silhouette of the woman holding the child.

Watched as they jumped into the water in a desperate bid to escape the rapidly building inferno.

All that Lena could see now was a steady stream of thick smoke billowing in a black haze out across the horizon, far out in the distance.

Hugging Roza tightly to her, Lena couldn't shake the guilt that consumed her: the haunting thought that it could have been her left on that boat.

That little boy could have been Roza. They had been selfish to leave them, to not at least try to save some of them.

Lena bowed her head in shame. She'd allowed them to die.

Her only consolation was that Roza was safe. Soon they would be in England.

CHAPTER SIXTEEN

'The King's Arms? It's not exactly the jewel in London's crown is it?' Ramiz sneered as Korab returned from the bar with his cousin Kush, placing three drinks down on the table.

Leaning back against the tatty leather seat, Ramiz eyed the suspicious-looking dark brown smears that were streaked down the ageing yellow paintwork of the wall in his booth.

Wrinkling his nose in disgust he moved over slightly. The light above him flickered – a mass of tangled wires poking out. Even the bulb looked ready to give up on the place.

'Well, it's better than the Jungle,' Korab offered; blushing, as he saw his cousin Kush flinch at the insult.

'Is it?'

Screwing his face up, Ramiz wasn't convinced. Noting the strong, acidic stench of piss wafting out from the toilet at the end of the bar, the place certainly didn't smell any better. Mind you, neither did he. He'd been in these clothes for five days. He was filthy. Desperate for a shower and a decent night's sleep, Ramiz figured that the place would have to do for now.

'What the fuck is this?' Taking a sip of his drink, Ramiz grimaced as the hot liquor hit the back of his throat.

'Brandy, my friend! If you close your eyes you can almost pretend it's the *Rakia* we have back home. It's not as sweet, but it has the same kick to it.' Kush offered a smile, trying to appear friendly, but catching Ramiz's sneer he could see that his intentions were wasted.

Knocking back the rest of the drink, Ramiz inhaled the cheap fumes, as the familiar satisfying warmth he was used to quickly turned to a fiery burning sensation. Scanning the pub, he eyed the only other customer in here; an elderly man, sitting propped up at the bar, his miserable face staring down into his empty pint. This place could do that to you, Ramiz guessed, make you want to drink yourself to death. Though, to do that you'd need a stomach made of iron because even the drink tasted like rat's piss.

In fact, the pub was a bitter disappointment; so far, the same could be said about London. The place hadn't come anywhere near to his expectations. So much for England being a free ride. The reality was that everything was overpriced and overrated.

Without money, life here was going to be a struggle. Ramiz could see that already.

The people here didn't seem overly welcoming either.

Here, in a place full of people all races, all cultures, Ramiz had been led to believe that England was a place of opportunity – only, the reality was anything but. People here looked right through him, as if he was nothing, insignificant. Kush had explained how England was now flooded with foreigners and illegals, and how many people here held nothing but contempt for them. Ramiz had felt it first hand – hostility coming off people in waves.

He'd even witnessed the discrimination back in the quieter coastal town they'd arrived in early this morning. Desperate to flag down a car, no one had wanted to stop and help them. Instead they were ignored as cars continued to whizz past; happy to leave them stranded by the roadside in the pouring rain.

The only vehicles that had slowed down had been work vans, with men leaning out, shouting abuse. Some jeering at Lena, while others directed their abuse towards him and Korab, telling them in no uncertain terms to 'go back to their own country'. In the end, Ramiz had forced Lena to stand with Roza while he and Korab stood further back, hiding inside the overgrown hedgerows.

His plan had worked. Within minutes of Lena standing there alone a car had finally stopped and Ramiz took no time in seizing his opportunity. Ambushing the vehicle, he threatened the male passenger with his gun.

It was funny how more compliant people could be when faced with fear.

Still, they were here now, and that was all that mattered.

'Korab told me of your set-up here, Kush. He said that you might have work for Lena?' Ramiz had made his intentions clear to Korab on the way here.

He had let Korab live, but the condition was that Korab now owed him. Though looking about the place now it didn't look like the gold mine that Korab had made it out to be. Apart from the old boy slumped at the bar the place was empty. The only noises came from the muted traffic outside and the blur of the TV that Kush had playing in the background.

Ramiz was convinced that Korab had spun him another line.

'I'd be willing to see how well she worked?' Then, pausing to look around, Kush added. 'Is she still tending to the child?' He didn't want to talk business in front of the girl. Things worked out better that way. The logistics of the way things worked around here didn't need to concern the girls. They just needed to do as they were told.

'She went to sort the child out. Enjoy the peace while it lasts!' Ramiz's voice was detached.

Lena had been in the bathroom for almost fifteen minutes, taking her time to tend to Roza. He was glad of the silence. The child's incessant whinging for the past few days had been like a constant droning inside his brain. His almighty headache had grown as much as his dislike for his daughter. He had no doubt in his mind that the kid was going to turn out to be just as difficult as her mother.

'I think the men would like her. Young, pretty, she'd be very popular. Sometimes the girls need a bit of persuasion though?' Kush said, raising his eyes.

Lena hadn't spoken much since they'd arrived. Silently, she'd sat and stared with disdain at both Ramiz and Korab, stubbornly refusing Kush's offer of food or a drink, even though she must have been hungry.

The girl would be difficult to break. He could tell.

'Don't you worry about that. Leave her with me.' Ramiz nodded.

He already had a plan. He knew her Achilles' heel.

The child.

'Lena will do exactly as she is told.'

Ramiz would make sure of it.

'What about rooms? Can we stay here?'

Kush shook his head.

'The rooms are all used by the girls. I'm the only person allowed here on the premises at night. I sleep down here in one of these booths so that I can oversee that there is no trouble.'

'We only need somewhere to stay for a couple of nights, that's all… We will sleep on the floor down here too; we'll be no trouble. Just until Lena has earned some money… ' Korab was begging now, desperate for Kush to agree.

Ramiz would not take no for an answer. Not after they had come all this way, but Korab didn't want to cause any trouble for his cousin.

Kush shook his head, adamant.

'I'm sorry, my friends. I can get you some clean clothes and make you some food, but I'm afraid you can't stay. Besides, this is no place for a child. A baby here would be bad for business.'

'Two nights, max.' Ramiz pulled back his jacket. His movement was small and subtle, but Kush instantly recognised the threat as his eyes rested on the exposed pistol tucked inside Ramiz's jeans. 'We are all out of options, so you best make the impossible, possible.'

Ramiz locked eyes with Kush now, the atmosphere suddenly heavy in the room. He could almost smell his cousin's fear.

'Two nights,' Kush said reluctantly. He knew when he was beaten. 'That's all I can do.'

He couldn't argue with a gun.

Ramiz smirked then. Leaning his head back against the booth once more, he relaxed – watching – as Kush and Korab continued speaking animatedly amongst themselves.

The two men were so alike they could have been mistaken for brothers. Both tall and gangly with crooked noses and chiselled cheekbones.

The conversation was boring, full of niceties and falseness. The usual bullshit family politics and talk of home that Ramiz didn't care for. It was their voices that he was listening to. Their thick Albanian accents. Nostalgic suddenly, Ramiz thought of home.

No doubt Drita would have been up to the house and found it empty by now. Ransacked.

Her son's rapid departure, with only a scribbled note left behind, would be like a knife to her heart. He knew that. Her only conciliation would be that at least she knew that he was still alive.

Pushing thoughts of his mother to the back of his mind, Ramiz homed in on the television screen as a welcome distraction. Recognising the scenery that filled the screen – the giant red Jubilee clock tower set in the centre of a promenade – he sat bolt upright. They had walked past that very landmark this morning. He remembered his irritation as Lena had stopped and stared up at the tower in awe. How she had run her hand over the words *Queen Victoria*, and had started to cry, overwhelmed that the journey was over and that they were now officially in England.

The camera zoomed in to the view of a news reporter standing on a sandy beach, her back to the sea. Behind her, in the distance, a lifeboat trawled the waters.

'Kush, turn it up. Quickly.' Lurching forward in his chair, Ramiz pointed to the TV screen.

Kush did as he was told without question.

Going to the bar for the remote control, he turned up the volume and stood watching, intrigued at what had caught Ramiz's attention. They listened as the reporter's voice filled the bar.

'A major search and rescue operation is underway after it is thought a boat carrying migrants into Britain from France has sunk just off the coast of Weymouth.'

Ramiz stared straight ahead at the screen, but he could feel Korab's eyes on him now. Ignoring him, Ramiz focused his attention back to the news piece as the reporter continued.

'The exact number of illegal migrants that were aboard the fishing vessel that, it is thought, had been heading towards the Jurassic coastline, is not yet known. Coastal guards and lifeboat crews have yet to find any survivors. So far, sixty people have been confirmed dead and it is feared the death toll will rise further. Officials say that at least a hundred migrants in total may have drowned in the incident.'

'Weymouth? Isn't that where you said you came in, Korab?'

'Turn it off.' Korab's voice quivered as he spoke, but his eyes remained fixed on the table.

All those people.

They hadn't made it.

He felt sick. Ramiz had insisted that the authorities would have seen the smoke, that they would have been rescued. Only they hadn't been. Thinking of the women and children on board, how they could have saved some of them, Korab hung his head down in shame.

'Turn it off!' Korab shouted now, startling the other two men. Kush did as he was told.

'Scary huh, my friend?' Kush said, sadly. 'You could have been on that boat. It was this morning wasn't it? Wasn't that when you arrived also?'

Sensing that something wasn't right, Kush was probing now.

Korab had paled; the tension in the room between him and Ramiz was so thick it was almost palpable.

'What is it, Korab?' Kush asked, concerned.

'Leave him be. He's just tired,' Ramiz insisted. 'Why don't you make yourself useful? Go and check on Lena.' Ramiz waved his hand dismissively. It was an order.

Kush didn't appreciate being spoken to like that but, aware that Ramiz had a gun in his possession, he didn't argue. Instead he hurried off, happy to get out of Ramiz's way, and left the two men in silence.

Korab finally spoke.

'We left them to die… '

'It wasn't our fault.'

Scrutinising Korab's face, Ramiz was agitated at the genuine emotion he saw there. Korab wasn't stupid; he would have known the score. What did he think, that trafficking people over the seas came without risks?

'There were children on board.' Korab shook his head now, astonished at the coldness in Ramiz's eyes. 'There was room in the motor boat to take more people. We could have made several trips; we should have at least tried.'

Korab had gambled their lives away.

Ramiz had ruined everything. If he hadn't shot the elderly man, the fire would have never started. The boat would have drifted aimlessly in the sea, but the coastguard would have found them all eventually. They could have all been brought to safety, and

Korab would be back in France now with his money. Instead, he was trapped here. Forced to endure Ramiz's company.

'You think that they would have done the same for you?' Ramiz sneered. 'You saw how desperate they were. They would have ambushed the boat. We would have all drowned. If we'd stayed any longer we would be dead now too.'

Ramiz shook his head; his glare cold, hard.

'It was every man for himself. It was them or us.' Ramiz raised his voice. His words were final. 'Pull yourself together, Korab! It's done.' Ramiz's voice was detached; the shock of what they'd just witnessed forgotten as quickly as it had been seen.

'Now, why don't you go and see if that cousin of yours can sort us out some food. I'm starving.'

Not wanting to rile his friend further, Korab did as he was told. His heart heavy as he went to find his cousin.

He'd been a fool to bring Ramiz here to his cousin's door, he knew that. Kush didn't deserve to get tangled up in Ramiz's web, but what could Korab do about it? Ramiz was holding both the money and all the control. They answered to him now.

He thought of his money back at the camp.

His only security – a world away from him.

He had nothing now.

He was trapped. They all were. Here, under Ramiz's watchful eye. Korab knew without a doubt that the man was far more dangerous and unhinged than any of them had ever imagined.

CHAPTER SEVENTEEN

Grinning as he leant over the balcony of the VIP area Joshua Harper scanned the club's main floor, shaking his head in wonderment as he spotted one of his men snorting cocaine from a dancer's pert buttocks. The party had barely even started and already his team were taking full advantage of his generosity – and why not? They'd earned it. This lot had come up trumps for him the past few months, raking him in an absolute fortune.

The celebration was long overdue. Off their faces on the best cocaine in London, his men were wasting no time in letting their hair down – or their trousers, judging by the amount of action that was going on inside some of the private booths.

Joshua grinned, glad that they were enjoying themselves.

This is what it was about. Work hard, play even harder. Men were simple creatures really. It didn't take much to keep them happy: a slap-up meal, the finest champagne, and the mesmerising sight of half-naked dancers sashaying around the room generally did it.

Parties at Harper's Palace were legendary. The gentleman's club was the crème de la crème of London's strip clubs, and Joshua wanted his men to make the most of everything that he had to offer. *Look after your workforce and in return your workforce will look after you*, was a mantra that had served him well over time.

The meet had gone smoothly tonight. The last of the monies had been collected up, and the next shipment organised. Joshua

Harper was a charmer, and he had the knack of making every single man on his payroll believe that they were the most important, indispensable person on his team. That they were each a vital cog in Joshua's wheel. Every man in here believed the hype. They were all desperate to be part of Joshua Harper's world. The money, the drugs, the beautiful girls.

Joshua liked to let them think that it was a free-for-all; that everything tonight was on the house. But there was always a price, and Joshua Harper's fee was of the highest. In return for his generosity, he wanted; no, he demanded, unfaltering loyalty.

It was the only way his business would work.

He was a good boss, and he expected his workers to return the favour.

He was no one's mug though. Piss him off and it was a whole different ballgame. Unwilling to suffer fools; he could be a grade A cunt if the mood took him. Tonight though, was all good. Downing the dregs of his Scotch, Joshua smiled as his gaze rested on Saskia.

He smiled again, watching her performing a lap dance in one of the booths.

He'd been right to take a gamble. Misty had completely transformed the girl. She was barely recognisable. Dark smoky eyes, ruby red lips and her hair tousled loosely with ringlets sweeping down over her shoulders. Nothing like the timid girl that had sat opposite him in his office just two days ago.

And boy, she could dance. Circling her slender hips in time to the heavy beat of the music that filled the club, she was seductively giving it all she had with one of her spectacular dance routines. Swaying in time to the beat of the music she ran her hands across her smooth skin.

Joshua laughed to himself then.

Vincent would have been the last person Saskia would have wanted to shake her arse at, especially after she found him in her house the other night. Still, give the girl her dues, if she was pissed off about the fact that she had to dance for him, she hadn't shown it. In fact, she hadn't batted an eyelid.

Joshua hadn't thought she'd last five minutes here. His plan was genius really. By offering her the impossible task of working here at the club he'd given her the semblance of choice. The illusion that he was prepared to give her a chance to prove herself. He'd thought that after she saw how hard it was she'd quit. Only it appeared that Saskia Frost was doing the complete opposite.

The girl was growing on him. Not Joshua's usual type by any standards, but he liked a girl who was up to the challenge.

If Saskia lasted the distance, he'd get his money.

If she didn't, he'd keep the house.

Whichever way their little deal played out Joshua was onto a win-win with this one, and he intended to have a bit of fun with it all in the process.

Smug now, he sipped at his drink, enjoying her little show.

Exquisite was the standard requirement for any of his girls, but Saskia Frost was something else altogether. The girl was in a league all of her own.

Every man in here had his eyes on her.

Every man, apart from his brother, it seemed.

Joshua frowned as he watched Vincent sitting impassively, staring through Saskia as if she was invisible. He hadn't been himself all evening; even during the meal he'd seemed off, like his head was elsewhere. Constantly checking his phone, preoccupied with fuck knows what.

It didn't make sense. They'd worked their nuts off for the past month. Tonight they were supposed to be celebrating, yet Vincent had a face on him like a slapped arse.

Confirming his suspicions, Joshua saw Vincent abruptly dismissing Saskia as he took his phone out from his pocket.

His brother's conversation played out, heated; Vincent's face thunderous. Whoever it was on the other end of the line was really riling the man up.

Hanging up, Vincent rubbed his temples, agitated, then with a darkening brow he looked up to the balcony to where Joshua was standing. Even from here, Joshua could see the anger glimmering in Vincent's eyes. Joshua held up his glass, motioning for his brother to come up and join him. Whatever it was that was troubling the man it was about time that Vincent filled him in.

'Pour us a couple of Scotches will you, Marnie?' Joshua smiled at the pretty young barmaid as he took a seat in the booth next to the bar. 'Make 'em large ones yeah?' Joshua added, as Vincent strode towards him. He had a feeling that they were going to need them.

'I see the delectable Saskia didn't "do it" for you?' Joshua mused as Vincent slumped down in the booth next to him, his huge frame filling the chair.

'I just ain't in the mood tonight, bruv.' Vincent shrugged. Then, seeing his brother's unconvinced expression, he added, 'they do my head in, the lot of them. Fake hair, fake tits, and until you cough up a bit of cash, even their fucking smiles are fake, yet women have the cheek to harp on about wanting to find a real man? What's that about, huh?' Shaking his head, Vincent reached for his drink, downing it in just a few gulps before raising his brows questioningly. 'Don't you get bored with it all?'

Any other bloke would have a permanent boner with the likes of Saskia draped over them, but then, Vincent wasn't like any other bloke. Vincent always told it how it was. He had no qualms in upsetting people.

'I dunno, Vincent, you could be missing a trick. They have their uses. It's a fucking cliche but it's true what they say, you can't live with 'em, you can't live without 'em.'

Vincent shook his head.

'I couldn't cope with some bird sitting in my ear giving me grief every five minutes. I like to be my own man. You remember the amount of aggro mum used to give dad. Fuck that shit!'

'Yeah, but come on, the old man took the royal piss out of our old woman. Always sneaking off for a bit of strange. It was no wonder she was constantly on his case.' Joshua raised his eyes. 'What about that old bird down the road. What did we used to call her? You know the one, parading around in mini-skirts with a face full of slap.

'Who, old Brenda the fucking bike? She was shagging half the bleeding street.'

'That's it! Brenda.' Joshua laughed. 'The old man was up her like a bleeding ferret every time mum left the house to play her bingo.'

Since their parents had died, he'd taken the role of head of the family. Taking Vincent under his wing, Joshua was determined to look out for his younger brother. He was all he had, at the end of the day.

Sitting back in his chair, he eyed his brother with seriousness now.

'So? Who was that on the blower just now? You having problems?'

'You could say that!' Turning to the barmaid, Vincent indicated for another drink. He'd been dreading this conversation all evening, but he couldn't put it off any longer. 'Though it's more a case of "we've" got problems, bruv… ' Vincent cleared his throat. 'We might have to cool off the op for a bit.'

'Good one.' Joshua laughed at Vincent's ridiculous suggestion, then seeing brother's face remain deadpan, he narrowed his eyes.

Vincent wasn't fucking about. Whatever was going on this was serious.

'We've just coined in over three million quid. Why the fuck would we cool it off now?'

'There was a fuck-up this morning with the shipment. The boat ran into some trouble.'

Taking his drink from Marnie before she placed Joshua's Scotch down on the table, Vincent circled his thumb around the rim of the glass, contemplating how to break the news.

'Trouble?' Joshua glared. He'd counted the money himself. It was all there... what the fuck was Vincent talking about? 'What kind of trouble?' Tapping the table between them with his fingers he felt suddenly agitated. Vincent had been here all evening. If something happened this morning why the fuck was he only just hearing about it now?

'There was a fire. A couple of miles out from the drop off point in Weymouth. The boat never made it. Apparently some dog walker reported finding a body washed up on the beach this evening. I only found out a few hours ago myself. The coastguard's scouring the sea for more bodies as we speak, but it's not looking good, bruv.'

'Are you fucking kidding me? I'd say it's a little bit more than a fuck-up, wouldn't you?' Joshua was fuming now. All fucking evening he'd been laughing and joking with his men, celebrating their good fortune, only to find out now that the operation was in jeopardy. 'A sinking ship is a fucking catastrophe. Why the fuck didn't you tell me sooner? How many people were on board?'

'A hundred, tops.' Vincent raised his hands up. 'I'm handling it. I didn't want to burden you with the minor detail unless I had to... '

'Minor detail?' Joshua gritted his teeth. 'Since when did a hundred fucking dead bodies floating in the English Channel become a minor fucking detail?' Shaking his head Joshua was fuming. 'Are you sure that there are no survivors?'

'The boat went down this morning, apparently. I'd say that any chance of finding survivors now is slim to none. The only thing they'll be fishing out of the water will be corpses.'

Joshua sat back in his chair, deep in thought, quiet for a few minutes as he digested the news.

Finally, he spoke again. Calmer, back in control.

'Nothing can be traced back to us can it?' This op was far too lucrative to shut down, but Vincent was right. They'd need to cool it. Lay low for a bit so that the authorities wouldn't be onto them.

Vincent shook his head.

'The fishing boat was bought privately – for cash – as per usual. Everyone on board had paid up. We made sure that no one carried any kind of ID on them; everything was kosher, like always. Done by the book.'

'Good!' Joshua interrupted. Leaning forward in the chair, relaxed a little. 'You're right. We're gonna have to cool things off for a bit. It's a fucking inconvenience but we don't have much choice. We'll lay low for a few weeks. Three maximum. Just until the heat's off.'

He was thinking now, his brain in overdrive.

'To be fair, the coastguard probably won't probe too much into it. This country's fucking overrun with immigrants as it is without another boatload of the fuckers.'

Joshua glared, his expression suddenly deadly serious.

'Next time the shit hits the fan, Vincent, I wanna be the first person to be told. Brother or not, this is my operation, my business. I brought you in on this because I need the muscle. You said you could handle it? Next time something like this goes down you do not keep me in the dark, do you understand?'

Vincent nodded. Heeding his brother's ruthless warning, he finished the dregs of his drink.

Joshua grinned, his composure regained as he focused on the money they had already made. In the grand scheme of things, a few weeks of laying low wasn't going to affect them really. It was unfortunate that people had died, but that was the business they were in. Those people were nothing more than collateral damage.

'Fuck 'em. We've got our money. Tonight's still a success. You win some, you lose some eh!'

CHAPTER EIGHTEEN

Rattling the door wildly as he stared out from the tiny gap, he let his eyes flicker frantically across the darkened room. He could hear the metal padlock scraping against the edge of the wooden doorway, but it held fast.

Trembling, he wrapped his arms tightly around his torso. He was beyond cold. Dressed in only his pants, the baggy waistband sagging at the narrowness of his hips, the soiled cotton material sticking to his skin.

The faeces had been warm at first, now they had gone cold and he'd been forced to sit in the damp pool of liquid. His bottom felt sticky and sore.

She'd be angry with him when she finally came. Angrier than she already was.

She loathed the way that he never seemed to be able to control his bowels, hated the sickly acidic smell that radiated off of him in waves.

She'd punish him for this, he knew that.

As if leaving him locked inside 'the hole' wasn't punishment enough. She was always so angry with him. For ruining her life: that's what she said when she repeatedly beat him with her shoe and the belt that was draped over the back of the bedroom chair. His eyes rested on the silver buckle now, gleaming like a brilliant gem as a thin sliver of moonlight from outside penetrated the darkness of the room. Only it wasn't a jewel at all, it was a weapon.

Running his fingers along his bony thighs he traced the tender red welts that she'd inflicted on him earlier.

His lips were cracked, dried up just like his throat.

Where was she?

When would she come?

Prepared for her wrath – but he was desperate for food and water. His stomach was hollow with an emptiness that made him feel physically pained. The void in his belly ached with such intensity he had no other choice but to try to antagonise her, to call out until she came. Even if it meant that he would forfeit any chance of being let out of here.

Maybe she had forgotten that he was in here? Locked away in the hole by himself.

Shouting loudly, he banged his fists against the wooden door.

'Mother!' he bellowed. 'Please, Mother. I'm hungry. Please.'

The bedroom door burst open.

He'd done it now. Finally, he'd summoned her to him. He listened as her footsteps stomped across the room, until she was standing just outside of the hole now, screaming wildly at him to shut up, her hands frantically unbolting the padlock.

She tugged the door open – a harsh yellow light flooding the tiny space.

He squinted then, startled by the brightness.

Pushing himself backwards he cowered up against the back wall, screwing his eyes up, shielding himself from the blinding light and his mother's presence.

He waited a few moments before he opened his eyes. She was there, looming in the doorway, her face mottled, her curly hair wild. Her eyes wide with fury.

The only emotions he recognised in her were those of anger and hate.

'Look at the fucking state of you. You fucking stink,' she spat. Her lips twisted in disdain at what she saw before her.

He was a mess. He couldn't remember the last time he'd washed himself, or sat on the toilet. Instead he'd been cramped in here – in this tiny space – day after day, left to fend for himself. His body was underdeveloped, emaciated. His ribs were jutting out of his chest, his collar bone prominent. His eyes were sunken in his head. His skin pale and gaunt. He looked more like a toddler than a boy of eight.

He was crying now. Thick, heavy tears rolled down his cheeks as he sobbed.

His heart heavy with emotion.

'Please Mother. I'm hungry… '

She clenched her fists in anger, incensed by the boy's brazen demands. 'I told you to shut up didn't I?' she screeched. Bending down, she grabbed him by his throat, hoisting him into the air, lifting him up so that he was eye level with her.

He struggled, kicking out. His eyes bulging in his head as he frantically gulped the air around him, desperately trying to release the pressure of his windpipe.

His tiny frail body was no match for hers. She squeezed him tighter and he saw the grin on her face as he convulsed in her grip – recognised the empowerment he'd given her as he gave into his fear.

Her eyes were manic now. The smell of the alcohol overpowering, even mixed with the sourness of her breath. She looked crazy, out of control. Like she wanted to throttle the life out of him. To put him out of his misery once and for all.

His lungs screamed for air, wheezing, sucking, but there was none to be had.

He gave in then, unable to fight anymore. His exhausted body suddenly limp as he gave himself to the darkness, slipping into unconsciousness.

He wondered if he was dead. It was like tunnel vision now. Like he was watching himself from afar as his tiny body was being dragged back into the hole.

She pushed his leg in with her foot; locking the door behind her before she left him alone once more.

He was right back where he started. Trapped in his hellish prison, lying limp on the floor, slowly dying of starvation.

No one would find him.

No one would ever know.

She'd told him that many times.

The walls started closing in on him, suffocating him. His body sprawled out in the tiny space as bugs crawled up from under the bare floorboards, feasting on his rotting flesh.

Springing bolt upright on the bed, Colin inhaled a deep breath of air, dripping with sweat as his heart hammered inside his chest.

It was a nightmare, he told himself, nothing more than a bad dream. A nightmare that constantly haunted him.

It was his mother's fault. She'd really pushed him tonight; triggering off his night terrors with her incessant bullying.

He tried so hard to bury the memories deep down inside of him, but they always found their way back up to the surface.

His mother might not force him inside 'the hole' anymore, but he was still imprisoned by her. Only, now the captivity he suffered was purely psychological.

He was trapped. Stuck in his mother's monotonous company, forced to listen to the constant barrage of cruel taunts.

The woman always seemed to come alive when she drank. Her eyes sparkled with a glint of something sinister as she passionately spewed the venomous poison from inside of her. All of it aimed at him.

'Why did they take her?' she had bawled, not waiting for an answer. 'She was my baby, my sweet little girl? Why? Why?'

Another of her breakdowns. Colin knew the warning signs well; he'd suffered enough of them over the years. His mother had never got over Karen's death.

'It should have been you,' she screeched. 'Look at you now, nothing more than a bitter disappointment… Forty years of age and still living at home with mummy. If Karen was alive, she'd have made me proud. She'd have been somebody. Not like you… '

Colin winced at his mother's venomous words. She wished more than anything that it had been Colin who had died. Not her precious daughter. She'd told him enough times over the years.

He'd only been three years old when his sister Karen was born. She'd only lived for a few weeks before she'd passed away. Cot death, they said.

Colin hadn't understood any of it. His mother, imprisoned in her own grief, had cut herself off from him. That was when she'd started drinking.

They'd left the cot in his room for weeks. Taunting him. Oblivious to the fact that Colin was petrified of it. Convinced that after killing Karen it might try and get him too.

Karen's death had affected them all. His mother the worst. Tonight she'd been incessant, bitter – her grief eating her up.

'You're just like him,' she sneered then. 'That useless good-for-nothing cunt. He should have taken you with him when he left; only he didn't want you either, did he!'

She was talking about his dad now. How he'd walked out on her, left her. Unable to cope with her drinking and her depression. Yet his mother had always blamed Colin.

Her voice, the high-pitched screeching, radiated through him, grating on his brain with her every word.

'Everyone left. Why the fuck didn't you?' she sneered. 'Oh that's right, you can't fend for yourself. I keep forgetting how you're special in the fucking head.' Mary cackled, remembering the words of one of the many social workers that had passed through her doors over the years. 'All those do-gooders dishing out counselling as if they were on fucking commission or something. Where are they now eh, Colin? No one gives a shit about you now, boy.'

She was laughing, mocking him. Just as she always did. Taking him to the edge and then letting him dangle.

Karen's death had affected him too. His father leaving meant Colin's life had been turned upside down. His mother had made every waking moment a living hell.

'Well, you're not completely useless.' Slinging her glass at him she added, 'run along, mummy's boy, and pour me another glass will you.'

Colin stood in the kitchen, his fists clenched in tight balls at his sides, an irritating twitch pulsating in the corner of his right eye, his chest tightening.

He was having to fight harder than normal to suppress the urge to pounce on the woman, to smash her ugly, thick skull in. Suppressing the years of abuse had made him feel weak and pathetic, but he could feel his anger boiling under the surface.

Then he saw the tablets discarded on the kitchen windowsill. They would shut her up. For a while at least. It was so simple he wondered why he hadn't thought of it sooner. All those nights he'd waited so patiently for the drink to take its inevitable effect. All the abuse he had endured while waiting for her to slowly drink herself into unconsciousness when the remedy to silence her vulgar mouth had been right in front of him all along.

Crushing up a handful of pills, he sprinkled the fine white powder into the glass before giving it a stir with his finger, praying that the quantity would have the desired effect. Then doubting himself, he crushed up a couple more, as generous with his dosage as she was with her hatred.

Walking back into the lounge he handed her the glass, but standing beside her in silence he felt suddenly anxious.

What if she recognised the bitter taste of the tablets?

He needn't have worried. Snatching the glass from him with her bony hand, her dark beady eyes didn't leave the TV screen as she greedily drank the concoction down in one go.

'I was wrong to say that to you, Colin,' she said now, staring up at her only son.

Colin felt his chest constrict at her words; his face flickering with confusion.

'You're not a complete useless cunt. You can pour a fucking drink.'

She roared with laughter, tossing the glass back at him. Colin had stood and watched as she had laughed herself stupid, wearing herself out.

It didn't take long for her eyes to close; the drugs working almost instantly. She was out cold. Splayed out in her chair in front of the television she was finally quiet. Finally silenced.

That's where he'd left her.

Pulling the duvet up around him, he stared down the length of his bed, over to where he'd dragged the dresser to cover the small doorway at the end of the wall.

The hole.

Colin had wanted to board it up, but mother would never allow it. He knew that she wanted it visible on purpose. Enjoying the discomfort it gave him.

All those memories he had of being locked away in there.

It was another one of her mind games, another way of her getting inside his head. Of controlling him.

Only, he had found a way to control her now. He'd wished he'd thought of drugging her sooner. Keep her sedated while he went about his business – tended to his secrets. He liked that. The thought of having something now that no one could take from him, not even his mother.

It made him feel powerful.

Lying back down, he buried his head in his pillow, smiling to himself as he closed his eyes.

He wasn't frightened anymore. Not now.

If the nightmares came again, Colin Jeffries would be ready for them.

CHAPTER NINETEEN

'Lena? Are you okay?'

Pushing open the toilet door, Kush grimaced at the smell. Even on a good day, after he'd mopped the piss-soaked vinyl floor and poured bleach down the toilet bowls, the place still reeked. Nothing he ever did seemed to mask the stench of customer's stale piss, but this smell was something else altogether.

Placing his hand over his mouth he fought not to gag as he made his way past the two empty cubicles.

He saw her then. Crouched on the floor below the sink; her face white with sheer panic.

She had Roza strewn across her lap, her dress covered in diarrhoea and vomit.

'Lena?'

'Help me. Roza's sick, really sick, please… '

Retching violently, Roza brought up the contents of her stomach – green watery bile spilling out all over the floor.

'I can't stop it for her, Kush. It just keeps coming… '

Patting the child's back hard, Lena looked distraught as Roza's retching was quickly replaced with gagging; a thick trail of mucus streaming from the child's mouth.

'Shit.'

Rushing to Lena's side, Kush crouched down on his knees next to her, his instincts taking over as he took the infant from her, tilting Roza upside down.

Gently he pressed her chest and stomach against his knee, as he rubbed Roza's back in small circular motions, increasing his pressure. But it was no use, the child was choking; her face puce as she made a horrific gurgling sound. Sliding his finger inside Roza's mouth, Kush hooked the substance, pulling it out in long stringy clumps of phlegm.

Still the child struggled to breathe. She was gagging for air, and he was running out of time.

'Go and get the phone, Lena, it's on the bar. You need to dial 999. Ask for an ambulance. We need to get Roza to the hospital.'

Sitting deadly still, her eyes not leaving her baby, Lena could hear Kush's voice, the alarm in his tone, but she couldn't move. Her legs felt like they were stuck to the ground.

'Lena! Go now!' Kush shouted. His voice suddenly commanding, breaking the trance. 'We're running out of time.'

Rising to her feet, Lena was moving towards the door, grabbing at the handle, but everything felt like it was in slow motion. Like she wasn't really here.

'Call 999. Tell them that we are at the King's Arms, Bridge Road, Battersea. Hurry.' Kush's voice echoed behind her.

Running through the bar, Lena repeated the address over and over inside her head as she made a grab for the phone – desperately trying to focus her eyes on the digits – her fingers stumbling frantically as she pressed at the numbers.

'What are you doing?' Ramiz was on his feet now. Seeing the look of alarm on his young wife's face; sensing her urgency as she grabbed at the phone. 'What's going on?'

Ignoring her husband, Lena pressed the handset to her ear and could hear the tone change as the phone began to ring.

Ramiz was walking towards her. She could see the gun down at his side; his hand curled tightly around it. Korab was up on his feet too now, aware that something bad must have happened.

'It's Roza. She's sick. We need to get her to hospital. She can't breathe properly. She's choking.' Lena was breathless now too; the panic still thick in her voice.

'No! No hospitals, Lena!' Ramiz made a grab for the phone.

Ducking out of his way, Lena stepped back, out of his grasp.

Her husband towered over her small frame; he could have easily overpowered her, but with the bar between them he was just out of her reach.

'Put the phone down, Lena. The hospital is not an option. People will ask questions; they'll take Roza from us. They'll send us home.'

Glancing down at the gun in his hand she saw his fingers twitch, before she returned his gaze, noting that his cold eyes held not so much as a flicker of concern for Roza.

'I cannot just sit back and do nothing, Ramiz. She will die.' Lena spoke with determination. Defiant. She couldn't get the image of Roza choking out of her head.

Ramiz would not stand in her way, not this time.

'You want to shoot me, Ramiz, then go ahead, shoot me, but I am getting my baby to a hospital. I will not let her die.'

A voice on the end of the phone answered then; the relief causing fresh tears to stream down Lena's cheeks as she blurted out the address she had memorised.

'I need an ambulance. Please, my baby is choking. She's sick.'

She stared at Ramiz as she spoke. Her eyes boring into his. Challenging him with every word as she recited the address.

It was done now. He was too late to try and stop her.

'How long, Lena?' Kush ran from the toilets into the main bar, his voice full of urgency. Roza's tiny body lying limp in his arms – he looked petrified.

'The ambulance is on its way… ' Lena said, her voice barely a whisper as she whimpered at the sight of Roza's drooping body; her child's eyes staring vacantly ahead.

Lena could barely talk. Roza looked almost lifeless.

She could hear the faint sound of the operator, still talking, still giving her instructions at the end of the line, but Lena was no longer listening.

She couldn't take her eyes off her baby, off Roza's wet, clammy skin. The raspy sound of her breathing, shallow, wheezy.

'Hold on for Néné, Roza! You're going to be okay,' Lena cried. Then looking at Kush for reassurance, she added, 'she will be okay won't she?'

Kush looked down, keeping his eyes focused on Roza as he gently patted her back; anything, so that he wouldn't have to look Lena in the eyes and lie.

Roza was almost lifeless now. He could feel her starting to slip away, sprawled in his arms, her breathing laboured.

Kush wasn't holding out much hope.

CHAPTER TWENTY

Aaron Miller was pissed.

Close to paralytic, in fact.

He'd only been in the firm for a month and already he'd had the privilege of experiencing one of his cousin's legendary parties that the other men had been raving about. Working in the firm was hard graft most of the time; the risks were big, but the rewards, judging by the huge tits on the busty barmaid in front of him, were plentiful, and Aaron was intent on enjoying every last second of tonight.

This really was the fucking life. Though now, clutching onto the bar next to him, he realised that perhaps he'd psyched himself up a little too early. Fuelled by whisky and many rails of cocaine he could barely stand up. Still, at least he knew how to get the party started, which was more than he could say for this bunch of miserable bastards.

'Right?' he slurred to the three men standing next to him. 'Whose round is it?'

'Are you going to ask that every time you order a drink?'

Jonjo grunted as he flashed Smithy and Ross a warning look not to react. Aaron Miller was a first-class cunt. How that fucking degenerate that was now propped up at the bar could be related to men like Joshua and Vincent Harper was beyond anyone's comprehension. 'It's a free fucking bar. You don't need to keep making a fucking joke about getting the drinks in.'

'Fuck me mate!' Aaron slurred, 'You not heard of those things they have these days called a sense of humour? You should look into getting yourself one… '

Smithy and Ross had their heads down, concentrating on their pints as Jonjo took a deep breath and tried to calm his temper. Making allowances for Aaron because he was Joshua and Vincent's cousin was one thing, but having to babysit the cocky little twat was quite another, and he was really starting to lose patience with this obnoxious prick.

'Don't you think that you need to slow down a bit, son? You can barely stand up.' Speaking through gritted teeth, Jonjo could see that Aaron was already half-cut; the kid was a lightweight. It wasn't even eleven o'clock yet and he was already pushing him to his limits with the cocky tirade of bullshit he was spewing. It was only a matter of time before he really pissed someone off, and tonight, Jonjo wasn't in the mood to be that someone.

'Slow down? Bollocks to that! I ain't even got started yet.' Aaron smirked as he turned away from the group, and then right on cue slipped and lost his balance, leaning against the bar for support. Dragging himself back up, he added, 'problem with you lot is you're fucking past it. Bunch of boring OLD wankers… '

Downing the last dregs of his whisky Aaron missed his mouth completely, the drink splattering down the front of his new crisp white shirt.

'Oh fuck it!' he groaned angrily as he wiped the stain, then, spotting the barmaid, he slammed his glass down on the bar in front of her.

'All right, darling, chuck another one in there for me will ya?'

Turning to the group of men behind him he shouted, 'Here lads, look at the bristols on this one eh?'

Ignored by the group of men, Aaron turned back to the barmaid.

'Can I help you?' Misty asked sarcastically, noting that Aaron was so engrossed in the sight of her breasts that he probably didn't realise she was actually attached to them.

'The question is… can I help you?' Aaron grinned, Misty's comment going completely over his head. 'You play your cards right, treacle, and this could be your lucky night!'

'Oh yeah, and why's that then? Gonna win a fiver on a scratch card, am I?' Misty smiled, not wanting to show the customer how boring his chat-up line was. She'd heard them all before, a million times over.

'A fiver?' Aaron raised his arms purposely, trying to make a point, as if he was really something special. 'Er, hello, you've just hit the fucking jackpot love!'

'No offence, lovey, but if winning you is akin to winning the jackpot then I'd rather just stick to making my own luck and live in poverty, if it's all the same.' Misty grinned at the drunk punter as he swayed unsteadily on his feet. 'Thanks for the offer though.'

Undeterred, Aaron grinned.

'Ohhh I like it! Playing hard to get are ya?'

Misty was bored now. Either this bloke was desperately trying to save face by ignoring her put-down, or her sarcasm had been completely lost on him. Going by how pissed the bloke was, Misty reckoned it was the latter.

'Ignore this one's banter, darling,' Jonjo interrupted loudly. 'He's not used to being in the company of ladies, you know what I'm saying?' he added with a wink.

'Oi! What do you mean I ain't used to being in the company of ladies? I ain't no fucking bender if that's what you're implying… ' Aaron slurred again now, disgusted with the innuendo that Jonjo had just chucked out about being some kind of shirt-lifter.

'Now who can't take a joke huh? Get him a glass of water will you Misty darling? Hold the ice though, he can't handle the hard stuff.'

Aaron gritted his teeth as the group of men continued to laugh at his expense. The girl behind the bar too. His colleagues were really starting to piss him off now. He might be tipsy but he wasn't fucking blind. He'd seen the looks that had passed between them. Raising their eyes at him, whispering about him behind his back.

All he wanted to do was have a bit of fun. Fucking old cunts, the lot of them.

They might all want to stand around like a boring bunch of bastards, but he was here tonight to party. With or without this lot.

'Anyway I don't know what you're looking at, Jonjo; I can't see any ladies around here. All I see are fucking slags. Wall to wall slappers putting it about and then playing hard to get at the last second. What's the matter, love, you not interested because I haven't offered you any money? How's a tenner sound? That's about how much you and your gammy snatch is worth.' Aaron laughed to himself now.

Jonjo was vexed then. It was all well and good having a bit of banter, but Aaron was being blatantly disrespectful now.

'Oi, watch your fucking mouth!' The warning tone in Jonjo's voice was clear to everyone around them. He'd heard enough. Aaron Miller was a fucking parasite. The sort of bloke that went through life hanging off other people's success. Taking whatever he could, but giving absolutely nothing back. The kid was too cocky for his own good; he had no respect.

'Watch my fucking mouth? I don't fucking think so. I know you're getting on a bit, Jonjo, but you ain't my fucking dad, mate!' Aaron laughed now, but it was clear to everyone listening that he was getting riled.

How dare they cunt him off, right to his face. Looking him up and down like he was a prize prick. If he wanted a drink he'd fucking well have one.

'Don't be shouting your orders at me, Jonjo. We ain't at work now you know.'

Who the fuck did Jonjo think he was? Just because he had worked under the bloke for the past four weeks it didn't mean that the bloke fucking owned him. Did he think that he could talk to him like a cunt and that Aaron would just swallow it? That he'd to be all, 'Yes sir, No sir, three fucking bags full sir.' Aaron had a free run to do whatever the fuck he pleased. Jonjo could go fuck himself.

'Watch your lip!' Jonjo warned, before turning back around and joining his mates. He'd had enough of Aaron's gob now. If the bloke spoke to him one more time tonight, he was going to fucking well lamp him one.

Seeing Jonjo turn his back on him, Aaron laughed. This was the kind of power that Aaron had – even Jonjo, who was a proper hard bastard, wouldn't be so stupid as to pick on Joshua and Vincent Harper's flesh and blood. Being the Harpers' cousin had given Aaron more than an in – it had given him free rein to do exactly as he pleased too and this lot would just have to fucking lump it. It didn't matter that he, Joshua and Vincent weren't particularly close. Just the fact they were related was enough to make people wary of him.

'As I was saying, stick another one in there will ya. Get one for yourself an' all.' Pulling out a wad of fifty pound notes, Aaron beamed at the girl.

Misty pursed her lips, unimpressed.

'No ta! I'm good, thanks.' Refusing the offer of a drink, Misty filled a fresh glass with water and plonked it down on the bar in front of him. 'Like Jonjo said, I think you've had enough.'

'I don't fucking think so.'

Pissed off that this tart was not only turning down his offer of buying her a drink, but she actually thought she could tell him what to do, Aaron pushed the drink back towards her, sending it flying. The glass tipped over, shattering into tiny pieces – the water splashing down the front of Misty's dress.

'Oops, don't realise my own strength sometimes. I'll have to watch that. Wouldn't want anyone to get hurt.' Aaron glared now, trying to look sinister.

'I'm sure.'

Rolling her eyes, Misty was trying really hard to keep her cool as she picked up the shards of glass from the bar. These men were all Mr Harper's business associates; she hadn't expected any grief tonight, but this bloke was trouble.

Misty could see it coming a mile off. Her guard was well and truly up now, and she wasn't the only one keeping Aaron firmly on the radar.

Tyrell Jones, the club's head of security, was at the bar in seconds; his expression thunderous.

He'd been watching Aaron Miller for the last ten minutes. This bloke had clearly drunk way more whisky than he could handle, and he was getting lairier with each glass. Tyrell could tell the bloke was goading for a bit of trouble, and if he wasn't careful he would be only too happy to serve some up to him.

'Everything all right here, Misty?' Tyrell's voice boomed over the bar.

Aaron bristled.

The burly black man was standing right behind him: so close that Aaron could feel his hot stinking breath on the back of his neck. He was making his presence felt. Letting Aaron know that he was watching him. It was a threat.

Well, Aaron wasn't even going to give this prick the satisfaction of acknowledging him; instead he kept his eyes on Misty. Watching her as she replied.

'No trouble babe, trust me, I can more than handle this one.'

Aaron smarted as Misty grinned.

The cheeky bitch was having a dig at him. Still cunting him off just because there was some big fucking gorilla backing her up. He was fuming at the girl's blatant audacity but knowing that Tyrell was still standing behind him, just inches away, Aaron didn't react. Instead he kept his eyes focused forward, pretending he hadn't even registered the narky bitch's comment.

'Yeah well, any problems, you just give me a shout. Okay?' Emphasising the word 'problems' Tyrell sauntered off.

Clearing up the mess, Misty rung out the cloth and wiped the water off the bar before getting a clean glass out. She could feel the man's eyes burning into her.

Still, Tyrell's warning had obviously done the trick. The bloke wasn't so cocky now. Instead he had been rendered silent. Standing there at the bar, with his chest puffed out, he looked like a deranged pigeon on steroids.

In the three years that Misty had worked the club, she had dealt with some of London's most notorious faces. Joshua Harper being right at the top. This bloke was nothing in comparison – just some cocky little wide boy – and going on his actions already tonight he wasn't going to last five minutes around here.

Unable to help herself, Misty couldn't resist one last comment. 'Here. A peace offering.' Banging down a fresh glass of tap water on the bar in front of him, Misty didn't bother to hide her smug smile. 'And that's the only thing you are getting from me tonight.'

Spotting Saskia on her break, Misty strode to the other end of the bar.

'You all right, Saskia?' Misty asked, glad of a distraction. She'd been wondering how Saskia had been getting on. She'd been meaning to keep an eye on her. Make sure the girl was okay. But the place had been so busy tonight that she hadn't had a minute to herself.

'My feet are killing me. Is there some kind of trick I should know about how to walk about in heels this high? Kicking off her six-inch clear plastic heels, Saskia sat down on the stool.

'Sorry lovey, what was that?' Misty asked, distracted – her eyes on Aaron at the other end of the bar.

The man stood glaring back at her.

'Is that bloke over there giving you trouble?' Saskia asked.

'He's harmless,' Misty spat. 'Just fancies himself. Fuck knows why though? I mean, let's face it, if sex appeal was dynamite the bloke wouldn't have enough to blow the cobwebs off his own balls would he!' Saskia couldn't help but laugh. Misty did too.

For Aaron Miller, the cackling sound that ripped through him was the final insult. What was it with people in this place cunting him off? Charging down the end of the bar, Aaron Miller finally lost it.

The first thing Misty felt was the burning sensation as Aaron Miller grabbed a fistful of her hair, ripping her hair extensions out in one fell swoop as he slammed the unsuspecting girl face down. Hard. Whacking her head off the top of the bar.

The attack happened so fast. Misty didn't know what hit her. Literally.

'What the fuck?' Aware she was screeching, Saskia panicked, hitting the man hard with the back of her fist. 'Get off of her—'

'You fucking cunt. Think you're so much better than me do you?' The man was on Misty now, smashing the girl's face repeatedly off the bar; the skin above her eyebrow splitting open on impact.

Seeing the blood, Saskia screamed for Tyrell. Then, pulling at Aaron's arms, she tried to wrench the man off of Misty, but he wouldn't budge. He was like a man possessed. Pushing Misty's face into the wood, his arm was locked like steel, refusing to let go.

Saskia was on him then. Jumping on his back, she clawed at Aaron's face, gouging at his skin as she dug her newly applied nail extensions deep into his flesh. Anything to get him to loosen his grip.

It worked.

In agony, Aaron let Misty go. His attention now on the deranged bitch that had clung onto his back, tearing strips off his face with her claws.

'You two-bit fucking whore!'

The girl wouldn't stop. His face was cut to pieces now, stinging. Swinging his elbow back he caught Saskia's cheek, whacking her with the full force of his strength, and she fell down on the floor onto her knees – in a heap.

In seconds, Aaron was down there too, lying next to her; his body pinned to the floor – squashed – underneath the seventeen stone mass of Tyrell Jones.

'Get the fuck off of me,' Aaron shouted.

The bloke was crushing him, dragging his arms up behind him, yanking them so far back Aaron thought the cunt was going to snap them off.

'That's enough, Tyrell. Get him back up on his feet.'

It was Joshua Harper: standing over them, sounding thoroughly pissed off. Now they'd know who they'd been messing with, Aaron thought to himself as he stood up, shrugging himself free of Tyrell's grip now.

'What the fuck is going on here?' Joshua stared as Saskia got up from the floor.

The girl looked a mess. Holding her face, Joshua could see that she'd taken a whack.

Misty looked worse. Her hair was all over the place, black mascara smeared down her cheeks. Visibly shaken up as she pressed a napkin to the large gash above her eye, she tried to stem the blood that was trickling down her face.

'This fucking no-mark hit Misty.' Kissing his teeth, Tyrell was doing all he could to keep his cool. He despised men who hit women. Gutless pieces of shit; they needed to be taught a lesson by a real man.

'Is that so?' Narrowing his eyes at Aaron, Joshua glared. 'Has this girl been causing you problems, Aaron?'

'Yeah, Josh, she was mugging me off. Winding me up… '

Joshua nodded as Aaron visibly relaxed. He knew once he explained things properly that Joshua would understand. These girls were nothing more than slappers. Fit for one purpose only, and this one had been way out of line.

'She was cunting me off, disrespecting me… '

Seeing Vincent standing at Joshua's side now, Aaron was back to his cocky self.

The club had come to a standstill. The music had stopped. Everyone's eyes were on him. This was his time to shine, to show everyone that he would not be made a mug of.

'I just lost it. She pushed me too far.'

Aware he had everyone in the club's complete undivided attention now Aaron spoke with conviction.

'So you took it upon yourself to teach one of MY girls a lesson by attacking her?'

'Sorry?' Aaron frowned then. Joshua's sudden change in tone confusing him.

His brain fogged by alcohol and cocaine, he realised he'd read this all wrong.

Joshua wasn't looking at him with understanding; he was looking at him like he was something he'd just trodden in. Scowling.

Backtracking now, Aaron tried to talk his way out of the hole he'd just dug himself.

'She was cunting me off, Joshua… ' Sobering up now, Aaron realised that he had royally fucked up.

Looking to Vincent, the younger of his cousins, Aaron hoped that he'd back him up. Another oversight.

Shaking his head, Vincent looked at Aaron with nothing but contempt. Aaron had made himself look like a class A cunt tonight and if he thought he was going to bail him out then he had another think coming.

Vincent should have known that something like this would happen. His cousin had always been a bell-end. The bloke had begged him for an in for months and stupidly, against his better judgement, Vincent had finally given in. He'd been the one to persuade Joshua to give the kid a chance.

They were family, after all. If you couldn't trust family, who could you trust?

He'd thought that by Aaron working alongside them both the kid would knuckle down, learn a bit of integrity, but he'd been wrong. Aaron was too much of a loose cannon. A fucking wide boy who had no respect for anyone. Tonight had proved that.

'Vincent, please, cuz! I didn't mean it… ' Begging now, his voice full of desperation.

He flinched at being called 'cuz'; Vincent was embarrassed to even be associated with the useless prick, let alone related. Joshua had given Aaron a chance, and Aaron in return had just royally cunted him off in front of the entire firm.

He was on his own now. Vincent wouldn't be able to help him.

'We're going to have to deal with this,' Joshua was speaking to Vincent now. 'Family or not… ' Vincent nodded.

It went without saying.

'Do what you have to, bruv. I'll take the girls to A & E. Get them checked over.'

'I'll take great pleasure in dealing with this piece of shit, boss,' Tyrell sneered, relishing the thought of inflicting some retribution on the piece of shit in front of him.

He took it as his personal responsibility to look after each and every one of the girls that worked here. This was his watch, and this little shit had overstepped the mark, big time.

Watching the exchange between the three men, Aaron shook his head, confused. He hadn't done anything wrong. It was the girl.

'What about her? She was laughing at me… ' His excuses sounded suddenly pathetic even to his own ears.

Joshua shook his head. Aaron Miller really didn't know when to shut up.

'Get this fucking cunt out the back – now,' Joshua ordered.

Tyrell did as he was told.

Vincent stood watching as Aaron, already defeated, let Tyrell drag him through the club without so much as a struggle. As if he'd already accepted his fate.

Cousin or no cousin, Aaron Miller was about to be taught the most brutal lesson of his life.

CHAPTER TWENTY-ONE

'Crash team! Her vital signs are fluctuating!'

The words were shouted with urgency, echoing around the tiny hospital room as Lena stared in horror – a team of specialists rushing into the room.

There were so many people. Registrars, consultants, doctors. It was hard to tell who was who. Standing haplessly in the corner as chaos erupted all around her Lena leant her back against the wall, as if without its support she would collapse.

Roza was sick. Really sick.

Clasping her hands tightly together to stop them from trembling it felt like the crisp white walls were closing in on her. Her worst nightmare was unfolding before her very eyes.

She felt suddenly claustrophobic, the already cramped room now full of extra equipment. A crash trolley, monitors. Tubes, alarms, cables. The room filled with a blur of noise. People shouting out instructions, machines bleeping. It was mayhem.

Korab stood beside her, his head down, his hand over his mouth – shocked at what he was witnessing. At the seriousness of the situation.

He was only here because Ramiz had forced him to come with her; a chaperone, to ensure that Lena wouldn't talk or run.

Ramiz had been a coward once more. Scared that the authorities would question them being in the country, he had stayed at the pub with Kush and sent Korab in his place.

Lena had her confirmation then that Ramiz had not an ounce of love for Roza. He'd watched without a flicker of emotion on his face as paramedics whisked her lifeless body away in an ambulance.

Korab was no better. Ignoring him as he loomed behind her, Lena didn't want the man anywhere near her. He disgusted her. Just the thought of him now, pretending to care about her daughter, about her, made her feel sick to her stomach. Stay focused, she thought to herself. She needed to be strong for Roza. Roza needed her.

Terrified, Lena looked over to where Roza lay inside the hospital's clear plastic incubator. Roza's breath, rasping, wheezy. She kept her eyes transfixed on her; scared to look away even for a second for fear that she might lose her if she did so.

An arm reached out and touched her. Recoiling at first, thinking it was Korab, Lena turned and stared at the nurse beside her.

'It's Lena isn't it? My name is Nurse Cheal. I want you to know that we are doing everything we can right now for your little girl; she's in safe hands.'

'Please? Will she be okay?' Lena begged, her eyes searching the nurse's eyes as if she would see the answer staring back at her.

'We need to know what Roza has been given. Any medicines? Do you know how long she'd been like this?' The nurse's words were urgent, controlled, but there was a softness in her eyes as she spoke.

'I haven't given her any medicine. Nothing.' Shaking her head. 'I guess she hasn't been herself for at least four days now. Though she only got really bad this morning.'

Lena faltered.

'Is there anything that you're not telling me, Lena. I really need as much information as possible. Is there anything else you can think of?'

Lena shook her head, unable to keep eye contact with the nurse. She wanted to say that Roza had only been like this since they had fled from Albania. That they had been travelling for days in the back of lorries and vans. That they'd spent the night on a boat. Freezing. Exhausted. She knew she mustn't though. Ramiz had warned her what would happen if she talked.

His words were still floating around inside her head.

They will take Roza from you.

They will send you back to Albania.

'We believe that Roza has been medicated, Lena.' The nurse persevered, not wanting to push the conversation, but she needed Lena to know the seriousness of the situation. 'We can wait for the toxicology reports to come back, but by then it might be too late. Lena, if there is anything you can tell me, anything at all, it just might help us to save Roza's life.'

'She hasn't been given anything,' Lena said, her voice full of certainty. 'I'm her mother, I would know. I haven't been able to feed her that well. My milk, it has dried up. I've tried so hard, please don't let my baby die.' Lena was crying now. Until the nurse had spoken of the severity of the situation Lena hadn't really comprehended the fact that Roza might actually die. 'Please, you must help her—'

Interrupted, the nurse turned to face the commotion in the room.

'She's going into respiratory arrest,' a voice across the room shouted out, panic erupting all around.

Lena didn't understand what the words meant but she knew that it wasn't good. Roza was gone from her vision now. Lost amidst the sea of people as the crash team moved in, huddling around the cot, desperately trying to save her child.

She couldn't move. All she wanted to do was to run to Roza's side, to pick her baby up and cradle her in her arms, protect her, but instead she stood paralysed with fear.

'We need oxygen.' Another shout came now.

They were losing her. Lena could see it in their faces.

There was another shout in the room. A flurry of movement – a shift in the atmosphere.

Running around to the other side of the room so that she could see Roza again, Lena began to cry hysterically.

Her baby's tiny body was limp, convulsing. Sporadically jerking about in her crib. Her skin had greyed, her lips tinged an icy blue. The crash team were doing everything in their power to keep her child alive.

As they huddled in around the child Lena lost sight of Roza.

You can do this Roza, Lena prayed. *You're a fighter, baby. You can do this.*

Helpless, Lena felt like she was suddenly floating outside of her body, responding in union to Roza's struggle. Her own chest constricted, her lungs struggling to fill with air.

If Roza died, Lena wanted to die right alongside with her.

'We're losing her,' someone shouted.

The words made Lena's blood run cold. Her legs buckling beneath her. Roza was losing her fight. Her daughter was going to die.

A sudden screech of an alarm filled the small room. Quickly followed by Lena's own harrowing scream.

CHAPTER TWENTY-TWO

'We're wasting our time sitting here you know. By the time you get that gash on your head seen to it would have probably fucking healed by itself.' Vincent Harper had the major hump.

Wedged between Misty and Saskia in the overcrowded waiting room of Chelsea and Westminster's A & E department he was starting to feel claustrophobic.

He hated hospitals with a vengeance, and it didn't help that they'd been sitting here like lemons for almost an hour and still they had yet to be seen.

'Fucking Christ! This place is a fucking safety hazard. If you're not sick when you get here, you know you're going to be by the time you fucking leave,' he muttered as the person across from him started coughing and spluttering their contagious germs everywhere.

Still, at least here he was out of Joshua's way. He wasn't sure he'd be able to stomach Aaron's reprisal. The bloke had acted like a prize cunt tonight, there was no denying that, but blood was still blood, and Vincent couldn't help feeling sorry for his younger cousin.

He was a bit soft like that. His cousin had always been able to manipulate him, even back when they had been kids.

Aaron was one of life's victims. Always down on his luck. The bloke had a way of making people feel sorry for him. That had been one of the reasons Vincent had put in a good word for him with Joshua in the first place, because he felt sorry for him. But barely a month in and Aaron had royally fucked everything up for himself.

People always thought it was Vincent who was the one to look out for between the two brothers. Him being the muscle, with the biggest mouth and the most volatile temper, but it was Joshua who was the real ruthless bastard.

Joshua was clever, shrewd – but what people underestimated was how ferocious he could be. His men carried out all his dirty work, as did Vincent, but it was Joshua who threw out the orders. He didn't take shit off anyone, family or not.

Agitated now as he thought of his brother and his cousin back at the club, Vincent tried to shrug it off. Casting his eye disapprovingly around the waiting room he shook his head in disgust.

'Ain't people got anything better to do on the weekend than hang out at a bloody hospital? I mean, look at them; it's like a social club for fucking degenerates. Do they congregate here after the pubs start kicking out do you reckon? Just so they don't have to go home to the fucking squalor they crawled out from… '

Grimacing, Vincent glared at one man over in the corner, passed out on the metal chair. Clearly worse for wear; a dark stain on the crotch of his jeans where he'd obviously pissed himself. Further down a woman sat slumped in a heap on the floor, semi-conscious, as her friend held a disposable sick bowl under her chin. Pointless really, seeing as the girl had already vomited all over herself, sick dripping from her hair.

'How much fucking longer are we going to have to fucking sit here!'

It was a statement not a question. Patience might be a virtue but it was something that Vincent certainly wasn't blessed with.

'I'll go and find out what's happening.' Sensing Vincent's mood, Misty stood up. Holding the blood-soaked tissue to the cut above her eye, her head was already pounding, and the last thing she needed was to sit and listen to Vincent harping on for another bleeding hour.

'No, no. You sit down. I'll go!' Saskia jumped up from where she was sitting now, desperate to make herself useful. Misty had taken a real pounding tonight. She looked awful. Her hair was sticking out in clumps where that arsehole had grabbed her, and she had a thick smear of congealed blood down her cheek. 'You shouldn't be walking about. Sit down. I'll go and find someone.'

Misty laughed then.

'I haven't had my legs amputated darlin', I've had a bang to my head. A little cut. It's an occupational hazard. I'm fine,' Misty insisted. Then nodding over towards Vincent she whispered, 'besides, I could do with a few minutes of peace – old moany bollocks here is going to be the death of me.'

Sitting back down, Saskia watched as Misty made her way over towards the receptionist's desk, surprised at how well the girl was holding herself together. The attack had seemed to affect her more than it had Misty. For all the glitz and glamour that Harper's Palace appeared to be, the attack tonight was a stark lesson of just how vulnerable the dancers really were.

She'd been lucky – she'd only got a thump – but that man could have killed Misty the way he'd continuously hit her head off the bar like that.

The club had security, but it had taken too long for anyone to notice what had happened. So much for the place being safe.

Jumping to his feet next to her, Vincent started bellowing, interrupting Saskia's thoughts.

'Oi! You dirty fucking cunt. Get the fuck out of here.' Towering over the elderly man sitting opposite them, Vincent was seething. His face was puce. His fists locked at his side. He looked like he was going to attack the man.

Saskia had no idea what the old boy had done to antagonise Vincent, but Vincent was making a spectacle of himself. Everyone was staring at them now.

'I said get the fuck out of here, go on… '

Standing up, confused, Saskia tried to step in between Vincent and the older man.

'He's about ninety Vincent, leave it… he's not doing any harm?'

The old boy had done nothing but shoot her affable smiles since they'd got there; he didn't look capable of harming a fly.

'Have a fucking laugh!' Vincent turned to Saskia and shook his head. This girl clearly had a lot to learn. 'This dirty bastard is only having a fiddle with himself under his coat while he's sat there gawping over at you.'

Horrified, and suddenly self-conscious, Saskia wrapped her jacket tighter and looked over at the old man, suspiciously. Vincent was right. She could see his hand on his crotch. His coat resting loosely over him trying to conceal what he'd been doing.

'Eww, you filthy bastard.' Saskia recoiled now.

'You heard me, you fucking perv, do one, before I fucking lamp you one. Otherwise you're going to need some serious fucking medical attention, you get me!'

The elderly man didn't need to be told twice. Humiliated at being caught out he got up from his chair and made his way towards the exit, sharpish.

Saskia sat back down then, mortified, and was glad when Misty returned a few minutes later.

'Right, do you want the good news or the bad news?' Misty asked, unaware of all the drama that had gone on in her absence, and plonked herself back down in her seat.

'The good,' Saskia said, hoping that Misty was going to tell them they could go home. Tonight had been nothing short of a complete disaster.

'The nurse on duty reckons that I'll probably only need a few stitches.'

'Ahh that's good.' Saskia smiled.

'What's the bad news?' Vincent said, his voice sounding bored.

'They are chock-a-block tonight and the waiting time to get seen is three hours.'

'Fuck's sake!' Vincent put his head in his hands. 'We've been sat here for an hour as it is.' He couldn't cope with another two; he'd end up murdering some cunt by then.

'Look. Why don't you two get off? Seriously? There's no point in all three of us dying of boredom. I'll hop in a cab when I'm done. I'll be fine.'

'I don't mind staying here with you?' Saskia said, dreading the thought of having to return to the club. She'd had just about as much as she could take tonight. 'I mean you might be concussed or something?'

Shaking her head, Misty wouldn't hear any of it. 'Seriously I'm fine. That bloke's come off a lot worse than me, trust me.' Catching Vincent's look, Misty pursed her mouth. 'Tell you what though, if you do want to do me a favour, I'd really appreciate if you went back to mine. My Boris will be doing his nut if I'm stuck here all night. Maybe you could keep the old bugger company for a bit. Just until I get back?'

'Boris? Er, okay, I guess…' Saskia suddenly didn't sound keen. She barely knew Misty, let alone feel comfortable about sitting in her flat on her own with her boyfriend. 'Or I could just give him a call?'

Misty laughed then. 'You could do, but I doubt he'd bother to answer the phone. Lazy bastard will be too busy lounging around the house, licking his balls…' Seeing the confusion on Saskia's face, Misty laughed. 'Boris is my dog!'

'Oh.' Blushing now, Saskia smiled. 'I thought… never mind.'

'The little bugger will probably be tearing the place up waiting for me to get home and let him out to do his business. I'd really appreciate it. Only if you don't mind though.'

Saskia nodded, glad to be of some kind of help as Misty reached into her handbag, retrieving her door key.

'Oh, here we fucking go again,' Vincent interrupted as he heard a loud noise from the other side of the waiting area.

Saskia and Misty followed Vincent's stare over to the commotion in the corner. A woman who had been previously lying on the floor was sitting up now, vomit projecting from her mouth.

'Fucking hell! Can't you go somewhere else and do that, like the toilets,' Vincent muttered, pulling the sleeve of his top up over his hands and covering his mouth. 'Fuck this.' He groaned. The woman had made the decision for him.

Misty was right. There was no point in them all sitting around like a bunch of cunts, waiting for a few stitches. Standing up, he reached into his pocket and pulled out a twenty-pound note.

'As soon as you've been seen get your arse in a cab. Okay!' Vincent said, getting up. The vile smell of vomit was filling the room now.

'Come on, Saskia. I need to get out of here before I start yacking my guts up too,' Vincent said over his shoulder as he made a hasty exit.

He couldn't wait to get out of the place.

CHAPTER TWENTY-THREE

Gathered at the nurses' station for a well-earned tea break now that the doctors had finally departed and normality had resumed on the ward, Nurse Sayers was doing what she did best: having a good old rant.

'It makes my blood boil – all these foreigners coming over here expecting to be given houses and benefits handed to them on a bloody plate. Funny how they are happy to fleece the NHS for free healthcare but as soon as there is any hint of trouble, "me no speak English". What a load of tosh! I mean, I know I've got a lovely complexion for my age, but by Christ, even a blind man can see that I wasn't born yesterday.'

Tonight had been a tough one for the nurses on shift. It always was when there was a little baby at risk, especially if drug abuse was suspected.

Thankfully, the doctors had managed to save the tiny infant, but Nurse Sayers's mood was still dark at the thought that they had nearly lost the poor little mite. It saddened her that these type of incidents were happening more and more lately.

'They don't really seem like a couple do they?' Nurse Roland chipped in. 'The man that's with her hasn't spoken a word since they got here. He's barely acknowledged the baby never mind offered any comfort to the mother, and the woman seems really guarded around him. I dunno, not scared of him, but indifferent. Like she'd rather he wasn't there… '

'Sounds like your typical married couple to me,' Nurse Sayers quipped. 'I know what you mean though, something ain't right. She's probably part of one of those gangs.'

'A gang?' Nurse Cheal asked as she looked around questioningly at the other ladies. It was her first week working in Paediatrics here at the Chelsea & Westminster Hospital and already she had seen and heard more than she had in the outside world in a lifetime. Working somewhere like here had been her dream. This was what she'd spent the last few years working so hard for; only, it was proving harder than she thought.

Tonight, she'd been thrown in at the deep end. While the crash team had revived baby Roza she'd been left to comfort the mother, Lena.

'You must have seen them. All those young beggar girls down in the underground stations. Out in all weathers that lot, begging for money.'

'Well, yes, I guess I have seen people begging… ' Nurse Cheal wasn't sure what Nurse Sayers's point was. 'Maybe she's homeless. She looked an awful state, didn't she? Her clothes are like rags, her hair and skin filthy dirty. Why would that make her part of a gang?' Nurse Cheal knew she sounded defensive but she couldn't help herself. The nurses seemed to have already condemned Lena. Even if the girl was a beggar that didn't make her a bad person. 'She looks desperate to me, like she's in need of some help. Maybe she was just doing what she had to for the sake of her child? Surely we can't condemn her for that?'

'That's just it though, my lovely. It's never about the sake of the child.' Nurse Sayers shook her head now. Nurse Cheal reminded her a lot of how she used to be when she'd first started out. Young, naïve. Thinking that somehow she could make a difference – before she realised what a sinister world they lived in and not everyone that came through those doors wanted to be helped.

'Have you ever seen any of those babies crying? The ones that those "mothers" are holding? I tell you what, next time you spot a girl begging on the underground take a proper look. Doesn't matter what time of the day it is, or how long they've been sitting there, those wee bairns never, ever cry. Most of them don't make a single sound, don't even open their eyes,' Nurse Sayers said, a sudden sharpness to her voice. 'Because they're drugged.' Seeing the shocked look on Nurse Cheal's face, Nurse Sayers continued. 'We've seen it too many times to mention. Those poor babies are plied with drugs and alcohol. Often it's heroin, but the gangs aren't fussy. They'll use whatever it takes to keep those poor mites sedated. Normally a concoction.'

'Jesus!' Nurse Cheal exclaimed, the shock clearly visible on her face. 'How could they do that to their own child? That is horrific.'

'Half the time the babies don't even belong to the girls. They've been bought on the black market, or even worse, kidnapped and then smuggled into the country. It's serious organised crime.'

'But surely the girls are victims too then?'

'Oh, don't even get me started.' Nurse Sayers was on one now. The events of the evening had well and truly rattled her. 'It's all about control. The men instil so much fear into those girls that they become unreachable. Even if the baby dies, which happens far too often – trust me – those girls still have to sit there and finish their day's work, otherwise they will be punished. Can you imagine? Having to sit there and hold a dead baby in your arms… ' She shook her head then, incensed. 'And all those do-gooders walking past, throwing money to them, oblivious to the fact that they are lining the pockets of a street gang. The whole thing sickens me to my core. It's inhumane.'

'But Lena seemed genuinely distraught. She was beside herself.' Nurse Cheal was doubting herself now; going against her better judgement. After all, these ladies had a lot more experience and insight than she did.

''Course she was distraught. Oh, I'd imagine the terror she felt was real all right. They all get scared when it starts to register that they could have a death on their hands.' Nurse Sayers shook her head. 'It's a hard lesson to learn, Nurse Cheal, but not everyone is as they seem. That girl in there is a liar. The toxicology reports have come back showing acute opiate toxicity. Opiate poisoning. Roza was drugged.'

'God! How awful. I really believed her when she said she hadn't given the child anything.' Nurse Cheal was sickened.

'Well, it's a lesson learned. People only tell you what they want you to know. The main thing is that baby's stable. Social Services are sending a case worker down here first thing in the morning.'

Nurse Sayers got up then, signalling that the tea break was officially over.

'I wouldn't wish being taken into care on any child, but what hope has the poor mite got with a mother like that? She's not fit to keep her.'

Peering out from the crack in the door of Roza's private room Lena could see the nurses all huddled around the station.

She could hear them too and bristled as she listened to them judging her. They were wrong. Wrong about her being part of a gang and wrong about her being a bad mother. She was a good mother; she loved Roza more than anything.

She hadn't drugged Roza.

When Ramiz had suggested it Lena had refused.

Suddenly she realised with horror what had happened.

Ramiz! Of course. It all made sense.

The couple of times he'd taken an interest in Roza on the journey and held her, Lena had thought that his sudden interest in their child had been out of character. Not only had he used their child to conceal his gun, but he'd been drugging her too! And now he'd almost killed her.

She'd heard what the nurses had said: they were going to take Roza away from her? Then what? Maybe they'd send Lena back to Albania? She might never see her daughter again?

Shaking, she watched as the nurses walked back towards the staff kitchen laden with empty mugs and half-empty packets of biscuits, while another nurse hurried off down the corridor to assist a patient whose alarm had just sounded.

Lena's mind was racing, her heart thumping inside her chest, as she began to pace the room, fighting back her tears as she felt the panic building inside of her.

She needed to get out of here, and fast.

She glanced over at Korab, still fast asleep on the chair; his jacket draped over him to keep himself warm, his head lolled to the side. Just the sight of him made her skin crawl. Ignoring the sleeping man, Lena turned and tiptoed back towards Roza's cot.

Leaning over the crib she reached out her hand, running her finger lightly over her daughter's cheek, relishing the warmth of Roza's skin beneath her fingertips.

Roza looked restful now. The grey tinge that had discoloured her skin had been replaced with a healthy pink flush. Her breathing was stable; her chest rising and falling steadily as she slept, with the help of a small plastic oxygen tube that had been fitted around Roza's head.

The nurses had assured her that it was just a precaution; that the wires and the monitors were purely so they could assess Roza's progress throughout the night.

Lena knew they were buying time; keeping her here until the morning. Giving her false hope, while all the while they just wanted to separate her from her daughter.

She knew what she had to do, but she needed to act fast. She had a few minutes, tops.

Rummaging around in the cupboard underneath the cot's base, Lena filled her bag with supplies: nappies, tissues, cotton wool, a spare blanket. Lena was careful not to make a sound as she filled the bag.

For a second, Lena doubted herself, wondering if she was doing the right thing. Maybe she *was* a bad mother? Taking her child from the hospital when she had just been so sick. Maybe she should just leave her here, and let the authorities take her.

Maybe then, finally, the child could have a decent life, have all the things that Lena would never be able to give her.

The thought hit her like a physical blow. She was unable to bear the thought of being apart from her child; the memory of Drita taking her still fresh in her mind.

Lena was Roza's mother. Roza belonged with her.

Reaching out, Lena's hands trembled as she hovered above the main power switch.

Apprehensive, she squeezed her eyes shut as she switched the button, waiting for a back alarm to screech out loudly, alerting Korab and the nurses to what she was doing.

But nothing happened. The room remained quiet, silent.

Lena stood deadly still, her chest constricted, her breath shallow.

The only noise was the sound of Korab snoring loudly.

Moving with haste now, Lena peeled the tape that had secured the tiny prongs underneath Roza's nostrils. Then she carefully lifted the transparent oxygen tube over the top of Roza's head before unclipping the probe from her daughter's foot.

Weaving through the tangle of wires that dangled from the cot's edge, she picked Roza up, wrapping her tightly inside the woollen hospital blanket. Roza didn't stir, fast asleep, still exhausted from her ordeal.

Making her way back over towards the door, Lena stood and peered back out into the dimly lit corridor once more. It was still empty.

Pulling the door open, gently, quietly, Lena took her cue. Creeping, she kept her footsteps light, making a sharp left towards the double doors at the end of the ward.

Everything was so quiet – nothing like the noise and chaos of the ward when she'd arrived hours earlier. Now there was just the odd sound of a beep in the distance, muted, echoing.

Picking up her speed, she was almost there, just another ten feet to go.

She was almost at the doors; her gaze fixed on the release button on the wall next to them.

Her heart thumped. Pressing the buzzer the noise made Lena jump. Making a grab for the silver handle, she pulled the door open. Just a few more seconds and she was out of here, free.

'Lena?' A voice behind her called.

She heard footsteps.

Glancing back, it was the nurse from earlier. The one that had comforted her.

Now though, her face looked full of concern, staring at Lena, then down at Roza; a frown spreading across her face. 'Lena, what are you doing? Where are you going?' Her voice got louder now. Panic ensuing as she realised Lena was trying to make a run for it – Nurse Sayers's words still inside her head. 'Lena, stop! Please, don't do this. Roza's not well. She needs to be here, with us. Please, Lena, let us help you?'

Lena shook her head.

The nurse was lying. They didn't want to help her. They wanted to take her baby. She'd heard them. All talking about her, judging her.

The nurse was shouting now. Running the length of the corridor. Hoping to stop Lena before she managed to get away.

The noise alerted the others; another nurse stepping out from a cubicle further down – the Ward Sister rushing out from the kitchen.

Lena needed to move. To run. Spotting the fire exit door that led to the stairwell she didn't bother wasting any time waiting for the lifts. Instead she ran as fast as she could down the narrow flight of stairs, clutching Roza tightly in her arms. Tripping in her haste, she stumbled down the last two runs. Dragging herself up, she was on the second floor.

She had no idea which way she should be heading, All she knew was that she needed to get as far away from this part of the hospital as possible.

She realised that some of the nurses might have taken the lifts and could be waiting for her at the bottom. She couldn't chance it.

Changing direction, she ran to the opposite end of the hospital. She'd find a different staircase. See if she could lose them that way.

So far, there had been no one else around. It was almost one o'clock in the morning, and most other patients had long been tucked up inside their beds. The only sound now was her, as she ran. Her breathing heavy, erratic; her feet rhythmically hitting the tiled floor – the noise echoing off the hospital walls.

Disorientated as she turned yet another corner, she lost her bearings, wishing that she'd paid more attention when Roza had been admitted earlier. The place was like a maze, everything looked the same; each sterile white corridor leading to an identical other like she was running in circles. There was another stairwell up ahead of her.

Lena could feel Roza stirring now, crying gently, still sleepy.

Taking the stairs once more, Lena made it to the ground floor in just seconds.

The sign above her read 'main entrance'. Following the arrows, just a few more minutes and she'd be out of here.

She was almost there. Almost free.

Turning the corner, her body slammed straight into something, into someone, stopping her in her tracks.

It was a man. His frame huge, heavy. Making her bounce backwards.

Clutching Roza tightly, something had to give. She dropped her bag to the floor.

Winded, Lena scrambled to her feet. Her only thought was for her daughter, but Roza, unaffected, didn't make a sound.

The man bent down to pick up Lena's bag, and Lena noticed the woman standing next to him.

She was young, pretty. Her hair blonde and curly, her eyes an icy blue.

She was speaking. Saying something. Lena could see her lips moving, her face etched with concern, but Lena wasn't listening, she was too distracted.

She could hear the voices behind her getting louder as they got closer.

Turning, she could see a nurse striding towards her, two burly security men at her side. Just two hundred yards away.

Shit!

Korab wouldn't be far behind either.

'Here, you dropped this.'

Turning back to the man, Lena gasped. Suddenly, it was if she'd had all the air knocked out of her.

It was him.

The man from the boat. In France.

Holding out the bag, Vincent stared at her, a flicker of recognition flashing in his eyes the same moment it did in hers.

'You?' What the fuck was the girl doing here?

'You know this girl?' the woman asked, unsure of what was going on.

'Please, I need to get out of here, please, they are going to take my baby… '

The security men were almost on her now.

The nurses would take Roza. They'd send her back to Albania. Just like Ramiz had said.

Lena tried to run past, tried to make it to the doors, but the man from the boat stood blocking her way.

The walls began closing in on her. She felt trapped. 'Please, help me. I need to get out of here.'

To her surprise, the man grabbed at her arm, shouting to the woman to get her arse in gear as he dragged Lena out towards the main doors.

'My car's just outside. Get a move on,' the man said.

Lena stopped resisting and ran now, grateful that the man and woman were helping her. She just wanted to get out of here. Get Roza as far away from the place as possible. Make sure that she was safe.

Reaching the black Range Rover in the car park, Lena watched as the man swung open the back door, the woman jumping inside.

She felt confused, a second of doubt creeping in once more.

'Why are you helping me?' she asked simply.

The footsteps behind them were still coming.

'Why not?' the man shrugged. 'Call it my good deed for the day! Now, you getting in or what?'

Lena wavered. Unsure.

'Well?' he asked, not in the mood for games.

Lena jumped in.

Slamming the door behind her, Vincent ran around to the driver's seat.

It looked like the night hadn't been a complete disaster after all. What were the chances of bumping into the girl from the boat? His head was spinning. If the boat sunk, but the girl had somehow survived, chances were that Korab and Ramiz might have survived too.

That meant that there were loose ends. Loose ends that could come back to him and Joshua.

Vincent needed to get this little situation sorted out, and pronto.

Jumping in his motor, Vincent shook his head in wonderment as he started the engine. If it hadn't been for Aaron acting like a fucking prick tonight, Vincent would never have even been at the hospital in the first place.

He'd never have seen the girl.

Turns out his cousin wasn't such a useless cunt after all.

CHAPTER TWENTY-FOUR

'Er, have I stepped into the friggin' twilight zone or something? What the hell is that and where did it come from?' Plonking her handbag down on the hallway floor as Boris sniffed around her feet and jumped up at her excitedly, Misty pointed to the baby in Saskia's arms.

'I know I've taken a clump to my head tonight, but the nurses at the hospital said the cut was only minor. Superficial, a bit like the no-mark that inflicted it on me. I only needed five stitches in the end but maybe the nurse had missed something? I think I might be hallucinating because that looks like a baby?'

'You're not hallucinating. This is a baby and her name is Roza.' Saskia exaggerated her whisper hoping that her friend would follow suit and keep her voice down. She didn't want to upset the poor child any more than it already was.

'You've got a kid?' Misty asked surprised now. She'd never even thought to ask Saskia if she had any kids; the girl was so young that it hadn't even occurred to her.

'God, no. She's not mine. Vincent just left me to it. Dumped her on me. She won't stop crying. The poor mite's been screaming the place down for almost an hour. Seriously, Misty, I'm so glad you're here, I can't seem to settle her. Look, I ain't happy about this little arrangement either, you know. She won't stop crying. I don't know what to do?'

Saskia was pacing the room as the baby bawled loudly in her arms.

'Where did Vincent get a baby? Why did he leave her with you?' Misty shook her head, confused. Saskia looked close to tears, and Misty had no idea what the hell was going on.

'Well, I'm just going to throw a wild guess out there that his childcare skills are probably right up there next to his flower arranging and cookery expertise.' Saskia shrugged. 'He couldn't get out the door quick enough; said he'll be back to speak to her tomorrow.'

'Vincent is coming back tomorrow so he can talk to the baby?' Rubbing her head now, Misty groaned inwardly.

She was definitely concussed. She must be, because none of this conversation was making any sense.

'No, he wants to talk to the girl. The baby's mother! He said to call as soon as she wakes up.'

'The baby's mother?' Misty stared, open-mouthed now. 'When she wakes up?' Misty repeated.

'Yeah she's asleep.' Saskia diverted her eyes away from Misty's. 'I don't know who she is. She literally ran into us at the hospital as we were leaving. Vincent seemed to know her… '

Staring at the empty sofa, Misty frowned.

'Oh no! Please tell me that you haven't let this woman kip in my bed, Saskia?'

'I can tell you that but… ' Saskia said with a small smile, trying to lighten the mood.

'Girl, are you fucking kidding me? I'm knackered. My head's banging and now you're telling me that, as well as having this sprog dumped on us, I've got some strange woman tucked up in my bed?' Stomping across the flat now, Misty pushed open her bedroom door and peered in.

'She's not a strange woman, Misty, she's practically a child. She can't be more than sixteen… '

Peering through the darkness, Misty could barely make out the girl's face as she slept. All she could see was her frame – long, slight – swamped underneath Misty's duvet. The rise and fall of the cover as the girl slept contentedly.

She was completely out of it. Sparko.

'Who the fuck is she?' Closing the door again.

'All I know is her name is Lena.' Saskia shrugged. 'Vincent seemed riled though. He kept asking her the same questions over and over again. It sounded like he was interrogating the girl. She wasn't making much sense, she was babbling. Talking in her own language. Poor girl looked a right state. I think he gave her something in the end to make her sleep… '

'Gave her something? Like what?'

'I dunno. He was rummaging around in your en-suite for ages; when he came out he told her he had something that would calm her down, help her rest—'

'My Xanax! No wonder she's sleeping through this racket. Jesus! It doesn't look like we're getting much sleep tonight then does it?' Misty sighed. 'Lena? I wonder who she is? The name doesn't ring any bells. Do you think it's Vincent's girlfriend?'

Saskia shook her head. Lena definitely didn't look like a girlfriend of Vincent's.

'I dunno, I don't think so. She sounded foreign. It was all a bit odd. She was being chased. Some nurse came charging around the corner, together with an entourage of security guards, and the girl just went nuts. She was saying that they were going to take her kid away from her. She was begging us to help her.'

'So what? Vincent Harper did his good deed for the day, did he?' Misty was suspicious now. 'Why would that man go out of his way to help her? He's not exactly the charitable type is he? What was he asking her, do you remember?'

'He kept saying the same name over and over… something like Conrad, or Korab… He said something about a boat sinking? That's when the girl really lost the plot. She was crying, shaking. He couldn't get any sense from her after that.'

'So he knocked her out?' Misty scowled. 'Typical Vincent.'

'He begrudgingly went out and got some supplies before he left. Some baby milk, and nappies and stuff. I think he just wanted to palm the kid off without us giving him any earache about it, but I haven't got a clue what I'm doing. She just won't stop crying…'

Misty could see that Saskia was on the brink of tears as well as she cradled the distressed baby in her arms and continued to pace up and down Misty's lounge.

'Here, give her to me.'

Taking the baby, Misty held her awkwardly in her arms. 'Hey little one,' she sang, trying her hardest to settle the child. 'Maybe something's wrong with her? I mean, they were at the hospital. Maybe Roza's sick?'

Saskia looked worried now.

'Well, I'm going to place my bet on the fact that this little thing has got a poorly tummy. Jesus, Saskia, how can you not smell that!' Wrinkling her nose up in distaste as an unpleasant stench of Roza's nappy wafted up her nose, Misty quickly passed Roza back to Saskia. 'Bloody hell! The little thing doesn't look capable of doing something that smells that vile does she?'

'I'm useless with babies.' Saskia winced. She didn't have a clue what she was doing, and changing a heavily soiled nappy was the sort of thing she had been dreading.

'Have you got anything to change her into? Did you say Vincent bought some bits for her?' Misty breathed through her mouth as she spoke.

'Yeah, there's a bag over there. What do I do though? I've never changed a baby before. I don't suppose you would give me a hand would you?'

'Er, no chance! I'm hardly bloody Mary Poppins am I!' Misty held her hands up as she trudged across the room and grabbed the carrier bag that Vincent had left, sliding it over to where Saskia was sitting.

There was no way that she was getting roped into looking after some kid. She'd already been through enough shit tonight without adding pooey nappies to the list.

'Vincent left you in charge so I'm afraid bum duty is down to you.'

'You're seriously not going to help me?'

Realising that Misty wasn't going to give in, Saskia got on with the task in hand. Laying Roza down on the floor, recoiling as she undid the nappy, she gagged.

Roza stopped crying.

'Well it looks like at least someone's happy to have that stinky nappy off,' Saskia cooed, as Roza happily kicked her legs out now. Her face relaxed.

'Ahh, look at her little face, Misty,' Saskia said. 'I think you were right. She must have had a poorly tummy? Is that why you were crying, little Roza? You poor little thing. You might be smelly, but you are gorgeous, aren't you, little one. Ahh, come and look, Misty. She's adorable.'

Seeing her friend looking so besotted Misty gave in, walking over to see what all the fuss was about. Gurgling and wriggling as her eyes flickered around the room, her little mouth making funny noises, Misty couldn't help but smile then too – Roza really was a little cutie.

'Could you just hold her feet for me while I clean her up?' Saskia asked now, seeing her friend soften. 'Please, I'll get it done so much quicker if you give me a hand.'

'Okay, okay!'

Reluctantly agreeing, Misty got down on her knees to help her friend. Taking Roza's tiny feet in her hands she held them up gently, while Saskia faffed about inside the bag searching for some wipes and a fresh nappy.

'Hello baby!' Misty cooed, still holding her breath to avoid the rancid smell.

Roza gurgled now, her eyes locked on Misty's. She smiled – the biggest smile that Misty had ever seen.

'Ah look, Sass, I think she likes me!' Misty grinned, turning to her friend, amused; her hands losing grip of Roza's bare feet as they slammed down into the soiled nappy. 'Great,' she groaned as she took in the sight of the yellow diarrhoea that had splashed all over her white dress. Roza was covered too. 'Well, I guess this sums up a perfect ending to a thoroughly shitty night!'

Saskia giggled.

'Maybe we should just move on to plan B?' she suggested.

'And what's that?' Narrowing her eyes, Misty raised her eyebrows questioningly.

'Let's just dunk her in the bath! Going by the state of you I think that's the safest option.' Saskia shrugged, then pointing at her friend's head she added, 'you should probably think about getting one too afterwards. You've got some, erm, baby poo in your hair!'

CHAPTER TWENTY-FIVE

Crouching on her knees in front of him the Russian girl was chunkier than Ramiz was used to. Her thighs and buttocks were heavy, her breasts full, curvaceous.

Just the sight of the woman made him hard. Nothing like Lena's flat, boyish chest. Unlike his wife, Anya was eager to please too. Obediently she took him in her mouth. Encased in total euphoria Ramiz allowed himself to relax. Tipping his head back, his eyes rolling as he gripped the girl's doughy flesh in his hands, kneading it roughly as he willed her to suck him harder. Faster.

He was enjoying himself. Sex with his prudish wife had been like fucking a corpse. Lena made no secret of the fact that she despised him. She only had to look at him and he could see the hatred pouring out of her. Her body physically recoiling when he touched her. The only sound that ever passed Lena's lips when he fucked her were the moans of pain when he purposely hurt her so that she had no choice but to cry out.

To beg him to stop.

It was his little game. If the bitch refused to give him a reaction, he had forced her to. She'd taken the fun out of that too eventually. When she clocked on to the fact that the more she resisted her husband's advances the rougher he would be with her, Lena had learned to comply. To lie there and let him do what he wanted with her.

Well, his prudish wife had her wish now.

Ramiz would never touch her again. Not now that she had lain with Korab.

She was tainted, dirty. Still, she wasn't without her uses. She'd be perfect for a place like this, he decided. The little set-up that Kush had running here was raking in the money. The man was smart.

The pub downstairs was a shit hole, that was true, but it served its purpose. It was just a front. The real money to be made was up here with the girls, and now Ramiz was experiencing first hand why.

Kush had a different girl in every room and punters coming and going all through the day and night. When Ramiz found out how much money was involved he'd made his interest in the place very clear. He wanted in.

He hadn't told Kush that yet though, but he would soon. Things were going to change around here. Kush was doing well for himself, granted, but Ramiz had real plans for the place. They were going to make some real money.

After he tested out some of the merchandise for himself.

Clasping a clump of the girl's hair now – Ramiz had picked well with this one – she was working hard to satisfy him. He was almost at his peak now. The point of no return.

He could hear Anya gagging. The strained noise vibrating in her throat only heightening his climax. He stared at her red face, her bulging eyes; her expression one of fear as she fought to breathe.

Ramiz shoved himself into her mouth more violently. Closing his eyes, he pictured the horror on Lena's prissy little face when she realised what he had in store for her.

All those men fucking her.

A young timid girl like Lena – her body being abused over and over again. She was going to make him a fortune.

He exploded then; the sudden rush of ecstasy releasing inside him as he emptied himself into Anya's mouth. He pushed the girl away from him, his earlier desire for her replaced with revulsion. She looked exactly what she was now. Cheap. Used.

Slumped on the floor, her sagging white belly hanging loosely over the top of her knickers, brash red lipstick smudged all over her face. She wiped him from her mouth with the back of her hand as she stared at him expectantly. She was waiting for her money, he realised.

'You think you're getting paid for that?' Ramiz smirked. 'That, Anya, was a lesson in quality control. Next time you'll work harder. Now go and get yourself cleaned up, you're making the place look dirty.'

Smiling to himself as he watched the girl gather her clothes and scurry out of the room, humiliated, Ramiz slumped back on the bed as he fastened up his belt.

Yes, this place could work out very nicely for him. First thing in the morning he would speak to Kush. Get the ball rolling. Kush would be keen, Ramiz was sure.

Maybe he'd even let Kush try Lena out for himself.

Smiling now, Ramiz had big plans for his wife.

Big plans indeed.

CHAPTER TWENTY-SIX

Waking with a start, surrounded by darkness, Ramiz felt disorientated.

He'd fallen asleep. Upstairs on Anya's bed.

'What the—?' He jumped as he spotted the shadowy figure standing next to him. Cursing as he realised it was only Korab, he relaxed once more.

'You're back?' Sitting up, Ramiz glared. 'Where is Lena? Downstairs?'

'No.' Korab tried to speak, but Ramiz had fixed him with a cold hard glare, his eyes penetrating. He was going to be angry. Ramiz had given him strict instructions not to leave the girl on her own. Not to let her out of his sight.

Reaching for the bedside lamp Ramiz flicked the switch.

He could see Korab properly now. The man was shaking, his eyes nervously scanning the room. Something had happened.

'The child, is she dead?'

Ramiz hadn't thought that the child might actually die. To be fair, he hadn't thought about Roza at all.

'She was really bad for a while though, Ramiz. She almost didn't make it. The doctors saved her life… '

'Good.' He realised then he was glad the child had survived. Roza was his bargaining tool. Threatening to take the child from his wife would be the only way that he could ensure that Lena would do exactly as she was told.

If Roza had died, Lena would have been no good to him.

'Where are they? Downstairs?'

Putting his shoes on, Ramiz stood up. The sooner he put his plan into action the better. He was looking forward to telling Lena what he had in store for her. Looking forward to the look on her face when she discovered her new destiny.

'They've gone Ramiz… ' Korab's voice shook, betraying him. His eyes were locked on Ramiz's gun, poking out from where he'd just tucked it inside his belt.

'She ran from the hospital, Ramiz. She took Roza. I only closed my eyes for a few minutes. I must have dozed off. I didn't think she would take the child. Roza was still wired up to the machines and monitors—'

'You fell asleep?' Narrowing his eyes, Ramiz pursed his lips. He must have misheard Korab. 'I told you to keep an eye on Lena at all times. Not to let her out of your sight, and you fell asleep?'

Korab nodded, feeling terrified now. 'I'm so sorry, Ramiz. The first I heard was the commotion in the corridor; the nurses and the security staff all chased her, but it was no use. She escaped.'

'If you're lying, I'll fucking kill you… ' Ramiz gritted his teeth, grabbing Korab roughly by the scruff of his neck and pinning him up against the wall. 'If I find out you helped her to escape, you'll have signed your own death certificate.' Snarling now, a thick vein pulsating above his right temple, Ramiz was seething. He should have just gone to the hospital himself. This would never have happened if he'd have been there.

Lena would never have run away; he'd have made sure of it.

Ramiz was starting to realise that if he wanted something done around here, it was best off him doing it himself. Korab was fucking useless.

'I promise you, Ramiz, I didn't know. When I realised that she'd gone I ran after her. I tried to catch up with her, but she was already out in the car park by the time I reached the main entrance.'

'And what, she outran you, did she? Is that what you're going to tell me next? That you couldn't keep up with a young girl holding a baby?'

Ramiz released Korab now. Letting go of him, he stared at him, hard.

There was no way that Lena could have got away. Korab could have caught up with her. He could have stopped her. There must be something Korab wasn't telling him.

'She got into a car!'

Ramiz was about to really lose his shit. 'What fucking car?' Ramiz asked. 'A taxi? A police car?'

'I think it was Vincent Harper's.'

'Who the fuck is Vincent Harper?' Ramiz shook his head. The name familiar, yet he couldn't place it.

'My boss.'

Korab hadn't been sure at first. Vincent was the last person he'd expected to see, but there had been no mistaking that big stocky frame. The broadness of the man's shoulders. Vincent hadn't seen him, but it would only be a matter of time before Lena told the man where he could find him.

'If Lena tells him that I'm alive and that I didn't even try and contact him, he'll be fuming.'

Korab knew the drill. The first thing he should have done when he made it to England was contact Vincent, but he hadn't. Instead he had gone along with Ramiz, and made his way to London.

'What the fuck would your boss want with Lena?' Narrowing his eyes, Ramiz bristled. Poking Korab hard in the chest, as the man looked down at the floor, he was starting to lose his temper now. This was all Korab's fault. If he'd just done as he was asked and kept an eye on Lena, none of this would have happened. 'What does he want?'

'He wants me.' Korab shrugged now. 'The boat sinking has been all over the news. Vincent would have assumed I was dead, that I had drowned like all the others. If Lena tells him that I'm alive, laying low, Vincent will be fuming. He's already questioned my loyalty once. He'll come for me.'

'Why is he here in London?'

'London is his home. His brother has a club somewhere in Chelsea. I have no idea how he found Lena.'

'Did he force her into the car?' Ramiz asked, trying to make sense of the news.

'No, she looked like she was going of her own free will. Like she was desperate to get away. The nurses were chasing her, the hospital security too… '

It went unsaid that Lena must have been desperate to have sought help from the likes of Vincent Harper. If her only other option was to come back here to Ramiz, she'd obviously decided to take her chances.

'You think he's going to use Lena to find you?'

Korab nodded. It was the only thing that he could think of, the only thing that made sense.

'We need to leave, Ramiz. Tonight.' Korab cringed at the tone of his voice; he hated that he sounded so weak and pathetic, but he was terrified. 'Vincent won't like any loose ends. I know how he works… '

Ramiz was fuming now. Silently, he shook his head. 'I'm not going anywhere.'

He had plans. He needed Lena back here, working, needed her to start making them some money.

'If this Vincent is coming for you, then let him. We'll be ready.' Ramiz was shouting again now. His voice loud with indignation.

Closing his eyes briefly, Korab felt his stomach churn. Ramiz just didn't get it. He didn't have a clue who he was dealing with. Ramiz might think that he was a force to be reckoned with but

Vincent Harper would annihilate him. The Bodi family had nothing on the Harper brothers. Men like Vincent and Joshua didn't mess around. They'd want him and Ramiz dealt with immediately. Korab knew that there was no point even trying to reason with Ramiz now, his mind was made up. Ramiz might want to sit this one out and wait for Vincent to show up, but Korab had no intention of hanging around. The first opportunity he got he was out of here.

If Vincent Harper was on his trail, Ramiz Gomez was the very least of Korab's worries.

CHAPTER TWENTY-SEVEN

Glancing at his Rolex, Joshua Harper rolled his eyes as he realised the time. It was almost four a.m. The party had only just finished and he was glad that everyone had finally gone. They'd taken their fill and left. Like vultures, greedily lapping up what was on offer, then disappearing.

It was just him now, alone in his office with a bottle of Scotch and his laptop and a major fucking headache.

There was no point going home to bed. He wouldn't sleep even if he did. Not after tonight's dramas. He was far too wired for that. Downing his Scotch, his mind was working overtime.

Aaron Miller had taken the brunt of his anger tonight. The bloke had royally fucked up by starting trouble in his club. Joshua could have let Tyrell deal with him; after all, that was Tyrell's domain. He was the muscle, the hired help; his job being to sort out anyone that got out of line in the club. But after his conversation with Vincent earlier, Joshua had felt riled up, relishing the chance of something to direct his anger at. Not only did Joshua feel the need to make an example of Aaron, he'd enjoyed every second of inflicting it.

Aaron Miller acting the cunt had given him the perfect opportunity to let off some steam.

By the time Joshua had finished with him his cousin had been nothing more than a crying, whimpering mess. All his earlier bravado had upped and legged it as he unceremoniously pissed himself.

Joshua had left the bloke begging for mercy, as if he was somehow doing him a favour by letting the bloke live. Staring down at his own trousers, he sighed. The fucker had made a right mess of his new Armani suit. It was splattered with deep red stains where he'd bled out all over him. He'd never get the claret out, it was destroyed. Though, as damage limitations went tonight, his suit was a small price to pay in the grand scheme of things.

Joshua had been stewing back in his office ever since. Nursing his swollen fist as he downed a few medicinal Scotches; for him the party was well and truly over.

The only people left in the club now other than him were his cleaners. He'd been watching them on the screen, trying to focus on anything other than the fucking headache he had at the top of his skull.

Being holed up in his office on his own for the past few hours hadn't been such a good idea, it turned out.

He'd been digging – scouring the net for as much information as he could get his hands on – but now that he had it he wasn't sure what the fuck he was going to do with it. All he did know was that unless he sorted this mess out, and pronto, they were going to be in some serious amount of shit.

Glancing at the CCTV monitor, he watched Vincent let himself in through the side door and head towards his office.

Finally. They had a fucking big problem on their hands and Vincent couldn't have timed his arrival any better.

'You all right, bruv?' Walking into the office Vincent picked up on the strained atmosphere straight away.

Joshua was staring at his laptop, his jaw clenched angrily. 'Sit down.'

Kicking out the chair opposite him, Joshua stared at him now.

Vincent sat down opposite his brother, a puzzled look on his face. Joshua had a right face on him. He looked like he'd had way too much to drink too, and Vincent knew only too well what a lethal combination that could be. Whatever reason Joshua had for summoning him back to the office, Vincent figured it had to be something bad.

Joshua wasn't into playing games, and the thunderous expression on his face only confirmed that.

'Look, bruv, if this is about Aaron then I just want you to know that I'm sorry I fucked up. I thought that if we gave him a chance, he'd sort himself out. He must take after Dad's side of the family, eh?' Trying to gauge Joshua's reaction, he continued, 'I guess there is no helping some people. He's nothing but a fucking embarrassment, bruv. He deserved everything he got.'

'Aaron was taught a lesson that he won't be forgetting in a hurry, but trust me, it's only because he's our cousin that I didn't kneecap the cocky little bastard. No one walks into my club and treats my girls like that. It's a fucking liberty. Especially in front of the rest of the men, publicly cunting me off like that. It's not good for business.' Joshua poured himself another drink, but he didn't offer his brother one. That gesture alone told Vincent all he needed to know.

Joshua was severely fucked off with him.

'Okay.' Vincent trod carefully. 'If Aaron's all sorted, what's the problem?'

Joshua raised his brow now, his face stern, fighting to keep his temper.

'What's the problem?' Joshua laughed. Manically. 'I'll tell you what the problem is, shall I?'

Turning his laptop to face Vincent, Joshua waited for him to say something as they both stared at the haunting image on the screen.

It was the tiny limp body of a toddler. The boy been found washed up on the beach at Weymouth. His lifeless form lay face down in the sand.

Vincent flinched, but he didn't look shocked or surprised, confirming Joshua's suspicions that he'd already seen the image. Of course he had. The whole fucking world had seen it. The harrowing photograph had already gone viral.

The image of the dead child was currently echoing its way around the world, headlining the front page of every newspaper, every TV channel, every internet post.

'I'd say this is a fucking problem all right, wouldn't you? Only, ironically you *didn't* say it, did you? You kept your fucking trap shut. When you said a body washed up on the shore yesterday you failed to mention that it belonged to a small child. Lay low? How the fuck are we supposed to lay low when the press is all fucking over this? It's all anyone's talking about.'

Joshua spat now, fuming, his fists clenched tightly to his side.

'They're illegals, bruv. Like you said, who's going to give a fuck? We're overrun with them... ' Vincent spoke with arrogance, repeating his brother's earlier words, but they sounded hollow now.

He hadn't told Joshua for this very reason. He was hoping that things would have died down by the time Joshua heard the full story. But the boat sinking was no longer merely local news. It had made the nationals too. The child's death had made people from all over the world sit up and take notice. The authorities wouldn't just sweep this one under the carpet.

Vincent knew it and Joshua did too.

'Who gives a fuck?' Joshua shook his head. The anger inside him was so immense now it was consuming him. He was fighting with every reflex in his body to control it. 'I'll tell you who gives a fuck shall I? The world and his fucking wife, that's who gives a fuck.' Joshua was raising his voice. 'This changes everything. A dead child cannot be ignored. No one's going to look at this kid with contempt. No one's going to say that that child's life didn't matter, that it was irrelevant. It's front page fucking news! The press is already having a field day with this. If any of this comes back to us, if anyone finds out about the op, we'll be fucking slaughtered. Crucified.' Joshua was bellowing now, his temper finally getting the better of him. 'It isn't a case of just laying low for a few weeks, Vincent, and hoping for the best. If our names are linked back to this, my name, I'll lose fucking everything.'

Joshua was furious. So far, Vincent was proving to be almost as useless as their poxy cousin.

'So, if there is anything else you need to tell me, anymore fuck-ups that I need to know about, you better fucking speak up now. 'Cause I have had enough of you keeping me in the fucking dark!'

Joshua sat back and glared. His eyes boring into Vincent's. He was doing what he did best: reading the man's every move. Absorbing every flinch, every twitch.

Vincent shifted uncomfortably in his chair.

'There might be a couple of other loose ends that need tying, bruv.'

'Loose ends?' Joshua shook his head.

Vincent raised his hands up. 'I didn't know about them until tonight, when I took Misty to the hospital, I promise.' Vincent looked nervous now as he spoke. 'I ran into one of the passengers from the boat. A young girl with a baby. She was at the hospital.'

'What?' Joshua tried to absorb what he was hearing. The last thing they needed right now, with the press all over this, was the chance of anyone talking. 'But you said there weren't any survivors?'

'That's just it, boss; I didn't think there were. This girl, Lena, she didn't even know that the boat had sunk…' Vincent rubbed his temples, agitated. 'I think she must have got off, abandoned the boat, and if she did, then she wasn't alone. She'd been travelling with her husband, some mad-looking Albanian cunt. They were both very friendly with one of the Calais brokers, Korab. I think they are here in London. The three of them and the kid.'

'You think?'

'I can't get any sense out of the girl, she's a mess… '

Joshua screwed his face up in disbelief. This was a fucking shambles.

'Why the fuck was your broker on the boat? Why wasn't he back at the camp in Calais?'

Vincent looked coy.

'He should have been, yeah, but our plans changed at the last minute. Korab pulled a bit of a sneaky one. It turns out that the girl and her husband didn't have enough money to make the journey, so Korab took it upon himself to make a deal with the husband. He slept with the girl in return for guaranteeing them a place on the boat.'

Joshua rubbed his head, agitated. The situation was getting worse by the second.

'I wasn't happy when I found out about it either, Joshua, so I thought I'd teach Korab a lesson. Make him earn his fucking keep. The skipper we had lined up was sick, so instead of sending one of my men I figured that it made sense to get Korab to do the crossing. I thought it would teach him a lesson: make him work for his money. I told him to dump the boat a few miles away from the coastline and to get his arse back to France in the motor boat. Same as we always do. Only I didn't hear from him again.' Seeing the baffled look on Joshua's face, Vincent continued, trying to explain. 'Next thing I knew, I was getting a call to say that the boat had sunk. I figured that he must have drowned alongside the others—'

'Until you ran into this girl!' Joshua spat. 'What's she saying?'

'That's just it; as soon as I mentioned about the boat sinking she just kind of freaked out. I could see by her face that she genuinely didn't know. She didn't really make much sense after that. It was like she had gone into shock or something. Like she was having some kind of a fucking breakdown.'

'Fuck's sake!' Slamming his glass down on the desk, it took all his restraint not to launch himself over the top of it and throttle Vincent. 'What sort of fucking Mickey Mouse operation are you fucking running here?'

Joshua was seething. This was not the way that he wanted his businesses run.

'I'm sorting it, bruv—'

'Sorting it? I don't fucking think so. This is a fucking mess!' Joshua stood up, launching his glass against the back wall – the glass shattering into pieces.

'Where's the girl now?'

'She's with Saskia and Misty, at Misty's place. The kid was doing my nut. Wouldn't stop screaming.'

'And you think that's wise? What if she starts blabbing her mouth off to the girls too?'

'She won't! Like I said, the girl was all over the place, boss, babbling on about fuck knows what in her own language. No one could understand a word she was saying. She wasn't making any sense. She took the pills I gave her and conked out. I'm going back around there in the morning, first thing.'

Joshua winced now, as he tapped his fingers agitatedly against his desk. Vincent looked his brother in the eye.

'I'm trying to fix it, Joshua. I will fix it. As soon as the girl is awake, I'll find out where Korab is and I'll get it sorted. It's already in hand, and I'll make sure he doesn't start running his mouth off either. The bloke's a fucking liability. Far too cocky for his own good. I should have got rid of him ages ago.'

Joshua was beyond agitated. 'How much does this Korab know about the op?'

Knowing that Joshua wouldn't accept any more bullshit tonight Vincent answered truthfully. 'He knows more than he was supposed to,' he said now with caution. 'He was a hard worker, bruv. The men liked him. He kind of just tagged along, fitted in. I think the men let their guard down around him, treated him like he was one of us… ' Korab getting so involved with his men had been a major oversight on Vincent's part. He was well aware of that now.

'Are you fucking kidding me? He's a fucking camp rat… ' Joshua glared, the prominent vein in the side of his head pulsating. 'What does he know?'

'He knows enough.' Rubbing his temples again Vincent felt like a prize cock. He'd worked so hard to prove to Joshua that he was up for the job and now, all because of one fucking broker, he'd royally fucked it all up.

'Like what? Enlighten me… ' Joshua probed.

'He knows the pick up and drop off points. A few names. The other men trusted him… '

'Well, if he's so trustworthy, why hasn't he made contact? Why's he just vanished into thin fucking air, huh?'

Vincent shook his head. 'There were at least a hundred people on that boat. If your bloke starts blabbing his fucking mouth about our business, we could be looking at a multiple murder charge.'

Joshua was incensed. This is not what he had wanted to hear. Gritting his teeth as he spoke, he got up from his seat. 'This is a major fucking problem, Vincent, and we both know how we deal with problems around here.'

Joshua's eyes were fixed on Vincent; staring at him with such intensity that he couldn't help feeling nervous as his brother opened the office door, ready to show him out.

'I pay you to sort out the mess; so, as soon as that girl wakes up I want you round there, sorting it. If you're not up for the job, then you know where the fucking door is. There can be no more fuck-ups!'

CHAPTER TWENTY-EIGHT

Waking up in unfamiliar surroundings Lena's eyes flickered around the room as she panicked, trying to gather her bearings.

Roza? Where was Roza?

The fancy furniture? An ornate cream dressing table displaying rows of expensive-looking bottles of perfume and toiletries? Sitting up, she caught her reflection in the mirrored wardrobe that stood against the wall at the end of the bed, recoiling at the barely unrecognisable sight that stared back at her.

She looked awful: her hair matted flat to her head, her skin, pale and sallow.

She was still dressed too. Looking down at herself she winced at the contrast of her heavily soiled clothes against the beautifully made-up bed she'd just slept in. Cocooned by thick fluffy cushions and pillows, the warmth of the duvet draped over her, her own clothes looked even more filthy in comparison, like rags. She could smell the fresh, clean bedding too. Like freshly cut flowers. Lilies or roses. The scent faint – not strong enough to mask her own stale smell. Confused, pulling back the covers, Lena swung her legs over the side of the bed and let her bare feet sink into the thick pile of the carpet.

Soft and soothing against her aching soles, it was a strange sensation. They didn't have carpet at home in Albania; all the floors were cold tiles.

She saw her ragged shoes then – the gaping holes in the leather. Cast aside, discarded on the floor as if they had been pulled from her feet.

She remembered everything. Last night, at the hospital, how she'd been running away.

Vincent. He had been there too.

He'd helped her? Him and another girl, slightly older than her. They'd brought her here.

Vincent had been asking her questions about the boat!

Lena remembered him telling her that it had sunk, that all those people she had travelled to England with had drowned. She couldn't remember much more after that. Everything had been a bit of a blur. In shock from the news, and exhausted after everything that had happened over the past week, it had all been too much. Her head had been spinning; the stress of the last few days catching up with her, overwhelming her.

Vincent had been questioning her about Korab and Ramiz too, she recalled. Asking if they were alive. If they had survived the boat capsizing.

She tried to answer, but she hadn't been able to; she'd been a mess.

He'd got angry, frustrated with her.

She remembered his tone as he had shouted at her to answer him, but his aggression had only made her worse. It had all been too much for her. In the end, he'd given her something. Some kind of tablets; he said that they would help her to get some rest, would help to calm her down. That the girl, Saskia, would watch Roza for her. That she was safe now.

Lena hadn't wanted to take the tablets. All she had wanted was her baby, but Vincent had made her.

Somehow she'd slept without her?

Making her way towards the bedroom door, Lena pressed her ear up against it, listening anxiously. Unsure of what she was about to walk into, she needed to find out where her daughter was.

It was only women's voices she could hear though; two of them talking, their voices in hushed whispers. Too low for Lena to make out what they were saying, but she suspected they were talking about her.

She heard Roza then too. Gurgling, cooing. Relief spreading through her, she was unable to stop herself; she pushed down the handle and opened the door. She needed to see her baby to make sure that Roza was okay.

'Ahh look, Roza, here is your mummy. It's Lena isn't it?'

The girl nodded.

She seemed even younger now in the cold light of day, Saskia thought. Just a child. She looked anxious too. The poor girl probably didn't have a clue what was going on. Walking towards her, Saskia offered her a friendly smile.

'Someone's been missing you,' she said softly as she handed Lena her baby.

Lena almost broke down then. Having Roza back in her arms, wide awake, alert. She looked a million times better than she had in hospital.

'We met last night. I'm Saskia and this is Misty.' Sensing the young girl's sudden emotion on being reunited with her daughter, Saskia sat back down at the table with Misty, giving the girl some space to gather her bearings. Lena hadn't said a word yet. Saskia wondered if she could understand what she was saying.

'You speak English?'

'Yes.' Lena nodded. 'I learnt English back home in Albania. In school.'

Lena thought back to Vincent last night. Shouting at her. His tone aggressive. She knew even more words now.

'What's that in her mouth?' Lena asked seeing a pink mound of plastic poking out of Roza's mouth.

'Oh, this is a dummy, or a soother. It helps babies to relax, gives them something to concentrate on to stop them from crying.'

Lena nodded, unsure of the thing, although Roza certainly seemed content. Her eyes were alert; she was looking right at her and Lena felt the connection between them. She was overjoyed that her little girl was well again.

'I hope you don't mind but I gave her a little wash in the bathtub last night. She had a bit of an accident, a bad tummy. I popped some clean clothes on her, and she was hungry too, so I've given her some milk. I didn't know how you were feeding her… I hope that was okay?'

'Milk?' Lena stared at Saskia's chest.

Saskia laughed then, her cheeks flushing.

'It's formula milk. Powdered. You buy it from the shop. It's very good. Apparently it has all the same nutrients in it as breast milk.' Saskia pointed to the tub on the side. The powdered formula that Vincent had bought. Wary now that maybe she had overstepped the mark. 'You just add hot water to it. I've made you up some bottles for today too… '

'Did she drink it?' Lena asked.

'Every last drop.' Saskia nodded. 'In fact, she's finished two bottles so far this morning, and I would put money on her taking another one too, if it was offered to her. She certainly has an appetite on her.'

Lena started crying then.

'I can't thank you enough for looking after her for me.' Lena had tears in her eyes, her voice trembled as she spoke. Hugging her daughter tightly to her, she kissed the top of Roza's head, inhaling the lovely clean smell as she did. She was so relieved that her daughter had her appetite back. She was going to be okay. Lena could feel it. Roza was over the worst.

'It was our pleasure. Roza was good as gold, wasn't she, Misty?'

Lena looked to the other girl now, standing over by the dining table. She smiled too, but she looked a bit wary.

'She's been an angel. Well, apart from one little incident involving a very dirty nappy… '

Misty couldn't take her eyes off Lena. Saskia was right: the girl was exactly that, just a child. She couldn't have been any more than sixteen.

'Do you fancy some breakfast? You must be starving, sweetie.' Sensing that the girl was probably hungry, Misty pulled out a chair. 'I didn't know what you'd fancy. I only have muesli in, but I can make you some toast—'

'Oh no, the muesli will be lovely, thank you.' Unable to even remember the last time she'd eaten, Lena sat down at the table and watched as Misty poured her out a bowl.

'Do want me to take Roza for you while you eat?'

Lena shook her head. She'd already been apart from her child for too long. She needed her close. Besides, the two girls had done enough for her already. She could take over again from here.

Spooning the cereal into her mouth she suddenly realised how hungry she was. Her stomach ached with a hollowness and she still felt heady from the tablets she'd been given.

Suddenly remembering the man from the boat Lena stared around the flat now, anxiously. There was no sign of him.

'Is everything all right?' Saskia asked, sensing the girl's unease.

'Where is the man from last night?'

'Vincent? He's not here,' Saskia said, watching the girl relax. 'He'll be here soon though. I said I'd call him as soon as you woke up.'

Lena stiffened. Saskia could see she wasn't comfortable with the thought of seeing Vincent again.

'There's no hurry though, eh? I can call him in a bit. You just eat up, honey. We can sort all of that out later.'

'Saskia?' Misty glared at Saskia now.

Saskia shrugged.

'What? We *will* call him, just not yet. Come on, Lena's only just woken up. Let's just let her have her breakfast in peace and get a shower first, yeah?'

Misty nodded reluctantly, then seeing Lena smiling again, she agreed.

A few extra minutes without Vincent breathing down their necks wasn't such a bad idea.

'Thank you.' Lena smiled 'I really appreciate your kindness.'

She was longing for a shower. She could smell the delicious clean scent radiating from her daughter, making her even more conscious of her own rancid stench. She felt sticky, dirty. As if her filthy skin and clothes were contaminating Roza.

'Wow, you must be starving, you practically inhaled that.' Misty smiled a few seconds later when Lena had finished the entire contents of the bowl in front of her.

'Help yourself to another bowl if you want?'

'No, thank you.' She blushed as she realised how intently the two girls were watching her; she didn't want to appear greedy. Not after everything that these girls had already done for her.

'How about a nice cup of tea then?'

Before Lena could refuse, Misty had placed a steaming hot mug of tea down in front of her.

'How are you feeling this morning?' Saskia asked as she casually took a sip of her own tea, savouring its sweetness. God knows she needed the caffeine after spending the night looking after little Roza. By the time they'd managed to settle her it had been almost four a.m. Saskia was exhausted. Still, by the look of Lena, it had been worth it. The girl had been in such a state last night she looked like she really needed a break.

'I feel much better thank you,' Lena said, suddenly realising that she wasn't just saying that either, she meant it.

Last night she'd been close to breaking point. Close to losing her mind. Since coming to England she hadn't been able to get the image of the boat sinking out of her mind, and last night had been the first respite from the nightmares.

'Ahh, it's amazing what a good night's sleep can do for you,' Misty jibed, still put out that she'd had to sleep on the sofa. If you could call it sleep, with Saskia and Roza sharing it with her.

'I'm sorry, I didn't mean to put you both out.' Sensing the atmosphere between the two girls, Lena shuffled awkwardly in her chair. She was a burden here. As was Roza.

'Oh, ignore her. You're not a morning person, are you Misty?' Saskia shot her a look then. 'It was no bother at all, Lena. You looked like you could do with the rest.'

Misty realised she was being rude. Saskia was right. The girl probably had enough on her plate. She didn't need to be guilt-tripped too.

'I was only joking.' Misty smiled now, feeling bad. 'Sorry, until the caffeine kicks in I'm super grumpy in the mornings.'

'Well, just so you know. I really do appreciate what you've done for me and Roza. I can't thank you enough for taking such good care of her. She's been through so much these past few days. There were moments when I didn't think she'd make it.' Lena's voice was thick with emotion.

'Can I ask you something?' Saskia hesitated, unsure whether or not she should try and probe further, but she was curious.

'Of course, ask me anything.'

Saskia took her time. She'd been thinking about Lena and Roza all night, replaying the scene at the hospital over and over in her head as she tried to work out the connection between Vincent and Lena. Lena didn't seem the type of girl that would know someone like Vincent, and the way that he'd been talking to her when he'd brought her back here had left Saskia feeling unsettled.

'Did you take her?'

'Sorry?' Lena was confused. Of all the things that Saskia could have wanted to know, that question had thrown her. 'Did I take who?'

'Roza?' Saskia didn't even want to say it, but it was the only explanation that she could think of. It was the only thing that would make any sense, that would explain why the nurses and the security guards had been chasing her at the hospital. Or why she was so desperate to get away.

'Is Roza yours, Lena? Last night at the hospital – you were running; the security guards were chasing you… Did you steal her?' Saskia felt awful even asking, but she had to know for certain.

'Of course she is mine!' Lena cried. Horrified that these girls would think so low of her. That they suspected her of kidnapping somebody else's child.

Looking down at Roza lying in her arms Lena fought back fresh tears. 'I would never do something like that: take someone else's child. I'm a good person. Of course she is mine.'

'I'm sorry, I didn't mean to offend you. It's just, I was trying to work out what had gone on. Why you'd been running?' Seeing the girl looking so distressed now, Saskia wished she'd kept her mouth shut. It was clear just by the way that Lena looked at her child that she loved her. They were so similar too; the same skin tone, same features, but still something didn't feel right. 'Why were you running then? Are you in some kind of trouble?'

Lena didn't answer. She kept her eyes down, focused on the floor.

'I heard Vincent asking you questions about a boat?' Saskia said now, trying to make her tone seem light, but secretly she was worried for Lena. Vincent had been acting erratically, as if he was on edge about something. The girl's presence had riled him. She wanted to get to the bottom of it all before he turned up this morning. She wanted to hear it from Lena.

'I just thought that maybe you might want to talk to us, you know, before he comes back—'

'What does he want with me?' Lena asked nervously.

'I'm not sure. I was hoping you could tell us.'

Lena shrugged. Shaking her head again. She had no idea.

'He was asking about someone called Conrad – or Korab?' Saskia said truthfully as she watched the girl closely. 'He was asking where to find him. He said that he would come back here today and you can take him to him.'

Lena was up out of her seat then; pushing the chair back behind her with such force that it tipped up, banging loudly against the tiled floor.

'Korab. I can't go back there. Please don't make me. Please. I need to go… ' Clutching Roza tightly to her, Lena was visibly shaking.

'Whoa, it's okay.' Getting out of her chair, Misty tried to comfort Lena; reaching out, stepping closer, but it was to no avail. She was only scaring the girl more.

Picking up the chair from where it had landed on the floor, Misty stepped back, reassuring the girl that she wasn't a threat.

'Please, don't make me go back there.'

Pushing herself up against the wall Lena had her guard well and truly up now as she stared at each of the girls, warily. Unsure of their intentions.

'We're not going to make you go anywhere,' Saskia said softly. 'We just want to help, Lena. You and little Roza. Talk to us, please? Maybe we can help you?'

'How do I know I can trust you?'

Lena looked at the two girls then. Scanning their concerned faces, she felt uncertain, unsure.

'Well, we haven't called Vincent yet, have we? Doesn't that show you that we're on your side?' Saskia spoke again. 'We just want to help you, Lena. Please, tell us what you are running from.'

Seeing the genuine concern on their faces Lena wanted so badly to believe them, to trust them.

'Talk to us, Lena. Let us help you. Sit down, have some more tea, and let's just talk, yeah? Please, what have you got to lose?'

Lena nodded then. Saskia was right. She had nothing left to lose. What if these girls really meant it; what if they would really help her? She had to try. Slowly, she sat back down.

'I don't want you to think bad of me. Thinking that I stole a child. I'm a good person. I love my baby… ' Lena began.

She told them. Everything. Her whole story, from beginning to end.

How she was taken, kidnapped. How Ramiz had kept her prisoner, forced her to marry him, to bear his child. About the Bodis, and how they had run. About the Jungle and Korab and about what he had done to her.

Then she told them how Ramiz had secretly drugged Roza. How he'd sedated her without Lena knowing. That Roza had been sick; she'd nearly died.

A whole year worth of anguish and grief came flooding out. The tears came too, spilling over with every word she spoke.

Misty and Saskia remained silent throughout. Shocked with what they were hearing. They wanted Lena to tell her story, to get it all out. Even when some bits were too hard to imagine; the bits that made them feel sick to their stomachs at what the young girl had been forced to endure.

Lena was just a young girl, still a child, yet already she'd been through a lifetime of woes. No wonder she was scared. No wonder she was frightened.

'And what about Vincent? Where does he fit in, in all of this?' Saskia asked when Lena had finally finished.

Lena shrugged.

'He is the man from the boat. In France. The one in charge.'

'In charge of what?'

'Getting us all to England.'

'How many of you were on the boat, Lena?' Saskia threw a bewildered look in Misty's direction. If what Lena was telling them was true, Vincent Harper was a very dangerous man.

'A hundred or so. Mainly men, but there were some women and children on board too.' Lena was crying now. 'They said that they would get us into England so that we could start a new life here.'

Lena had wondered at first how much these girls knew, but she could tell by the look on Saskia's face that she genuinely hadn't known about Vincent's business dealings. About the boat. The trafficking.

'There was a fire on board. I thought that help would come, that the people would be saved… but last night Vincent told me that it had sunk. That everyone on board drowned… ' Lena struggled to get her words out now. A lump forming in the back of her throat; her voice heavy with emotion. Just knowing that all those people were dead now made her feel physically sick to her stomach.

'There was a woman on board. She begged me to help her. To take her child. He was only a little boy, but we couldn't. Ramiz wouldn't let us. He said that if we helped, they would ambush us; he said that we would all die. So we left them.'

Lena was staring now, as if in a trance as she remembered the sight of the woman dangling her child over, screaming for help.

It was a vision that would haunt her for the rest of her life.

'Oh my God.' Saskia looked at Misty now. Both girls exchanging a look of realisation. 'You're talking about the boat down in Weymouth?'

They'd both seen a news report on the TV two days ago about a boat carrying illegal migrants. They'd heard about a little boy washed up on the beach. Everyone had. It must have been that boat that Lena was talking about. What the fuck was Vincent doing involved with it all?

'We were so busy saving ourselves we just left them all to die.' Lena looked down at the floor, filled with shame.

'You couldn't have done anything, Lena,' Saskia said now, her voice quiet, soothing. 'Like you said, your husband Ramiz made you leave them. You weren't in control. It's not your fault.'

Lena shook her head, unconvinced. Saskia was just being kind, but she knew the truth. She should have spoken up. Made Ramiz listen.

'Last night, Vincent kept asking me who else survived. Who I'd left the boat with. About the broker from the camp, Korab.' Lena's voice trailed off then as she remembered the irritation in Vincent's voice. 'Korab and Vincent work together. What if this is all a trick and Vincent is just planning on forcing me back to Korab and Ramiz? If I go back to Ramiz now, he'll never let me go. It will be worse than ever. He'll take Roza from me. I know he will.'

Lena knew that Ramiz would for ever punish her for trying to escape. Her life would be worse than she could ever imagine. Worse than she'd ever endured before. She couldn't go back to him, not now she'd finally managed to escape.

'We'll tell Vincent about Ramiz, what he did to you, to Roza.' Saskia sounded hopeful now, but looking to Misty she noticed her friend didn't look so convinced. 'We'll make him understand, won't we, Misty?'

Misty didn't answer, instead changing the subject.

'Look, why don't I run you a nice shower, babe. Let's concentrate on getting you and Roza sorted yeah? We can deal with everything else later when Vincent gets here.'

Nodding gratefully, Lena stood up and followed Misty back through to the bedroom.

'You're going to be okay, Lena, I promise you,' Saskia spoke now, wishing that there was something she could do, anything that would help. 'We're going to help you. Ramiz can't hurt you anymore.'

Smiling gratefully as she clutched Roza tightly to her Lena wished more than anything in the world that Saskia's words could somehow be true, but she knew the truth.

Ramiz had told her from day one that the only thing that would free her from him was death. That there was nowhere to run, nowhere to hide.

Lena knew that Ramiz would find a way to get to her.

One way or another.

CHAPTER TWENTY-NINE

Standing underneath the hot flow of cascading water Lena closed her eyes, relishing the warmth that trickled down over her naked body. She'd scrubbed her skin raw, lathering the sponge with soap, intent on washing every part of the last few days clean away from her.

Ramiz, Korab, the Jungle, the boat. All of it, swept away down the plughole along with the rest of the dirt and grime.

Looking out through the open en-suite door she could see Roza's tiny body in the middle of the double bed; her tiny legs kicking out excitedly as she cooed and gurgled to herself. Lena smiled, despite herself.

Oh to be so carefree. So unaware of all the violence, the harsh reality of their world.

Turning the water off, Lena stepped out onto the shower-mat, her body shivering as the cold air hit her, and she quickly dried herself with a towel before pulling on the oversized jumper that Misty had left for her, hugging it tightly around her body. It swamped her tiny figure, but at least it was clean and warm. Anything was better than the rags she'd been wearing earlier. She'd been mortified when Misty had gathered up her clothes from where Lena had discarded them on the floor, noticing that Misty had desperately tried to hold her breath while she spoke so that she didn't have to inhale the overpowering stench of them. Lena had cringed when Misty had politely offered to wash them for her. They both knew that the heavily soiled clothes were beyond redemption.

Throwing Lena's clothes into a black sack she'd insisted that Lena scour her wardrobe and pick out whatever she wanted. Lena had never seen so many clothes.

Such an array of bright and beautiful material. Shiny, sequins, leathers. Lena wasn't used to the cut of most of the outfits – the low necklines and tiny skirts – so she'd selected a pair of plain black leggings and an oversized navy jumper.

Standing in front of the sink now, she ran her fingers through her dripping wet hair, inhaling the delicious fruity scent of the shampoo as she scrutinised her reflection.

A ghost stared back at her.

She'd lost weight. Her skin was sallow, her face gaunt. The bruise around her eye from where Ramiz had hit her before they had left Albania had almost gone now. Faded into nothing, as if it was never there.

The woman staring back at Lena in the mirror wasn't a woman she recognised.

She didn't feel like herself anymore.

She'd spent the past year just surviving, trying to get through each day.

How had it come to this?

Ramiz had taken everything from her. He'd tried his best to destroy her, snatching her away from her old life, her family, from Albania. He'd forced her to leave behind everything she'd ever known and loved.

Almost daily, subjecting her to his incessant beatings, the rapes; it was no wonder that she'd lost sight of herself.

He would break her eventually; Lena knew that without a doubt. By using the only thing she had left. Roza.

Picking up the pointy nail scissors that she'd found in the drawer, Lena took a deep breath. Hesitating, just for a second, before weaving the sharp blade through her thick, dark hair.

She began cutting – watching with fascination as big chunks of her hair fell to the floor all around her. She chopped until there was nothing left, just a short cropped creation. Almost boyish. The floor was covered in hair. Scooping it up in handfuls she threw it all into the bin. She'd thought that cutting off all her hair would make her feel sad, but it hadn't.

She felt just the opposite. She felt almost human again. Lighter, empowered.

For the first time in a long time Lena was starting to feel like she was back in control again. Of her own mind, her body, her child. She had a real chance now of finally being free from Ramiz.

A chance of making sure that Ramiz could never find her again.

If he did, he'd be intent on making it a living hell. Even more unbearable than before – but Lena had no intention of letting that happen.

CHAPTER THIRTY

Mary Jeffries was awake.

The first thing that hit her was the rancid, overpowering stench of the drains. Gagging, she sat bolt upright in her armchair, still wearing yesterday's clothes. She wondered how long she'd been here? All night? Her head felt fuzzy, her thoughts too cloudy to allow her to remember. She felt as if she'd been in some kind of a trance, a time warp.

Disorientated, she rubbed her pounding head as she tried to recollect the previous evening's events. It couldn't be that hard to recall what she'd been doing, she thought; she did the same bloody thing every night that she had for the past God knows how many years.

She must have been doing her usual evening ritual of watching her soaps, wedged in her armchair, drinking herself into a stupor.

It was slowly coming back to her. Colin had been there. Skulking about in the background as always. She remembered that she'd been angry with him, but then that was hardly a revelation. Colin had handed her a drink. Standing over her with that irritating, gormless look on his face.

That was her last memory. She couldn't remember anything else after that.

Pressing the remote control the TV guide showed that the time was now nine thirty in the morning. How could that be?

If that was right, then she'd been out cold for over twelve hours?

Impossible. She hadn't slept a full night for years: a decade, at least. She knew damn well that she could drink herself into oblivion on a daily basis – as she often did – and the booze would be no match for her insomnia. Even if she managed to pass out she'd normally wake after a couple of hours. Something wasn't right.

She was ill. She knew it. It had been happening so often to her lately.

Passing out, losing her memory, giant chunks of time missing from her mind.

She was old. Ill. Dying. She didn't need a doctor to tell her. She knew. It was the only explanation; the only thing that made sense. One day soon she would close her eyes and that would be it. She wouldn't be waking up. Despite her lifestyle, Mary was scared senseless at the thought of death. Staring down at her wrinkly skin on the back of her hands she winced, as if she was seeing them for the very first time. The skin was loose, slackened, so pale that it looked almost transparent. The only colour came from the clusters of brown age-spots and the blue veins that bulged prominently. She had got old and she wasn't quite sure when it had happened.

Feeling the usual familiar flutter of anxiety grip her inside she got to her feet.

Fuck this bullshit. She needed a drink.

Walking slowly, she made her way out to the kitchen. Her feet felt like she was bouncing, like she was outside of her body. Floating.

Reaching the worktop she picked up the vodka bottle. Examining it, she tilted it left and right, as if the liquid that sloshed about inside was nothing more than an optical illusion. The bottle was still half-full. She grinned; half-full, that was the optimist in her. Half-empty was for pessimists, isn't that what they said?

She wanted to laugh then, at all those fancy psychiatrists she'd seen over the years, all the shit they spouted. What the fuck did they know? She was the most pessimistic person she knew. Yet stick half a bottle of vodka in her hand, in any alcoholic's hand, and of course they would look on the bright side.

Perplexed, she realised she was losing her focus again, forgetting what she had come here for. She did that a lot lately, lost her train of thought. Her mind going off on a tangent. She felt like she was slowly going mad.

Staring at the bottle, something didn't sit quite right with her. Why hadn't she finished it? That was odd in itself. She would never have slept until it was all gone. She drank until there was no more. That's what she had always done. The half that she'd consumed wouldn't have been enough to knock her out – she'd built up a tolerance over the years.

Tablets? As soon as the thought crossed her mind, she knew. Insomnia, depression, anxiety, arthritis. You name it, according to the doctors, she had it. She never bothered taking the stuff; what was the point? She was sixty-five years old for Christ's sake, riddled with all sorts. Her liver was probably going to pack up any day now; shoving tablets down her throat wasn't going to suddenly save her. No, sod that. Self-medication was the only thing that made her feel better – the type that came in the form of a bottle of booze.

Pulling open the kitchen drawer, she frowned. It was empty. Completely bare.

She didn't understand. They had all been there. Packets, pots, bottles. Maybe she'd moved them, tucked them away somewhere.

She started looking frantically about the kitchen then, opening cupboards, lifting saucepans. She even looked behind the ornaments and picture frames that cluttered the windowsill, ignoring the thick film of dust she disturbed as she moved things about.

They were gone. Everything was starting to make sense to her now; the reality of the situation hitting her like a bolt of lightning.

Colin.

It had to be.

All this time she convinced herself that she was ill, dying. All the constant nausea, the blackouts – the blocks of time that were missing from her mind that she couldn't account for.

She'd thought she was sick. Really sick. Dying. Drowning herself in alcohol to rid herself of the anxiety that had all but consumed her, and all this time her bastard son had been lacing her drink with cocktails of medication. Purposely drugging her.

But she needed proof. Solid evidence. She needed to find the packets of tablets.

Grabbing the bin she yanked it across the floor; spilling the contents out onto the lino as she scoured through the slimy remnants of the last few days' dinners: scraps of leftover food congealed on discarded microwavable plastic cartons.

Still she found nothing.

His room?

Storming out to the hallway she reached Colin's bedroom door. It was locked.

Bolted with a padlock as it had been for some years. The dumb bastard had taken to locking himself away. It was ironic really: the fact that, in order to stop his mother from locking him inside 'the hole' he'd taken to locking himself away in his room.

That was how thick he was. The boy was a fool, so stupid that he didn't even realise that by locking his mother out he was still locking himself in. He'd become his own prisoner. But the triumph was still hers.

She was older now, frailer, and Colin had grown so big, so tall.

She hadn't used 'the hole' as a punishment since he was a boy; instead she'd found new ways of punishing her son.

Purposely fucking with his head; the same way that just him existing fucked with hers.

Him locking himself away in his room meant that the fear was still there. She still had him.

She needed to get into his room, to find the tablets, to show that bastard that she was onto him. That she wouldn't be outsmarted. All she needed was the evidence, then she'd ram it down his throat and have great pleasure in doing so.

Determined now, Mary went to the cupboard under the stairs. Flicking the switch on she rummaged around in the boxes that were stacked at the back. Old tools that had been discarded, never used. A rusty screwdriver, a pair of pliers.

Bingo! A hammer tucked away inside a box. It hadn't seen the light of day for years.

Back outside Colin's door now she lifted the hammer high above her head and hit the lock with all of her strength. Fuelled with anger and determination, it only took three attempts. The bolt buckled, then the lock snapped off, falling to the floor.

She was in. Opening the door the rancid stench of rot and decay hit her with full force. Reminding her of rotten cabbage, the blocked drains seemed even stronger in here, which was strange as they were at the back of the kitchen. She'd have to send him outside later. Get him to sort them out once and for all.

They were a health hazard – but then again, so was Colin's bedroom.

Her eyes quickly scanned the heaps of clothing left piled up around the room before settling on the desk in front of the window. She spotted the tablets straight away, packets and bottles piled high; the bin full of the empties.

She'd been right all along. That fucking bastard had been drugging her. She was going to punish him for this.

She looked over towards 'the hole'. Colin had dragged a shelf in front of it, trying to disguise it, to pretend that it wasn't there.

Then she was back to looking at the clothes, the mess, the clutter.

Noticing the strange objects that lined the outskirts of the room, Mary recoiled in horror. Her eyes must be playing tricks on her; perhaps the drugs still inside her system were making her delirious.

She started to gag now, uncontrollably. Her already fragile stomach fought the urge to expel its contents.

For the first time in nearly forty years Mary Jeffries was rendered stone cold sober.

Unable to stop herself she threw up, emptying her stomach all over the floor until she felt hollow, empty. She was shaking, mumbling loudly, frantically, until her words escaped from her mouth in nothing more than a strangled scream.

Then she heard it.

The small noise behind her.

Turning, she saw Colin standing in the doorway.

He'd been watching her. His eyes expressionless, fixated on his mother as he drank in her reaction. Relishing her horror.

'What have you done?' Her voice was barely a whisper now. 'What the hell have you done?'

Colin laughed; the sound contemptuous.

For the first time in his life he was mocking her, enjoying her terror.

'You're not right, Colin. You're sick in the head! You're a monster, a freak!'

Colin just shook his head with certainty. He'd suffered a lifetime of abuse in this woman's hands. The damage inside him was inconceivable, irreversible.

She was right. He was a freak. A weirdo.

He was everything that she had made him.

Moving towards her, his eyes devoid of emotion, he was going to make sure that his mother would never tell a single living soul.

CHAPTER THIRTY-ONE

'All I'm saying is that this is none of our business. We should just keep our noses out of it, Saskia. We don't know anything for sure. I don't mean to sound like a bitch but Lena could be lying to us? Who knows what her motives are? Let's just wait for Vincent to get here, yeah?'

Gathering up the breakfast things, Misty busied herself putting the dirty crockery in the dishwasher, her back to Saskia. She was growing tired of the conversation.

Saskia was getting ahead of herself now. Worried about Lena, she was talking about confronting Vincent when he got here. She was utterly naïve. Saskia didn't have a clue what she was getting involved with. Vincent Harper's business was exactly that, his business, and he wouldn't appreciate Saskia trying to involve herself in it.

He would be here any minute, and Misty was desperate to try and talk Saskia down before that happened. She could really do without any more drama today.

Lena wasn't their problem.

'So you're saying that you don't believe her? You think she's lying to us?' Saskia shook her head, disbelieving. Still sitting at the table, Saskia was stewing over Misty's sudden change of attitude since Lena had left the room. 'After everything you just heard? Vincent is trafficking people, Misty. You just heard it for yourself.'

'What I just heard was the story of a very scared, desperate girl. A girl with a small baby who has been drugged that's just admitted she is here in England illegally. I'm just saying that we don't know all the facts.'

'So, you think she's spinning us some kind of story?'

'I don't know, Saskia, but like I keep saying it isn't any of our business. We shouldn't be getting involved. We've done our bit…'

'Done our bit?' Saskia was incredulous now. 'What's that then? Just hand her back over to Vincent? You heard what she said about that boat. If what she is telling us is true, then Vincent is responsible for all those people that died. Joshua Harper too.'

'Enough!' Misty turned and faced Saskia, her tone deadly serious. 'Throwing around accusations like that could land you in a whole heap of trouble. I know that you're just trying to help the girl, Saskia, believe me, I really do, but you really don't know what you're getting yourself involved with. So just let Vincent come and do his thing and don't get involved. Okay?'

Saskia was silenced then.

Misty's tone was sharp, her voice fuelled with anger but there was something there in her eyes too. Guilt.

'You already knew didn't you?' Saskia was staring at Misty now, intently. 'When Lena told us about the boat, about all of those people being trafficked, you didn't react. No look of shock, disgust, nothing. You already knew!'

Leaning against the worktop, Misty let out a sigh.

'Look, whatever goes on at Harper's Palace is none of our concern. We work there, that's it. Ignorance in this world is bliss, Saskia, trust me. If they even think that you know about their private business, you'll be putting yourself at risk too. So please, for your own good keep your opinions and, more importantly your assumptions, to yourself.'

'Who are you people?' Saskia felt sick. Misty had known about this all along. None of this was a shock to her.

'That's who all those men were, the night of the private party. They were his workers, his traffickers? I danced for them, Jesus Christ!' Closing her eyes she realised – she was part of it.

She'd danced for them, entertained them. Criminals. Villains. Crooks.

'Oh come on, Saskia, who did you think they were? DJs? Waiters? Joshua has a lot of other business ventures. Not just the club.'

'Business ventures?' Saskia raised her voice, stunned at the coolness of Misty's tone. 'A hundred people were on board that boat, Misty; a hundred people are dead now. There's probably even more than that, others that we don't even know about. Joshua and Vincent have blood on their hands. That's not a business venture, that's murder!'

Saskia couldn't believe how gullible she had been. Dancing in the club, thinking that the worst things around her were pervy men and a few lines of cocaine. This was worse than she could have ever imagined. How could Misty just act like everything was normal?

'Oh my God, that's why Vincent brought her back here isn't it? He doesn't give a shit about helping her; he's just clearing up his mess. Make sure that nothing comes back onto him and Joshua. Lena's in danger isn't she?'

'You're just second-guessing.' Misty walked over to the table and sat down opposite her friend. 'Seriously, Saskia, I know that you are angry right now, but please, trust me, you mustn't get involved in this.'

Saskia couldn't believe what she was hearing – how selfish Misty suddenly sounded.

They'd both seen how genuinely scared Lena was. Of Vincent, of Ramiz.

'It took a lot of courage for Lena to confide in us. We promised her that we would help her… '

'And we have. You were great with Roza last night. We gave her somewhere to rest, some food. Shit, I've even let the girl raid my wardrobe, Sass.' Misty offered a small smile then, adding sadly, 'we can't do any more than we've done already… We can't get involved in this. I won't get involved in this.' Placing her head in her hands Misty looked defeated. The conversation was over.

Misty wasn't prepared to help Lena. She was just going to hand her back over to Vincent. *Ignorance is bliss.*

'Okay,' Saskia said sadly. Deflated, she felt like she'd had the air punched out of her. 'Well, I'm going to go and see if Lena needs any help with Roza while she's getting ready.'

'Seriously, Saskia, I know it sounds harsh, but there is nothing we can say or do. This is Vincent's business not ours. We've done as much as we can for Lena.'

Saskia didn't bother to reply.

Getting up, she made her way to the bedroom to check on the girl and the baby.

Misty was wrong. They hadn't helped Lena at all.

They were no better than Vincent and Joshua.

In fact, if anything they were even worse.

They'd made Lena a handful of empty promises and now they were going to throw her to the wolves.

They had betrayed her.

CHAPTER THIRTY-TWO

Opening her front door, Misty barely got a chance to step aside before Vincent charged his way in, rudely barging past her. He looked like shit. Like he hadn't slept. He was still wearing the same clothes he'd had on the previous night, his eyes bloodshot, his face unshaved.

'Rough night? You should try looking after a baby… ' Misty mumbled sarcastically under her breath as she followed him through to the kitchen.

Vincent ignored her. He wasn't in the mood for Misty and her smart mouth this morning. He needed to speak with this girl. Find out if Korab and this Ramiz cunt had survived. Then he needed to get this mess cleaned up once and for all.

'Where's sleeping beauty then?'

Noting the three mugs of tea on the kitchen table, but no sign of the girl, Vincent glared at Saskia. Another one with an attitude problem.

'She's in the bedroom, changing Roza's nappy. She'll be out in a second.'

'Do you want a cup?' Misty asked begrudgingly, wondering if maybe Vincent just needed a dose of caffeine in the morning to stop him from being such an obnoxious bastard.

'This ain't a social call. I've got things to do. Lena!' Vincent shouted now, dismissing Misty's offer. 'What is she, fucking deaf? Get her out here.'

'Well, she's not going to come out here if you speak to her like that!' Saskia said tartly, getting up and making her way over towards the bedroom door. 'The poor girl's a nervous wreck.'

Misty shot Saskia a warning look. She knew Vincent better than Saskia did, and she knew he would tear Saskia apart for talking to him like that.

Heeding the warning, Saskia tapped her knuckles lightly against the wood.

'Lena? Are you done? Your tea's going cold out here… '

No answer.

'Lena?'

Trying the handle then; the door wouldn't budge. Turning to Vincent, Saskia shrugged, unsure of what to do. 'She's locked it?'

'Lena!' Something was off. Vincent sensed it immediately. 'Get out of the bloody way.'

Losing his patience, Vincent shoved Saskia out of the way and grabbed at the handle, jiggling it hard. He lost his rag then; slamming the weight of his body into the wooden panel several times before he managed to force the door open, whacking it loudly against the bedroom wall.

The loud bang echoed around the room.

It was empty.

'Where the fuck is she then?'

Staring past the mess – the unmade bed, the piles of clothes strewn in a heap on the floor – Vincent's eyes rested on the open window. The large pane had been hoisted open, and the floor-length curtains billowed wildly in the breeze as rain pelting into the room formed a small puddle on the floor.

The girl had fucking gone!

'Are you fucking kidding me?'

Storming over to the window, Vincent looked down past the metal stairwell that ran down the outside wall, his eyes scanning past the fire escape and along the alleyway that ran the length of the flats.

There was no one about. She'd fucking legged it. The girl had done a runner.

'For fuck's sake!' Banging his fist on the window frame, Vincent was beyond fuming. This was all he fucking needed. Joshua was going to have a fucking field day with this one. 'I asked you two dozy tarts to do one thing. One fucking thing, and you couldn't even do that right!'

Nervous now, knowing how volatile Vincent's temper could be, Misty was trying her hardest to defuse the situation.

'She couldn't have got far. She was only here just a few minutes ago,' Misty began. 'Honestly Vincent, she said she was just going to change Roza; she was only in here a few minutes. I made her a cup of tea… ' Misty was panicking now, as she could see the look on Vincent's face.

'Bullshit.' Pointing at the pool of water on the carpet underneath the window from the rain that was pouring in, Vincent didn't believe her. 'She's been gone more than a few minutes. What were you two fucking doing? Drinking tea and having a fucking mother's meeting while the girl fucking took her chance and legged it?'

Vincent glared before he stormed back into the kitchen, not in the mood to wait for the girls' pathetic excuses.

'How hard is it to look after a fucking kid and a baby? Even a pair of slags like you can do that, surely?' Vincent sneered, looking at the girls as if they were nothing more than dirt on his shoe.

He was incensed. Fuming. If he'd known how incapable this pair of bimbos were, he would have stayed here the night himself and kept an eye on the girl. He was angry with himself now. That's what he should have done. Then they wouldn't even be having this fucking conversation right now.

'We did what you asked us to do. How were we supposed to know that the girl was going to do a runner?' Saskia was getting annoyed now. How dare Vincent talk to her and Misty like this?

Vincent strode across the room then, stopping just inches away from Saskia. Looming over her, Vincent was purposely trying to intimidate her, and it was working.

Saskia felt wary.

He leant down towards her and, to her surprise, he laughed. He found the gall of the girl in front of him nothing but amusing. Saskia clearly had no clue of the trouble she had fucking well caused.

'You must be fucking deluded, love. If you did what I asked you to do, then that fucking bird would still be here, wouldn't she.' Vincent rubbed his head. 'You must have said something to her? Scared her off?'

'Us?' Saskia raised her voice.

Misty could see that Saskia was close to losing her temper and doing something that she'd regret; she wanted to head her off before that happened. 'We didn't really speak to the girl,' she quickly interrupted. Remembering what Saskia had told her about how they had found her last night, the state she had been in, she decided to play it to her advantage. 'She wasn't making any sense, mumbling stuff in her own language. She was a bleeding nut job.'

Misty could see the doubt in Vincent's face now. She was convincing him.

'Look, we made her a cup of tea. It's still hot. She can't have gone that long. She probably legged it just as you arrived. We had no idea.'

Misty held Vincent's stare. She could feel his eyes were boring into hers; staring right through her as he tried to suss out if she was lying to him.

'You two had better not be fucking spinning me a line, 'cos if I find out you had anything to do with her legging it there'll be fucking trouble, do you hear me?'

He could smell bullshit from a mile off. He didn't believe the girls – not for a second. Still, standing here arguing about it would only get him nowhere fast. The fact remained, the girl had done a runner. This was a fucking mess. The last thing he needed was some neurotic fucking illegal immigrant running about and causing shit for him, especially with the mood Joshua was in.

'Fuck's sake!' Furious now, he slammed his fist into one of the kitchen cupboards, shattering the wooden door to pieces, making the girls jump with fright. 'Right. You two, get your fucking coats on, you're going to come and help me look for her. She ain't going to get very far with no money and a sprog in tow, so hurry up and move your arses.'

Seeing the mood Vincent was in, Misty and Saskia didn't argue. Fetching their shoes and jackets they did as they were told without so much as a word, while Vincent stood pacing the kitchen.

He should have known that something like this would happen. He should never have let the girl out of his sight. She was his only lead to finding that bastard Korab and he'd only gone and fucking lost her. Another fuck-up to add to his growing collection.

He needed to find her and fast; otherwise his brother would have his fucking nuts for this.

CHAPTER THIRTY-THREE

Huddling inside the shop's doorway Lena didn't bother to make herself comfortable. There was no point. She'd done that in the first one only to be shooed away.

She wasn't welcome, here, or anywhere. It hadn't taken her long to work that out. People around here didn't seem to care that it was pouring down, that she was soaking wet, or that she had a baby to care for. They saw her only as vermin. To them she was just unwanted rubbish cluttering up their doorways.

The last man had been horrible to her. Threatening, aggressive. Lena had thought that the shop was closed: its steel shutters were down; the lights all switched off. She thought that she'd be safe to seek refuge in the doorway. Grateful for some respite from the treacherous rain, she'd huddled at the back trying to keep Roza dry.

No sooner had she sat down she'd been back up on her feet again: the door behind her swinging open, the aggrieved shopkeeper shouting abuse and obscenities at her, moving her on.

'Dirty immigrant, tramp, scrounger.'

He was saying what everyone she passed was thinking. At least earlier, when the shops had been open she hadn't stood out so much. Lena had taken her time, wandering into every shop. Trying her best to stay out of the rain, to keep Roza as warm and dry as possible. She'd managed to blend in with the rest of London's shoppers, but it hadn't stopped the dirty looks. She could see the suspicion on people's faces. A foreigner that didn't belong here. A shoplifter, a pickpocket.

She felt guilty then. That's exactly what she had become.

She still couldn't believe that she'd left her bag behind in Misty's flat. She'd left the flat in such a rush to get away before Vincent arrived that she just hadn't thought straight, and by the time she'd realised it was too late. She couldn't go back for it. Vincent would have caught her.

She'd felt sick about it all day. How could she have left something so important behind? She'd tried breast-feeding, but her milk had completely dried up now.

Screaming hysterically, Roza had been hungry. The nappy she had on was soiled. Lena had been forced to steal then. Taking her chance in a chemist, while the old lady behind the counter had her back turned, she'd grabbed a baby's bottle, some cartons of ready-made formula, and shoved a pack of nappies under her arm, then she'd ran, the woman's voice shouting after her.

Consumed with remorse afterwards, Lena's only consolation was that at least Roza had eaten. She'd been desperate. She'd had no choice.

Back outside in the rain now, the shops were all closing up for the night. It was getting dark.

Peering out from her soggy hood, the rain continued to fall mercilessly around her.

Lena stared over to the tall white building across the road; the warm yellow glow of light spilling out like a beacon against the blackening skies, making the police station look suddenly inviting.

Inside, she could see people moving about. Answering phones, tapping away on their computers.

Battling with her conscience, Lena didn't know what to do. Ramiz had warned her that the authorities wouldn't help her, and the nurses at the hospital had proved him right, but she was slowly running out of options. She thought about telling the police about Ramiz. About how he had kidnapped her. How he had drugged their daughter. Maybe they would believe her?

Jumping as a sudden clap of thunder exploded above her head, Lena looked up, startled by the vivid flash of lightning that ripped through the dark, heavy clouds.

The rain came down faster then. Lashing, torrential.

She couldn't stay out here much longer. Roza was tired, hungry, and cold, crying once more, Lena held onto her tightly; her arm swaddled around her child down inside her jumper in a desperate bid to try to soothe her. She wanted to break down and cry alongside her too.

She was so tired. Tired of running, tired of hiding.

Taking one last glance up at the black sky that loomed above her, the thick heavy clouds, the downpour that showed no sign of easing off anytime soon, she took a deep breath and made a run for it. Weaving in and out of the traffic that was at a standstill in the busy London road, her feet splashed in the puddles, water slapping against her legs as she ran.

The flat ballet pumps that Misty had given her were soaked through, the leather cutting into her skin. Blistered and raw she winced with every step she took.

It didn't help that she'd been walking around in them all day, round and round, in aimless circles. Getting nowhere fast. The pain was excruciating now. Yet it was the only part of her that she could still feel.

Soaked through to the skin and shivering from the cold, every other part of her was numb.

Running up the flight of steps that led to the main doors, she pulled the big glass door back and stepped inside; the sound of the rain silenced now. Replaced with voices. Lena took in the sea of miserable-looking faces ahead of her occupying the row of chairs that lined the wall in the reception.

There was a man standing behind the desk talking to a woman. Walking towards them, Lena waited her turn. Pulling the soggy hood off her head, she was glad of the warmth of the place if nothing else.

Roza was still crying, but it was more of a grizzle now. Her eyes were closing, her mouth tightly clamped around her new dummy. Lena willed her to sleep, just as the lady in front of her shouted loudly, making both Lena and Roza jump once again.

'I want someone out here now to tell me why my Jack's been fucking arrested. He ain't done nothing wrong. Haven't you lot got anything better to do than lock up innocent boys? No wonder there's so many fucking criminals out there.'

Lena could smell alcohol emanating from her. The bitter acidic smell was so strong the woman could have bathed in the stuff. Staggering, unbalanced, she stepped back, causing Lena to step back too, out of her way.

'Your Jack isn't exactly an angel is he my love?' The man behind the desk laughed. 'He's in here that often that the custody officers are thinking of inviting him to our Christmas party… '

'Oh, you're a fucking comedian an' all! Well, doesn't that make a change. A bit of variety from the usual clowns you get working in here.'

'Why don't you go and take a seat, Mrs Andrews? Someone will be with you shortly to deal with your enquiry.'

'I'll tell you what, I'll make a deal with you. I'll go and sit nicely in the corner if you go and fuck yourself. How about that huh?' the woman squawked.

The woman was shouting now. The drink fuelling her temper, she was making a scene. Aware that she had all eyes on her, she wasn't going to let the officer get the better of her.

'I'm not going to ask you again, Madam. Take a seat or you're going to find yourself arrested too, for being drunk and disorderly.' The officer sounded bored now, and his patience was wearing thin.

'Oh you'd fucking love that wouldn't you,' the woman shrieked, slamming her fist against the protective glass in front of the man. 'Two for the fucking price of one. Mother and son. What are you? On some kind of fucking commission? Fucking jobsworth prick.'

'That's it. I warned you,' the officer said.

Everything happened so quickly then.

The officer pressed an alarm and two officers came rushing out to the reception.

Pushing the woman down to the ground, they managed to restrain her, before dragging her back up onto her feet and leading her away through the side door.

Clutching Roza to her protectively, Lena had stood right back, out of the way.

Shocked at what she had just witnessed, the voice behind the desk pulled her back from her thoughts.

Looking down at Roza, Lena started to doubt herself. What if the police didn't help? What if they punished her, accused her of being a bad mother? What if they took Roza away from her and sent her home back to Albania without her?

She'd been stupid to come here.

There was too much at risk.

'Miss?' the officer repeated, looking down at the baby in her arms. His face concerned now. 'Can I help… ?'

'No sorry, I shouldn't be here… I made a mistake—' Before she finished the sentence Lena had already turned on her heel to leave. She could hear the man still talking to her, confusion in his voice as he called after her.

Grabbing at the door, Lena ran down the steps. Soon she was back out on the street again; standing in the middle of the pathway as people rushed past her under the shelter of their umbrellas as if she was invisible. Next to her, on the road, cars lined up bumper to bumper, making their way home. Back to the warmth of their houses. Back to their families. Faces peering out, looking right through her.

She was back to where she started. Back out on the busy London street, out into the pouring rain. No idea what to do, or where to go next.

She had absolutely nothing now. No one to help her and nowhere to go.

For a second she thought about Ramiz. Maybe he was her only option? At least, if she went back to him Roza would have somewhere warm and dry to stay. They'd both have food to eat.

Even in her complete desperation she knew that she couldn't go through with it though. Ramiz was dangerous. Reckless. He had already almost killed Roza once, and Lena had no intention of ever giving him another opportunity to hurt their daughter. She was going to have to find her own way now.

Somehow.

Out here on London's streets.

Surrounded by people, so many people, but completely and utterly alone.

CHAPTER THIRTY-FOUR

'We're not going to find her, you know; she could be anywhere by now.'

Vincent Harper may have the hump, but he didn't have anything on Misty's sulky mood. Annoyed that she'd been lumbered with some strange girl and her baby all night, not only did she have to give up her bed for the girl, now she was having to spend her day traipsing around half of London looking for her too.

Glancing at her watch, she saw it was almost six p.m.; they'd been searching for Lena all day. She wasn't in the mood for this shit anymore.

'Did I ask for your opinion?' Vincent spat. 'Just keep your gob shut and your eyes open. Do you think you're capable of doing that much, at least?'

Turning back to the busy road in front of him, Vincent slammed his foot on the brakes and bellowed just as an elderly man stepped out in front of his Range Rover. 'Get out the way you fucking cockblanket!' Vincent wasn't in the mood for any of this shit today either. Joshua was going to have the raging hump when he found out that he'd somehow allowed the girl to give him the slip. He was already treading a thin line with him as it was – he couldn't afford anymore fuck-ups.

He needed to find the girl, fast.

'Besides, how far is she going to get, huh? She's got no fucking money and a sprog in tow.'

Pursing her lips and folding her arms, Misty shrugged. It was clear that Vincent wasn't giving up his search anytime soon.

'Who knows, but we've already looked everywhere. Twice. We're going to have to call it a day soon though; we're both working tonight. Joshua will do his nut if I'm not there to sort the girls out,' Misty reasoned.

Vincent bit his lip. He knew Misty was right and that just irked him even more.

He'd been driving around for hours, getting this pair of dozy cows to search in almost every coffee shop, park and public toilet this side of the river, and it was turning out to be a complete waste of time. The girl had completely disappeared off the radar.

She'd vanished into thin air; but there was no way that Vincent was going back to the club without her.

'We ain't fucking stopping until we find her,' he snarled. 'Now shut your trap and keep a fucking look out, there's a good girl.'

Misty looked at Saskia now and shrugged. Vincent was a stubborn bastard.

'Well, you can explain to Joshua why we're late then.'

'Oh I'll explain all right. It wouldn't surprise me if you two had a hand in all this anyway. I mean, why else would the girl do a runner? Are you sure you didn't put the idea in her head? What did she say to you both? And don't give me no more of your claptrap; she must have said something.'

''Course we didn't say anything. Why would we get involved with some random girl? We got enough of our own shit to worry about…'

Leaning her head against the window, Saskia tried to zone out as Misty and Vincent continued to argue amongst themselves. It was the third time they'd driven down Wandsworth Road now and Saskia was busy distracting herself by staring out at all the passers-by. Watching them all laughing and talking as they bustled up the high street, window shopping, strolling in and out of cafés. Carefree.

Saskia couldn't help but feel envious of them. Just normal people, living their normal lives. She'd been like that not long ago, until she'd found herself trapped into this crazy world. What the fuck was she doing mixed up in all this?

She missed her dad so much right now. He had been her rock. If he was here, he'd know what to do. She sighed then, shaking her head, as the realisation hit her. It was because of her dad that she was in this mess in the first place.

Staring across the road, something caught her eye.

A girl. Standing in a shop doorway. Her hood pulled up obscuring her face. Holding a baby in her arms.

It was Lena. Saskia was sure of it. She was standing thirty feet away from them, while Vincent obliviously continued his lecture.

Suspicious of her and Misty's involvement in Lena running, he wasn't going to let up. 'If I find out you two girls helped her, I swear to God, this will not end up pretty for you—'

'She's there. Look! I see her. That's Lena. She's just gone into the underground… Stop the car.' Sitting forward in the seat now, suddenly alert, Saskia was pointing ahead of them, towards Vauxhall Tube Station.

'Are you sure?' Vincent asked, taking no time in waiting for Saskia's answer as he cut across the traffic coming the opposite way and pulled up outside the station.

'It was her. I'm sure of it. She's wearing a big oversized navy jumper, with the hood pulled up.'

'My bloody jumper,' Misty mumbled.

Vincent grinned. Pulling his car up on the kerb, he ignored the disgruntled drivers beeping their horns behind him. Maybe he'd been wrong about these dumb bitches. Maybe they hadn't helped Lena after all.

'Get your fucking arses out then and go and fetch her,' he ordered. Then, opening his door he added, 'on second thoughts, fuck that! You two fucking muppets can stay here and keep an eye on the motor. You'll only end up losing her again otherwise. I'll go and get the girl my fucking self.'

CHAPTER THIRTY-FIVE

Someone was shouting.

Fuck!

The thunderous voice was so loud that it penetrated through the floorboards; even from upstairs in one of the bedrooms Kush Malik could hear the commotion clearly.

It was Ramiz. Drunk, sounding off again. The man was out of control. Only this time Kush had a feeling that the man had really lost it. He was bellowing about something.

Hurrying down to the bar Kush rounded the corner, only to be met with the sight of a paralytic Ramiz leaning over the pool table, pinning down one of Kush's regular customers by his throat with a pool cue.

'What the fuck is going on?' Kush shouted now as he took in the scene before him. Ramiz was out of control. His face puce with rage; spittle shooting from his lips as he shouted wildly in the man's face. 'Ramiz, what are you doing?' Wiping the sweat that had gathered on his forehead, Kush winced as he heard the nerves in his own voice.

He hated himself for being so weak, but that's exactly what he was. He was powerless. This was his pub. His venture. He'd worked hard to build up his business.

Yet Ramiz was destroying it all. Fuelled with anger at Lena disappearing, the man had become unbearable. He did nothing but drink all day and throw his weight around.

That's why Kush had retreated upstairs to one of the rooms, to get away from the man – only it seemed Ramiz had no intention of letting Kush have any peace.

'This man refuses to pay, so I'm teaching him a lesson... he needs to learn some respect. Remember who he is dealing with... ' Ramiz sneered over his shoulder to Kush, while jabbing the pool cue down harder against the man's windpipe.

The man was thrashing about wildly under Ramiz's weight as he fought to breathe, his face going bright red under the strain, but Ramiz didn't seem to notice or care. He was beyond reasoning. A law unto himself, he was now taking out all his pent-up anger on one of Kush's customers.

'There must be some kind of a mistake,' Kush said, desperate to talk Ramiz down. 'This man is one of my most loyal customers. He has been coming to the pub every week. He's never given me any kind of trouble, Ramiz. He always uses the same girl. Pays the same price.' Kush was shouting now. Desperate to make Ramiz listen to him before he ended up killing the man. He already looked close to losing consciousness, his eyes bulging in his head.

'Enough, Ramiz. You've taught him a lesson.'

To Kush's surprise, Ramiz did as Kush asked and let go. The man rolled away from Ramiz to the other side of the table, rubbing his throat as he greedily sucked at the air around him.

Wheezing, strained, finally he spoke. 'You nearly fucking killed me?'

Sitting up, traumatised, he stared in horror at the two men in front of him – his confusion quickly turning to anger. 'I paid.' Pointing his finger at Ramiz the man was shaking violently. 'This animal told me that it wasn't enough. That I need to pay more. When I wouldn't pay, he attacked me.'

Kush looked at Ramiz now to see if what he was hearing was true.

'You're not charging enough.'

Ramiz's lip curled up in distaste as the man shook. He was petrified of him and so he should be. Kush should be too. Things were about to change around here. It was about time that someone upped the stakes. There was money to be made, real money, and from what Ramiz had seen Kush didn't have the balls or the brains to get the maximum potential from the place.

'I put the prices up.'

Kush felt his heart sink in his chest now as Ramiz's grimace turned into a sneer.

Ramiz was challenging him. This was his way of showing Kush that he was muscling in on his little enterprise, convinced that no one would dare stop him. That he could do as he pleased.

Kush closed his eyes in dismay. Not only was Ramiz armed, he was also unpredictable, desperate. The combination made Ramiz an extremely dangerous man. He'd been a nightmare the past few days. Constantly paralytic, he was drinking the bar dry, abusing Kush's customers, mistreating the girls. Kush had been trying in his own way to pacify the man, but he knew that he had only been stalling for time. Ramiz had been asking too many questions about the business, about the girls. He wanted to know how much money Kush was making.

Kush had told him as little as he possibly could, while every day praying that Lena would return. Then he could tell them that they had to move on, that they couldn't stay here.

It had been wishful thinking though. Clearly Ramiz had no intentions of leaving now, and he wanted in on Kush's business. Deep down Kush knew that there was nothing he could do to stop the man.

Ramiz had all the power, and he knew it.

'Our prices have gone up.' Defeated, Kush couldn't look his customer in the eye. 'You need to pay up.'

Incredulous, the man shook his head. This wasn't the deal.

'What kind of a fucking place are you running here? We had an arrangement. You can't just change the price to suit yourselves—'

The man had barely got his sentence out when the pool cue struck him. There was the sickening crunch of wood cracking against the man's skull and a thud as he fell back onto the table. Unconscious. Ramiz had whacked him so hard that Kush was surprised he hadn't taken his head clean off. Blood was pouring from the side of his face.

But that wasn't enough for Ramiz.

'This is what happens to people who don't pay. This is what happens when you fuck with us.'

Taking the cue, he pummelled the man repeatedly with it. Battering him. Stabbing the end of the stick into his flesh, puncturing his body, his face, until there was nothing left but a bloody red pulp.

Kush couldn't move. He just stood and stared. Tasting the bitterness of the bile in his throat as he swallowed it down. There was blood everywhere. Ramiz was covered too: his clothes, hands, face. It was like something out of a horror film.

Terror enveloped Kush's entire being as he realised just what he was dealing with here.

Ramiz stopped then. As if something inside him had suddenly clicked. As if he'd just come out of a trance. His vicious outburst was over. Seeing the look of terror on Kush's face, the battered bloodied man beneath him, Ramiz laughed, maniacally, the crass sound filling the air. Reaching into the inside pocket of the man's blood-soaked suit pocket, Ramiz took out the man's wallet. Fingering the notes inside, he shot a look to Kush.

'He should have done as he was told.'

The message was loud and clear.

This was Kush's warning too.

Staggering over to the bar, Ramiz poured himself out another brandy, downing it in one go.

Kush saw Korab then; until that moment, he hadn't even realised that the man was in the room. He was sitting in the corner, in one of the booths, silently terrified of the monster they were dealing with, just as Kush was.

Ramiz clocked him too.

'Don't just fucking sit there,' he slurred, his eyes blurring out of focus; he was so drunk he could barely see, barely stand. 'Get this shit cleaned up. It's bad for business.'

Petrified, Korab did as he was told.

Walking over to where his cousin stood, Korab shook his head in wonderment, heart sorry for what he'd brought to Kush's door.

The two men said nothing. They just exchanged the same knowing look, as Ramiz stood at the bar and poured himself out yet another drink.

The man was out of control. The more he drank, the more volatile he became.

Ramiz had shown them what he was capable of; he wouldn't hesitate in inflicting the same reprisal on anyone who stood in his way.

No one would be spared. Not even Korab and Kush.

CHAPTER THIRTY-SIX

Crouched down on all fours inside the pitch-black cavity Colin could feel his excitement building. This was his favourite part. He was almost finished, almost at the best bit. Relishing the fleeting moment of anticipation.

It had taken two hours, but it had felt much longer than that.

Hammering the chisel with force the strong steady blow fractured the wood and it split. It was only a sliver of a crack, a thin jagged slice, but it was all he needed for the saw to slot down inside it. In his element now he hacked at it tirelessly, dragging the hacksaw back and forth as he scoured a deep gouge into the timber.

Backwards, forwards, backwards, forwards. His shoulders throbbed; the dull, gnawing pain quickly erupting into an excruciating, burning ache, but still he persevered, picking up his speed, adrenaline surging through his body.

He was almost there. The sweat was pouring off of him now; his hair stuck to his forehead, beads of perspiration trickling down the sides of his face. Putting all his strength into each stroke he relished the fierce scraping sound as the serrated blade finally broke through the oak veneer.

He'd done it.

The saw's thin jagged teeth were now firmly embedded in wood beneath it. He was pleased to feel that it was chipboard. Solid oak would have only impeded his task, and it had already taken him far too long as it was.

Colin thought of the mound of mud that he'd stacked so carefully up on the tarpaulin above him. He'd dug it all out by hand. The soil had been slack, still unsettled from today's earlier backfill; nonetheless, the task had still been a gruelling one.

He was pleased with his speed tonight. He'd broken a new record, beat his best time. Spurred on by his anger at his mother, no doubt. He'd envisaged her face with each vicious stab his spade made to the soil. Spearing the ground over and over again he'd destroyed the earth until there was nothing left.

He felt focused, motivated. Excited.

Severing the last bit of wood now with his saw the panel became loose, dropping down into the casket with the final cut.

Reaching down, Colin picked up the chunk of wood. Discarding it, he threw it to the other end of the grave. Then, he reached his hands back down inside the coffin, his fingers brushing against the fabric inside.

He'd done it. Alone in the darkness, in the dead of the night, he had found the treasure that he had been looking for.

He smiled then, a rare genuine moment of happiness engulfing his entire being.

His mother underestimated him, as everybody else did. Still, that suited him just fine. Their misjudgement only worked in his favour in the long run. If no one knew his secrets, then no one could ever take them from him, and that was just the way Colin Jeffries liked it.

CHAPTER THIRTY-SEVEN

Circling her hips in time to the rhythm Saskia plastered a smile onto her face as she finished her final dance of the night. She was late. Still, she wasn't getting away with finishing even a second early, not with this tightwad as her last customer.

The man sitting in the booth in front of her had spent more time glancing down at his watch, making sure that he'd got his full four minutes' worth, than he had spent looking at her.

Hearing the music to her final set coming to an end, Saskia happily gave the man one last final wiggle before jumping down from the podium. Not bothering with the usual false niceties of saying goodbye, she made her way across the main floor to the dressing room. If she hurried she could still make it.

She could feel Vincent Harper watching her; his eyes boring into her as he took in her every movement.

He'd been in a bad mood all evening after not being able to find Lena at the underground station earlier. Riled that she'd somehow given him the slip once again, he'd driven the girls back here and had sat, in prime position at the main bar, watching them both like a hawk for the duration of the night.

He was trying to intimidate her, trying to put her on edge but Saskia wasn't going to give him the satisfaction of knowing that it was working.

Turning his way, she forced herself to look at him. He didn't look away. Instead he stared back at her coldly. Saskia looked away first. A cold chill making its way up her spine as she shuddered.

The sooner she got out of this place the better. Saskia hated the club and everything it stood for. She felt so foolish now. So stupid that she'd allowed herself to be sucked into it all. The glitz and the glamour of the place. Expensive magnums of champagne; the girls all immaculately groomed.

It was all a facade. Fake, every bit of it.

The club was a front. A money-making machine trading off people's misery, and Saskia couldn't wait to get away from the place. These people made her feel sick. Joshua, Vincent, even Misty. They were all just in it for themselves.

The only reason Saskia was here tonight was because Vincent had driven her here; she'd had no choice. He hadn't taken his eyes off her all night either, not for so much as a second. Still, she was done now. Her shift was over so she was free to leave.

Glancing back over her shoulder as she rushed down the corridor towards the changing rooms she'd half expected to see him following her, lurking somewhere behind her in the shadows.

He wasn't though, and finally Saskia relaxed, thinking that he'd given up with his constant suspicions. Vincent had been relentless earlier. Questioning them both; convinced that she and Misty had helped Lena escape.

Pushing the changing room door open, Saskia was glad of the sudden silence away from the hustle and the noise of the club, the blinding lights of the main stage.

Even if the place did look like a bomb had hit it. Looking around at the chaos she saw the piles of clothes scattered across the floor, coats and bags discarded on every chair. The air was thick with the lingering smell of perfume and hairspray from earlier. Still, at least she was on her own; she didn't have the energy to make small talk with any of the other girls.

Stepping out of her heels she pulled her jumper and jeans on over her underwear. She didn't even bother to wipe away her make-up tonight. Instead she swept her hair up into a bun, pinning the loose strands back before grabbing her bag.

'Oh, you leaving already?' It was Misty. Walking in as if right on cue; catching Saskia before she left.

'I'm just going to get off; I'm knackered,' Saskia said, averting her gaze. Rooting around inside her handbag she pretended to look for her phone. Anything so that she didn't have to look Misty in the eye.

She couldn't. She was still too annoyed with her. She wasn't the girl that Saskia thought she was.

'Here… ' Holding out the envelope, Misty knew that Saskia was still angry with her. 'There's a grand in there. It's the money from last night's party too. Think Joshua is making up for the little incident with Aaron.'

'He's making up for something… ' Saskia muttered. Taking the envelope she tucked it into her bag without saying another word. It was hush money.

Joshua Harper was just trying to keep her sweet. They both knew it. Saskia had seen Misty going into Joshua's office earlier this evening. She wouldn't be surprised if it had been Misty's idea to give her extra money; after all, Misty was the one in charge of keeping all the girls here happy. She was a pro at it. Saskia wondered if Misty had told them; if she had repeated everything that Lena had said about the boat, the trafficking.

There was no point asking her. Misty didn't have any loyalty towards her; she was only loyal to the job. To this place and Joshua Harper.

Saskia knew she couldn't trust her.

'I've got to get going. I need to get my head down. See you tomorrow.'

Grabbing her handbag, Saskia threw the strap over her shoulder. Snubbing Misty as she started to say something. Saskia wasn't in the mood to hear it. She needed to get out of here.

The place felt dirty, contaminated.

She felt dirty.

Hurrying out of the main doors, she made her way down to the bottom of the steps and didn't stop until she was back out on the King's Road. The icy breeze hit her; she wrapped her jacket tightly around her, glad of the fresh air. It felt like she could breathe again.

The skies were clear; the torrential rain from earlier had finally stopped. Glancing at her watch, she started to walk back up the King's Road and towards Albert Bridge.

The roads were quieter now, almost empty. An odd taxi whizzing past; a few dregs of people still spilling out of the clubs.

It was a stark contrast to the chaos that would erupt in a few hours' time when the Monday morning commute began. She couldn't even think as far forward as tomorrow though. Her mind was still focused on tonight.

She wasn't done yet. Picking up her pace, Saskia felt full of determination then. That something good would come out of all this mess. She'd make sure of it.

Misty might be capable of making promises with no intentions of keeping them, but that wasn't how Saskia did things. She was a girl of her word.

Tonight, she'd done exactly what Misty had told her to do on her very first night. She'd put on an act so good she could have earned herself an Oscar. Working the stage without a care in the world she had danced her arse off tonight. She just hoped she'd done enough.

Hurrying now, she started running.

She just hoped she wasn't too late.

CHAPTER THIRTY-EIGHT

Patting the mound with his spade, Colin was almost finished. He was pleased with himself. The ground looked undisturbed, exactly as he had found it.

It was the only time that he didn't mind doing the backfill – when he knew that the casket below him was empty.

All he had to do now was arrange the wreaths once more, so that everything looked just so, to ensure that his colleagues would be none the wiser that the ground had been disturbed.

He could barely contain the excitement that bubbled inside him as he thought about his newly placed treasure in the wheelie bin beside him.

This was the moment he lived for. This one perfect moment.

The shrill clang of metal behind him made him jump, his joyous triumph rudely interrupted. Caught by surprise at the sound, Colin threw himself flat onto the ground.

The gate was locked? He was sure it was. He'd locked it behind him. Just as he always did.

He heard the noise again then. Louder this time, more urgent. Whoever it was sounded determined to get in.

He remained deadly still, his breathing slow, controlled, as he allowed his eyes to flicker through the darkness.

Nothing. No movement, only that noise.

Clang. Clang.

It was the main gate, the thick metal chain rattling against the railings. Someone was trying to force it open, trying to get into the cemetery.

A terrifying thought crossed his mind then.

They knew? His colleagues? The police? They must have been watching him, lying in wait ready to catch him in the act? Beads of perspiration trickled down Colin's face as his heart raced inside his chest.

He couldn't get caught. They'd lock him up. Leave him to rot. He could feel his chest tightening at the thought of being locked away again. Panic surged through him.

Desperate now, he reached out his hand, frantically smoothing the dent in the wet soil. Carefully sliding the sheet of tarpaulin next to him, he quietly folded it, then pushed it, along with his shovel, under the generous mound of wreaths around the grave. He prayed that if they caught him here it would be too dark for them to see that the grave had been disturbed.

Shit, thought Colin, realising they'd see the bin beside him. If they looked inside, he was doomed; the evidence would be there for all to see.

The noise at the front of the cemetery had stopped now, he realised.

Instead, he heard something else. Something nearer, by the fence to his side. Someone was climbing over the railings.

He saw the faint outline of a person, the shadowy silhouette. Then he heard footsteps, close now.

Lowering his body down into the wet, slimy mud, so that he was completely flat, Colin pressed his face down into the soil, praying that he would be camouflaged by the night. Swallowed up by its darkness.

He could taste mud on his lips, his tongue, could barely breathe, but still he didn't move. Whoever it was they were right behind him. He could hear twigs breaking nearby, leaves rustling as the footsteps continued. He waited for a hand to reach down and grab him, for a torch to be shone in his face.

But then the noise slowly began to fade. Then there was nothing.

Curious, Colin looked up, apprehensive of what he might see. Expecting to be surrounded by the police, he hesitated, surprised.

It was just a girl. She was walking right past him. Oblivious to him. She looked like a ghost, at first, her pale white face lit up by the moonlight, enough for Colin to make out her features. She was young, nothing more than a child. She was holding something in her arms too. A package of some kind.

He relaxed then. His body slumping back down onto the cold, slushy ground, as the girl made her way through the sea of gravestones. She wasn't here for him; his secret was safe.

But why was she here?

His eyes watched as she walked, cautiously, towards the main office at the back of the cemetery.

No, no, no!

He remembered then; the office door, he'd left it unlocked. He had planned to go back there before he left. Return the shovel to where he'd got it. Lock everything up. It was too late to stall her; the girl had already reached the doorway and looked around suspiciously before quietly slipping inside.

She was going to ruin everything. He needed to clean up, to put away the tools he'd used. To lock everything up. But now he'd have to wait it out. Wait for her to leave.

Crouching patiently on the ground, he tucked his freezing cold hands inside his sleeves. Losing track of time as he waited – all the time watching. He was starting to feel anxious. On edge.

He needed to finish what he'd come here to do and the girl was hindering that.

Slowly, he got to his feet. There was only one thing for it.

He'd have to deal with this girl himself.

CHAPTER THIRTY-NINE

Someone was following her. She was sure of it.

Stopping outside the black metal Albert Gates of Battersea Park, Saskia turned.

Her eyes scanned the street. A row of cars standing in darkness. A sea of abstract shadows cast out from the street lamps above danced eerily on the pavement around her.

A noise. She'd definitely heard something. She jumped, hearing the loud high-pitched scream, but it was just an urban fox tearing open a rubbish sack as it rummaged through the contents that were now strewn across the street. Closing her eyes she cursed herself for allowing herself to feel so scared.

A night under the watchful gaze of Vincent Harper had turned her into a paranoid wreck. Her nerves set on edge; she was being overcautious, letting her mind play tricks on her.

She needed to pull herself together. Concentrate.

Reaching up she shook the gates – just in case – but she already knew that they would be locked. The council locked them every night, at ten thirty sharp. Supposedly to keep the scallywags out. The rebellious teenagers, gangs, the local waifs and strays. The gates weren't much of a deterrent, she thought; if people wanted to get in they just climbed over. Which was exactly what Saskia was going to do.

Checking that the road was completely clear, Saskia pulled herself up onto the rubbish bin. It wobbled beneath her as she tilted her weight onto one leg, swinging the other up onto the bar. Carefully resting her foot between the gold ornate spikes, she kept her balance before pulling herself up.

It was like being at the club and working the pole. Twisting herself around the metal she was over the gate quickly. Dropping down onto the wet grass, her trainers squelched in the mud but she got to her feet knowing she'd have to run. She could get to the cemetery in under ten minutes by cutting through the park – less than half the time than if she'd walked all the way around.

She thought of Lena then and prayed that she'd still be waiting for her. She'd said three a.m., and it had already gone half past.

She'd been so shocked that morning when she'd gone into the bedroom to check on the girl, only to find Lena dressed in Misty's clothes, her hair cut short, with her legs dangling out the window. Ready to make her escape.

Saskia had startled her but had seen the look on Lena's face. Fear, pleading, then confusion when Saskia had told her that she wasn't going to stop her from leaving; that she thought she was doing the right thing. That she should run. That she shouldn't trust Vincent.

Saskia hadn't told Misty about the exchange. Instead she'd calmly gone back into the kitchen and made them all a cup of tea, hoping to stall a bit of time before Vincent arrived so that Lena could get a head start.

Even earlier today, when she'd spotted 'Lena' in the underground – it had all been a ploy. She'd been throwing Misty and Vincent off Lena's scent and making herself appear as if she had no motive not to find the girl.

Vincent had been harder to shake off than she had anticipated. Suspicious, he hadn't taken his eyes off her all night.

Saskia was glad that she'd told Lena to wait for her after she'd finished her shift. It was only now, in the dead of night, that Saskia could get away without raising anyone's suspicions. Greenwood Cemetery had seemed the ideal place. Tucked away out of view from the main road, Vincent would never think to look there.

Only, Saskia hadn't factored in the heavy, incessant rain. The place had no real shelter, nowhere for Lena and Roza to keep dry and warm. Lena would have had no choice but to go somewhere else. Saskia just hoped that Lena had gone back there, for three a.m., like she had said. She needed to hurry though, as she was late. Running faster, she could just make out the outline of Greenwood Cemetery up ahead in the distance.

CHAPTER FORTY

Standing outside the doorway Colin listened intently. The office was silent. He couldn't hear a sound. No noise, no movement. The main light was still off too – the place in complete darkness.

The girl was definitely here though; he'd watched her go inside with his own eyes and he hadn't seen her come back out.

What was she doing?

Curious now, Colin stood waiting for a few more minutes, unsure of what he should do. He couldn't just leave her here. He needed to clear up after himself, to put the tools away that he'd used. Otherwise he'd start to arouse suspicions that he'd come back here at night. Then people might start asking questions and he couldn't have that.

A thought crossed his mind then: what if the girl had seen him? Maybe she had and now she was hiding. He started to feel twitchy now. Irritated. The girl's presence here was messing everything up.

He was going to have to go in there and see what she was doing.

Placing his shovel down, he leant the handle up against the wall before carefully tiptoeing inside the building. He knew his workspace off by heart.

Scanning through the darkness, he could just make out the outlines of the office furniture. The desk appeared untouched. The computer screen was still black, switched off. Piles of paperwork, the phone, the staff lockers all still neat. Organised.

Everything was exactly as Colin had left it earlier. Everything, apart from the far back corner.

His eyes looked down to where the pile of coats had been taken off the hooks on the wall and scattered across the cold floor tiles. For a second he thought his eyes were deceiving him. The coats moved. Then he spotted the girl beneath the pile. Blanketed under the sheet of darkness inside the makeshift bed she'd made for herself. She was curled up in the foetal position.

The brightness from the moon coming through the window above her, shining down on the girl's face, left Colin transfixed.

She was already fast asleep.

He couldn't take his eyes off her. She was sleeping so peacefully, her eyelids fluttering; he wondered what thoughts were going around her head as she dreamed. What vivid images were flashing through her mind? A tiny frown appearing then, a deep crease etched just above the girl's nose. A nightmare perhaps?

He couldn't let her stay here. He should wake her, he thought. But what if he startled her? She might feel scared and start to scream. He'd have to be careful. Gentle, friendly.

He'd tell her that he'd been patrolling the cemetery. That she needed to leave.

That she was trespassing but he didn't want any trouble. If she left quietly, he wouldn't call the police. Scare tactics, but subtle. That should do it.

Stepping nearer, Colin leant towards the girl. Reaching out his hand to shake her, he stopped himself.

He stared at her, hard. She was so pretty. Doll like. In sleep, more so. Sweet perfection.

He was so caught up in the vision of the girl, the sudden screech that suddenly rang out in the room made him jump. Startled, Colin stepped back and hid behind the door, his heart pounding inside his chest.

Still the girl didn't move. She was still fast asleep, her only movement the gentle rise and fall of her chest underneath the coats, her breathing still relaxed. He thought that maybe she'd been sleep-talking, but the noise hadn't come from her.

Colin waited, still wondering if perhaps the girl had called out in her sleep, tormented by her dreams.

He kept his eyes on her, and when the loud squawk filled the room again he knew for certain that it hadn't come from her this time.

There was a sharp, sudden movement at the girl's side. A jolt underneath the material that covered her. Something was moving. A dog perhaps?

Colin stepped forward, quietly, carefully.

The noise came again now. A gurgle.

Leaning down, Colin held onto the edge of one of the jackets, lifting the material up to see what was underneath. He stepped back, amazed; a shocked noise escaping his mouth at the sight of the tiny baby.

A girl.

She was wide awake too. Staring up at him, a face full of innocence and wonder, she seemed to become suddenly alert. Her voice loud as she screeched excitedly, her legs kicking out. The girl was stirring now. Waking to comfort her child.

Then she saw him. The tall silhouette looming over them in the darkness.

The girl was suddenly aware that she was no longer alone. Scared, her eyes wide like saucers, her mouth opened and she screamed.

Grabbing Roza protectively, Lena pushed herself backwards, away from the man that loomed over them.

He was close too. Close enough to touch her. Terrified, Lena felt the cool wall behind her, realising with panic that she was boxed in. There was nowhere to go, nowhere to run.

'It's okay. I'm not going to hurt you.'

Sensing the girl's fear Colin stepped back, not wanting to alarm her.

'My name is Colin. I work here. It's okay, don't be scared.' Colin's voice was quiet, calm.

He smiled at her.

'I was checking up on the place. We've had vandals here, at night, taking people's gifts and mementos from the gravesides, generally making a nuisance of themselves—'

'I promise you, I haven't touched a thing.' Lena protested her innocence. 'I was just looking for somewhere we could sleep, me and my daughter. Somewhere to shield us from the cold and the rain… '

Colin nodded as if he believed her.

'What's your name?'

Lena looked at the man warily. She was scared, her eyes darting to the open door behind him. He was standing directly in the way of any hasty exit she might try and make so she decided her best option was to comply.

'It's Lena. My name is Lena.'

'Hello, Lena.' The name suited her. It was pretty. He could hear the lilt in her accent. Eastern European, he guessed, though her English was almost perfect.

'You can't stay here, I'm afraid,' Colin said quietly. 'It's trespassing; if anyone saw you coming in here, they might have called the police. You're going to have to leave.'

Lena started to get to her feet then. Dragging herself up off the floor as if she was on autopilot. The fight and determination gone from her. *Here we go again*, she thought to herself, back out onto the streets of London, traipsing around looking for somewhere warm and dry to stay.

She thought of all the people she'd met today. The ones that had sent her away from their shops and doorways. The ones that had called her names, spat at her. She couldn't go back out there, alone in the middle of the night, with Roza. She couldn't face it.

'Let the police come.' Lena started to cry then.

She wished more than anything now that she'd handed herself in earlier when she'd had the chance. Instead, she'd thought of Saskia and how she'd promised to meet her. How foolish she had been to believe that the girl had wanted to help her. Three a.m., Saskia had said; only she hadn't come. It was just another broken promise. Lena was tired of it all. Of running, of hiding. She just wanted it all to stop. She was freezing cold, her hands almost blue. What sort of life was this for Roza? What sort of life was this for anyone?

'Please, call them. Let the police come. Let them take me… I can't do this anymore. I just want to go home to Albania.'

The girl was sobbing hysterically now.

Colin shook his head, confused. This wasn't what was supposed to happen.

He'd thought that at the mention of the police she'd just leave. Of her own free will – while she still could. He didn't think that she would break down. She must be desperate. Homeless? A runaway?

There was no way that he could call the police. They'd ask too many questions. It would be too much of a risk. He didn't know what to do. This was all going wrong.

'I have somewhere you can stay… It's not far from here. You can stay until the morning.' Colin shrugged then.

It was a stupid idea. He regretted his words as soon as they left his mouth.

'You'll help me?' Lena spoke now through her sobs.

This man was a stranger. She should be wary, but he seemed kind, and right now she didn't have any other options. He was her only chance of getting somewhere warm for the night. Anywhere would be better than here in the cemetery.

Colin felt anxious then. He hadn't expected the girl to agree.

'Just until morning,' he reaffirmed. 'A few hours.'

He thought about the wheelie bin and the tools. How he needed to move it all.

It would be getting light soon, but he needed to get the girl out of here, fast.

'Okay!' Lena nodded, glad to have somewhere to go, for Roza's sake. She was her only priority.

'Okay,' Colin echoed.

Shit!

Mother.

He'd have to keep Lena away from mother. This wasn't ideal. It wasn't ideal at all, but he was running out of time. He needed to get the girl away from the cemetery. Taking her to his flat was the only option.

'It's just around the corner. A few minutes' walk.'

Watching now as Lena gathered up her belongings and her child, Colin tried to convince himself that everything was going to be just fine. It was just a few hours.

She'd be gone in the morning. Not much longer now, and everything would work out just as he had planned.

CHAPTER FORTY-ONE

Slipping down underneath the broken railings, Saskia pushed herself through the gap in the fence. The rain had eased off hours ago, but the ground was still saturated. Crawling on her hands and knees through the hedgerow, she was covered in mud.

Cursing silently as she stood up, she wiped some of the brown slush down her already caked jeans, as she immediately scanned the cemetery.

The darkness didn't deter her. Even blindfolded she could have found it; she knew the location by heart. She'd been here so often over the years.

Making her way to the back of the graveyard towards her parents' plot, covered by the beautiful yew tree, Saskia weaved between the headstones.

Daniel and Angeline Frost.

That's where she'd told Lena to meet her; only she wasn't here.

Of course she wasn't here. The place would have been terrifying for the girl. Alone, in the dark, surrounded by death, gravestones, ghosts. That and the fact that there would have been nowhere to keep warm, no shelter from the rain. It had been stupid of Saskia to even suggest the place.

Sitting down on the wet grass beside her parents' headstone she was crestfallen.

Saskia thought about going home, back to that big lonely house all by herself again.

She was doing everything in her power to be able to keep it. Only, the thought of going back there now was filling her with dread.

Clutching her handbag tightly to her side, she shook her head as she thought about the money Misty had paid her.

It was dirty money. Blood money. She didn't want it. She didn't want any part of it.

These people, this life. Not now she knew what was at stake.

The house wasn't going to make her happy; it wasn't going to bring her father back. It was just bricks and mortar. An empty shell. It certainly wasn't worth all of this.

Crying now, Saskia sunk her head down in her hands. It was all such a mess. Getting involved with Joshua Harper and the club. She was caught up in the middle of it all, mixed up with these people. They were dangerous. Ruthless. But she had no idea how she was going to get out of it.

She'd have to walk away. From the house, from everything. She had no other choice. Her head was pounding, consumed by her thoughts, so that the sudden noise startled her. She looked around. Nothing. Then it came again.

Footsteps? Could it be Lena?

Turning, she could see movement over by the cemetery's office. The building was still in darkness, no lights were on, but there was definitely movement in the doorway. A shadowy figure.

Standing up, Saskia was filled with hope. Lena. She had come after all. Thank God. But walking towards the figure she realised it wasn't Lena at all. It was the outline of a man. Tall, wiry. Thinking fast, Saskia sunk back down to the ground, hiding behind a headstone.

She watched the man making his way down the steps to the pathway, a smaller figure walking alongside of him. Daintier, slight; a girl with a large coat draped over her shoulders. She was holding something in her arms. Lena. Saskia had no idea who the man was though.

She wanted to call out. To tell Lena that she was here, but she couldn't. She was afraid to call out, remembering what Lena had told them about her husband Ramiz; about him having a gun.

Instead she stood watching, unsure what she should do as the two figures made their way down the pathway towards the cemetery's main entrance. The street light shining down on them both now, illuminating their faces. The man looked familiar. As if Saskia had seen him somewhere before? His skin white, pale. Not Ramiz then.

Maybe he was a police officer? But he looked too nervy, too awkward. They were at the main gates now. The man unbolting the chain. He had a key? He worked here. Saskia was sure of it. She'd seen him before, when she'd been sitting at her parents' graveside. He had been tending the graves nearby. An odd man; his eyes always beadily watching.

What was he doing here with Lena in the middle of the night?

Lena walked through the gate, then stood waiting as the man locked it behind them.

She didn't seem distressed.

Shit! They were leaving.

Getting up, she ran to the side fence, to the hole that she'd crawled in through.

She needed to get out of here, and fast. To follow them.

Scampering back through the maze of headstones, Saskia sunk to her knees, ducking back underneath the broken railings, ignoring the sludge as she squeezed her way back into the muddy verge of the park.

She needed to get round the front, to the main road, to keep Lena in her sights.

She ran faster and, turning the corner, felt relief spread through her as she saw them once more. The two figures up ahead in the distance, walking side by side. They were on foot. That was something. She could follow them.

Walking fast, she kept herself tucked in against the hedgerows, hiding amongst the shadows as she hurried along. Her eyes fixed on them both, concentrating.

She didn't hear the noise behind her until it was too late – the tread of footsteps catching her completely off guard.

A strong arm grabbed at her, wrapping itself tightly around her. She opened her mouth to scream, but a hand clamped over her mouth, silencing her, before dragging her down to the ground.

CHAPTER FORTY-TWO

Apprehensive as they walked in awkward silence through the heavily built-up housing estate, Lena hugged her daughter close to her, hoping that she was doing the right thing.

Her feet throbbed as she walked. Swollen and blistered. She winced at every step as her soles hit the pavement, her toes frozen cold.

Roza must be frozen with the cold too. Lena could feel her shivering despite being wrapped up in layers of clothes and blankets. She felt so guilty then; she'd tried so hard to keep Roza from getting wet today, but the downpour had soaked them both. If Colin hadn't offered to take them in, they might not have made it to morning. Though now they were almost there Lena was doubting that Colin's flat was going to bring her much refuge. Colin seemed preoccupied too. Hummed loudly to himself as Lena followed him; the noise sounded strained, disjointed.

He hadn't spoken a word to her since they'd left the cemetery. Looking up at the two tower blocks as she walked, she wasn't sure what kind of a place she'd expected the man to live in, but it hadn't been one like this.

Looking around at the filth, the dirt, as she walked along the pathway of the large communal garden that ran right through the centre of flats, she couldn't help but think how rundown and derelict the place was. The grass littered with rubbish. Carrier bags, empty beer cans, sweet wrappers.

Passing a bench, Lena could see that it was part of a memorial. What was left of it. The brass engraved plaque was sprayed with graffiti, clinging to the scorched remains of the wooden slats that had been clearly set on fire. Nothing looked sacred.

Everything here had been defaced, destroyed.

Lena had expected London to be so much more glamorous than this. Back home in Albania she'd heard so many stories about royalty that lived here in England. About places like Kensington Palace. The Changing of the Guard. The Queen. The royal princes. Yet so far all Lena had seen was poverty, and lots of it. Depressing-looking tower blocks. Grey skies. Rain. Gloom. The people here seemed miserable, hostile.

They'd come all this way to England, her and Ramiz, for what? So far, life was no better here for them than it had been at home. She still felt like a prisoner, still felt as if she was trapped. Only now she had even more people to run from: Ramiz, Korab, Vincent. She was no freer now than she had been back home. In fact, if anything she was worse off. Alone in the middle of the night, with only this strange man helping her. Desperate to keep Roza from getting ill again. From dying of hypothermia. Lena was doing everything in her power right now to keep herself from falling apart. She needed to keep focused. Stay strong.

Reaching the main doorway of one of the tower blocks, Colin slowed down. Pulling the door open they both stepped into the cold, echoey hallway. Lena looked around at the grey concrete steps, the black metal handrail. It was all utterly stark, gloomy. Above them a bulb flickered. A strobe of bright light flashed erratically, casting shadows all around them as they walked. Ignoring the lift, Colin made his way up the concrete steps and Lena followed.

She could see him better now in this light. The back of him anyway. He was filthy. Covered in thick smears of mud, his trousers were caked, the back of his jacket too. He was a lot older than her. Catching the side of his face, she saw his skin was blotchy, lined, his hair thinning, a large bald spot in the middle revealing his scalp.

Reaching the first landing Lena held her breath, shielding herself from the strong acidic smell of urine that dominated the passageway. Though she soon realised that the puddles of yellowy piss were the least of her problems as she looked down at her feet, the floor littered with broken bottles, shards of glass, discarded syringes. The place was disgusting.

By the time that Colin stepped out onto the balcony where his flat stood she'd counted five flights of stairs. Five rancid, pissy landings. Out on the balcony now, the rush of cold air hit her and she gratefully gulped it down. Taking in the view as she walked, she tried to gather her bearings.

It was still dark outside, but the warm glow of the street lamps below lit up the area enough so that Lena could work out roughly where she was. She could see the cemetery from here, or at least the boundaries of it. The high gates and hedges that surrounded the graveyard's perimeter.

From up this high London looked almost welcoming. The darkness of the night creating an illusion, a favourable blur, blotting out the dirt, the grime. Hiding its stark, ugly truth.

Colin stopped walking, as they were outside his front door now. Eyeing the blue flaky paintwork, Lena saw the remnants of food that were smeared down it. Eggs? It had been sprayed with graffiti too; she couldn't read the writing though. The bright scrawl was too faint, patchy, as if someone had tried to scrub it away.

The silence was unbearable now; Colin still hadn't spoken.

Lena wondered if maybe he was regretting his offer to help her. Regretting letting a stranger into his home. If he was, he didn't say. He didn't say anything at all in fact.

Instead, he fumbled inside his pocket, looking for his key. Opening the door he stepped aside politely, allowing Lena to walk in first, ahead of him. Grateful to be finally inside, out of the cold, Lena stood just inside the small, pokey hallway, looking anxiously around her.

The first thing that hit her was the smell. Putrid, vile, like rotten vegetables.

'The drains are blocked.' Finally, Colin said something. Unfazed, he repeated his mother's perpetual diagnosis as he helped Lena take off her coat; hanging it up on the coat hook for her.

Lena nodded, not wanting to appear rude. The stench was overwhelming. Even worse than the smell at the Jungle, and that was saying something. She felt nauseous. Unable to control her reflexes, she gagged. Then again. This time she could taste the bile at the back of her throat. Swallowing it down, she covered her nose with her hand as she concentrated on breathing through her mouth. Colin looked at her blankly. She felt embarrassed then, as if she'd just insulted him. Insulted his home.

'You can't go in there,' Colin said firmly as he saw Lena look towards the lounge door, to where the noise of the TV blasted through. 'Mother is sleeping. She doesn't like to be disturbed.'

Lena nodded. Wondering how anyone could sleep through such a loud noise. The television was blaring. She was surprised that the neighbours hadn't complained, but then, from what Lena had already seen of the estate, this place didn't look like anyone took any notice of what went on.

'My room's through here.'

Opening his bedroom door, Colin led Lena through. The place was a mess, clutter and chaos everywhere. Clothes scattered all over the floor; a heap of paperwork adorned the desk. Books stacked up in piles, boxes full of junk. The noise was quieter in here, but the smell still lingered.

Colin closed the door behind them.

The noise startled Lena as she realised that they were alone. Alone in a bedroom with a man she hardly knew. She felt apprehensive once more.

Colin must have felt it too, because he didn't move. Instead, standing over by the door, nervously.

'You can have the bed. Get some rest.'

Lena nodded. She eyed the bed now. Unmade, messy; the blankets looked dirty, stained, but it was better than the cold hard ground of shop doorways and cemeteries. Sitting down on the edge of the mattress she lay Roza down beside her. Unwrapping the cold blanket from her, she placed her underneath the duvet, tucking it around her to keep her warm.

She took her own shoes off, placing them on the floor, then dipped underneath the covers too, pulling her knees up to her chest as she hugged herself. She shivered violently, unable to get warm. It was as if the cold had got right down inside her bones. But she didn't want to lie down yet, not while the man was still here. She'd wait for him to leave first.

'I've got to go back out,' he said. 'Can I get you anything before I go? Something to eat? Some water?'

Lena shook her head. Glad that the man wouldn't be staying. She was ravenous. She hadn't eaten since the previous morning, but she didn't want food. She just wanted him to go so she could sleep. She'd given Roza her last bottle just before they'd gone back to the cemetery. She'd be okay until morning.

Beyond exhausted, all Lena wanted to do was curl up and close her eyes.

Just a few peaceful hours where she wouldn't have to worry about anything or anyone. She wanted to forget about how cold she was, forget about the rumbling deep in her stomach.

'I won't be long,' Colin said quietly.

Then he was gone. Closing the door behind him.

Lena breathed out a long slow breath she hadn't even realised she'd been holding. She felt the tension in her back soften.

She was relieved that he'd finally gone and listened as he moved about outside.

The lounge door opened, the TV blasting out for a few minutes, then the door closed again and it was quieter once more. He was back out in the hallway now. She could hear him pulling his jacket back on, ready to go back out into the cold. To finish his night shift at the cemetery.

Laying back against the pillows, she pulled the covers up around her and waited for the warmth.

Then she heard the scrape of metal. The sound of a lock bolting shut. Sitting up, Lena was suddenly alert.

He'd locked her in?

Hearing the front door close, Lena jumped from the bed and crossed the floor in a panic. Pulling down the door handle the metal moved in her hand, but the door remained closed. Wrenching down the handle again, she tried to pull it open, but it wouldn't budge.

She banged her fists loudly against the wood then, pounded with every ounce of energy that she had left.

Her fists felt raw, bruised. She'd thought that maybe she could alert his mother. Wake her from her sleep. Maybe if she made enough noise, she would hear her and come and let her out, but it was no use; the TV was too loud. It was drowning her out.

The window, she thought. But, of course, it was locked too. The glass thick, double glazed, frosted, so that she couldn't see out and no one out on the balcony could see inside.

Scanning the room for some other way that she could get out, she spotted the other doorway in the corner of the room, peeping out from behind the large dresser. She didn't hold out much hope, thinking that it might be a closet, a cupboard, or if it was a door it would be locked, but she had to at least try.

Grabbing hold of the corners of the dresser she pulled at it with all her strength, dragging it across the floor, pulling it clear of the door.

She ran around and yanked at the handle. It opened, but all hope was gone.

It was just a cupboard. Bleak, bare. Empty, apart from a tiny doll: an old-fashioned doll that lay discarded in the corner.

Lena crouched down on the floor, despair spreading through her. She wanted to scream, to cry.

Her eyes focused now on the doll.

It was dirty, naked, just its white soft body and its plastic limbs. It had an eye missing too.

Lena shivered.

Then she saw the scratches down the walls. Gouges set deep in the paintwork.

Fingernails? Like someone had tried to claw their way out.

Sliding down to the floor, Lena started to cry. She was scared. She had been so stupid, so thoughtless coming here. So desperate that she'd put her own and Roza's lives in the hands of this stranger. No one even knew that she was here. Now she was trapped. There was no way out.

She was completely at Colin's mercy.

CHAPTER FORTY-THREE

Saskia's body slammed down to the cold, damp grass. Struggling, she kicked out, trying to fight off her assailant, but at this awkward angle she was at a disadvantage.

Her attacker had struck from behind. Whoever was holding her had the upper hand; they had caught her unawares and they were stronger than she was too.

She was being pulled backwards now, being forced down on the ground inside the bushes. Closing her eyes, Saskia felt a sharp sting of thorny twigs scraping across her face, ripping at her skin. She was being pulled further inside the undergrowth.

Cold droplets cascaded down her neck, her back, from the rainwater on the leaves above her as they were disturbed.

Her assailant stopped moving then.

Saskia was on her stomach. Face down, her face in the ground. The heavy weight of something on top of her – her attacker was on top of her now. Pinning her legs down too. But Saskia wasn't ready to give up just yet. Kicking her legs out forcefully, she had to fight. She wanted to scream, to shriek, to bite. Whatever it took to break free. She wasn't just going to lie here and do nothing. She couldn't.

The hand hadn't moved from her mouth; it stayed there, clamped tightly.

Then she heard a voice whispering in her ear.

'Don't move.'

Saskia recognised the voice instantly.

Misty?

What the fuck? Anger surged through her then, but still she couldn't talk because of the hand around her mouth, gripping her.

'I'm going to let go, but promise me you won't make a sound,' Misty spoke quietly. Her voice almost a whisper; her tone deadly serious.

Saskia nodded, but it was a lie. She was going to bloody kill Misty for doing this. For terrifying the crap out of her. Saskia had thought she was going to be beaten, or raped, or worse still – murdered by some crazed psychopath.

She'd lost Lena now too. What the fuck was Misty playing at? Misty moved her hand, and Saskia spun around ready to give her a mouthful.

'Fuck, he's here. Don't move, Saskia. Don't say a word… '

Misty held a finger up to her lips, signalling for Saskia's silence. Her eyes flashing with urgency.

Saskia could see by her friend's expression that she wasn't messing about, so she did as she was told. She didn't move. Didn't speak. Lying on the ground, side by side in silence, hidden under the shrubbery, they heard the crunch of gravel nearby.

Peering out through the leaves and branches, Saskia could see a pair of men's boots.

She'd seen them before.

Vincent's.

He was here.

Flashing a look to Misty her friend didn't respond, but remained completely still, her eyes staring ahead.

Willing Vincent not to see them.

Vincent stood there for a few moments, then turning on his heel, he walked away, further up the pathway.

Peering in over the hedges, his eyes searched through the darkness past the headstones. He was looking for someone. Her, Saskia realised. Seconds later he was back. His boots standing directly in front of where they were both hiding. Saskia winced as she watched him come nearer. Closer. He'd found them.

Closing her eyes, daring not to breathe, she was waiting for him to tear through the bushes, to grab her, hoist her out by her hair. Her heart was thumping inside her chest. Her body sticky with perspiration. They could run, she thought. They could get up now, and just run. As fast as they could. Before Vincent got them.

Misty's arm pressed down on Saskia's shoulder, as if she was reading Saskia's mind, and she shook her head. A warning.

Then Saskia heard Vincent's voice.

'It's me.'

He was on his phone. Relief spread through her. He hadn't seen them.

'I've lost her, bruv.'

Saskia felt sick then as she listened in to Vincent's call. He was on the phone to his brother. He'd been following her – on Joshua Harper's orders, it seemed.

'She climbed the railings and cut through the park. Don't take a fucking genius to work out that she ain't here to feed the fucking ducks. I'm gonna put my money on her meeting the girl. She knows where she is, without a doubt… All right bruv, I'll buzz you in a bit.'

The conversation was over.

'Fuck sake!' Vincent muttered angrily before he started walking away.

The girls waited in complete silence until the car engine started and Vincent drove off.

'Jesus Christ!' Saskia rested her face down in the ground.

That had been close. Too close. She felt Misty relax beside her too.

'You scared the shit out of me.' Saskia finally spoke. 'How did you know where to find me?'

'I followed you too,' Misty said. 'Look, I shouldn't be telling you this, but they think you know where Lena is. Joshua dragged me into the office earlier, practically interrogated me. He wanted to know what we knew. What Lena had told us. He thinks that we helped her escape. I told him the truth, that we had nothing to do with it, but he obviously didn't believe me if he sent Vincent to follow you.'

Misty crawled out of the bushes now. Wiping the leaves and mud from her face and hair, she stood up, brushing her clothes down.

She looked a mess. Her top was ripped and her feet were bare.

'I nearly impaled myself following you over that park fence. Girl, you can bloody run. I could barely keep up! What are you doing here anyway?' Misty stared around the place, shivering. The place gave her the creeps. 'I know it's hard for you, babe, missing your dad and everything, but I'm sure he wouldn't want you here on your own in the middle of the night.'

Saskia stared down at the ground then. She wanted to tell Misty the truth, the reason she was really here, but she still wasn't sure that she could trust her.

'You're not here for your dad are you?' Misty said as the truth finally dawned on her. 'Joshua was right, wasn't he? You know where Lena is, don't you? But what was all that about earlier? When you saw Lena going into the underground station… I don't understand. Why would you tell Vincent that you saw her, if really you were helping her get away?'

Saskia could see that Misty looked genuinely hurt then.

She obviously wanted Saskia to trust her and something in her eyes told Saskia that maybe she could. Misty was here wasn't she? Trying to help her.

Saskia relinquished then.

'She wasn't going into the underground station. She was behind us, going the opposite way down Wandsworth Road. I lied to throw him off, so that he wouldn't see her. So that he'd think we were telling the truth too. It was a double bluff.'

'Why didn't you tell me you knew where she was? You had me looking for her all day.'

'I wasn't sure that I could trust you; I thought you'd tell Vincent. You said we should stay out of it, but I just couldn't, Misty. I just wanted to help her... ' Saskia shrugged, feeling suddenly guilty about lying to Misty now.

'I know what it's like to have no one, Misty. That feeling of complete helplessness. Lena is just a young girl. A victim. I couldn't make a promise to her and then just break it.'

Misty nodded.

'I wasn't being a heartless bitch when I told you to stay out of it, Saskia. I was scared. You don't know what Joshua Harper is capable of.' Misty spoke softly now. 'A while back, when I first started working at the club, one of the girls, Shanice, she was caught ripping Joshua off. She'd been taking money from the till, skimming a bit here and there from the punters. I don't really know the ins and outs, but I know she was a single mum and that she was in a lot of debt. That's why she worked at the club. She wasn't really there by choice; but then I guess none of us are really are we? Anyway, Joshua found out about Shanice and, as you can imagine, he was livid. It had been going on for months apparently. Right under his nose. The girl turned up dead a week later. One of the others girls found her. Slumped in the toilets, with a needle sticking out of her arm.'

'A heroin overdose?' Saskia asked.

'Apparently so.' Misty shrugged

'Apparently? What do you mean?'

'Shanice was a good girl. I know she took the money, but she was desperate. Her little boy was autistic and she was trying to get as much money as she could as she'd found a special school for him. It was all she had spoken about for weeks. How she wanted to give him the best life she possibly could. How she was going to do everything she could to make it happen. She wasn't into drugs. She'd told me how her parents were both addicts. Her mother an alcoholic, her father a junkie. She said she'd seen it fuck all their lives up and that she'd never do that to her own kids. Shit, the girl was so adamant not to turn out like her parents, she didn't even drink. She was a teetotaller. Wouldn't even have a nightcap with us girls after our shift at the end of the night. She only drank orange juice.'

Misty shook her head.

'We all knew that it wasn't right, but none of us could prove anything, and even if we could have none of us voiced our suspicions. We were all too scared. Joshua had made it very clear what happened to people who crossed him.'

Misty looked at Saskia now, tears welling up in her eyes.

'I was telling you to stay out of it for your own good. Joshua and Vincent are dangerous. They live by their own rules—'

Before Saskia could respond, a shrill noise rang out behind the girls, rendering them both silent. They ducked back down to the ground.

'Fuck. Is it Vincent?' Misty asked now.

Saskia peered over to the main gate, her eyes homing in on the figure as it removed the chain.

'No. It's the man from earlier,' she whispered 'He took Lena with him, but he's back now and he's on his own? Lena's not with him?'

Misty peered through the leaves to where Saskia had pointed. She saw him then too. Tall, broad, dressed all in black. Alone in the cemetery, in the dead of night.

They watched in silence as the man made his way across the cemetery.

'I've seen him before. He works here.'

'What the fuck is he doing here at this time of night?' Misty murmured quietly as they watched him drag the wheelie bin down the path behind him. 'Brings a whole new meaning to moonlighting doesn't it, gardening at this time of night. Bit fucking weird if you ask me.'

He was so close now that Saskia could see his face clearly. She had a bad feeling.

'Where's Lena? We need to follow him, Misty. Find out where Lena is. I think she's in trouble.'

Watching, the man wheeled the bin out onto the street. Locking the gate behind him once more, before looking around to make sure that no one was watching him.

He made his way along the pathway.

'What the fuck do you think he's got in there?' Misty said with a shiver.

Saskia shrugged, her eyes still fixed on the man as he walked. Dragging the bin behind him with force.

Whatever it was it looked heavy.

'I've got no idea, but something is telling me that, whatever it is, it isn't going to be good.'

CHAPTER FORTY-FOUR

Lena's fingers were red raw, the skin sore, peeling. Her short nails, chipped, broken.

The door was loose now though. She wedged the metal bracket that she'd snapped from the struts underneath the bed back into the gap between the door frame and, prising the slip of steel through, she bent it towards her, putting pressure on the hinge.

She almost had it. She'd already broken one, but this one was proving much harder. She wasn't going to give up though.

Digging the rod in further, she twisted her arm around, wincing as she caught her skin on the edge of the sharp metal. A trickle of blood slithered down her wrist. Ignoring the pain that shot through her, she bent the bar again. A little more leverage.

Then the metal bar broke, slipping out of her hand. The door was still held up by the solitary, stubborn hinge at the top and the padlock that Colin had bolted on the other side.

Determined, she couldn't give up now. Sliding her fingers underneath the slim gap under the door she pulled with every bit of strength that she had. Yanking the wood backwards and forwards, she flinched as her fingers smashed against the rough grooves of the door bar beneath. She heard the crack as the wooden frame splintered, the hinge finally breaking, and the door flew open, launching Lena backwards into a heap on the floor.

In pain but victorious, as she saw the door hanging crookedly from the single padlock, a gap now big enough for her to climb out of, she knew she didn't have much time.

Scrambling up from her knees, she swaddled Roza inside her blanket.

Outside in the hallway she could hear the loud music blaring from the other room. Disorientated, panicked, she made her way to the front door, but she was too late. Stopping suddenly her eyes fixed on the pane of glass in the middle of the door and the dark shadow that lingered on the other side.

Colin was back. He was at the other side of the door, searching for his keys.

Alarmed, Lena turned around. Her mind racing. She was five floors up. In a flat. The front door was her only way out. Colin's mother!

She remembered then. Lena would wake her up, beg her to help her. The woman wouldn't want the girl kept against her will. She'd want to help.

Grabbing the door handle, Lena rushed inside; closing it behind her to buy herself an extra few minutes.

She heard the front door close.

Colin was inside the flat.

Lena stared, looking for somewhere to hide. Anywhere. Only, now she was in the lounge she realised something was very wrong.

Her skin prickled. Her senses all seemed to come to life at once, overwhelming her, as her head began to spin.

The smell in the room was so overpowering, so vile, it hit her like a physical blow. The sound of the TV was deafening.

There were people here, she realised.

All sitting at the table. Only they weren't people at all.

They were dolls.

Dressed in funny-looking clothes. Bright dresses, hats and wigs. All of their painted-on expressions looking blankly ahead. Big, exaggerated, blue cartoon eyes, thick red smiling lips. Life-size dolls, all sitting at a party. A huge chocolate cake sat in the centre of the table. Surrounded by fancy cups and saucers. A teapot. The tea had long gone cold now though; Saskia could see a thick layer of scum floating on the surface of each one.

She shuddered then as she noticed the flies. So many, a constant buzzing.

She'd mistaken the sound for just the TV at first, but now she could see the room was full of the insects, all buzzing around. Swarming the room in a frenzy as they flitted from the food to the dolls.

Then to the other armchair in front of the TV.

Lena saw her then. A pair of thin mottled legs sticking out from the chair.

The woman had her back to her. The chair's high back obscuring her view.

She was facing the TV, directly in front of it.

'Please, help me,' Lena cried, running over to the chair. Begging, pleading, but then she stopped, unable to comprehend the horror that greeted her.

The old woman's face was twisted, contorted. Her skin tinged a deathly grey.

She was the only one in the room that didn't have a big red smile painted onto her face.

She was dead.

Clutching her baby close to her, Lena buried Roza's head into her chest, instinctively shielding her baby's eyes from the gruesome sight in front of her.

She turned as she heard the sound of the door behind her.

'You should have stayed in the room like I told you.' Colin was in the doorway. 'That's why I locked you in.' He looked sad, his eyes full of pity.

'I was scared. I'm sorry. I won't say a word I swear… I'll pretend that I haven't seen any of this… ' Lena was begging now.

Colin shook his head. Staring at the table he looked over to his dolls; his face lighting up with affection.

'They'll take my dolls away from me. They won't let me keep them. I'll be all on my own again.'

Lena followed his gaze. His dolls?

She thought of tonight, in the cemetery. Alone, in the middle of the night. The mud. Covering his clothes, his boots, his hands. The smell in the flat, that rotten stench of sewage.

Her ears started ringing, her eyes dark, peppered with shining white spots.

She was going to pass out.

The realisation hitting her with such force that her brain couldn't take it in.

The dolls.

They were real.

They were children.

Mummified human remains.

This freak had dug them up.

Lena tried to speak, but her words were caught at the back of her throat. The room started spinning, round and round, whirling so fast she felt like she'd momentarily left her body.

She could still feel Roza in her arms. Desperate to cling onto her, she held her daughter for dear life as her legs gave way and she fell to the floor.

Lena knew nothing then.

Only darkness.

CHAPTER FORTY-FIVE

Rubbing his hands down the front of his trousers, Colin Jeffries wiped away the beads of sweat that had formed on his palms. He felt sticky, dirty; he needed a shower. There would be time for that later though. Right now, he had better things to do. He had waited for this moment for days.

Carefully plotting and playing and finally getting his mother out of the way, and then the girl, Lena, had almost ruined it all for him.

Still, he'd dealt with her for now. Making his way towards the bed, Colin knelt down beside it. An excited thrill rippled through him as he took in the sight of his newest doll splayed out in the centre of his bed.

This one was beautiful. By far the prettiest of them all. Exquisite. She looked like a sleeping angel. He even approved of her clothes; he couldn't have picked better himself.

A blue and white checked dress that sat just above her knees, finished off with frilly white ankle socks and pretty navy shoes adorned with a cute little bow. It was simple, but perfect. Not like some of the clothes that the dolls had been dressed in. Garish, immodest. The children these days dressed too old for their age. A heel on their shoe. The hemline of the skirts too short. Their faces painted with make-up.

This was just perfect though.

He stared at her face now in awe.

Her eyes were closed; her thick, full lashes resting on her porcelain skin. Her hair was long, chestnut-brown, cascading down over her shoulders.

With a trembling hand Colin reached out to touch her.

Closing his eyes, he gasped loudly as his fingers caressed the soft, natural curls. Twisting the ringlets around his fingers, he opened his eyes; his nose wrinkled as he noted the stark contrast of his wrinkly, coarse hands against his new doll's perfectly smooth waxy complexion. It only emphasised even more how perfect she was.

They all were. Each dolly unique in its own way.

There were seven in total in his beautiful collection. He knew every detail there was to know about them. Their birthdays, their favourite songs. He knew everything about them because he had saved them; he had brought them back to life.

They were his. All his. No one could take them from him now. No one.

Lying down on his bed next to the doll, Colin smiled over at her as he compared the differences in their forms.

Mother always said he was like a big, stupid oaf. His large six-foot frame was cloddish, clumsy. The girl looked so tiny next to him. Colin scanned her fragile, delicate features and instantly he felt better.

Oh yes, she was already his favourite by far.

Burying his nose into the mass of wavy hair he inhaled her scent.

No, no this simply wouldn't do.

Shaking his head, he drew back with a grimace. Sitting up sharply, screwing his face up, instantly repelled. Disgusted at the sharp, unforgiving smell of lavender that filled his nostrils, he felt his palms go clammy, his stomach churn. He hated the smell of lavender.

His mother's signature scent.

He was going to have to bathe this one – wash that dreadful smell out of her hair.

He was annoyed now – the thought of his mother agitating him.

She ruined everything. Even now, after her death. Her cruel words, her wicked taunts still lived on inside him.

He'd stood up to her in the end though. Wrapping his hands around her throat he had throttled the life out of her, strangled her last disgusting mouthful of air right out of her. He hadn't taken his eyes off her while he did it, not once. Surprised in the moment that he'd actually enjoyed it. The power; the control of finally standing up to the woman who had done nothing but abuse him his whole life.

A monster, that's what she'd called him. Those were her last words to him. Her final insult.

Even as she slipped away, as her life flashed before her very eyes, she still didn't get it.

She had done this.

She had made him this way.

If anyone was the monster it was her.

Getting up, Colin left the room, returning just minutes later with a bowl of fresh water, a towel and some shampoo. He needed to get rid of that smell. To make his doll perfect once more.

He would bathe his new doll, then he could comb her luscious long hair, before tucking her into bed next to him. His first night with his dolls was always Colin's favourite. That was when they were at their best. They didn't last long after the first night. A week at the most. It was such a shame.

Colin had learned that the hard way with the first few dolls he'd brought back here.

Despite the embalming process, despite the girl's veins being flushed with formaldehyde, it only prolonged the inevitable.

Exposed to the elements; the air, the moisture, their bodies soon started to decompose. He couldn't bear how their skin would start to rot; their bodies shrinking as their fluids seeped out from them. Then the decay would set in. That smell, that godawful smell. He tried so hard to preserve his dolls the best way he knew how. Wrapping them in bandages, covering every inch of them, even, eventually, their beautiful faces.

For him that was the saddest part, but deterioration was inevitable.

Dead was dead. At least they were out of the cold ground now. Out from the dark.

No longer alone. They didn't need to be afraid anymore.

He would look after them now, each and every one of his beautiful dolls.

Singing to himself as he started combing the doll's hair, Colin Jeffries smiled to himself.

Today had turned out to be a great day.

He had the most perfect addition to his growing collection.

Violet Jackson was everything he had wished for and much, much more.

Lena woke up. It was dark, cramped.

Unable to stretch her legs out, she could barely move. The space around her was tight, restricted. Her knees were drawn up to her chest; her back against a cold, dark wall.

The smell of rot was lessened now. Instead she could smell the overpowering dampness. The air was thick with the smell of mould.

Dazed and confused, she had no idea where she was; no recollection of how she had got there.

Something was next to her, on the floor, next to her thigh.

Roza.

Relieved, Lena reached out to touch her daughter. Wanting to scoop her up in her arms, to comfort her child, expecting to feel the warmth of her child's body, the soft mop of her hair.

Instead she felt the coolness of plastic limbs – a soft padded body. It was the doll that she'd seen earlier.

She knew where she was now. She was inside the cupboard in Colin's bedroom. The harrowing scene from earlier filled her head as she remembered.

Colin, his mother, all of those dolls.

Roza? Where was Roza?

Pulling herself onto her knees, she leant forward, her eye drawn to the crack of light that shone through the gap in the cupboard door. He hadn't blocked her in completely; the dresser was still over in the middle of the floor. The light from the bedroom flickered.

There was movement. She could hear voices now.

Colin's. That low, disjointed humming sound. He was singing to himself again.

Placing her eye to the crack in the door, Lena could see the child then. Splayed out on the bed, her skin waxy, her eyes closed. As if she was sleeping.

Only she wasn't sleeping, Lena knew that.

The child was dead.

Colin sat down on the bed next to the girl. Singing to himself. The lilt to his voice deranged, almost as if he was in some kind of trance.

His eyes were fixated on the dead child as he concentrated on brushing her hair.

Lena was horrified. The poor girl. Snatched from her grave. No one even knew she was here. Her family would be mourning her, grieving her loss, unaware that her grave lay empty. That this monster had exhumed her body.

A sudden movement on the bed caught Lena's eye.

It caught Colin's too.

Stopping what he was doing, he put down his brush, his attention caught on something else now. His face showing intrigue, fascination. Then Lena watched in horror as the man picked up Roza, comforting her as she started to cry.

He looked startled by how tiny she was. How precious.

'It's okay, Karen,' he sang softly. 'You're back home with me now. You're back home with your big brother Colin. You don't need to be scared anymore. I'm going to look after you.'

Rocking the baby, Colin smiled. 'No one will take you away from me ever again.'

Hugging Roza to his chest, he kissed her gently on the forehead.

That's when Lena started to scream.

CHAPTER FORTY-SIX

'What the fuck was that?' Misty stared at Saskia.

They could both hear the noise loud and clear. A blood-curdling scream coming from inside the flat.

It was Lena.

'We need to get in there.'

Scanning the front of the flat, desperate now, Saskia looked for a way to get inside.

Greenwood Estate was notorious in Battersea. Overrun with gangs and the unemployed, the place looked like a prison, the windows of the flats all secured with metal bars. The only way in was through the front door and neither of them were strong enough to break it down.

'What about the police?' Misty said now, her hand reaching inside her bag, fumbling for her mobile phone.

'We haven't got time. You heard that noise. By the time the police get here who knows what that psycho would have done to her. We need to get inside.'

Misty knew that Saskia was right. They had to move fast.

Staring at her friend's hair, still pinned up in a bun from how she'd tied it up after working at the club tonight, Misty held her hand out. 'Give me a couple of your hair grips.'

Saskia looked at her friend, confused.

'You want to get in there yeah, then give me your grips. Do you know how many times I've locked myself out of my flat? Too bloody many. I'm a pro. Come on, I need two.'

Doing as she was told, Saskia picked out two clips from her hair, passing them to her friend.

'Here, hold my bag.'

Stepping towards the front of the door, Misty twisted the metal in her fingers as she expertly bent one of the grips at its end, then the other one halfway down. She got to work, slipping them inside the lock; her hands shaking nervously as she tried to keep them steady.

The flat had gone quiet now.

'Is it working?' Saskia asked as she watched Misty fumbling, sweeping the barrel with the second grip, her fingers moving fast as if she was working to some kind of sequence.

'Fuck!'

She dropped one of the pins.

Bending down, Saskia picked it up for her. 'Here.'

Misty had to start the whole process again; the pressure of getting inside the flat getting to her now as they heard another shrill scream ring out.

'I can't do it. It's not bloody working.'

Her hands were shaking so hard that she couldn't get the momentum right.

'Just give it one more try,' Saskia said. 'Please Misty… '

'Okay, okay.' Misty knew she couldn't give up. She wanted to get inside the flat as much as Saskia did.

Twisting her fingers around in circular motions, moving the second pin slowly with the first.

Click.

'You little beauty!' Misty grinned as the lock sprang open.

They both looked one to the other, willing each other to pluck up the courage to go inside. Pushing the door ajar slowly the girls cautiously peered inside the dark hallway; the overwhelming stench of the place hitting them with such force they recoiled.

They both listened out, suddenly hearing something much scarier than the screaming they'd heard before. An eerie silence.

Were they too late?

CHAPTER FORTY-SEVEN

'Well, well! Isn't this fucking cosy.'

The voice coming from behind shocked them both.

Turning around, Misty and Saskia stopped dead in the middle of the hallway as they were met with the sight of Vincent Harper, leaning against the open doorway, a conceited smirk spread across his face.

'Fancy seeing you both here? Fucking uncanny, huh?'

Seeing the shocked expressions on the two girls' faces, Vincent could only laugh.

These two really were as thick as shit.

'You two must have thought that you were really clever, thinking you pulled a fast one on me. Only I've been onto you.'

Vincent stepped inside the house now. His voice low, controlled.

'The pair of you wear that much cheap fucking perfume you could have gouged my fucking eyes out and I'd have still been able to sniff the pair of you out playing fucking hide-n-seek in those bushes down at the cemetery.' Tutting now, Vincent shook his head as he spoke. 'Thought I'd have some fun didn't I; thought I'd play you two conniving bitches at your own game. Even pretended to call my brother up and make out I'd lost you. He doesn't even know I'm here. That's what a clever cunt I can be. I fooled you both, huh? Made you both think that I'd buggered off when really I was around the corner. Give people enough rope and they always hang themselves in the end.' Vincent stared from Misty to Saskia, smugly.

It never ceased to amaze him how conniving women could be, but he was always one step ahead.

'Where is she then?'

Saskia nodded her head inside the flat.

'Something's not right. We think she's in trouble—'

'Oh she's in trouble all right. The amount of bleeding aggro that bloody girl has caused me today. I've turned half of London upside down looking for her—' Vincent pushed his way past the girls now.

'Wait!' Stopping Vincent mid-sentence, Misty's voice sounded urgent, panicked. 'There's someone in there with her, a man. She's in real trouble, Vincent... '

'Is that so?' Vincent grinned now. Tonight was just getting better and better.

Saskia must be talking about the other two Albanian numb-skulls that he'd been looking for. Korab and Ramiz. Three for the price of two. This was fucking child's play.

Pulling out his gun, Vincent nodded towards the doorway behind him, indicating to the girls to leave.

'You two have caused me enough bleeding grief today an' all. Stay out there, out of my way,' he ordered, pointing to the front door. 'I'll deal with this.'

Seeing the gun in Vincent's hand the girls did as they were told. At least with a gun, Vincent had the upper hand.

Right now, he was the only hope they had.

Treading carefully through the hallway so that he didn't make a sound, Vincent screwed his face up in disgust.

The flat was fucking disgusting. Not only was it dingy and outdated, decorated like something his old granny would have lived in, but it smelt fucking rotten. Like something had died in here. Damp, mould. Rotten vegetables. The smell was rancid.

Coming to the first doorway, Vincent peered in, noting that the door was hanging off its hinges. The wooden doorframe was split, damaged, as if it had been forced open.

The bedroom was empty. The bed upturned, broken. Books, clothes and other crap covered every inch of floor space. The place was a shit tip.

Wrinkling his face in disgust he continued down the hallway. Reaching the next door, he could hear loud voices blaring out, a TV? Someone was in there.

Opening the door Vincent stepped inside the room with caution, looking around, taking in everything all at once. His eyes went straight to the table.

Giant dolls, like mannequins, sat staring back at him, garish expressions drawn on their white fabric faces.

Freaky as fuck.

The stench in the room was unreal. Vincent heaved. Spitting out the watery phlegm onto the carpet.

The girl from the boat, Lena, sat at the head of the table. She was clutching her child tightly to her as she stared back at him. Her body rigid. Unmoving.

The only good thing that Lena could focus on was that, for now, she'd been given Roza back. She wasn't going to do anything to jeopardise that.

'Where's Korab?' he asked her.

Lena didn't answer. She looked as if she was in a trance. The way she was staring at him made Vincent feel on edge. She looked terrified.

Only it wasn't his presence here that had had that effect on her.

It was something else – something much more sinister.

Vincent saw the woman then.

Dead. Slumped in the armchair behind Lena.

This was the cause of the stench, he realised. The flies. There were so many flies.

'What the fucking hell is going on here?'

Lena still didn't move.

She didn't dare; just stayed deadly still. Obedient. Submissive. Doing exactly as she'd been told to do. Staying put in the chair that Colin had dragged her into. He'd told her if she didn't stop screaming he would kill her. He'd make her join the rest of his dolls. And he'd meant it too. Taking the cake knife from the table, he'd held it to her throat; a crazed look in his eyes. He'd only stopped himself from killing her when they both heard Vincent entering the flat.

Colin was still here though, hiding in the room.

Lena's eyes flicked towards the door, the subtle movement giving the man's hiding place away.

Turning… Vincent was too late.

Colin had already stepped out from the door, stunning Vincent momentarily as he lifted his gun, ready to aim, fire.

He wasn't fast enough.

Colin struck out. The full force of his punch sent Vincent reeling backwards.

Reaching down on reflex, Vincent placed his hand to his side, protecting the dull ache in his ribcage. He felt the blood then. Warm, sticky, as it pumped out from his body.

The bright glare from the TV lit up the room as Colin came towards him once more. Vincent caught the flash of silver in Colin's hand then, as he lifted it high above his head, ready to strike him with the blade for a second time.

CHAPTER FORTY-EIGHT

The pain was immense, engulfing Vincent's entire body, immobilising him completely. If he could just reach over to where his gun lay, just inches away from him on the floor…

But Colin was standing over him now; the knife raised above his head. Vincent didn't have time to try and reach it. He needed to act fast. The blade lunged towards him once more as Vincent rolled to one side, grabbing Colin's wrist as he struck out, crushing his knuckles with every last bit of force he had left in him. A crunch of bones inside his grip. Screaming in agony, Colin finally dropped the knife.

Vincent had the edge now.

This cunt wasn't Korab or Ramiz. Vincent didn't have a clue who this man was. All he knew was that he was fighting for his life, and he was going to take great pleasure in taking this fucker out.

Fuelled now with rage at being attacked, Vincent pulled the man down onto the floor, fighting ferociously.

The man was tall, but there was nothing to him. He was awkward, clumsy. He wasn't a fighter.

Vincent was on top now. The pain in his side was searing through him, making him feel weak, heady, but he wasn't giving up just yet.

He couldn't.

Grabbing the man roughly by the back of his head with both hands, he began slamming his skull repeatedly off the floor as hard as he could. Vincent had him now. Reaching for his gun, Vincent pointed at the man, ready to finish him off. Then a sharp jab of the man's knee caught him off guard as it punted him straight between his legs.

The gun went off.

Seeing the two men fighting on the floor, Lena looked over towards the doorway.

If she ran, she might just make it, but it was too much of a risk.

The two men, writhing around the floor as they fought, were blocking her way.

Vincent still had the gun in his hand. There was blood all over the carpet now.

Scared that she was going to get caught in the crossfire Lena scrambled down onto the floor, shaking uncontrollably as she cowered under the table. Clutching Roza tightly, she looked on in horror as the two men continued their struggle.

Vincent was winning. He was overpowering Colin. Blinded by rage, he had beat him almost unconscious. But he didn't see that Colin had reached out and grabbed the knife once more; that he was bringing it up towards Vincent's face.

Lena did though and screamed. The noise ringing out in the air.

Confusion spread over Vincent's face as he registered what had happened.

The blade had sliced into his flesh, opening up his throat.

Lena stopped screaming then, engulfed with fear as she watched Vincent slump forward onto the floor, a sickening gurgle coming from his throat.

He was dying. Choking to death on his own blood.

Lena was crying hysterically now. Tears streaming down her cheeks. Sobbing.

Then she saw Colin moving. He was back up on his knees, covered in blood.

The knife was still gripped in his hand as he looked straight at her.

CHAPTER FORTY-NINE

'We need to get in there!'

Hearing the second gunshot ring out as they stood huddled together outside on the balcony, trying to stay warm, Saskia looked to Misty, her expression flooded with pure panic.

Vincent had been in there for ages.

Something must have happened.

'We can't! It's too dangerous, Saskia. You heard what Vincent said. He knows what he's doing, let him deal with it.'

'But you heard that. Two shots? What if he's hurt Lena?'

Saskia was deadly serious now. After what Misty had told her about Shanice being found dead at the club, who knew what Vincent and Joshua Harper were capable of? What if this was all part of their plan. That the first chance they got they would make Lena disappear too? She couldn't just stand here and do nothing.

Lena was in there. Roza too.

A third gunshot ran out loudly then. Echoing.

'What the fuck is going on in there?' Saskia cried as she shrugged Misty's firm grip from her arm. 'We can't just stand here. Come on.'

'Sass! Fuck sake!'

Following her, cautiously, Misty couldn't let Saskia go in there on her own.

The flat had gone silent now. Treading quietly inside both girls stared at the broken door hanging off the bedroom that they passed, apprehensive of what else they might find waiting for them.

Reaching the lounge Saskia pushed open the door, letting out a loud shriek.

'Lena?'

There was blood everywhere. The floor covered in thick pools of the stuff. Splayed out in the middle of the room was Vincent.

Dead. A jagged gash across his throat. A stream of blood.

The man from the cemetery was beside him, a few feet away. A knife in his hand.

'What the hell has happened in here?' Saskia asked, horrified, as she tried to make sense of what she was seeing.

'Jesus Christ!' Misty was standing directly behind her then, her hand covering her mouth. Her eyes were open wide, trying to process the scene in front of them through her shock.

'Lena?' Saskia spoke again, this time her voice softer as she looked to Lena standing in the middle of the room, the gun still in her hand.

'Lena? He's dead. They're both dead.'

Lena looked as if she was in a trance. Staring down at the man from the cemetery, she was still aiming the gun directly at him.

'Lena?'

'He was coming at me,' Lena said, her voice shaking. 'He had the knife in his hand. All that blood. I saw the way he looked at me. He was going to kill me.'

Lena trembled as she spoke. The memory haunting her.

Colin had got back on his feet, his eyes boring into hers as he made his way towards her. Unsteady, determined, the bloodied knife still in his hand.

That strange look in his eyes as he came closer.

Lena hadn't had time to think straight; her instincts had taken over. Leaving Roza underneath the table, she'd made a grab for Vincent's gun and pulled the trigger.

'I didn't mean to kill him,' she said to Saskia now. 'I just didn't want him to harm me and Roza. I didn't know what else to do… the children… there's something very wrong with the man.'

A strangled sob escaped from somewhere deep in the back of her throat as the realisation of what had just happened hit her.

She'd killed a man.

Colin was dead.

Vincent was dead too.

'What the fuck… ' Misty was looking around the room now – past Vincent and the man from the cemetery – to the table display of the strange life-sized dolls. 'Children?'

Saskia followed her gaze. Then they both looked over to the chair, their eyes fixed on the elderly woman, dead in the armchair.

'I'm going to go to prison. They'll take Roza… After everything that's happened, I'm still going to have my daughter taken from me.' Lena was weeping now, defeated. The fight leaving her body. She was ready to finally give up.

'No, Lena, you're going to be okay. I won't let that happen,' Saskia said, determined that she would somehow make this right for Lena. 'This wasn't your fault. None of this was your fault.'

Saskia looked around now, scared. Lena was crying hysterically.

'Lena? Where is Roza?' There was no sign of the baby and, concerned that she'd yet to see the child, Saskia stepped forward to look for her.

'Don't!' Lena turned to face Saskia. Tears rolling down her cheeks, her arm still out rigid, she aimed the gun at the two girls. 'Don't move.'

Startled, Saskia stopped dead. 'Lena, please. You're safe now. It's us. We're not going to hurt you. I promise.'

Lena shook her head.

'What do your promises mean?' Saskia had already broken her only promise. Why should Lena trust her now? She had to protect herself. Her child. 'I waited for you, like you said. You didn't come.'

'I did, Lena. I was there. I was late, but I did come. That's how we found you here at the flat. We followed you and the man from the cemetery. I kept my word. You can trust me; you're safe now, Lena.'

Saskia saw the flicker of doubt in Lena's eyes. Then the sound of Roza's gentle cries filled the room, and they could see she was under the table.

The noise seemed to jolt Lena out of her trance and, seeing the girl soften, Saskia inched her way towards her.

'You're safe, Lena. I promise. I'm going to help you.'

Lena lowered the gun then. Saskia nodded to Misty to go to Roza.

'I can't do this any more. I can't… ' Lena was inconsolable now. Shock, relief, a thousand emotions flooding her at once. Overwrought from it all she finally broke down.

Reaching out to the girl Saskia wrapped her arms around her.

'It's over, Lena. You're safe now.'

CHAPTER FIFTY

'This place is like something from the house of fucking horrors.'

Staring down at Colin Jeffries's body, Joshua Harper felt nothing but contempt as he finally broke his silence.

The gory scene before him sickened him to his stomach. It was grotesque. Monstrous.

He couldn't take it all in. None of them could.

Death, blood – the children.

What the fuck had been going on here?

Even Jonjo and Tyrell, two of the hardest fuckers Joshua knew, had been rendered speechless at the harrowing scene they'd been met with.

They'd seen it all over the years, but walking in here tonight had completely floored them all.

Joshua just couldn't register the fact that his brother was dead. He felt numb. He was in shock. He must be.

The gruesome image of his brother sprawled out on the floor with his throat cut open would be etched on his mind for ever. The sight had shaken him to his core and, unable to think straight, his men were having to lead him.

'Boss, the boys have taken Vincent's body out to the van. We're going to need to get out of here now so the other boys can come in and get on with the clean-up op. They're going to make sure that we remove any trace of Vincent being here. We can't risk him being associated with any of this… ' Tyrell Jones chose his words carefully. 'This.'

He was referring to the children; his voice raw with emotion as he stared over to where the 'dolls' sat eerily around the table, the sight of them making his skin crawl. He thought of his own kids at home, tucked up safely in their beds.

'Fuck man! Their parents don't even know that they have been taken from their graves, snatched by this monster, I just can't even imagine—?'

Joshua shook his head, quietly. Everything about the scene before them was incomprehensible.

'The Old Bill are going to be all over this, boss. We can't just make it all disappear. The kids need to be put back where they came from… '

Joshua nodded.

Of course the Old Bill would be all over this; the press would be too. This was big.

A headfucker of heinous quantities.

Of course, they couldn't make any of this just disappear.

The authorities would make sure that these kids were put back from where they had been taken. Laid to rest in peace – again. This monster needed to be outed for his disgusting crimes.

The only thing Joshua and his men could do was make sure that Vincent wasn't associated with anything to do with any of this mess.

'We'll get one of our boys in blue down here first. At least if the first copper on the scene is one on our payroll we can keep a better eye on what happens. What about the neighbours? Did anyone see or hear anything?'

Tyrell shook his head. 'See no evil. Hear no evil. Literally. Next door is empty; the one down from that is some old bird on her own. She said she didn't hear a thing. The woman's deaf as a fucking post.' Raising his brow, Tyrell grinned. 'Turns out you can get a lot for a grand around these parts. The old biddy was that keen to earn a bit of dough I thought she was going to apply for a fucking job at the club.'

Tyrell was trying to lighten his boss's sombre mood, but he could see Joshua wasn't listening to his jokes. He wasn't in the mood for anything. He looked disgusted, staring down at the dead man with a look of pure hatred on his face.

'Fucking piece of shit!' he finally said, turning his lip up in distaste as he looked down at Colin on the floor, blood seeping out all around him.

Tyrell couldn't agree more.

'The fucking nutter can burn in hell as far as I'm concerned. If it wasn't for these kids, I'd happily get the fire started an' all. Burn this fucking place down to the ground with this sick fucker still inside.'

Joshua nodded. Burning in hell was too good for this bastard. If Joshua'd had his way, the man would have died a slow torturous death. Still, that had been out of Joshua's hands.

He thought of the girls then.

'Where's Misty now?' Joshua asked, trying to focus. He needed to snap out of this mood, gain back some control. Vincent was dead. There was nothing he could do to bring him back.

Right now his priorities were to sort this mess out. His heart could wait until later.

'Jonjo's taken her out to the car. She's pretty fucked up boss. Then again, what girl wouldn't be after seeing this huh? She knows her stuff though. She knew not to call the Old Bill. The only person she rang was me.'

Joshua nodded, hearing the affection in Tyrell's voice. He was right. Misty had come up trumps for him. She could have freaked out and called the police, but the girl had kept her head. She knew how much loyalty meant to Joshua.

That was something at least.

'What about the Albanian girl? You want me to go out and look for her?' Tyrell asked now, as Joshua started to walk towards the front door.

Joshua shook his head.

'What's the point?' He shrugged, his shock subsiding. Sadness swept through him as the realisation hit that his brother Vincent was really dead. 'She isn't going to cause any shit for me now, is she? She's murdered a man. She'll be long gone now, and if the girl's got any sense she won't so much as even look back.'

Misty had told Tyrell how Colin had attacked Vincent, killing him. Slitting his throat. Then Lena had picked up the gun. She'd shot him. Dead.

It wasn't the slow agonising death that Joshua would have wished on the murderer of his brother, but it was the ultimate price.

Lena had killed him. For his brother. For herself.

As far as he was concerned Lena had earned her freedom.

Seeing the bewildered look on his boss's face, Tyrell tried to hold it together for him. He'd never seen the man look so defeated.

'Come on, boss, let's get you out of here. Yeah?'

Joshua nodded.

Tonight, he was grateful that for once someone else was taking control.

CHAPTER FIFTY-ONE

Walking up the rickety dirt track, Korab pulled his scarf up to cover his mouth, tugging his hat down as the strong winds whipped around him. He was glad of the cold weather though. It gave him a reason to hide under layers of clothes. His perfect disguise.

Vincent Harper might be as far away as England, but the man had eyes and ears everywhere. He didn't miss a trick. The other brokers working at the camp would give Korab up in a second if it meant that it earned them brownie points with men like Vincent. He couldn't believe he was back here now, after six days of being away. It felt like a lifetime, as if he was seeing the place for the very first time. The Jungle on the border of Calais. It was nothing more than a desolate piece of wasteland: a makeshift shanty town.

Getting back here had been the easy part. Much easier than he'd anticipated. The lorry driver that he'd flagged down had practically laughed in his face at Korab's strange request to take him back over to France. He'd said that he'd had plenty of people try their luck to be taken over to England, but Korab had been one of a few that had begged to be smuggled back. The five hundred pounds Korab had offered him for the journey had sealed the arrangement. The man had gladly taken his money. Delighted at not only getting paid to go to a place he was already going, but also to put one of the fuckers back where they came from.

Korab felt guilty: he had taken the money from out of his cousin Kush's till and he'd also left Kush alone with Ramiz.

He'd been cowardly, he knew that. Sneaking out in the middle of the night without saying a word to anyone… but he couldn't. Ramiz wouldn't have just let him waltz out of there. The man was unhinged, out of control. He'd never have allowed Korab to just walk away from him. That's why Korab had taken his opportunity to escape. The first chance that he'd got.

He just prayed that one day Kush would forgive him for burdening him.

Reaching the top of the winding dirt track, Korab was finally back at his tent. What was left of it.

It had been ransacked, just as he'd expected. The news of him going to England, of the boat capsizing, would have spread around the camp like wildfire. The other residents of the camp had homed in like vultures, taking everything. All that was left were a few wooden sticks that had marked out the tent's structure and some broken pallets that had once lined his camp's makeshift walls.

Everything else was gone. His bed, the mattress, the sheet of tarpaulin. There were just a few items of clothes left and some broken ornaments. Tracing the steps, he tried to map out where his camp bed had once been. He could still see the markings in the ground, the indents from where its legs had dug into the mud. The familiar mound. A tiny glimpse of a strap.

Bending down, he started scraping his hands through the soil, moist from being exposed to the elements. Raking at the ground, the dirt gathered under his finger nails. He stopped when he felt it.

The soft canvas bag. That's what he'd come back for. It was still here. Still buried in the ground: the perfect hiding place.

Closing his eyes, Korab's body relaxed, filled with sudden joy, relief.

The bastards hadn't found it. He was elated. Overjoyed that his journey had not been wasted. They hadn't found his stash of money. Digging faster now, with new-found optimism, Korab listened out for noises around him. If people here found out that he had money, a lot of money, he'd become a target. He'd seen men fight to the death here over much less. Scraps of bread, the last cup of fresh water. Eleven thousand pounds would be enough to get lynched.

This money was his lifeline. His one and only saving grace. He'd been skimming money off the top of his collections since he'd started.

Vincent Harper and his men paid him a good wage, but nowhere near enough for a new life in England. So he'd been taking a few pounds here and there; stashing it away religiously, while living under the guise of a man in dire destitution. Eating the same rations as everyone else here. Dressing in the same rags.

Korab had it all planned out. As soon as he had enough money saved up he was going to send for his family. They would all make it across to England. Though that plan was ruined now. Korab would have to take his money and leave tonight. His dream of England was over now. The place had promised to be so full of prospects and opportunities, only it hadn't been any of those for him. And with Ramiz in London, Korab didn't want to go back. He'd already made his mind up. He was going to make his way over to Greece. Try his luck in Kos, where he'd heard migrants had been flooding in their droves. He was going to use the money he had to start up his own business.

He was done with being a camp rat and lining the pockets of others. He was going to cash in for himself, be his own boss, answering only to himself. The money he had saved up gave him options.

Pulling the bag out now from the soil, Korab sat back on the muddy bank.

It was starting to rain. Icy cold droplets pelting down around him, but even they couldn't dampen his spirit.

He felt refreshed, happy. Away from men like Ramiz and Vincent he would make his own fortune.

Unzipping the bag, he thought of all the things that he would do once he was settled. He'd send for his family. His children.

They could be together once more. Finally, living in squalor, this poverty, would all be worth it.

But reaching his hand inside the bag Korab's hands felt only the bare material.

Throwing himself down on the ground, he searched back inside the hole, scraping his fingers through the mud once more. Digging frantically at the earth. It had to be here. Why would someone from the camp take the money and leave the bag? It didn't make any sense. It must have fallen out?

Desperate, frantic, he searched until his hands were raw. But his efforts were futile.

Behind him, he could hear sheets of tarpaulin from the tents all around him flapping angrily as the wind picked up. The rain was lashing down now, his clothes soaked, stuck to his skin. Raindrops dripped down his face, mixing with his tears.

Korab's money was gone and so was his only hope of getting away from the camp.

CHAPTER FIFTY-TWO

Slipping into the front seat of his Beamer, Joshua Harper nodded at Jonjo to give him a minute.

Turning to Misty, Jonjo offered a small smile. He had no idea how this was going to play out for the girl, but he hoped that his boss went easy on her. She'd had a shock tonight. Witnessed things that even Jonjo had found hard to stomach.

Joshua was unpredictable though and, as much as Jonjo had seen a lot of shit go down over the years, the death of his boss's brother wasn't something he had ever anticipated having to deal with.

Joshua's eyes looked empty, as if the light behind them had been extinguished.

Doing as he was told, Jonjo got out of the car.

'I'm so sorry about your brother, Joshua. Really I am.' Misty spoke quietly now. She hadn't liked Vincent, not really. But seeing him tonight laid out on the floor, all that blood, she couldn't imagine how Joshua must be feeling right now.

His face said more than his words. He looked tired, old. Like suddenly tonight he'd aged ten years. Filling the awkward silence in the car, Misty continued speaking.

'That man was crazy. Would have killed me and Lena too, if Lena hadn't shot him. He had all those things in there, dolls, children? What sort of a sick fucker does that?' In shock, Misty was mumbling now. She didn't know what else to do.

So far Joshua had barely said a word and it was making Misty feel nervous.

Finally, he spoke. 'What the fuck was he doing here?' Joshua asked. 'Here on the Greenwood Estate in some shitty little council flat?'

Remembering what Vincent had said earlier, about him pretending to make the phone call to Joshua, Misty realised that Joshua didn't know he'd followed her and Saskia. He didn't know anything.

Vincent had died tonight, and now it would only be Misty's version of events that Joshua would have to go by.

She better make this good.

'Vincent said he'd had a tip-off that Lena was here. He asked me to come with him. I think he thought we could do a good cop, bad cop routine, you know? He said it would be better if I came as I could coax the girl to come with us, without causing any more dramas. Only, we had no idea what we were walking in on…'

Joshua rubbed his throbbing head as Misty continued.

'That man in there, those dolls? He was crazy. Vincent fought a good fight, but the man took him by surprise. He would have killed me too, if Lena hadn't shot him…' Joshua closed his eyes now.

This was all his fault.

He should not have told Vincent to pursue the fucking girl in the first place. They should have just let her be. She was more fucking trouble than she was worth.

He'd pressurised Vincent to look for her, and now this.

His brother was dead. The girl was nowhere to be seen, and he had a whole load of shit on his hands.

'Do you know where this Lena went?'

Misty shook her head.

'I have no idea. She just took off. After killing that bloke I don't think we'll be seeing her again any time soon, and she certainly won't be talking to anyone that's for sure. Not now she's shot someone.'

Joshua nodded his head. He'd been thinking the very same thing. It wouldn't be in the girl's interest to talk.

'What about Saskia? Was she with you?'

'Saskia? The new girl? Why would she be with me? She clocked off as soon as her shift finished.' Misty shrugged, praying that her version of the story sounded convincing.

The silence between them lengthened as Joshua tried to process what Misty was telling him. His head was spinning. He felt sick to his stomach.

His brother's death had floored him. For the first time in his life, Joshua Harper didn't know what to say, what to feel.

'Are you okay?' Misty asked seeing Joshua's face pale, tears brimming in his eyes.

''Course I'm not fucking okay. Vincent just had his throat cut open… He's fucking dead… ' Caught off guard by his sudden loss, Joshua had tears streaming down his face now.

Grabbing a tissue from her handbag, Misty passed it to him. Embarrassed, Joshua wiped his face. Trying to pull himself together.

'I'm going to shut the club for a while. I need a fucking break from all this shit,' he said now, his voice solemn.

He'd had enough. The club, the boats. He'd made his fortune. He was done.

'Can you sort the girls out for me? Just give them a week's pay. I'll get Jonjo and Tyrell to sort everything else out.'

''Course,' Misty said, offering a small smile. 'Anything I can do to help; you know you've only got to ask.'

Joshua appreciated it.

There weren't a lot of people he trusted in this world, but Misty had proved herself loyal to him to the end. She was a good girl.

'I'll get Jonjo to take you home. And thanks, Misty. I know tonight must have been horrific for you, but you did the right thing not involving the police. Calling me first. I'll make sure that you are looked after for that.'

Joshua got out of the car then. Forlorn, he made his way back over to where Jonjo stood.

Misty sunk back in the chair, her heart pounding inside her chest. Her palms were sticky with perspiration.

Joshua had just bought every word of her story, and why wouldn't he?

She had no reason to lie to him, did she?

CHAPTER FIFTY-THREE

It was light now. Morning had arrived.

Peering out from her hood as the rain eased off now, Saskia could see the sun peeping out from between the bare branches of the trees as she made her way back through Battersea Park.

Reaching the gate, she climbed over the black iron railings. Paranoid, she scanned the road before she crossed. Exposed, no longer being able to hide under the blanket of darkness, she quickened her pace, worried that any car that passed her might be Joshua or one of his men from the club.

Misty had told her that she would make things right. That she was going to keep Saskia's name out of it, but she still wasn't sure. However, she wanted to trust Misty now. After everything they had all been through she wanted to believe that Misty had meant what she said about this being the way that she could help Lena, by taking all the blame herself.

Even if she did, Saskia wasn't sure that Joshua Harper would believe her. He might still come looking. She was paranoid now, but she couldn't help it. Not after everything she had gone through in the last few days.

There was no one around yet. It was still too early. The morning commute would start soon though. She was almost home.

Reaching the front gates of her house, Saskia made her way up the pathway and, turning the key in the lock, she stepped inside. Taking a minute to gather herself, she took a deep breath, then she stepped into the lounge – where Lena was waiting.

The girl was already on her feet. Her eyes alert. Her body guarded.

'Sorry, I didn't mean to startle you.' Saskia pulled her hood down. 'It's only me. Here, I got it for you... '

Pulling out Lena's bag from her jacket, Saskia handed it over. It had been stuffed right at the back of Misty's wardrobe. Buried under piles of Misty's shoes and handbags. Saskia, in a hurry to get back to Lena, hadn't even bothered to check the contents, but whatever was in there, Lena had certainly not wanted anyone to find it.

Now wasn't the time for questions. Saskia could see that Lena was too fragile. The girl needed a break. She'd been through so much. Saskia was surprised that Lena hadn't had some kind of breakdown.

She'd cried for an hour solidly when Saskia had first brought her back here a few hours ago.

Saskia didn't want to push her. Not now. Not when she knew the girl was so fragile. So instead of asking what was inside she took a seat opposite Lena.

The room was silent. Lena sat down then too.

'How is Roza?' Saskia asked.

'She's good. Sleeping.'

Lena looked irritated. On edge. Now that she had her bag back, Saskia suspected Lena was eager to leave. She couldn't blame her either.

The further away Lena could go right now, the better.

Reaching down to her own bag, Saskia placed the envelope that she'd tucked down inside on the table between them.

'I meant what I said when I told you that I want to help you, Lena. It's not much but, here, I want you to take this.' Holding out her earnings, Saskia smiled warmly. 'This is why I was late to meet you last night. I had to work so that I could get you some money. It's enough to get you home, to your family back in Albania… I want you to have it. Please.'

Saskia had tears in her eyes now.

She wanted Lena so desperately to see that she really cared – for her to believe her when she told her that she wasn't alone – that Saskia would help her, but she could still see it so clearly in Lena's eyes.

The doubt.

The mistrust.

It was as if nothing Saskia said or did would make her trust her.

'I can't take your money… ' Lena shook her head.

'Please, I want you to,' Saskia insisted. 'For Roza—'

'I don't need it.'

Saskia couldn't understand.

'I'm offering you a way home, Lena. The money, it will get you there.'

Reaching down to the bag at her feet, Lena unzipped it and slid it over to Saskia, willing her to take a look inside.

'I have money of my own.'

'I don't understand? Where did you get this?' Saskia asked, eyeing the bundles of creased euros.

'It's mine,' Lena said now, her voice full of conviction. Then, seeing the suspicious look on Saskia's face, she felt the need to justify herself. 'Do you know how often I have prayed for someone to help me and Roza? To get us away from Ramiz. To help me get back to my family? It's been over a year now since I was taken. Néné and Bàbá probably think I am dead. My brother Tariq… I don't even know if he is alive… ' Lena's voice was full of raw emotion. 'Back at the camp, in France, when Korab did what he did to me… I was on the bed. I did what I used to do with Ramiz. I tried to block out what was happening to me. I play a game in my head. A memory game of the things I can see around me. So that I don't have to focus on what is actually happening to me.'

Lena sat back down on the chair now. Reaching out her hand to where Roza slept peacefully next to her, she ran her fingers through her auburn curls tenderly, before continuing.

'He had me pinned down to the bed, and there was a slit in the canvas. At first I was counting the stones in the mud, then I noticed a small mound of mud. It looked like it had been disturbed. I could see a tiny bit of black fabric sticking out… '

Taking a deep breath, Lena looked like she was back there, then. Reliving the painful memory of what she had endured. Tears blurred her eyes as she spoke.

Remembering.

'Afterwards, after he'd finished what he did to me, he left me alone for a few minutes to tidy myself up. I kept thinking about the mound of earth. I had an urge to look. Find out what it was. So I dug at the soil with my hands and pulled out a strap. A strap from a bag. A bag full of Korab's money. He had been hiding it.'

Lena stared at Saskia now, hoping the girl would understand.

She wasn't a thief. She wasn't a terrible person.

She had been desperate. Desperate to get away from Ramiz and Korab. Desperate to save herself and Roza any way she could.

'I felt like the money was for me. It was the help that I'd been praying for. My chance to finally get away. So I took it and hid it inside Roza's bag. I figured that, by the time that Korab realised his money was gone, we would have been halfway across the English Channel. Only, the plan changed, and Korab was forced to sail with us, and by the time we reached England Roza was so sick. I took the first chance I could to run, and well, you know the rest… '

'But you didn't take the bag when you ran?'

Lena shook her head, still angry that she'd forgotten something so important.

'I was in such a hurry to get away before Vincent came back,' Lena said honestly. 'I had no intention of meeting you in the cemetery. I only agreed so that you would let me go. So that you wouldn't raise the alarm. But then when I realised that I needed my bag—'

'That's why you went there?' Saskia said sadly. 'For your bag?'

She had been silly to think that Lena would trust her. Of course she wouldn't. Why would she? Everyone this girl had come in contact with had hurt her, or used her. Why would Saskia be any different?

Only she *was* different. She genuinely wanted to help.

'I waited for you, and when you didn't turn up I didn't know what else to do. If we'd stayed outside any longer, who knows what would have happened. Roza would have frozen… Colin, he said he'd help me. I think he meant it too. If I'd stayed in the bedroom, and not seen… '

Lena shook her head now, as if trying to shake the haunting images of those poor children from her mind. She couldn't even finish her sentence.

'It sounds like we're both going to be having fresh starts,' Saskia said, gently now. Reassuring Lena that she was still on her side. 'Look, I meant what I said about helping you. I want you to believe me. I'm not from this world either. Me and you, Lena, we're two of the same. The club, Joshua Harper, Vincent. I don't want to be any part of any of it.'

She looked sadly around the room at her family home.

'All I wanted was to keep my home, but you know, without my dad here, it's nothing. Just an empty shell. I'm done with it all. It wasn't worth this.'

Saskia had tears in her eyes then.

Lena was listening intently, tears in her own eyes too.

She was obviously still frightened of something. Still holding back.

'I'm sorry about everything that happened to you, Lena. I just wish there was something I could do to prove to you that I just want to help you.'

'You have helped me already. Don't you see?' Lena looked her right in the eye now. Speaking only the truth.

Saskia had helped her.

She believed in her. She had listened. That alone had meant the world to Lena.

'It has been a whole year since Ramiz kidnapped me. In that time, I have been beaten, berated, worn down to almost nothing. I have had to watch my every word, my every move. He almost broke me. I guess that I stopped believing that there are good people out there. People without motive, people like yourself with only good intentions. Kind people.' Lena was openly crying now. 'You have a good heart, Saskia. You had faith in me and for that I'm truly grateful.'

Saskia smiled then warmly.

Glad that somehow she'd made a difference.

'There is one last thing you could help me with though… ' Lena asked now.

'Of course.' Saskia nodded. 'Anything. Anything at all.'

'Can you watch Roza for me?'

'Of course. I'd love to.' Saskia beamed.

The fact that Lena was trusting her with her daughter spoke volumes.

Lena stood up then.

'Before we leave, there is one more thing I need to do.'

CHAPTER FIFTY-FOUR

Squeezing her way in through the bathroom window, Lena stepped down onto the toilet seat, then onto the ground. Her feet landing softly, she trod lightly across the tiled floor towards the door that led out to the bar.

Pushing the door open, she peered out through the gap, scanning the main bar.

Kush was fast asleep, lying in the booth under the bay window, his head thrown back as he snored loudly. She could see Ramiz's jacket next to him, strewn over the back of one of the bar stools.

He was still here somewhere. Upstairs?

Lena knew what went on here. She'd heard Kush telling Ramiz and Korab all about the girls and the money that they made for him. Of course, that's where her husband would be.

Lena made her way quietly through the bar, tiptoeing. The pub was silent.

It was almost seven a.m. now; the girls would probably be sleeping. Kush had said that they all worked until the early hours.

Reaching the top of the steps, Lena made her way along the corridor to the one door that was already ajar.

He was there, naked, spread out on the bed. The room was filled with the lingering stale stench of body odour – and something else. Brandy? Sex? Ramiz probably hasn't even washed since he arrived, Lena thought to herself as she looked over to where her husband lay. Hygiene had never been high on her husband's agenda.

The girl next to him was naked too. A pair of tiny black knickers lay next to her on the duvet. The girl started to stir now, as if suddenly aware of someone else's presence in the room. Glancing up at Lena, bewildered, she did a double-take as she saw Lena standing there next to the bed.

Placing her finger on her lips, Lena indicated to the girl to stay quiet. One look at the girl's battered face, her purple swollen eye – Ramiz's trademark – and Lena knew that the girl would comply. Her husband had a penchant for violent sex.

The rougher the better, as Lena recalled.

She nodded at the girl to leave.

The stern look on Lena's face, the coldness in her eyes, told the girl that she didn't need to be asked twice. Grabbing her clothes from the floor the girl gladly scarpered from the room.

Lena was alone now. Standing at the end of the bed, looking down at her husband.

The monster who had stolen the end of her childhood from her.

The animal who had beaten, raped and humiliated her.

The man who had drugged and almost killed their only daughter.

Here he was, laid out in all his pathetic glory. Drunk and naked. His mouth gaping open; a pool of dribble forming under his chin.

Lena wanted him to see her, to know that she was here. That she wasn't scared of him anymore. Jabbing her husband's leg with her fist, she watched as Ramiz gradually opened his eyes.

Finally awake, his initial confusion was replaced by a cruel grin spreading across his face as he realised that his wife had come back to him. Remembering the girl lying next to him in the bed, he smirked.

'Have you come to join our little party, Lena?'

When he realised that he was alone now, that the girl had gone, he looked back to Lena and sneered.

'I knew you'd come back eventually. You can't survive out there without me.' Not bothering to cover himself he placed his hand over his genitals, touching himself as he spoke – knowing that Lena couldn't stand the sight of him – enjoying how uncomfortable his lewd act would make his prudish wife feel. The disgust on Lena's face would only gratify him more. He could feel himself getting hard.

Then he saw the gun.

'What the fuck are you doing?' Ramiz almost laughed now. Pushing himself back on the bed, he stared at Lena in wonderment.

'You crazy woman!' Glancing over to his dresser he saw his gun still there on the side.

'Where did you get that gun?' Ramiz asked now. Faltering. A look of uncertainty crossing his face.

Lena hadn't just picked up his weapon in a moment of anger; she'd come here armed. Her intent was clear.

Lena didn't answer him.

Instead she held her arm out straight and aimed Vincent's gun at Ramiz's chest.

'Put it down, Lena. You're being stupid.'

She saw it then. Just for a fleeting second. Ramiz had composed himself quickly, but the flash of fear in his eyes had definitely been there.

'You are a coward, Ramiz. You should have accepted your fate. Then none of this would ever have happened. The ancient *Kunan* law teaches that spilt blood must be met with spilt blood. The Bodis wanted their retribution but you wouldn't give it to them. Instead, a coward, you ran.' Lena's voice sounded alien even to her own ears. Yet, it was full of certainty now. Like she was seeing everything clearly for the very first time; seeing exactly what Ramiz was. In all his naked glory. 'If being married to you has taught me one thing, it's that I'm not prepared to spend my life running from my demons.' Lena spoke now with conviction.

'Demons?' Ramiz laughed, shaking his head as he realised that Lena was referring to him. The woman was acting crazy. 'I have given you everything, Lena. A marriage, a home, a child. It's you who is the demon. Ungrateful. Insulting. Throwing everything back in my face. You are weak, Lena. Weak and pathetic. Go on, shoot me. I dare you. Shoot me!'

Ramiz was getting angry, aggressive.

He was goading her now. Just as he always did; testing how far he could push her.

This was the real Ramiz. The Ramiz that she knew and hated. He was making it easier for her and he didn't even realise it. He hadn't asked her how or where Roza was. She knew that he genuinely didn't care. Their child was just another means to an end for him. Another pawn in his sick twisted game.

Pressing her finger lightly against the trigger, relishing the cool metal against her skin, her hands trembled, her eyes filled with tears.

Then, she froze; thinking of the image of Colin coming towards her, the bullet tearing through his chest.

All that blood.

She willed herself to find the courage, to finally break free from this man. But Ramiz was laughing now; throwing his head back, full of confidence once more. He mocked her.

'You see! You can't do it, Lena. You're not strong enough. That is why I chose you in the first place. That day on the street when I took you? Because I could see exactly what you were. A stupid, weak little girl – and that is all you'll ever be.'

CHAPTER FIFTY-FIVE

Stepping off the minibus, Lena clutched Roza to her side as she stared out over the city's main square.

Beautiful Shkodër.

It looked exactly the same as before she'd left, before she'd been taken. Life had just carried on, as if she'd never been away. Children ran past her, laughing, playing. The market stalls bustled with fresh fruits and vegetables, and people were everywhere. The sound of the traffic, loud, chaotic, filled her ears as a battered old Mercedes beeped its horn at the horse and cart that had slowed its journey.

Smiling as she made her way up the rubble-strewn pathway that crept up the side of the city's edge, Lena took it all in, soaking up every second of her culture as the warm late October sun beat down on her.

It was good to be back.

Clutching Roza in her arms, she felt nostalgic at the sights and sounds.

The breathtaking view of the mountains that rose up in the east just off in the distance. Her eyes drank in the sight of brightly painted houses, vibrant purples, yellows and pinks, scattered like little gems across the mountainous landscape.

Ahead of her she could see her own house set at the top of the hill. Rickety, worn.

Strewn with rubbish outside. A bald tyre. Empty boxes.

To Lena it was the most beautiful vision of all.

Walking up the old familiar dirt path that led to the front door, she was trembling now. Not knowing what to expect.

Would her parents be here?

Reaching for the handle, shaking, she'd barely had time to register that the front door had opened. Shrieks of pure joy filled the air. Screaming, crying, laughing.

It was Néné, crying hysterically, chanting, pulling her into her open arms.

Bábá came running then too; both of her parents disbelieving what they were seeing; wrapping their arms around their daughter as if they would never let her go again. Néné reached out her arms for Roza. Tears cascading down her face as she held her beautiful granddaughter for the first time.

She didn't speak then; the moment too precious. Heartbreaking and beautiful both at the same time.

Then Lena saw him standing at the back of the room. The look of shock on his face as he saw her.

He smiled.

Tariq. He was alive. Running to her, they embraced. Néné, Bábá, Tariq and Roza, all of them together in the same room.

Overcome with emotion, Lena fell to her knees, crying once more. But this time her tears were of joy, of love.

She was finally back where she belonged. Back home with her family. She didn't need to run anymore. Ramiz was gone for good.

Vengeance for him had finally come.

An eye for an eye, spilt blood met with spilt blood.

She'd done it.

Lena Cona had finally set herself free.

LETTER FROM CASEY

Thank you for choosing to read *The Taken*.

I can't tell you how much I appreciate reviews from my readers. Not only is it great feedback for me but reviews can really help to gain the attention of new readers too. So, if you would kind enough to leave a short, honest review, it would be very much appreciated!

When I first started writing *The Taken*, I was unsure in what direction the story would take me. As always with my writing process, I had a character in my mind's eye before I had the actual storyline. Only in this case I had two characters fighting to tell their stories. Lena Cona and Colin Jefferies. Two very different characters, set worlds apart. My challenge was to find out how the two stories intertwined, and how their paths would eventually cross.

Harrowing in places, but a journey nevertheless and one of which I really hope you enjoyed.

I'm currently working on the next book so if you'd like to stay in touch and find out about the next release, you can sign up to my new release email in the link below:

www.bookouture.com/casey-kelleher

Or if you just want to drop by and say 'Hello' you can find me on Facebook, Twitter and my website.

Casey x

OfficialCaseyKelleher

@CaseyKelleher

www.caseykelleher.co.uk

ACKNOWLEDGEMENTS

Many thanks to my lovely editor Keshini Naidoo for not only giving me the opportunity of publishing *The Taken* with Bookouture but also for her fantastic editorial skills too. Your brilliant ideas and suggestions really helped to shape *The Taken* into what it is today. Thank you so much!

I'd also like to thank Oliver Rhodes, Kim Nash and the rest of the Bookouture team. I'm absolutely thrilled to have joined the Bookouture CrimeSquad.

A special thanks to Christian Threader for answering all my questions on burials and cemeteries. Also to Artan Prifti for your information on Albanian terminology and Louise Fennell for her gambling expertise.

As always I'd like to thank my extremely supportive friends and family for all the encouragement that they give me along the way.

The Cooper's, The Kelleher's, The Ellis's.

The Besties, The BW Girlies, The AH Girlies.

Too many of you to mention by name!

Finally a big thanks to my husband Danny – my hero, and our three children Ben, Danny and Kyle.

My world!

Printed in Great Britain
by Amazon